CLOAK
OF THE
VAMPIRE

CLOAK OF THE VAMPIRE

BOOK 1

Cloak
OF THE
Vampire

SAPIR A. ENGLARD

Montlake

Text copyright © 2024 by Sapir A. Englard

Published by Montlake, Seattle

www.apub.com

Amazon, the Amazon logo, and Montlake are trademarks of Amazon.com, Inc., or its affiliates.

ISBN-13: 9781662522260 (paperback)
ISBN-13: 9781662522253 (digital)

Cover design by Faceout Studio, Amanda Hudson
Cover images: © Hakan Filiztekin, © By Shin jungeun, © anny ta, © By Dany Kurniawan / Shutterstock; © Nenov / Getty; © Danielle Skinner / ArcAngel

Printed in the United States of America

For Gil, my ginger lass

TRIGGER WARNINGS

PROLOGUE

They were fighting. Again.

It hadn't even been two weeks since I moved to this dilapidated studio apartment on the shitty side of town, and yet I knew far too much about the neighbors I'd heard but hadn't yet seen.

For instance, they *loved* having pretty loud sex. In this six-story walk-up apartment building, where the walls were paper thin, there was no such thing as privacy. The groaning and moaning of the couple who lived next door and the banging of their bed's headboard against the half-crumbled wall kept me awake at night, staring bleary eyed at the ceiling. *They must like it rough* was only part of what went on in my head. It was an endless cycle of fighting and make-up sex.

I sighed and closed the magazine I was attempting to read. I got off the bed and took two steps to the 1970s-era galley kitchen. The entire apartment was the size of my childhood bedroom, but I didn't complain; anything was better than . . . *there.*

Besides, the rent was cheap, which was just as well, considering I was living on minimum wage.

I just wished I didn't need to hear everything happening behind these damned walls.

"You stupid bitch," a male voice was now snarling. *"You said it was the last time!"*

"Austin, please—" the female tried to say, breathing heavily.

But he cut her off. *"You really think apologizing is good enough?"* The man screamed, and a shattering noise followed. *"You're so fucking stupid. You think you can do better than me? Do you really think that idiot cares about you? He only wants to fuck you, just like every other guy you let cozy up to you!"*

Grimacing, I poured water into the kettle and placed it on the tiny stove to heat it up. That man was one hell of an asshole. I'd known guys like him before. They tried to compensate for their tiny, wrinkly dicks by emotionally manipulating their partners. They didn't listen. They merely screamed, threw their weight around, and tried to intimidate their women into submission. They only thought with their balls, and nothing more. This woman should dump his ass, pronto.

"We were just talking, Austin," the woman sobbed. *"Please . . . I promise I didn't do anything . . . I wouldn't . . . I love you . . ."*

I rolled my eyes, feeling bile rise in my throat. That guy was such a tool. How could she love him?

I pressed my palms against the kettle, feeling it warming up, as the man snapped back, *"If you really loved me, you should've listened when I told you to never speak to another man again unless it's for work. And even then, he can talk to me about booking you if that's really what he wanted. But no"*—he laughed bitterly—*"you just had to piss on my requests and try to show how you can actually think for fucking yourself. You're nothing without me. Nothing. You hear me? No man will want you after I'm done with you."*

Wow. That man really thought highly of himself. I mean, look where we lived. The kettle grew warmer, as if agreeing with me.

"It won't happen again, I promise," the woman begged, whimpering. *"I'll never talk to him or anyone again. Just . . . don't leave me . . ."* Her voice broke. *"Please don't leave me . . ."*

The kettle became too hot for me to touch.

"Stop yammering on and on, you fucking bitch. What you need is a fucking lesson," the man said, and suddenly, there was a noise and then

a scream. The walls vibrated as a large object . . . or rather *someone* . . . hit it.

The kettle's whistle was ringing in my ears as I abandoned my apartment and raced next door. There was a crashing sound, a cry, and an almost animalistic growl that made me throw open the unlocked door and run inside.

What I saw caused me to freeze. It was like no time had passed, and I was sucked back to a dark, cold basement. I shook the memories away and focused on the scene unfolding in my neighbors' apartment. I couldn't save them back then, but I sure as hell could save her now.

A woman was lying on the dirty floor, curled into a fetal position with her arms over her face. Blood trickled from her black, long, messy hair, and she was shivering, crying.

My eyes trailed up to the man who loomed over her, tall and slender with his hands fisted and bloody. His face was the epitome of rage when he saw me standing there, as if I had rudely interrupted his performance.

"Who the fuck are you?" he said menacingly, his hands fisted so strongly his knuckles turned white. The look in his eyes was strangely overwhelming.

I didn't respond. I was too busy trying to hold myself back from smacking this stick figure of a guy right in his skinny, ghoulish face, not letting him intimidate me into submission. I'd gone up against worse monsters than him. This motherfucker was going to get it.

"I said," he said, starting to turn toward me, "who the fuck are you, and what the fuck are you doing in my place?"

My, not *our*, I noted, and I finally found my voice and barked out, "Step away from her."

The whistle of the kettle rang throughout the hallway like a fire alarm.

His eyes widened. He seemed incredulous. "Why should I, when she fell and hurt herself?" He suddenly crouched and extended his hand toward the woman, but she flinched.

Of course that's what he would say. "Step away from her," I repeated, curling my hands into fists. I had to restrain myself. It had barely been a couple of weeks since I left everything behind and started this new life of mine. I couldn't throw it all away at the first hardship I encountered.

But I also couldn't let this woman stay there. She looked so small, so fragile, lying on the floor, with her pale skin coated in red. My chest tightened. And even if this man did hit me, too, I couldn't leave her.

Ignoring the man, I walked over to the woman and squatted. "Hey," I said quietly, "can you stand?"

She tensed and lowered her arms. She was beautiful, but her beauty was marred by an ugly wound on her forehead that kept on bleeding, and purple-blue bruises over her left eye and cheek. Her nose, too, seemed broken.

She looked at me, but she didn't seem to really see me. There was too much horror in her emerald eyes for her to be able to see I was there to help.

"Come on," I said, grabbing her arm gently and helping her up. She let me, rising as well, and then I turned to the man, who stared at me with evident displeasure. "I heard you hitting her," I informed him, my voice low and threatening. "I live next door, you see. I recorded your fight tonight and all the noises I heard, including our little conversation."

I paused, leveling a meaningful look on his scowling face, and then said, "Don't you dare follow us, or I'll end you."

The woman leaned her entire weight on me as I wrapped my arm around her waist and half carried her toward the door. But then the man's hand was on my arm, and he growled "Nosy bitch" before he made a move to grab the woman.

But I wasn't having any of it. I whirled around, used his hold on my arm to grab his arm in return, and twisted it. He gasped in pain, but I strengthened my hold.

"You don't want to mess with me, bastard, or you'll regret the day you were born," I warned, locking his gaze with mine. For a moment, I could swear his eyes glowed with wrath, but then he curled his lip, and the moment was gone.

I wanted to do far more than just twist his arm. I wanted to grab his neck and crush his windpipe, a residual result of my extensive martial arts training. I wanted to see the whites of his eyes bulge with pinpricks of crimson. I wanted to see him opening and closing his mouth, trying to get a sound out to no avail. I wanted to cut his forehead, show him what his girlfriend felt when he did those things to her.

Some part of me hoped he would push me, that he would give me a reason to do all these things. But then he let me go as if my arm was on fire and stepped back, wincing in pain as he caressed his newly bruised arm.

"Bitch," he hissed.

Pulling my violent instincts in and locking them in a cage, I showed him my back, took the woman, and stepped out of the apartment, closing the door behind me.

And if he followed me, I would make him pay.

CHAPTER 1

I'd rather be anywhere else on a Friday night than the Hole. But Cassidy was my friend. The first friend I'd made since starting my new life away from my hometown. The moment I rescued her from her abusive relationship and we became fast friends, I promised to attend every show Cassidy was in, and I was proud that I'd kept up the commitment in the past three years. I would keep on doing so, too, even if it meant hanging out in places like this.

I wasn't one to go clubbing, but at least the other nightclubs where Fourcorns performed weren't as sleazy as this shithole. And at least I wasn't alone. Skye was the other friend Cassidy had roped into attending her shows.

"I got this new under-eye-bag concealer; wanna try it?" Skye asked, glancing at me. She was the only person who could disguise an insult inside an offer to help.

At once, I gave her the fake bright smile I'd perfected throughout the years. "Thanks, but it's fine. It's not like there's anyone here I need to look well rested for," I said, my attempt at making a joke failing.

She shrugged and shook her head as if how I looked was a personal affront to her. "Working night shifts in that *grocery store* sure takes its toll."

The mockery in her voice was palpable, and normally, it would take more than a gibe at my chosen occupation to get to me. But today had been shitty enough already, what with a customer filing a complaint about me to my boss because I refused to accept her expired coupons, and being in this hellhole now, it was hard to keep up my act. I needed that job. I'd worked my way up to shift manager in a matter of months. And the extra two dollars per hour really made a difference.

She harrumphed loudly and checked her phone, the brightness of the screen blinding in the dim light of the club. "It's almost ten already. When are they going to start?" she said, not really talking to me. It wasn't like Cassidy's band ever went on when they said they would.

Murmuring an unintelligible "I have no idea," I turned to the bar and asked for a glass of water. The bartender took my order but kept his eyes glued on Skye. He waited a few moments for her to notice him before sighing and returning to work when she didn't. It wasn't surprising, really; she was pretty, and she had men fighting for her attention on a daily basis. And there was a time when she would have appreciated his interest. But now she was with Tyler, and unlike the other men she'd dated, Tyler knew how to play her to keep her.

"Cassidy texted," Skye said as I sipped my water. She eyed my choice of liquid in disapproval. "They're on in five."

Thank God.

As shitty as this club was, it was packed. Cassidy's shows were never this packed, so I had to imagine it was the drink specials that had brought the crowd in tonight.

Skye started scrolling and tapping on her phone, ignoring the people pushing and shoving around her as if they didn't exist. As usual, she was ignoring me, which was great because I was not in the mood to talk, at least not about makeup. Instead, I hoped for some air; the place was too stuffy, and the people too stinky. I wasn't claustrophobic per se, but it was too much even for me.

Before I could tell Skye I was heading out, something moved to my right, and my spine stiffened. Surreptitiously, I took a long sip from my water and glanced sideways to see what it was. What I found made my entire body freeze.

A man stood there, leaning his back against the bar. He was extremely hot, with shoulder-length dark-brown hair, dark eyes, tanned skin, and a face that was both sexy and completely expressionless. His broad shoulders accentuated his tall frame and muscular figure, both evident even in the dark trench coat he wore. I instinctively moved in his direction, focusing entirely on him and ignoring the hair standing up on the back of my neck. There was an intense sense of danger in the air now that he was mere feet away.

Run, my instincts told me. *Run, and don't look back.*

I couldn't move, though. My eyes were glued to him as if watching him might turn off the eerie warning bells in my head. It wasn't a creepy vibe I got from him; I'd encountered my fair share of creeps before. This was something else entirely, and I wasn't sure I wanted to find out what it was. So shifting from foot to foot, I watched him, sneaking long glances I hoped no one noticed.

He ordered a beer and sipped it. Such a normal thing to do, but something about it seemed so calculated that my instincts were now roaring at me to flee. But I stared at him too long, and he must've sensed it because his eyes were suddenly on me.

I schooled my face and gave him a neutral smile before swiveling my head back to Skye. "Let's go up to the front," I told her, blood rushing to my ears, making it hard to breathe. "We can't see anything from here."

Thankfully, Skye was so lost in texting she simply hummed a positive "Sure" and let me lead us away from the man, whose eyes I felt on my back for a few long minutes.

Fourcorns was a great band for one reason only: Cassidy.

My friend had the voice of an actual angel. She could sing any genre she wanted. Hell, she even knew how to rap, and she did it well too.

She was crazy talented, so why she was slumming it with this band, I would never understand.

Not that I would ever tell her that. She could never appreciate compliments from someone she didn't respect.

I knew nothing about music, but even I could hear when the drummer lost his rhythm sometime during their first song and when the electric guitar wasn't entirely in tune. Cassidy didn't seem to care; she was lost in performing the songs she'd worked so hard to write.

Thanks to Cassidy's otherworldly voice and amazing stage presence, the crowd adored them. It also helped that Cassidy was as beautiful as Skye, if not more so. She wore a tiny black dress plastered to her curvy figure; its contrast with her ivory skin seemed even brighter under the stage lights. Her charcoal hair flowed down to her waist in manufactured curls, and her bright-green eyes were accentuated by smoky makeup. She looked absolutely gorgeous, and she knew it.

By the time the last song came on, I was so ready for it to be over with. I loved watching and listening to Cassidy sing, and I could do it for days on end, but the Hole was wearing me down, and I wanted to be back at my apartment, in my bed, listening to an educational podcast.

Finally, Cassidy said into the mic, "Thank you, Hole! You guys were awesome" before she and her band departed the stage. I was beyond relieved.

Skye, who'd been texting throughout the concert, put her phone back in her purse and said, "Let's go."

We headed backstage and found Cassidy alone in the dressing room. Skye was the first one to hug her. "You were unbelievable!" she squealed, as if she had been listening as intently as I had been.

Cassidy hugged her back, laughing. "Thank you," she said, as if she didn't already know how we all felt about her.

I gave her a shorter hug and said, "I can listen to you sing all day long."

She smirked. "Of course you can. I'm amazing."

And ever modest too.

"Where are the guys?" Skye asked, eyes darting around in anticipation. She might have a boyfriend she was obsessed with, but she still liked ogling eye candy.

"They went to buy some drinks." Cassidy sighed. "I don't want to drink, though. I'm tired. I want to go home."

Skye flipped her blonde hair back. "You're not going home without celebrating another successful gig, Cass!"

"Come on, Skye," Cassidy said, her smirk falling. "I'm not in the mood."

I frowned. "What's wrong?" Just a second ago, she was fine. Happy, even.

Cassidy sighed again. "Come on, let's get out of here."

Skye tried to argue, but Cassidy seemed to have her mind all made up. We left the club, and once we hit the street and clear air blasted my lungs, I felt infinitely better.

As we waited for Skye's cab to arrive, Cassidy said, "I think Shawn has a crush on me."

Cassidy thought every member of her band had a crush on her, or used to. Now, it was Shawn, the guitarist and arguably the second most talented of Fourcorns. Last time, it had been Emery, the drummer, who, I was positive, wasn't interested in girls.

"Go for it," Skye said. "It's been a while since you got some."

"But I'm seeing Ollie," she retorted, "and Bryan. Dating two of them at once is so energy consuming as it is. I don't need a third."

"It's fun, though." Skye grinned. "If Tyler wasn't so perfect, I would've done the same. I *did* the same."

Cassidy leaned against a light pole and took out a cigarette, lighting it up. I never understood singers who smoked, and I understood Cassidy less because she actually wanted to have a career in singing, and smoking wouldn't help her achieve that.

"I'm just tired, you know?" She inhaled the smoke deeply. "I know I'm hot, and I know I'm talented, but come *on*. Stop falling for me already."

"You need a Tyler," Skye advised sagely. "That will solve all of your problems."

"No, it won't," Cassidy replied irritably. She then turned to look at me. "What about you, Aileen? Anyone in your life, for a change?"

She knew the answer to that question already, but she still asked every time we met. It had become almost a habit for her. And like every time she asked, I acted as if it was the first time and manifested a blush, shaking my head and murmuring a soft "No."

She rolled her eyes and exhaled smoke into the night. "When are you ever going to start dating? Have sex? You can't stay a virgin forever."

If she only knew. "I . . . I don't . . . ," I stammered as I tried to figure out something evasive to respond with.

"Leave her be, Cass." Skye snickered. "Some people are just meant to be alone. It's not as if she doesn't have opportunities to meet guys. Whenever we're out, she's out. But she gives off this vibe that makes her so unapproachable," she said as if I wasn't standing right there.

"Yeah, I suppose so." Cassidy snickered, too, then gave me a once-over. "Seriously, though. You could be hot if you just tried, Aileen. You're pretty, in your own way. It wouldn't hurt for you to show a little skin, put some makeup on, run a brush through your hair. Maybe get some highlights or something. These baggy clothes aren't cutting it."

What she called *baggy clothes* were tights and a long-sleeved, V-neck tee with a sweater. If I didn't show even a small patch of skin, it wasn't good enough for her. But again, I was immune to her insults. It took far more than that to crack me.

Thankfully, I didn't have time to come up with a response since the cab arrived. Skye hugged us, told us she loved us (yeah, right), and took off.

Cassidy and I lived in the cheap part of town. Or at least it used to be cheap. Before, you could rent a sixth-story one-bedroom walk-up for like six hundred dollars a month. But developers swooped in and put in fancy stores and coffee shops, and now, you couldn't get a studio apartment for less than nine hundred dollars.

Which was why it had been such a big shock when Cassidy had wanted to move out of our shared apartment about six months ago, considering apartments were hardly affordable for a single person.

We first met when I'd just moved into the apartment next door to the one she shared with her then boyfriend, Austin. We moved in together after she left her abusive relationship, and I thought all was well. But one day back in April, without warning, Cassidy moved a couple of streets away from me. It was as if she was hiding something from me. Or someone. Or perhaps she simply couldn't stand living with me anymore.

Now, we walked together through the neighborhood. As usual, I accompanied Cassidy back home first before heading back to mine. I had adopted this protector mentality when it came to Cassidy, and even though she hated being a victim, she would never admit that she liked that I watched out for her.

Things were so different between us when Skye wasn't around.

As we walked, Cassidy said, "I really think you should start taking better care of yourself."

I didn't tell her that hooking up with guys didn't count as taking care of myself, so instead, I retorted, "Thank you for worrying, but you don't need to. I'm happy with my life."

She snorted. "How could you be happy, working in that store all the time and having no actual social life except for when Skye and I are hanging out?"

"It's a quiet, modest life," I told her, feeling a tad bit more defensive than usual. "I like it." *And for people like me, it's the best and only solution.*

"What about painting?" she asked out of nowhere. "You used to love those painting classes you took a couple of years ago."

Love was a very loaded word. "I still paint from time to time," I murmured reluctantly, "but those classes are expensive . . ."

She threw her hands up. "I give up," she said, annoyed. "Do whatever you want. Work shitty jobs for the rest of your boring life for all

I care. I don't know why I even bother since you seem so content with having no life at all!"

Cassidy had a problem comprehending different perspectives. She never bothered looking for the little nuances and experiences that made each person perceive the world in their own unique way. She couldn't grasp the idea that living this life gave me a sense of freedom I'd never dared dream of in the past.

So I didn't care to explain.

She deflated at the lack of response and gave a mighty huff. "I can't believe you love being like this, being so . . . so . . ." For once, she was at a loss for words in trying to describe me.

"I'm happy," I told her, forcing out an amicable smile. She wasn't wrong. I knew my life was far from good. My job sucked and didn't pay well. My only friends were Cassidy and Skye. I hadn't bought anything new to wear in years, and if it were not for Cassidy, the only places I would ever go were work and home.

But it was *my* life, and I *was* happy—or at the very least, happier than I'd ever been before. The simple act of coming home from work and putting my key into the door of an apartment that was mine meant a lot to me.

Lips pursed, she didn't speak to me until we reached her building. "I'll see you tomorrow," she said, moving past me to the building's entrance door.

"See you," I retorted quietly.

I was about to leave when Cassidy suddenly said, "Can I ask you something?"

I turned around and stared at her, frowning. "Sure."

I couldn't read the expression on her face, nor the look in her eyes, when she asked, "If you were to never see me again, would you miss me?"

My spine stiffened in shock as I searched her face. But she looked away, fiddling with the hem of her dress as if she was embarrassed by that question. Which she probably was; Cassidy had never been insecure when it came to me. In fact, if anything, she took me for granted.

I'd tried so hard to show Cassidy my support and loyalty. I'd done everything in my power to give her the sense that she was a huge part of my life, an inseparable part of my life, even. But it appeared I was wrong. Perhaps I was so broken that my attempts came out as nonchalant, or stoic.

But I cared about her. I cared about her so, so much. And it hurt that Cassidy was oblivious to my feelings.

Whatever she was thinking didn't matter, though, because I chose to answer her with the utmost sincerity. "You're my friend, Cassidy," I said, which, despite everything, was the truth. "Of course I'd miss you."

Our friendship might be a complicated one, but Cassidy was a part of my life. She was like a sister to me at this point. If she left and never returned, I would feel the loss.

She didn't seem convinced, though, if her puckered brows were anything to go by. She turned her back to me and inserted the key. "Thank you," she murmured, pushed the door open, and shut it behind her.

I stared ahead, completely baffled. Most of the time, I understood Cassidy. But this time, I was at a loss.

Shaking my head, I restarted my walk back to my place and decided to forget about it. Cassidy tended to get forlorn more often than not. All I could do during these tough times was be there for her.

She would've never done the same for you, a little voice whispered in my mind, but I ignored it. It didn't matter what Cassidy would or wouldn't have done for me. It wasn't like she had any idea what I was going through, or who I truly was.

And I intended to keep it that way.

CHAPTER 2

It was the beginning of October and already relentlessly cold, as fall tended to get in New England.

Huddled in my comfy hoodie, I went to the local bar several streets away. Cassidy was probably already doing the sound check even though her show wouldn't start for another few hours. I wondered if she was going to wear her usual skimpy attire, considering the Banner Bar wasn't known for its good heating, but then again, it was Cassidy. She could wear a swimsuit in the middle of January if it meant it would bring bigger crowds to her shows.

Skye wasn't there yet, so I chose a table close to the stage, settled in with a glass of orange juice, and watched the soccer game playing on the TV screen across the bar. So much for rushing my much-needed shower, thinking I was going to be late.

With nothing left to do, I was staring around the bar when I noticed a man walking in. He was tall and muscular with broad shoulders, and he was wearing faded jeans, combat boots, and a dark trench coat, with its hood up, concealing his face. He settled at the bar and discussed something with the barman. He didn't take off his coat, which was a damned shame because from what I could see of his body, he seemed like a snack.

My ogling was cut short when Skye dropped her purse on the table and plopped her ass on the seat in front of me.

"Tyler almost didn't let me hang out with you girls tonight," she said in her own way of saying hello. "Stupid man. Wanted us to stay in and watch a movie. *Again*. As if I don't have other things to do."

You love it when he pulls shit like that was what I thought. What I said, however, was, "He really loves you."

She smiled dreamily, as though she hadn't just talked shit about him. "He does, doesn't he?"

I was spared from responding when I saw Cassidy heading over to us. As I suspected, she wore jean shorts that showed half her butt, a black crop top, and thigh-high black boots with extremely high heels. It was a wonder she could walk as straight as if she was wearing flip-flops.

"Hey," she greeted us with a surprisingly somber face. Usually before a show, Cassidy was high on nerves and excitement. This wasn't like her.

Skye didn't seem to notice. "Oh, my god," she said, looking her up and down. "You look *gorge*, Cass."

"Do I?" she said, and there was something seriously aggressive about her tone that was so out of character, she seemed to realize it herself and put on a forced smile. "Thanks, Skye."

Completely oblivious, Skye grinned back. "When's the sound check?"

My eyes darted to Cassidy, and her eyes were no longer on us. She was holding her phone, staring at the screen with hard eyes. "In thirty," she mumbled as she typed something on her phone and then bit her lip, as if waiting for a response.

"Then sit with us," Skye prompted, and Cassidy reluctantly did so.

That's when I felt the side of my face burning. Someone was watching us. *Me.*

I sipped my juice as I let my eyes roam over the room. They landed on the man I'd seen before. His face, still hooded, seemed to be turned in Cassidy's direction, focused on her in a way that gave me pause. He wasn't moving, and he seemed to be staring at her, but something told me it didn't stem from interest or anything like that. He seemed to be . . . waiting.

When I averted my gaze before he could catch me staring, I felt again as if someone was watching *me*. But when I looked around, no one seemed to be looking my way. Why would they, with Cassidy and Skye around? No one ever looked at me, and if I was being honest, that was just fine.

". . . so I said, 'Ty, you *know* Finn hates that you bust his balls in public,'" Skye was saying. She'd been rambling on and on about her possessive boyfriend, Tyler, after Cassidy sat down. "And you know what he tells me? 'No one calls my woman a bitch and gets away with it.'" She sighed. "I was like *Holy shit, that's so hot*, so of course I dragged him to the nearest room and—"

"Fucked his brains out," Cassidy cut her off with a dry, uninterested tone.

Skye shot her a look. "You sound disappointed," she noted flatly.

Cassidy raised her eyes from her phone and turned to her. "I know what Tyler is capable of," she said, green eyes glinting ominously. "Been there, done that, did not buy the T-shirt."

Silence spread across the table, and I stared at Cassidy, gaping. This was the one topic we never talked about. It was an unwritten rule, so much so that we never even mentioned it, not since Skye started dating Tyler. It was for the sake of their friendship, after all.

But Cassidy, already in a peculiar mood, seemed to throw caution to the wind.

Skye folded her arms and glared at her. "What the hell is wrong with you?"

As if she'd been waiting for this, Cassidy jumped to her feet. "What is wrong with *me*?" she repeated, angrily incredulous. "Why do you think I care about what you and Lil-Dick Tyler are doing every moment of every day?"

My heartbeat escalated. This had never happened before. For the three years I'd known them, Cassidy and Skye had never fought, not even once. For Cassidy to not only confront Skye about anything but also seemingly purposefully pick a fight with her about Tyler, the most sensitive topic between the two of them, was not just out of the ordinary; it was downright bizarre.

Concerned, I glanced between the two of them. "Cassidy," I said quietly as Skye rose from her seat, her pretty face twisted in rage. "Skye, both of you, sit back down—"

"Oh, don't you fucking start, Aileen!" Cassidy sniped at me. "You know I'm right! You're just as sick as I am from constantly hearing about Tyler and how good he fucks her!" She shot a vicious glare at Skye. "Besides, you know why he's with you, don't you?"

Skye gasped, obviously hurt, and I felt my heart kicking in my chest.

"Cassidy, don't—" I started, but she wouldn't have any of it.

Cassidy leaned over toward Skye, her eyes full of blazing emotions I couldn't quite decipher, as she hissed, voice venomous, "Everyone knows that whenever he sleeps with you, he wishes it was me."

That did it.

"How dare you!" Skye snapped, angry tears filling her eyes. "You stupid slut!"

I stood up, eyes jumping around the room. We were drawing too much attention for my liking. It was enough that there was that man staring at Cassidy. We didn't need for this to become even more of a spectacle. "Calm down, both of you," I said quietly. "Let's sit back down and talk it out."

Cassidy threw her phone on the table. "As if I'm going to stay and 'talk it out,'" she said, mimicking my voice exaggeratingly. "I'm gonna go get some air. Don't fucking follow me, either of you."

I grabbed her wrist. "Cassidy, wait—"

She threw my hold off and strode outside the bar.

Skye grabbed her purse. "What a cunt," she hissed furiously. She turned to look at me. "Are you seriously going to stay and watch the show after what she just said to me?"

"Skye, stay," I said as gently as I could. "You know Cassidy didn't mean anything she said. It's just the nerves talking." Though I wasn't so sure about it. I'd never seen Cassidy lose it like this before. Not since her breakup with Austin.

"Whatever," she said, glaring at me now. "Keep being her little pushover minion, for all I care. I'm out of here."

She stormed out of the bar, her blonde curls waving behind her.

I slumped in my seat, wondering how the hell things had deteriorated so quickly.

Choosing to wait for Cassidy to come back, I walked toward the bar and ordered tap water. I drummed my fingers on the counter as I drank, and the more minutes that ticked by, the more anxious I became.

What was taking her so long?

The band was already getting settled on the stage, but Cassidy was nowhere in sight. It wasn't like her to be late for anything when it came to the band. Nothing about today was like her, to be honest.

I sipped the last drop of water in my glass and instinctively glanced toward the man who'd been looking in Cassidy's direction.

He was gone.

My heart kicked in my chest. *Don't panic,* I told myself. *Maybe it's just a coincidence. Maybe Cassidy is simply in the toilet, and I'm worried for nothing.*

First, I walked out of the bar, but the street was completely empty. Cassidy was probably in the restroom, then. I went back inside, walked toward the toilet, and entered the room.

Fear gripped me when I saw Cassidy wasn't there.

A cold wind caressed the nape of my neck, causing my ponytail to sway a little. Urgency burning through me, I turned to the window and saw it was open . . . and wide enough for a person to climb through.

Without thinking twice, I pulled myself onto the ledge, using the sink right beneath it, and looked out. The window led into a deserted alley, and I debated whether to jump out. What if Cassidy was already backstage, and I'd simply missed her? What if my instincts were wrong?

The problem was I'd disregarded my instincts before, and that had resulted in deadly consequences I still had nightmares about. I was learning not to ignore past mistakes if I didn't want another innocent person to get killed.

Especially not Cassidy.

Decision made, I jumped out the window and landed roughly on my feet. My knees ached from the impact, slight shock vibrating through my body, but I ignored the sensation and scanned the alley. There were dumpsters to my left and the main road to my right. *Where should I go?*

A noise to my left followed by a masculine hissed curse was the answer. I crouched behind one of the dumpsters and peeked from behind it, trying to listen beyond my thundering heart.

The man from the bar was holding Cassidy against the wall. He loomed over her, his lips pressing against hers.

The logical thing would've been to call the police, if not back when I hadn't found Cassidy in the bar, then right now. But I couldn't get involved with the police. I couldn't have my name associated with anything having to do with law enforcement, and even though I could have left an anonymous tip, Cassidy was running out of time.

If you were to never see me again, would you miss me? she'd asked merely two days ago.

My heart beat like a drum in my ears. I had to do something.

When Cassidy went limp in the man's hold, I couldn't help the gasp that left me. My hand squeezed my phone. I was frozen in place as I watched the horrible scene unfolding before me.

Time seemed to slow down. The man's eerily aglow neon-blue eyes stared at me, like he was trying to decide his next move. He was breathing heavily, stepping closer to me, his eyes blazing as he scanned me from head to toe. His black boots hit the ground in reverberating thuds I could feel vibrating in my bones. Like a deer caught in headlights, I stood rooted in place, horror and fascination flowing through me in equal measure at the sight of this tall, gorgeous man making his way toward me.

I shrieked when the man was suddenly right in my face as though he'd teleported over to where I was. All I could do was stare, wide eyed, as he ripped the phone from my hand and clutched it so hard it broke apart and fell to the ground in little electronic pieces.

Now that he was so close, he seemed faintly familiar. It was only when my instincts started yelling at me to *RUN!* that I realized where I'd seen him before—a couple of days ago, in fact, in the Hole. But I couldn't run. My body was locked in place, unable to move, as if held there by his sheer will, an invisible force I was sure was there while I struggled against it in my mind.

He didn't say a word when he suddenly pushed me to the ground so that I was flat on my back. He leaned down and grabbed my chin in an unbreakable hold. As he hovered over me, his trench coat fell around him, casting a weird shadow.

And when I tried to move, I couldn't. I could move only my eyes, and even then, I couldn't blink.

Panic unfolded inside me, rattling so much that I felt all kinds of terrible memories rise to the surface of my mind. It was like the nightmares kept repeating themselves.

I couldn't save Cassidy.

I couldn't save myself.

I was helpless.

Utterly helpless.

The basement flashed before my eyes. The blood. Ash. The belt in my hand. The hazel eyes of my father, so similar to mine and yet so alien, bright with fervor as he delighted in forcing me to participate in his abhorrent activities.

And here I was again. Unable to move. To help either my friend or myself. But it wasn't fear holding me in place. It was . . . *him.*

Then something astonishing happened.

His lips landed on mine.

Everything in me wanted to thrash against him. But all I felt was groggy instead, as though he was drugging me the longer his lips were pasted against my own, unmoving. My eyelids grew heavy, falling like drapes over my eyes, breaking the contact with his eerily glowing ones. Soon, my entire body became limp, exhausted, as if I'd just finished running a marathon.

Before I could form another thought, reality fell away, and my mind was no more.

My body hurt, but it wasn't a great pain; it was almost like I was on painkillers, which numbed a much more unbearable ache.

I was lying in a hospital bed, but the bed wasn't between four white walls. It was in the middle of a field of an endless expanse filled with red flowers and green, healthy grass, with a deep-purple sky full of tiny stars.

The colors were vivid, the flowers like pinpricks of blood across the plain. I wanted to get off the hospital bed and marvel at the sight. But when I tried to, I couldn't. Bound to the bed rails by leather straps with gold buckles that cut into my wrists, I wasn't going anywhere. When I tried to move my hands, I realized there was something else wrapped around my left wrist. It looked like an old, battered wristwatch. My heart gave a large thud in my ears, as if it recognized the watch, but my mind was too foggy to figure out what it was about the watch that bothered me.

Out of thin air, a dismembered head dropped onto the mattress before me. Even in my delirious state, I knew who it belonged to, but surprisingly, it didn't freak me out. I'd known the day would come eventually when I would see this face again.

A voice echoed loudly in my head.

"Drink it."

I frowned.

Drink what?

A gash appeared on the head's cheek, crimson blood spilling down its face onto the white sheets. *"The blood,"* the voice insisted. *"Drink the blood."*

Funny that a severed head appearing out of nowhere didn't quite make me feel as strange as the thought of drinking someone's blood. I stared at the head for a few frozen moments, feeling a distant sense of sadness. I didn't want to drink the blood, but somehow, I knew I had little choice in the matter. Whatever or whoever had brought me here was not going to be taking no for an answer.

"Drink it," the voice said once more, louder and more forcefully than it had before.

Looking around, I saw the belts were gone, and my hands were free, all but for the shabby wristwatch. My body was compelled to move before I made up my mind. My torso leaned forward, and my lips brushed against the wound, my tongue flicking out to lick the blood. *It doesn't have the metallic flavor blood usually has,* I thought with growing wonder. It was like water, tasteless yet so vital; I was suddenly desperate for it, as though I'd been wandering in an endless desert, parched for so long, and had finally found an oasis.

I put my entire mouth over the cut and sucked.

Stillness came over me, freezing my heart, chilling my veins. The more I sucked, the colder I felt, and while it was disconcerting, it was eerily alluring, pulling me in, tempting me to feel . . . *more.*

My hands found hair and pulled, bringing the skin impossibly closer as I licked and devoured every crimson drop my tongue could find. Ironically, a frosty kind of heat lit up inside me, making me feel as if my own blood was suddenly on fire, the flames spreading across my body, causing me to shudder at their force.

It was a war of heat and frost, fire and ice, that made my body feel more alive than it had ever been. I felt so light, like everything that had been bothering me, all of my problems and regrets, had been lifted up and thrown away, leaving nothing but a wicked, awe-inspiring sensation of invincibility.

I had no idea how much time had passed before there was no more blood for me to suck. I pulled back, lamenting the loss of the rush, and the severed head disappeared into dust.

Finally, I lifted myself off the bed. But my feet didn't touch the flowers or the grass; instead, they went right through.

I fell down an airless, dark void as oblivion took me under once more.

CHAPTER 3

It was deathly quiet when I awoke. I tried opening my eyes, but my lids weighed a ton. It'd been a while since I'd felt so weary. Something was wrong.

But then the memories came so quickly and hard that they slapped me awake at once. Ignoring the heaviness, my eyes snapped open and darted around.

A man holding Cassidy, kissing her, that man right in my face, pressing his lips against mine, then nothing.

I was in a small, unfamiliar room furnished only with the twin bed I was lying in. The floor, walls, and ceiling were made of wood. There was only one small window that let me see the night sky. Pushing down the thin blanket that covered me, I put in a lot of effort to sit up. Using my fingers as a brush, I untangled my loose bed head ponytail, brushed it until the long brown wavy strands were less of a mess, and pulled them back up.

My body begged me to lie down again and go back to sleep, but I refused its whims and forced myself up on my feet. After my knees stopped threatening to buckle under the exhaustion, I toddled to the door on the opposite end of the room. When I turned the door handle and pushed, I found that, unsurprisingly, it was locked.

Sighing, I took my hand off the handle and began to make the long trip to the window when the door suddenly opened, and in walked the towering man who'd assaulted Cassidy and me. I saw him clearly now, thanks to the lamp dangling from the ceiling.

He wore the same trench coat he'd had on at the Hole, where I'd seen him the first time, and his eyes were midnight blue. He was *that* man, the one with the terrifying presence who called all my survival instincts to rapt attention, yet when he moved, like a predator stalking his prey—slow, silent, and careful—I couldn't help but be hypnotized.

He closed the door behind him and faced me. "Name," he said, his voice low, rough, and commanding.

I might've been inexplicably tired, but my mind had completely woken up. "I would like to understand what is going on," I said in a formal tone, ignoring his order. My heart thudded in my chest as everything in me yelled to flee, to run, that this man was dangerous.

But I had to ignore the voice of reason since there was nowhere to go anyway. Not with his tall, muscular body blocking the only exit. Besides, since I had no idea where exactly I was, running seemed like a dumb idea. At least until I found Cassidy, and we could both get out of here.

The man stared at me for a long moment. Then everything blurred as he swiftly and quickly pushed me against the closed door, his fingers digging into my shoulders. I gasped, wincing at his hard hold, but said nothing.

"Name," he repeated, growling.

"Aileen," I let out, breathless. Goose bumps burst to life over my skin as I was hammered by both nerves and awful, *awful* exhilaration.

He's not hitting you, he's not hitting you, he's not hitting you . . .

"Full name," he said.

"Aileen . . . Henderson," I replied, my voice trembling even as my heartbeat seemed to slow. I forced my muscles to relax one by one, moderating my breaths. *Calm down, Aileen; you've got to calm down . . .*

"Age," he commanded.

"Twenty-one," I retorted.

"Country of birth."

27

"United States."

"State?"

"Maine."

"Ethnicity."

That was an odd request, but I responded nonetheless, even though everything in me rebelled against it. "Scottish, Egyptian, Ukrainian."

"Education."

"Some high school."

That made him pause. His face, previously brutally expressionless, contorted for a moment in what seemed like anger before regaining composure. "When did you drop out?"

It seemed like he wasn't expecting to have a high school dropout on his hands, if I went by his asking a question instead of barking orders. "Eleventh grade."

He moved on, returning to said barks. "Talents."

"None."

Another pause. Then—"Hobbies."

This was a tricky one. I liked painting, but I wouldn't consider it a hobby. My passion for it was . . . complicated. "None," I said, seeing as I didn't have any notable talents or interests.

He released me and stepped back. "The name's Ragnor, but you will address me as *my Lord*," he said curtly. "Sit. We need to talk."

I wanted to laugh. Call him *my Lord*? Who the hell did he think he was?

But one look at his harsh, unyielding face, and any humor I might've felt deserted me.

Even though the last thing I wanted was to do as he ordered, I groggily crossed the room and obediently sat down on the bed. He crouched before me until we were eye level. "I'm a vampire," he said, voice neutral as he delivered the blows. "I gave you the Imprint, meaning you're now a vampire too. With me so far?"

My throat was instantly dry, and for a split second, I wondered if this could be a sick joke—he didn't *give* me anything; he only took everything away. The thing was, he was deadly serious.

Seeing as I wasn't exactly responsive at the moment, he continued. "I will send someone over soon to give you paperwork to sign and explain everything else. Meanwhile, do not attempt to run away." His eyes suddenly flashed an unnatural bright-neon-blue color. I froze in shock. "I would know if you did, and you do not want to anger me."

He straightened and strode out of the room, then locked the door again from the outside.

I'd never been into those books, TV shows, or movies everyone seemed to love about the supernatural, including vampires. But if I had to choose a favorite mythological creature to be a fan of, I would probably be team werewolf.

Sitting on the bed in the small room, I tried to make sense of everything. First, I tried to wrap my head around the vampire thing. Magic was an extremely abstract concept, one I hardly believed in, and the existence of any sort of fantasy race was reserved for moral-inducing fairy tales.

Yet Ragnor didn't seem to be lying. He'd looked as if he believed every word he'd said. I raised my hands to my neck, feeling for a bite mark. Wasn't that how people got turned into vampires? But I found nothing.

How had his eyes glowed like two beacons of light staring right into my soul? No one had eyes like that. And how could I be here now, wherever this was, when I was just with Cassidy in that alley behind the Banner Bar? How could I be seriously contemplating the existence of vampires? And *me*? Did he expect me to believe I was an actual vampire too?

The door opened, and into the room walked a stunning woman carrying a stack of papers. She seemed to be in her midtwenties, with seafoam green eyes and waist-length dark-auburn curls bouncing effortlessly with every step she took. She had a voluptuous body, and she moved with the confidence of someone used to getting their way.

She kicked the door closed and sat on the bed next to me. "I'm Margarita," she said in a slightly accented voice. "I work for Vampire Resources. I got the dry details from our Lord and fixed up some paperwork for you to sign."

There were so many things wrong with what she just said that I didn't know where to start. But most importantly—"Reverse it."

She looked at me as if I had just sprouted a new head. "What?"

"The vampire thing. Reverse it," I clarified. If I was going to buy into this ridiculous story, I wanted out. I was not going to become some mythological creature.

She cocked her head. "You newbies never cease to amaze me," she said, her eyes narrowing with disapproval. "If it wasn't clear, then no, it's impossible. Once you're given the Imprint, it's for eternity."

Not life. *Eternity.* "Am I immortal?" I asked, trying to make sense of the nonsensical.

"Yes, unless you do something incredibly stupid," she responded and put down the paperwork on the bed. "Listen, you're a vampire. As our Lord, Ragnor Rayne, must've told you, he gave you the Imprint, which is the essence that allows every human inflicted by it to transition into a vampire. This is an irreversible condition; you will be a vampire until the day you die," she added with a sharp look.

She grabbed a couple of papers and handed them to me. "Here are some mandatory forms you need to sign before I can proceed with the briefing. Take notice that if you choose not to sign, you'll be Leagueless."

"Leagueless?" I asked, still trying to process what was happening to me.

When she responded, she seemed impatient, as if I had asked the dumbest question in the world. "If you're attacked, kidnapped, tortured . . . you're on your own."

I looked down at the forms. Vampires were the hunters, weren't they? But then again, so were humans. Both were monsters in their own right, and both could probably become the prey.

Gritting my teeth, I said, "I want to read it first."

"Be my guest." She shrugged.

The title read "League System Agreement." Below were a bunch of clauses entailing what living as a Leagued vampire meant: follow every order and rule, drink only blood provided by the League sources, work for the League in order to maintain the Leagued vampire status, attend all mandatory League events, complete the Comprehensive Newcomer Three-Month Course, and so much more that it made my head dizzier than it already was. The only thing I needed to know was that a League meant some sort of vampire community. At the bottom of the page, in big letters, it said, "By signing, you agree to all of the above."

The next page was a Secrecy Agreement detailing that the Vampire Society was, in fact, a secret—shocking, I know—and that any violation of the agreement would result in immediate expulsion from the League ranks, rendering one Leagueless, thus doomed to fend for themselves. It was basically a standard NDA—nondisclosure agreement—only if you violated this one, they kicked you out and left you alone in the world with no protection, no home.

"Do you have legal backing for all of these?" I inquired, keeping my voice steady as, inside me, the realization, the full understanding of what was going on, was beginning to sink in, and I didn't like it. I didn't like it one bit.

"We have our own judicial system," Margarita replied dryly. "Here in the Rayne League, our Lord's word is the law."

Ragnor hadn't lied. This woman wasn't lying to me either. On the off chance they weren't some vampire-worshipping conspiracy theorists, if I didn't sign the forms and then returned to my life, I might die sooner rather than later. In the myths, vampires had many weaknesses: sun, garlic, and mirrors, to name a few. Say they were telling the truth. What if those weaknesses applied now?

"I want proof," I said, holding Margarita's gaze. "I've been assaulted and kidnapped by your *Lord* and told some shitty fantasy story about vampires, but I have no bite mark on my neck or anywhere else, and I'm not craving human blood." I paused, panting as I worked myself up into a prepanicked state. "So give me proof."

Margarita studied me for a few quiet moments before giving me an annoyingly secretive grin. "Sign the papers first."

I wanted to throw said papers in her face. I wanted to storm out of this place and go back home to my dump of an apartment. I wanted to return to my blissfully boring life, where I didn't follow my stupid friend into a dark alley, wasn't kissed by a stranger, and wasn't told that vampires existed and that I was now one.

Yet I couldn't shake the nagging feeling in my gut that told me the best route was the one I was most reluctant to take.

My situation reminded me of the poem "The Road Not Taken," by Robert Frost. It was the last literary piece I'd studied in English class before I dropped out, so I remembered it vividly. In the poem's case, it's about the importance of one's choices through life and how these choices shape one's journey through life.

I had a feeling that in my case, though, the choice wouldn't simply reshape my life. It would destroy everything I'd ever been and would never mend everything it broke.

"Time is ticking," Margarita murmured, tapping her watchless wrist.

"Fine," I said, reaching a bitter decision. Grimacing, I took the pen she'd given me and signed the damned papers.

She took the papers and looked at me. "You're now officially Leagued. Congratulations, and welcome aboard."

"Talk," I spat.

She finally did. "Being a vampire doesn't change the fact you need to eat normal food or sleep. The only difference is the liquid substance you now require; blood is your new water."

She rummaged through her bag and took out a bottle full of what could've passed as red wine but was most likely blood. Handing it to me, she said, "Make sure you drink at least one bottle every day."

After eyeing the bottle suspiciously, I uncorked it and put it to my lips. Ignoring the slight nausea I felt at the thought of downing actual human blood, I closed my eyes and took a sip. To my surprise, it was as tasteless as water. Just like Margarita had said.

"Now, let's start with weaknesses," she said, smiling sharply when I lowered the bottle from my lips. "We have none; although, much like most people assume, we prefer nighttime over daylight, for no other reason than that vampires are pretty much nocturnal and are most productive at night. Garlic, mirrors, all that bullshit? Not true. We can't get sick, guns aren't effective on us, and the only way to kill us is by beheading or carving our hearts out. We can be maimed by simple blades, and we have no aversion to stakes, whether wooden or silver.

"That's everything you need to know for now," she finished. "The rest you will learn in the Comprehensive Newcomer Three-Month Course, but until then, you're all set. You have a few more things to sign and read through—residential rules, life as a Leagued vampire, and so forth. I'll leave the paperwork for you to go through; then I'll send someone up here with some food. Meanwhile, rest." She rose to her feet, tucking the signed forms under her arm. "Your body must still be exhausted from the Imprint, and you need to regain your strength. Tomorrow night we're going to get you all settled."

She was already at the door before she turned back to me and smiled once more. It wasn't a nice smile. In fact, it was downright evil. "Again, welcome to the Rayne League, and congratulations on your successful Imprinting."

When Margarita was gone, I was left staring at the door and feeling empty while my head filled with wild thoughts.

After I went through the rest of the forms and reading material, it took me a while to finally make sense of everything. I found a blank paper at the bottom of the stack and wrote down the most urgent details I had on my mind:

Vampires are real, and they have glowing eyes.

I'm a vampire.

Cassidy must be a vampire too.

Ragnor Rayne is a fucking prick.

CHAPTER 4

I felt much better when Margarita picked me up the next evening. I'd slept throughout the day and woke up feeling moderately energetic. The only thing missing was a shower and new clothes.

As Margarita walked me out of the room, I mapped out the place in my head. It was a small warehouse located in some sort of unfamiliar industrial area, which led me to wonder where I had been taken and how long it had been since the night I was supposedly given the Imprint. Was it yesterday? A week ago? Even longer than that?

Margarita and I passed a few closed doors, and I wondered if Cassidy was behind one of them.

Speaking of which—"Where is Cassidy?" I asked, breaking the silence. Realizing she might not know who I was talking about, I clarified, "My friend. You know, the one you took along with me. Or didn't you?"

Margarita glanced at me briefly. "That's none of your concern. Just know that she's fine."

I grimaced, and her face turned stony. I wouldn't get anything else out of her, it seemed like, but I refused to give up. "Tell me," I said, voice low.

She paused and turned to me. "I don't think you understand your position, newbie," she suddenly said, and her eyes glowed again. "You don't get to bark orders as you see fit. You're not entitled to any sort of information. In this place, the hierarchy is very clear." She stepped closer to me, and even though she was shorter than me, she somehow managed to look down her nose at my face. "I'm a Lieutenant, the Lord's second-in-command, and your rank is the equivalent of a foot soldier."

Glowering at her, I folded my arms. "I don't give a shit what your rank is," I informed her. "I just want to know where the fuck Cassidy is."

Her eyes narrowed. "Your insolence will be reported. My Lord is not the forgiving kind."

She resumed her walk, ignoring my request, and I debated whether I should stand my ground and throw a tantrum until she told me what I wanted to know. Yet, unless I shook her until she answered, it seemed she wouldn't budge.

Irritated, I followed her. *Not to worry,* I thought. *I will find out soon enough.* Or so I hoped.

Margarita stopped before the warehouse entrance door before crouching down, feeling up the floor. She caught a hidden handle and pulled up a trap door, revealing a staircase. "Follow me," she instructed.

We climbed down the staircase until we reached a barely lit, dark, small room with brick walls. There was an elevator, and the only way to order it was by handprint. "You don't get to have your handprint installed until you're a year old for security reasons," she explained off-handedly as she pressed her palm to the monitor. It flickered green, and soon the elevator arrived; its metal doors opened.

Margarita leaned back against the elevator wall with folded arms as we began to descend. Meanwhile, my mind was on Cassidy, and my chest tightened. Her life, much like mine, wasn't great, and yet she must've been forced to give it up like I had been, because of Ragnor Rayne. She wasn't the type who liked losing control over her life. It was the single thing we had in common.

After her parents died years ago, leaving her in the hands of her abusive aunt whom she'd escaped from right into the arms of her abusive ex, she strived to get ahold of her shitty life and make it better. She may have had no meaningful relationships in her life, what with Skye being her comfort friend and all the guys she saw being nothing more than a passing fancy, but she was in charge. Despite Fourcorns being a trashy band, it was *hers* to use as a stepping stone toward her dream to become a solo artist. And while I, too, was merely a pebble under her shoe, another person to discard once she reached stardom, she still wanted me around. Needed me to be there when she was in danger.

It was a lonely life, but it was a life of her choosing. Just like I'd chosen mine.

And yet it was forever gone. Cassidy, wherever she was, was probably going through the same thing I was. She probably woke up disoriented, scared out of her mind. She probably was interrogated by Ragnor in the same rude, abrupt manner, with violent force, which Cassidy couldn't really handle.

Yet I wasn't there to do the one thing she relied on me for as a friend. I wasn't there to protect her.

Would I lose her, like I lost everyone else?

There was an entire underground city beneath the warehouse, which seemed to spread out for miles. The city was like a mix between a labyrinth, a shopping mall, and a medieval-style ship, with marble floors, brightly lit caverns, and wooden walls.

Margarita gave me the grand tour of the place. We started from where we exited the elevator. "This is the entrance hall," she said in a somewhat bored tone, gesturing dismissively at the room, which was more like a terrace overlooking the entire place from above. "The elevator here is the only exit."

She led me toward an escalator heading down. It was one of dozens of escalators that I could see with the naked eye. It was almost like a high-tech version of Hogwarts.

We reached the floor below, and she motioned toward closed mahogany doors. "This is the cafeteria," she said and passed it by, not bothering to show me inside.

We arrived at a corridor with a few doors. It was dimly lit, with dangling lanterns and smooth marble floors. "Here you have the classrooms," she explained, sounding less bored now. "One of them is reserved for the Comprehensive Newcomer Three-Month Course—or CNC for short—while the others are designated for different divisions of the League."

"So, it isn't the only course you offer?" I asked, unable to hold back the sarcasm. "Do you have a League syllabus?"

Margarita shot me a glare. "I would suggest getting rid of this tone sooner rather than later, *noob*," she murmured warningly.

I glared back, lips pursed.

The corridor led to another escalator leading to the floor below. That floor looked far more high tech than the rest; while the floor was parquet and vintage lanterns lit up the space, some of the walls were partially transparent, with what looked like offices behind them. "This is the Vampire Resources department." Margarita motioned toward the large place. There was a note of pride in her voice. "As the head of this department, I have thirty workers who do all the work I'm not always able to. They're efficient and well behaved."

It sounded like she was speaking about well-trained dogs. She even looked at me expectantly, as if wanting me to show my amazement at what seemed to be her pride and joy.

I managed to grit out a dry, unfeeling "Wow."

"I know, right?" she said, seemingly oblivious to my tone this time. Smirking, she turned to me, her eyes glinting ominously. "Fortunately, I don't foresee you ever working for me."

That worked for me as well.

We passed a corridor and took an escalator back to the upper floor, though to a different section. "There's the Archive there." She pointed at an obsidian door. "Access is granted only to people who complete the CNC, much like most of the League's facilities."

She stopped and turned to me. "The Rayne League's main focus is knowledge. We trade in it, mine it, and protect it," she said. "Knowledge is very powerful, and our Lord makes sure not to hand it so freely to those who don't deserve it."

I didn't care much for reading, but it sounded a bit too extreme. "He sounds paranoid," I said before I could think twice.

Margarita's face contorted in annoyance. "He's not paranoid," she snapped. "He's smart. Smarter than you will ever be. He understands what makes the world tick and the psychological tendencies of people, and so he's careful." Her eyes were flashing vehemently, full of awe, reverence, and . . . affection.

Someone has a crush.

Not that I cared. "Everything points to the contrary, though," I sniped back, my anger getting the better of me. "If he's so careful, how come he just randomly gives the Imprint to people like Cassidy and me? Vampires are powerful, aren't they—or rather, we? So, isn't he far more careless than you give him credit for?"

Her lips stretched into a smile full of teeth. *Like a shark.* "Aah, noob," she murmured, looking me up and down in amused disdain. "You'll find out soon enough just what kind of man Ragnor Rayne is."

Her patronizing tone made my blood boil, but she was already walking, conversation done.

She took me to one of the lower floors, and we arrived at what looked like a hotel hallway. "These are the shared-residence wings," she said, bored again, while leading me to one of the doors. "You will share this suite with two other newcomers like you."

When we stopped, she shoved a piece of paper into my hands and said, "This is your weekly schedule starting tomorrow."

I looked down at the spreadsheet. It was a timetable for the CNC.

"As for your stuff," she continued, and I snapped my eyes back up to hers, sudden tension making my spine go stiff. "We'll bring over all of the essentials and clothes from your former apartment."

Narrowing my eyes, I said, "Former?"

She gave me another sharklike grin. "You didn't think you would go back there, did you?"

I clenched my hands into fists. "How do you know where I live?" I asked as dread filled my gut. Here was another thing I was forced to give up. Not that the apartment was that important to me, but it's what it symbolized that mattered: the freedom I would no longer have.

"We have your purse," she replied dryly. "We found the address there."

My heartbeat quickened. *I threw away the other keys, and I burned those articles, didn't I? They wouldn't be able to find anything . . . would they?*

In one of the forms, I'd signed my new lease with the Rayne League and forfeited my old apartment lease. At the time, I hadn't thought they would go to my apartment and snoop. It was the last time I was signing any sort of contract without legal advice.

Margarita informed me that the legal department would take care of all the bureaucracy involved and that I should settle into my private room—one of three in the suite—abide by the schedule, and all else would be explained during the Comprehensive Newcomer Three-Month Course that started tomorrow.

"For any questions, don't hesitate to ask your teacher," she said, then flicked her fingers. "Dismissed."

She turned on her heel and left, her red curls bouncing down her back as she strode away.

I was relieved to finally be rid of her.

My new apartment—or rather, suite—was tidy and nice, with a common area full of plush sofas, a TV, a gaming console, and a shelf full of both video and board games. My room was small, with a double bed, a desk, and a modest walk-in closet. I searched for a restroom but found none; there was only a shower. Didn't we have to pee?

My hunger also worked differently; even though it'd been almost twelve hours since my last meal at the warehouse, I wasn't exactly starving. It just felt like mild annoyance. But since night lunch wasn't until another hour, I went to my room, closed the door, sat on the bed, and for the first time since I woke up after the attack, I let myself truly *feel*.

Buried deep inside, a blinding rage rose to the surface. My nails dug into the sheets of the bed, aching to do something, to claw into anything. My entire body shook uncontrollably as the rage rampaged through my veins, making my blood boil and my head explode.

It had taken everything in me to find my freedom. I'd worked so hard to put the past behind me and live an absolutely ordinary life that made me feel content and comfortable. Then in a matter of moments, all that I'd achieved, everything I'd built from scratch, was ripped out of my hold and thrown away as if my blood, sweat, and tears were all as insignificant as a grain of sand in the Sahara desert.

I knew what being caged and locked meant. I knew what it was like to be thrust into a situation where you had no control over anything, when you didn't choose to be there, and where you had no way out.

It was why I'd fled my hometown when I was eighteen to find solace in a different city, starting from scratch with only fifty dollars to my name. Why, for the first week of my new, free life, I'd worked all kinds of jobs to scrape enough money together to rent that tiny studio apartment.

And yet I'd been utterly relieved. It was like a weight had been taken off my shoulders. I no longer had to watch as horrors unfolded before my eyes and take multiple showers a day as if they would get rid of the filth that was far more than skin deep. I preferred sleeping behind dumpsters for a week straight rather than going back, where all the memories wouldn't just haunt me but drive me mad, agonizing and suffocating me until I died.

So, yes, my free life was a poor, stinky one, but it was *mine*.

And in less than one minute, Ragnor Rayne had stolen it from me.

I'd never before hated someone as much as I did Ragnor Rayne. I wanted to find him, put my hands around his neck, and pull his head clean off. I wanted to see him dead for what he'd done to me. Because it was all starting to sink in—me being a vampire and never again a human—and I detested Ragnor for forcing me into this new life, or rather, this new *existence*.

He stole my life, so I would take his. I would kill him with my bare hands the first moment I got the chance. I would teach him a lesson. I would plot, bide my time, and get stronger until I could get my revenge. No one would ever make me feel helpless again.

Fucker's not the only monster on the premises.

CHAPTER 5

The cafeteria was surprisingly underwhelming.

Located on the top floor of the underground city, it was big enough to seat two hundred people, which was about the number of vampires in the room when I walked in.

The room resembled a modernized crypt, with arches everywhere and a dome made of glass, through which a fake night sky was shown by a projector to give us the sense of being outside. The floor was made of dark, depressing marble, contrasting with the peaceful image of the skies above.

The buffet offered different cuisines—from Italian to Vietnamese—and had a whole stand specifically for eight water jars, only instead of water, they contained the different blood types.

There were long tables, round tables, small tables, and even single tables ready to seat loners. I made a beeline to an empty single table and settled down. As I was eating the spaghetti carbonara and broccoli I picked from the buffet along with a glass of AB negative (its jar seemed to be nearly empty, so I figured it might be the best), I watched the other vampires in the room and made some mental notes.

Most of them looked around my age, but of course that was deceptive if I considered everything I knew so far about vampire anatomy (which, granted, wasn't a lot). Some, however, were older, in their early to midthirties, but that was the extent of the looks-wise age range.

What really threw me off was that they struck me as normal people and acted accordingly. There were cliques, groups of friends, and couples. Almost no one was sitting alone; it felt like the League was more like any modern high school rather than some sort of a militaristic dictatorship.

I hated it.

I'd worked hard to have the life I had before Ragnor Rayne came along, even going so far as to switch my name. I'd built that life with meticulous considerations, learning everything I could in order to improve my physical and mental health. I ate nutritionally sound food, made a couple of friends so my social needs would be met, worked a stable, nonhazardous job (despite one instance of attempted armed robbery), and made sure to pay on time what few bills I had.

Knowing I would most likely keep an emotional distance from whichever friends I made, I chose to suppress and express my feelings by playing video games.

Now I had to work with unknown parameters in this stupid new life I was forced into if I wanted to maintain some semblance of stability.

During lunch, I made a list of what I needed to do. Food wasn't a problem; the cafeteria's food fit my criteria. For social needs, I would soon begin this stupid course and might be able to find some superficial friends there. I had to make sure they were as shallow as Skye and as self-involved as Cassidy, though. As for mental stability . . . that I would have to figure out.

Those were the first priorities. I had to establish all of the above if I wanted to keep being the *me* I had worked so hard for.

When I returned to the suite after lunch, there was a woman in the common room. She looked as if she was only a couple of years older than me, and since Margarita said this suite was for newbies, it must've been her true age. She had a sandy-brown bob with long fringes, freckles, and a long pointy nose that stood out on her heart-shaped face. She was also taller than me, with a willowy figure and olive skin.

She raised her eyes, and her brown ones met my hazel set. "Hello," she said in a surprisingly strong voice.

"Hey," I responded. "I'm Aileen. I'm new."

She nodded. "Me too. I'm Zoey," she introduced herself. "I was given the Imprint a week ago. What about you?"

I shrugged, giving her a small smile. With how overwhelmed I'd been, I completely forgot to ask Margarita about it. I would have to find an opportunity to ask her, though.

She frowned. "You don't know?"

My smile slipped. "You sound surprised."

She seemed to consider something before shaking her head. "Never mind," she said, then offered me a grin. "How long have you been on the waiting list?"

Waiting list? "The what?"

"Waiting list," she repeated. "The list you get on to get the Imprint? I've been on it for the last three years, and I started thinking I would never receive the Imprint until our Lord came to my house the other day and told me I was finally through the sorting."

I tried to process the information and failed. What the hell was she going on about? Neither Ragnor nor Margarita had mentioned a fucking waiting list!

"Oh, yes," I lied instinctively, nodding as if I knew what she was talking about. "The list. I've been on it for a while too."

Zoey sighed dreamily. "I can't believe I'm finally here. I was afraid at first, you know? I wanted to be in the Rayne League—it's the safest, most renowned League, after all—but you can't choose which League will take you. Thank God I'm not in that creepy, sleazy Lord's League. I met Renaldi in one of those events, you know? I felt him staring at me, and I mean *staring*. I was dressed pretty modestly back then, and yet I felt him looking at me as if he was seeing me naked!" She shuddered.

"I heard he had a thing for brunettes, so lucky for both of us, we're here instead."

I understood nothing of what she said. Meeting a Lord before getting the Imprint? Attending an event with other vampires? Being in the dark regarding which League you would belong to? What the hell was going on?

"Yeah, lucky," I murmured.

She perked up. "Anyway, I'm really happy. I just woke up yesterday, five days after my Imprinting, and I feel so great, you know? I'm where I want to be, turned into what I want to be, and it's like everything is finally falling into place . . ."

As she went on about her thoughts and feelings, my mind was racing. Something was off here. Because if there was a waiting list with people signing up of their own volition to become vampires, then why the hell did Ragnor give the Imprint to Cassidy and me without receiving our consent?

Or maybe . . . maybe it had been just me?

Thinking back to that awful night, I realized Cassidy had been acting strangely. She'd been agitated, so much so that she picked a fight with Skye, something she'd never done before. Then she'd stormed off without another word—uncharacteristic behavior. Despite how she acted, Cassidy avoided drama at all costs. Then when I found her in that alley, she was held against the wall with Ragnor kissing her . . .

It occurred to me that I hadn't seen what came before then.

Could she have been on that waiting list?

My heart stopped. No way. This couldn't be possible. Why would she do that? Why would she give up her life in exchange for this . . . this *existence*? Did she really hate that life? Sure, it wasn't perfect, but I thought we understood each other. I thought we were of the same mind when it came to being free!

Don't jump to conclusions, the voice of reason whispered in my ear. *She probably wasn't on the list. There's no rational reason for her to be on that list, after all. How could she have learned of vampires' existence?*

"You're coming to the class tomorrow, too, right?" Zoey's voice snapped me back to attention, and I released my hands, feeling calmer. *Right. Cassidy would've never been stupid enough to go out of her way to find some secret society to belong to, let alone be on that list.*

When I gave my new roommate a distracted but affirmative nod, she seemed excited. "It's going to be great. I met some of the other newcomers—a couple of them are really hot too. It's gonna be a blast!"

Yeah, right. "I can't wait to meet everyone," I lied.

A door opened, and into the room walked a girl who was probably nineteen. She was the youngest I'd seen so far; all the vampires I'd seen up until now seemed to be my age and up. She had round cheeks and large blue eyes that gave her an innocent, doe-like, naive look. Her hair was strawberry blonde and so smooth and long that it reached her knees in a neat braid, like a horse's tail. Her skin was pale with a rosy tint, and she was short and thin, almost waifish.

Her huge eyes went to Zoey first before they turned to me. "Tansy," she said in a soprano voice that was surprisingly somber.

"Aileen," I greeted back, unsure.

She cocked her head. "Your pronunciation is off," she said somewhat dreamily.

I figured she was thinking of the popular *Eileen*. "It's a Scottish name," I explained, "so it's pronounced a little differently."

"Huh," she said. "Are you also new?"

I was about to reply, but Zoey must've missed her own voice because she answered in my place. "She was given the Imprint only a couple of days ago. She's also joining us for the course tomorrow."

"Oh," Tansy muttered. "I'm new too."

"We were given the Imprint around the same time," Zoey informed me. "Tansy was on the waiting list for merely *one year* before she was accepted, the bitch. But I hold no grudges, though." She winked at the other girl, and while her voice was light, I could tell she was actually jealous.

Tansy stared at Zoey for a few awkward moments before she said, "The list is long," nodded at me, and went back into her room.

Zoey threw me a meaningful look. "She's a bit of an airhead," she murmured softly. "I don't recommend reading too much into what she says."

I wasn't as curious about the girl as Zoey was. I had enough bullshit to deal with and little energy to spend on unimportant mysteries, not when the greatest mystery weighed heavily on my mind, making my heart rate kick up to dangerous levels.

Had Cassidy been on the waiting list all along?

After morning dinner, I decided to look for Margarita. I didn't see her in the cafeteria, and since she talked so proudly about how she worked for Vampire Resources, I decided to look for her there.

The large VR—Vampire Resources—office looked like any regular office, if it was built in medieval times; dark marble floors and dimly lit lanterns accompanied me as I strode through the place toward the front desk. There was no one there, however, and the office itself seemed deserted. Perhaps work hours were already over?

Grimacing, I walked to the first door I found and opened it. The small office within was empty. I headed to the next door and did the same, but again, it was vacated.

When I reached for the handle of the third door in the office, I heard voices coming from within. I froze when I heard a man's low voice saying, *"Are you questioning me, Margarita?"*

A chill went down my spine. That voice.

"Of course not, my Lord!" Margarita replied with what sounded like desperation. *"All of us will abide by anything you decide, even if protocol dictates otherwise . . ."*

I froze.

"*I could give two shits about protocol,*" Ragnor Rayne said in a voice on the verge of an actual growl. "*And if you prioritize protocol over your Lord's word, then you're not the woman I thought you were.*"

"*Nothing's changed, my Lord! I am still that woman!*" Margarita protested vehemently, and there was a slight accent to her voice, which became thicker as her panic rose. "*I don't give a damn about that stupid noob, or anyone else! I only care about you!*"

"*I don't need you to care about me,*" he said, voice almost cruel. "*I only need your obedience.*"

Margarita sucked in a breath so loudly I could hear it through the door. She was hurt, I could tell. I would be, too, if I had been rejected that strongly by the man I liked.

"*Why didn't you kill her?*" she suddenly asked in a voice so soft I almost didn't hear it. There was an undertone to this question, a subtext I couldn't decipher, and its lack of an answer put me on edge.

I stopped breathing, waiting for Ragnor to respond. Seemingly hours later, he finally did. "*That's for me to know.*"

Anger filled my veins, and I would've thrown the door open to confront the asshole had I not heard footsteps from inside growing closer, and *the Lord's* voice saying, "*We're done here.*"

I stepped back just in time for Ragnor to open the door. He was wearing that long trench coat that seemed to be his signature attire, with faded dark jeans tucked into black combat boots. His shoulder-length hair curtained his hard face, and his midnight blue eyes found mine and narrowed.

He closed the door behind him and turned to face me fully. "Got anything to say?" he asked in a low murmur, folding his arms.

I gritted my teeth as I felt the rage climbing up my body, lighting my nerves on fire. I wanted to throttle his thick neck. I wanted to kick him in the groin. I wanted to dig his heart out with my bare hands.

I tried to force some words out, but my entire body was tense, ready for action, and I couldn't speak. I wanted only to act.

He took a few steps until he was merely inches away. "Well?"

His proximity shot lightning through my spine. I schooled my face before my eyes had a chance to widen in response. "You were talking about me," I blurted; though, when I thought about it, they hadn't mentioned my name. And yet who else could it be?

His eyes narrowed. "Eavesdropping is not tolerated in my League, Henderson."

I took a step forward until only an inch separated us. "I would think Imprinting on someone against their will would be the most important between the two," I said quietly, not averting my gaze from his, "but I guess we have different priorities."

His hand was suddenly around my neck. He wasn't suffocating me, but his hold was resolute, and the touch, the warmth of his hand, elicited a gasp. "What am I to you?" he asked in a deep growl that made the hairs on my arm stand on end.

"Someone who forced this whole bullshit on me," I hissed through gritted teeth.

His hold tightened just enough to be a warning. "I'll give you one more chance. *What am I to you?*"

I knew what he wanted me to say, and for a moment, I debated spitting in his face instead. But his eyes were suddenly neon blue, and as if he turned on a switch, I felt him emitting that terrible, *terrible* aura that made my heart kick into high gear, and my brain urged me to *run, run, RUN!*

Everything in me screamed at me to flee, but I couldn't move a limb. I was frozen with sudden irrational fear, and the two contradictory urges made my muscles tighten and my throat dry, making me feel caged in my own body, claustrophobic in my own skin.

You won't win, a voice of reason told me. *You're not strong enough yet. He can tear your head off with his mere hand if he wants to. You have to give up.*

I swallowed hard, closed my eyes, and, trying to ignore the horrible fear he incited in the very core of my being, I said, "My Lord."

His lips brushed against my ear, and I shuddered in barely contained rage at my defeat. "Don't you ever forget it."

He was gone by the time I opened my eyes, taking that terrible, overwhelmingly intimidating air with him, snuffing it into thin air as if nothing ever happened. My hands traced my neck, following the ghost of his touch.

CHAPTER 6

According to my schedule, I had two weekly classes, each four hours long. The thought of having to sit in a classroom with only one ten-minute break made me break out in hives. There's a reason I dropped out of high school.

But I needed all the information about vampires I could get so that I would have as much ammunition ready as I could for the time I chose to act against the man who'd given me the Imprint without my consent and who seemed to be doing so consensually with everyone else.

When my suitemates and I entered the classroom, it was already half-full. Zoey broke away from Tansy and me and went to sit with a group of people who were already chatting enthusiastically and greeted her with hugs and smiles.

Tansy headed to a quiet corner in the back of the room, pulled a book out of her backpack, and started reading. I took a seat in the middle row, next to the wall. I wished I had a book with me, too, so I could've at least pretended to be doing something other than feeling the discomfort of being in a classroom again.

More new vampires entered the room. Almost everyone seemed to be in their midtwenties, but a few looked as young as me. None looked as young as Tansy, though.

My concerns rose to the surface when I overheard a couple of men talking in the row in front of me.

"Gotta say, I'd already given up on receiving the Imprint by the time our Lord came knocking," one of them said.

"Why?" the other asked. "You must've known that once you signed the contract, you were going to get the Imprint eventually. There's no *out* clause."

"Of course I knew that, dumbass." The first guy rolled his eyes. "I was just saying, five years on the list is a hell of a long time. See that girl in the corner?" They turned to look at Tansy. "Rumor has it she was only on the list for *one year*."

"Some people are lucky bastards," the second guy murmured bitterly as they turned back around.

Everyone had been on this waiting list, it seemed.

Where the hell was Cassidy? She was a newbie, too, wasn't she? She should be here in the Comprehensive Newcomer Three-Month Course. I really needed to see her, too, so she could confirm to me that she hadn't been on that damned list. That she hadn't even thought of such a thing. That everything that had happened had been pure coincidence.

Perhaps something had gone wrong with the Imprinting process. What if she hadn't survived? What if she'd died?

If Ragnor'd killed her, he would regret the day he'd been born.

As I was thinking about all the possible horrible things that could have happened to Cassidy, a man who was probably in his late twenties walked into the classroom. He hadn't spoken a word yet, but his thick eyebrows, black eyes, mocha skin, heavy beard, and thick ebony hair drew me in immediately. The expression on his face was light, but the overall look was very intimidating.

By now, all of us were seated in our places, and the man addressed the class as he leaned back against the front of the wooden desk and crossed his feet. "The name's Abe," he said, "and I'm going to be your teacher. If you've found yourself here, you are a Common. I've already memorized your names, so if you expected an icebreaker, you're in for a disappointment. You will, however, have time to socialize with one another outside this classroom."

A few students in the front rows mumbled something inaudible, making Abe smile.

"No, the Gifteds have a different kind of course. Who can tell me the difference between Common and Gifted?"

Zoey's hand shot up to the sky, a predatory, excited look on her face. Abe glanced at her and said, "Yes, Zoey?"

She flushed as though his knowledge of her name was special despite what he'd just said. "Gifted vampires had talents while human, and once they were given the Imprint, that talent transitioned into some sort of magical ability." Zoey paused as if she'd just shared some deeply intelligent revelation. Though, for me, this was new information. Margarita hadn't mentioned anything about being Common or Gifted.

When no one reacted, she continued. "Common vampires do not have extra powers but will acquire the acute sense and formidable strength of a full-blooded vampire within a year of their Imprinting."

Zoey sat back in her chair, looking smug and satisfied.

"Correct." Abe nodded. "I'm a Common vampire such as yourself. I'm fifty years old in vampire years, and I grew into my full vampiric potential after a few months of hard work. You can do so in as little time, too, if you're as determined as I was."

He started pacing, locking his hands behind his back. "There are some rare cases when Commons develop certain abilities that turn them into Gifteds, but that can only happen when you're far older in vampire years. So for now, you're all Commons, and you'll probably remain that way."

Zoey shot her hand back up, and Abe gave her a nod. "There's also the Sacred, right?" she asked, eyes shining with curiosity.

Abe grinned. "You're an inquisitive one," he said. "Yes, that's true. In addition to Common and Gifted, there are the Sacred. Do you know what it means, Rittman?"

Zoey flushed with pride. "Yes, Margarita told me," she said, almost puffing out her chest. "Sacred are the oldest vampires in the world. They have certain abilities. Much like . . . *magic*."

"This is true." Abe nodded, then turned to look at us. "But in order to explain it better, let's go back to the Gifted."

Leaning against his desk, he said, "Gifted vampires make up fifteen percent of the vampiric population. They are ones who excelled in a particular area back in their human life—it could be artistic or even scientific—and when they were given the Imprint, that talent of theirs adjusted to their new state in certain ways."

Cassidy came to mind with her magnetic stage presence and ethereal voice, and I was suddenly cold, bile rising in my throat. *She wouldn't,* I thought almost desperately.

"Let me give you an example," he said. "One of our vampires is a man who'd been a talented gardener back in his human life. When he was Imprinted on, he gained a certain affinity with the plants he tended to, an affinity that allowed him to somehow communicate with the plants and understand what they needed in order to grow healthy and strong. You won't get a better harvest than what he provides. That's just one example out of many, and each case of a Gifted vampire is individual and depends on the person's talent and sometimes personality. Two talented musicians won't necessarily develop the same Gift as vampires—take pianists, for example. One might develop a keener hearing, but nothing more, while another might be able to enchant people with their playing."

The bad feeling in my stomach grew stronger.

"Then we have the Sacred," Abe said, face turning serious. "The Sacred are rare; there are only about ten of them in the world at the moment. They are very old vampires, as Rittman said, and very powerful. They possess magic—not something like it, but actual magic that turns them into something close to gods."

Unsurprisingly, Zoey raised her hand again. When she got Abe's approval, she said in a quiet, reverent voice, "The Lord is Sacred, isn't he?"

"Yes, he is," Abe said quietly, giving us an alarming look, as though he was telling us to watch our backs.

He straightened and resumed his pacing. "I'm here to teach you everything you need to know about your new existence," he explained, changing the subject so quickly I got whiplash. "You'll study Vampire–Human History, Vampire Biology, Vampire Physics, Physical Education, and Personal Development.

"You've been waiting for a long time to be here," he continued, and for a fleeting moment his eyes met mine, "but *patience* is key. We have three months to cover everything, and you can rest assured you won't be lacking in knowledge once the course is over."

He paused and gave us all a small but confident smirk. "Let us begin."

For two hours, Abe talked about our new biology. As Margarita had already explained, the water that made up around seventy percent of our bodies had been replaced with blood. And like the water that we needed to drink as humans, we now needed to drink blood. The surprising thing was that we could choose which type of blood to drink, meaning we could drink from animals as well as humans. And apparently, the older you were in vampire years, the thirstier for blood you would get.

We then proceeded to talk about our fangs. We could show and hide our fangs at will. "Since we don't need to hunt for blood anymore," Abe explained, "evolution allowed nature to help us hide our identity."

Abe then made us practice extending and retracting our fangs until it became second nature. It was freaky feeling my fangs grow long and pointy, their sound like the unsheathing of a sharpened blade, then returning back to normal, but it was even freakier to see and hear all the vampires in the class doing the same.

If I had any lingering doubts about the existence of vampires, they were gone after that little exercise.

Afterward, Abe launched into a scientific explanation of vampire anatomy, but by that point, I had lost focus. Science had never been my favorite subject, and while it was interesting to learn about it in a vampiric context, I got lost in the terms and descriptions.

When it was time for the ten-minute break, Abe left the class, and Zoey jumped to her feet. "This is so exciting!" She beamed. "We'll never be sick again! Think about it—so long, runny nose!"

"The wait was *so* worth it," another girl said, grinning.

I turned to look at Tansy, who was in her corner, staring into space while practicing the extension and retraction of her fangs.

"And the *teacher*!" Zoey sighed. "He's so sexy, very fuckable."

One of the guys she was talking to gave a snort. "In your dreams, maybe," he said. "I've been here for two weeks already, and believe me, I've tried. I wouldn't get my hopes up if I were you."

"And you would think that since our Lord chose us, he'd be a lot nicer," another girl said, pouting.

"We need to earn our place, remember?" one of the guys said. "We must work to earn our stay in the League. Maybe if you fail at your job, you're kicked out?"

This was just silly. "He can't kick you out," I said.

Zoey and her companions swiveled to stare at me. "How come?" Zoey asked, frowning.

"There was a specific clause about it in the League System Agreement form we all signed," I replied, and when their faces remained puzzled, I inwardly rolled my eyes. Didn't anyone read the contracts before signing like blind fools? "Unless you breach the Secrecy Agreement, you won't be kicked out of the League System. It's illegal for a Lord to do so based on you failing at your job, for instance."

The guy sighed in relief, but Zoey still seemed concerned. "What happens, then? If we are of no use to the League?"

I shrugged, unable to provide an answer. I honestly had no clue, but my gut told me there was something in this question that was worth looking into. Not that I'd planned on being useless; I wanted to stay in this League for one very clear reason, and being useless wouldn't help my cause.

When the break was over, Abe returned to the classroom. Another man followed him inside, wearing black jeans, a black turtleneck sweater, a black leather jacket, and black boots. He had curly black hair that stopped right below his earlobes, bright-turquoise eyes, and a handsome, clean-shaven face. His body was like that of a swimmer, lean with broad shoulders, and he had a golden tan that seemed to be natural.

My breath caught, and my mind blanked out.

I barely heard anything Abe said. He was probably introducing the man to the class, but no introductions were needed, not for me.

The man's eyes did a quick sweep over the class but didn't for a moment rest on me. Could it be that he didn't recognize me? My face hadn't changed that much in the past few years—and neither had his.

I was deeply flustered and also completely and utterly scared. This man was one of the very, *very* few people who knew things about me I'd rather keep hidden. His being here was more than just an ill-fated coincidence. It was extremely bad news.

I was somehow able to maintain my outward composure, and it took all my effort to return my focus back to whatever Abe was saying.

". . . show us his abilities," the teacher completed his sentence and gestured over to the man.

To . . . Logan, my first and last boyfriend.

I watched as Logan took a step forward. "Like Abe here already said, I'm Logan, and I'm Gifted," he said, his tenor voice too familiar, yet it sounded like a stranger's. "When I was human, I was really good at soccer, a rising star, a prodigy. When I was given the Imprint, the talent seemed to be more inherent than I would've thought."

He turned to Abe. "Can I kick your desk?"

Abe sighed as if he knew firsthand what agreeing to Logan's request meant. "Buy me a new one, will you?"

Logan smirked as he glanced over at the class meaningfully. Then he raised his leg and kicked the desk. It was almost a love tap, gentle and slow.

But that love tap resulted in the desk hitting the wall and shattering into a million splinters.

The class was deadly quiet as Logan snickered and gave us an unfamiliar devil-may-care grin. "My power lies in my legs, but I also have better stamina than most vampires. All because I was a talented soccer player."

"Logan will be your gym instructor." Abe grinned evilly when he saw the dread on some of the faces. "Don't worry; he's not going to kick any of you. The only thing he will kick is your butt."

Logan grinned, too, as his eyes moved over the class. Again, they didn't linger on me once, yet it seemed like his grin wasn't as lighthearted when he turned to look back at Abe.

Then Logan said, "I'll see you in a couple of days," before he turned and left the room.

That's when I made a split-second decision and shot to my feet. "I'm thirsty," I said aloud. I couldn't say I needed to use the toilet; one thing I had listened to was Abe's explanation about how our digestive system worked now. The blood and food we consumed did not translate into nature's call; instead, they were transmuted into energy.

While Abe turned a questioning look at me, I strode toward the door and left the room before he could give me permission to do so. Logan was already halfway down the hall, and I had to jog to catch up to him, my footsteps echoing off the floor.

He must have heard me coming and turned around to face me. Despite my standing a few feet in front of him, his face remained expressionless, and his eyes were unreadable. Before I could think twice, I said, "You know who I am, don't you?"

His eyes trailed down my body before shooting back up to meet my gaze. They were no longer a calm green blue; they were glowing neon. "So?" he asked, his voice low.

My heart thudded in my chest as anxiety made my veins freeze over. I opened my mouth and closed it like a fish, not knowing what to say now that I had his undivided attention.

What could I say, really? *Hey, long time no see! Can you please keep your mouth shut about me? Thanks!*

His eyes grew cold when I didn't speak. "What do you want, Aileen?"

His saying my name was like a sucker punch to my gut. "How are you here?" I blurted out, my heart booming in my chest. "What happened to you?"

It didn't seem to be what he expected me to say, and his face twisted with anger. "I could ask you the same fucking thing."

My head was a mess, and I tried to collect my thoughts, to figure out something to say. Before I could, Logan strode toward me. He stopped an inch away, glowered down at me, and spoke before I made sense of this recent development.

"Let me be clear," he said quietly but menacingly. "Here, we don't know each other. We are complete *fucking* strangers who don't share a past." Logan's voice was angry and emotional. It was like he had waited a long time to unleash his hatred on me, and now that he had the chance to do so, he wasn't holding back.

"I . . . Logan, I . . ." I didn't know what I was going to say. I wanted to say everything and nothing at the same time.

"Yes, Aileen"—he cut me off and smiled coldly when my eyes widened—"I'll keep your fucking secrets, as long as you stay *the fuck* away from me."

He stepped back, giving me a disgusted look. "That's the least you can do after everything you did. Am I clear?"

I stared at him with something akin to shock. Because this Logan was more than a vampire. He was an entirely different person from the boy I used to know.

His eyes flickered when I didn't respond. "I said," he snarled, "*am. I. Fucking. Clear?*"

My heart dropped, grief overcoming every other emotion I felt at that moment. "Crystal," I somehow managed to reply. And when he turned his back to me and walked away, I felt like I had lost Logan all over again.

And the worst thing was, I deserved it.

CHAPTER 7

The next day, Zoey, Tansy, and I were about to head over to breakfast when Tansy pointed at a neatly folded paper that had been pushed under our suite door and said, "Let's read this first."

Re: Temporary Work Assignments

Dear Suite 2304,

While you attend the Comprehensive Newcomer Three-Month Course, you will be expected to work like all vampires in this League. You'll be assigned a permanent job once you finish the course, but in the meantime, your assignments, which begin immediately after breakfast, are as follows:

- Zoey Rittman: Library Assistant. Meet Sanu at the Archives.
- Tansy Contos: Vampire Resources Assistant. Meet Maika in her office on the third floor.
- Aileen Henderson: Kitchen Associate. Meet Lon in the cafeteria.

Best of luck!

Maika Russo

Deputy Director, Vampire Resources

"Shit," I murmured. I was expecting that—it *was* written in the agreement. But kitchen duty? I could hardly even make instant noodles.

Zoey sighed. "Nothing comes free."

As the three of us headed to the cafeteria, Tansy said in her natural, dreamy voice, "I like Margarita."

From the disgusted scowl on Zoey's face, it seems that made only one of us. "Well, lucky for you to get a job at her office, then."

Tansy shrugged, nonchalant. "A job is a job," she said.

"I wonder why we were given these specific jobs?" I thought out loud, glancing at Zoey. "I don't think anyone could ever accuse me of being a good cook."

Like Tansy, Zoey shrugged. "I guess we'll have to wait and see."

In the cafeteria, we found a table with Gus and Jakob from our CNC class. The two of them, I learned, had been neighbors in one of the finest districts in their city, leading me to question what they were doing here in the first place. I didn't voice it, though; the two of them seemed to be content where they were.

Unlike me.

"What job did you get?" Zoey asked them at one point.

Gus replied, "I'm an Archives Assistant, while Jakob, the bastard, got a job in one of the Lieutenant's offices."

"Lieutenant?" Tansy asked, cocking her head.

"Every Lord has a couple of Lieutenants, a second-in-command, if you will," Jakob explained. "I read about it in the classroom reading material." He seemed proud of himself. "I'm eager to learn everything I can and explore the League that's going to be my home," he added, his eyes bright like a kid's on Christmas morning.

"Who are the Lieutenants, then?" Zoey inquired.

"Our Lord has two." Jakob shrugged. "I got Margarita from VR, and I have no idea who the other one is. Anyway, what did you three get?"

"I got Archives too," Zoey said, smiling at Gus. "We can go together."

"Vampire Resources," Tansy responded, and before I could, too, she answered for me. "Aileen's in the kitchen."

Everyone gave me sympathetic looks. "Kitchen duty is rough," Jakob informed me as if I didn't already know. It seemed that even Maika Russo had it in for me.

"I'm fine with hard work," I said blankly, determined not to show them how anxious I was about it.

"It's not the Sisyphean work that's hard," Jakob said, face somber. "I've been here for a couple of weeks now, and I've seen the way the kitchen staff is treated." He paused, almost dramatically, before murmuring, "It's not good."

Zoey nodded gravely. "I noticed it too. It seems like most people don't consider kitchen duty as something honorable, or respectable at the very least."

That didn't sound good, indeed. "Well, I don't have much of a choice, do I?" I murmured a tad too bitterly as Ragnor's face came to mind. I began to think all kinds of murderous thoughts just then.

Once breakfast was over, our group disbanded, each heading to start their new jobs.

I approached one of the apron-clad cafeteria ladies as she cleaned off the table next to ours and said, "I'm looking for Lon. I start work here today."

The lady jerked her head toward a double door behind her. "Go to the kitchen. Lon's there."

I did as she said and went through the door, which led to a dish-washing room. There, a man was yelling at one of the workers. I waited a few feet away until he finished scolding the girl, who had tears in her eyes. When she noticed me, she wiped the tears on her white apron and ran into the kitchen.

Stepping forward and taking a guess, I asked, "Are you Lon?"

He whipped his head around to me, his eyes glowing a freakish neon-yellow color. "You're one of Ragnor's new girls," he barked.

"Yes," I said, schooling my face into a blank expression despite fuming at being called one of Ragnor's new girls like I was some fucking possession of his. "I'm—"

"I don't care for names," he cut me off harshly. "For me, you're number two forty-nine. Come," he said, waving me forward and walking quickly through the gigantic kitchen. "I'll show you the ropes once, and then you're on your own. Learn quickly, ask questions if you don't understand, and pay attention. Show up late or fail to follow instructions, and you can forget about a warm and fuzzy recommendation. Understood?"

No, I didn't. "Recommendation?"

"For the Auction! You need a glowing recommendation for the Auction," he growled before shaking his head and throwing up his hands. "I don't have time for this. Every quarter, you noobs get dumber and dumber. Come!" he said louder this time as I struggled to keep up with his frantic pace around the kitchen as cooks, bussers, servers, and other staff buzzed around.

Unsure how to respond, I simply followed him inside the kitchen, where he shoved a white apron into my hands, sniped at me to put it on and get to work, and left in favor of yelling at another worker.

This was going to be a blast, I could tell.

Putting on the apron, I turned to a frightened-faced worker cutting veggies so quickly I was half-scared he would cut his finger off and asked, "Where should I start?"

He shoved a cutting board my way, handed me a knife and a huge pile of onions, and whispered in a horrified tone, "Just do *something*."

So I did. I cut eight large onions as tears burned my eyes and ran down my face. When I was done with that, I tenderized some steaks in all different cuts and left them out to get to room temperature. Then I helped prepare gallons of Alfredo sauce, making sure each cook had a supply that would carry them through tonight's dinner, and when that was done, I cleaned the dishes that had piled up.

No one talked while they worked except for the occasional "Order up" alert from the cooks. Lon paced from one part of the kitchen to another, raining absolute terror down on us with his menacing growls and yelling. It was either the presentation was off, or the temperature of the meat was wrong, or maybe someone ordered meat sauce and *not* marinara. He questioned how we had managed to hold down jobs as humans if we were so inept. He wondered aloud how he would make it with such idiots working under him, and vowed to have a talk with Maika for assigning such complete losers to work in the kitchen.

But the worst part was his tasting of the food, which almost always resulted in us having to remake entire servings after he dramatically threw the food into the trash with an almost theatrical "People, I have had shit that tastes better than that!"

Gordon Ramsay looked like a cuddly teddy bear next to Lon.

I kept my mouth shut and did what I had to do. Every time Lon shouted or poured a pot full of sauce down the drain, my anger grew. But Lon was just a cog in the machine. He wasn't the one responsible for it all, for me being here. He wasn't the one who was going to pay for what they did to me and to Cassidy.

Close to lunchtime, Lon began calling workers by their numbers without yelling, for once.

"One hundred! Two thirteen! Sixty-seven! Twenty! One ninety!" Lon read from a list he held in front of his acne-scarred face.

One by one, all those he called paled as though they'd seen a ghost. They each quickly lined up in order in front of him, awaiting his commands.

I turned to the girl working at the island next to mine and asked softly, "What's going on?"

She glanced at me in fear. "He's selecting lunch servers."

That's it? "Why the fuss, then?"

She didn't have time to respond before Lon called, "Two forty-nine!"

Knowing he referred to me, I left what I was doing, wiped my hands on my apron, and met him where he stood. He didn't even look up from his paper when he said, "Follow one ninety."

Number 190 introduced herself as Jada as I followed her out of the kitchen and into the cafeteria. She was tall and Black with a mass of pretty dark curls surrounding her head like a halo. Her stunningly pale gray eyes were friendly when she told me, "Don't worry about Lon. He might be an ass, but at least he's upfront about it."

I snorted out a chuckle. "You sound as if you *like* him."

Jada returned with her own snort. "Don't be daft," she said. "I'm just trying to find the silver lining, is all."

She took off her dirty white apron and put on a new black one, motioning for me to copy her. As I did, I said a bit bitterly, "Doesn't seem like there's one."

She gave me a sympathetic look. "Well, true," she said quietly, "but if it makes you feel better, I can try and push Lon to assign you to dishwashing duty next time."

I tried not to scrunch my nose. "That doesn't sound any better," I said as we scurried over to the buffet.

"You'd be surprised," she said with a grin. "Out of all the jobs I've done around this place, dishwashing is the best."

"All the jobs?" I asked while we unloaded the Lon-approved food from their pots and pans onto the huge plates.

Jada gave an amused huff and spilled a bit of sauce on her hand. She licked it absentmindedly as she said, "Not all vamps here have fixed jobs." She sucked on her thumb before she washed her hands, picked up a saucepan, and poured the contents over the enormous bowl of pasta. "Some of us, like me, refuse to hold a single job for long."

I frowned and, with shiny silver tongs, picked up a duck dumpling as I mulled over her words for a moment. "So you're like the League's freelancer of sorts?"

"I prefer the term jack-of-all-trades." She grinned. "I'm lucky, you know. I haven't heard of other Lords who allow for such leeway."

That made more questions pop into my head, but Lon's shout of "Move your asses, or I swear to God you'll be working in the kitchen until the day you cease to exist!" interjected before I could say anything.

Jada and I quickly finished our duties, and then all the servers stood in a row. "We're here to serve only the higher-ups—Lords, their Lieutenants, and anyone with a director title and above," Jada whispered to me. "I suggest you keep your mouth shut unless they speak to you; then take their orders and serve them their food." She paused and gave me a serious look. "Never take orders from anyone not seated at a leadership table."

Sounded fun. "All right."

A boom sounded from the kitchen, and then Lon strode toward us. "Five and six," he told one of the servers, then continued down the line in the same manner. "Seven and three. Four and ten. Eight and nine." He then stopped before me and gave me a stern once-over, his eyes examining me up and down and then left to right. "One."

He moved on, and Jada gave me a pitying look and murmured, "You've got real shitty luck, Aileen. You better be careful. Table one is the worst."

Oh. "I've got only one table, though," I whispered back, relieved. Maybe Lon was going easy on me since I was new.

"It's like ten tables combined, unfortunately," she hissed back, then muttered half to herself, "Eight and nine again. Fuck me . . ."

"Who sits at table one?" I asked her, sure it couldn't be all that bad.

She gave me a rueful smile. "The Lord, his Lieutenants, and anyone worthy enough to eat with them."

Fucking wonderful.

CHAPTER 8

It was 1:30 a.m., and table one was still empty. I kept my distance as the rest of the tables filled up around me and waited not so patiently for the vampires I was assigned to serve showed up.

As I did so, I couldn't help but feel a stifling, awful aura about the cafeteria. There was something ominous now that hadn't been there before. It was as though the place had done a one-eighty in the past few hours I'd spent in the kitchen, and now it was this cruel and unyielding jail. The smell of food did not help the nausea creeping into the pit of my stomach.

When the table-one guests finally walked in, there were only a few other people left in the cafeteria. Jakob, Gus, Zoey, and a couple of other classmates sat at a table near the kitchen. They were so deep in conversation that they didn't notice me, but they all turned their attention to the door at the very same time.

The first guest I saw was one of the best-looking men I'd ever seen. His burnished golden hair and brilliant honey gold eyes drew me to him. His sun-kissed bronze skin and body roped with muscles on a six-foot-fourish frame made him impossible to ignore. The way he walked, self-assured and confident like an experienced model on the runway, was hypnotizing. He was really terribly beautiful.

Next to him, Margarita walked. Her catlike green eyes were bright, matching the emerald color of her dress, and her waist-length dark-auburn curls bounced effortlessly with every step she took. She moved with the confidence of someone used to getting their way, laughing at everything the man said.

But they weren't alone.

Logan accompanied the two, head down as if he had heavy things on his mind. The trio settled in at table one, chatting, while the beautiful man whispered in Margarita's ear, making her smirk as though he was the funniest person in the world.

Reluctantly, I walked to the table, aware of the other servers' pitying eyes following me. When I reached the table, I took out a small notepad and a pen from the apron's pocket and asked, "Ready to order?"

The group of three turned to look at me. I made sure my face was passive and relaxed as I waited for them to speak. I noticed the beautiful man raking me with his gaze, then turning back to Margarita, seemingly uninterested in what he saw. Margarita's face twisted as if I had asked the dumbest possible question, then turned her attention back to the man. The chatty woman from two days ago was gone, it seemed.

Logan was the only one who responded, though he did so without looking up at me. "We're waiting for our Lord."

His dismissive tone caused my spine to stiffen, and I nodded rigidly. As I backed away from the table, I could hear Margarita murmuring loudly enough for me to hear, "I can't believe Ragnor gave the Imprint to *that.*"

The beautiful man whispered a response in her ear while looking right at me, but I couldn't hear the rest.

Margarita sneered and said, "No, Magnus." She took another look up and down my entire body this time, before shaking her head in disbelief.

Just as I was about to head to the kitchen and escape the scrutiny of those two and the disdain of Logan, the doors to the cafeteria opened. In walked Ragnor Rayne.

He wore his signature trench coat, black trousers, a black shirt, and black boots. His dark-brown hair brushed his shoulders, a little wavy as though he hadn't bothered blowing it out after his shower. As he walked, again in that predatory way, he cast his midnight blue eyes around the room like he owned it. I was so struck by his presence at that moment. My heart beat like a war drum in my chest, and I could feel an angry flush coating my cheeks. I remembered my last encounter with him a couple of days ago at the Vampire Resources office. It made my blood boil.

Here he was walking into the cafeteria without a care in the world while I was stuck here, working a job I didn't choose, living the life he'd forced on me.

His eyes suddenly met mine, and a lightning bolt shot through my veins. I forced myself to look anywhere but at *him*. Instead, I settled on studying the woman by his side, but that was a mistake. How could I not have noticed her until now?

Cassidy.

All thoughts of Ragnor melted away under a new wave of shock. Seeing her after everything that had happened threw me off completely. She looked the same as the last time I'd seen her, like nothing had changed; her charcoal hair was as silky smooth as it had always been, her green eyes brimmed with satisfaction, and her skin was still as unblemished as always, if not more so. She even wore the same revealing clothes she'd always liked.

The only thing different about her was her disposition. She was radiant with happiness and contentment, as though the dark cloud that'd always been hanging over her head was gone under rays of sunshine. The way she held herself was more assured and relaxed, confident in a way that was far from the fake arrogance she'd always adorned herself with. In fact, Cassidy was the most exuberant I'd ever seen her.

This could only mean one thing: Ragnor hadn't randomly given her the Imprint. He hadn't been attacking her in the alleyway that night. No, it was with full consent that Cassidy had received the damned Imprint.

And that meant she had been on the waiting list.

A sharp pang of betrayal sliced through my chest. Why hadn't she told me anything? Cassidy would've never kept secrets from me before. What the hell had changed? Why would she discard her freedom as if it mattered shit?

And how dare she be so carefree and happy about it when I was so miserable?

But then again, was it really *discarding* when she most likely consented to it?

I took a deep breath and let it out slowly. *I've got to calm down,* I told myself. *I can't let myself lose it here.*

The guests at table one were on their feet when Ragnor and Cassidy settled down, and a hush came over the room. This time when I glanced at Zoey's table, she and the others were staring at me. And they weren't the only ones; I was now the center of attention in the cafeteria. Everyone seemed to be holding their breaths as though they were waiting for a good show to start.

With a bucketload of effort, I managed to pull on a feigned composure while, inside, my mind was a thunderstorm. For a second time, I made my way to *table one*. My eyes were supposed to be on my notepad, but from the corner of my eye, I could see Cassidy staring at me with big, wide eyes full of shock. Her mouth opened as though she wanted to say something, but then she closed it, frowned, and looked away.

At once, I was overcome by an urge to slap her face. *How dare you.* The thought reverberated through the thunderstorm in my head. *How dare you drag me into this bullshit while you sit here like a fucking princess and I serve you like a maid?*

Logically, I knew she hadn't really *dragged* me. I'd gone after her of my own volition. But my anger was a culmination of everything, because in our three years of friendship, I'd been a much better friend to her than she had ever been to me. I helped get her out of sketchy situations, helped her shitty band get gigs, and let her walk all over me just so she could be happy.

And somehow, even after I risked my life to save her, gorgeous Cassidy was now cozied up with a vampire Lord, utterly at peace.

My hands shook slightly as I asked, "What can I get for you?" Thankfully, my voice remained steady.

"Why don't you show us a little smile?" Margarita said, and when I looked up, her eyes were on me, calculating. Gone was the woman from two days ago who showed me around and lied by omission, acting as if my situation were normal. Sure, she hadn't been that nice then, but now she was downright mean.

"I'm here to take your orders, ma'am," I replied with as much calm as I could maintain, knowing that everyone, including *Cassidy*, was looking at me.

"My order is a smile." Margarita put on that sharklike grin of hers.

I stiffened as red edged into the corners of my sight. *What the hell is this bitch's problem?*

"I would like steak and some risotto," Logan cut in, sending a warning gaze to Margarita before looking back at me with evident impatience. "If you could also add some mushrooms to the risotto, that would be great."

I scribbled it down immediately, hoping they would all follow Logan's lead and place their orders without incident. Margarita nodded to Logan as if to say she would be nice from now on. She then curled her lips into a fake smile and said, "I'll have what he's having, and I would also like for you to give me a fucking smile." She smirked. "Noob."

Deciding that arguing with her was completely unnecessary for my already shaky well-being, I took a deep breath, flipped my hair out of my face, and gave her a chilly, apathetic stretch of the lips.

Her delight immediately changed into a murderous look. "Show some respect, *Aileeeeeennnnnn*. I'm a *Lieutenant*."

The way she said my name and the entitlement written all over her face told me everything I needed to know about her, if I hadn't already gotten the memo before. The fact that no one stopped her made me madder than before.

Removing the smile from my face, I gave her a nod and said, with just the right amount of mockery, "I respect you."

That seemed to enrage her. "You little *twat*—"

"That's enough, Margarita," a low voice rumbled.

I turned to look at Ragnor, whose eyes were on me. A chill went down my spine when his gaze held mine, followed by a spark that shot fire through my blood. I couldn't turn away, and I wasn't sure I wanted to.

"Three medium-rare steaks and a bowl of pasta," Ragnor said before licking his lips and keeping his eyes on me.

Someone suddenly cleared their throat, taking me out of my locked-eyes connection with Ragnor. It was Cassidy.

I slowly moved my eyes from Ragnor to Cassidy. Our eyes clashed, and she held mine for long moments. It was as if she was trying to determine whether I was going to acknowledge our shared past. When she finally spoke, all she said was "I would like steak too."

And just like that, I realized that the lives we had before were gone. Erased. Friendships? Lovers? Teachers? No one cared about that but me. Cassidy was a struggling musician up there. Here, she was in cahoots with a powerful vampire Lord, seated at his side at *table one*, and being waited on by someone she used to know—and if I'm being honest, didn't really like all that much. She didn't owe me anything, so waiting for her to say something other than what she did was moot. Down here, Cassidy didn't *want* to know me.

It seemed as if I was the only one holding on to the life above, and despite the circumstances, despite the anger and betrayal, this had to end. Now.

As though my body had switched to autopilot now that I finally understood how things worked down here, I found myself gritting out, "With our Lord ordering three steaks, we're out. My protein recommendation is chicken breast."

"I'll take the chicken, then," Cassidy said with an exhausted sigh as if she had just negotiated to free a hostage. She could be overly dramatic when she didn't have her way.

There were so many things on the tip of my tongue that I wanted to say. Instead, I wrote down Ragnor's and Cassidy's orders on my notepad.

"Is that all?" I asked, looking at everyone seated at table one.

The beautiful man quietly placed his order without incident, and I quickly scribbled it down on my pad.

When I looked up, Cassidy was still staring at me. In her eyes, I finally saw what I hadn't seen before.

Panic.

She was begging me with her eyes to not say anything. Not here, not now.

It didn't take a genius to figure out Cassidy's motivations, seeing as she'd just shown up on the arms of the Lord of our League *and* was important enough, apparently, to sit at *table one*.

Our marginal friendship from before was now a distant memory. All of it flushed down the fucking drain now that she was no longer a poor lead singer of a shitty band living in a shitty neighborhood waiting to become a vampire.

First Logan, now Cassidy. Despite being surrounded by hundreds of vampires, I was truly fucking alone.

After I finished writing down the rest of the orders, I turned on my heel and left, staring straight ahead and ignoring the pitying looks of my classmates and the mocking ones of the rest of the League.

CHAPTER 9

It was close to dawn when I finished my first cafeteria shift. Even Lon was gone. I ripped off my apron and threw it in the laundry bin before washing my hands in an attempt to wash away this awful, *awful* day.

I had been ridiculed, taunted, yelled at, cursed at, and stared down. I had endured watching Cassidy and Logan laugh and eat and carry on like they didn't have a care in the world.

I left the kitchen, wishing the place would be set on fire, and was just walking out of the cafeteria when a familiar voice said, "Good job today."

With as high strung as I was, that comment sent me over the edge. I whirled around, enraged, and was sending a punch straight to the speaker's face when he caught my wrist, grabbed my other wrist, pushed me backward as though I weighed nothing, and shoved me against the wall.

That's when I came face to face with Ragnor Rayne, the reason for all my pain.

His eyes were a cool midnight blue and his face was as intimidatingly blank as always. Now all I could think about was him. His hold on my wrists was strong, but he wasn't hurting me. His touch seemed to set my skin on fire. His palms were so rough and warm.

"Nice attempt," he said in a low voice, glancing at my much smaller hand still balled in the fist that was meant to strike him, before returning his gaze to my face. "But consider this a warning. If you ever try to hit me again, I won't be so forgiving."

"Let me go, asshole," I snarled, despite feeling my body start to give in.

With lightning speed, he freed one hand, and used it to grab my neck. I found myself wishing he'd grabbed me hard enough for it to hurt. For a split second, I was vulnerable to him, as my body was betraying me.

"Be careful, Henderson," he said, his eyes no longer so cool and his breath quickening. "Or—"

I didn't wait for him to finish. Wild thoughts that shouldn't have manifested ran through my head. So I used my free hand to attempt to punch him once more, but in a blur, he turned me around so that my front was pinned against the wall, my arms were behind my back in a shackling hold, and his thighs pressed against the backs of mine, completely immobilizing me.

I inhaled sharply as our bodies were twisted up and pinned together in a way that they should not have been. When he suddenly tightened his hold, he pressed closer until I could feel him in ways I wished I couldn't feel.

Something pooled in my belly, something I refused to acknowledge. I wanted to run as far away from him as possible.

Yet I couldn't.

And when I felt his breath near my ear, I regretted striking him in the first place.

"Are you done?" he murmured against my ear, not angry but rigid, nonetheless.

As if. Ignoring all the warning bells in my head, I decided it was now or never. "You have no right," I spat out, growing furious. "You have no right to make life here difficult for me after what you did to me."

I squirmed beneath his hold, each movement bringing our bodies together even more.

Ragnor's silence and resolute hold infuriated me further. "You stole everything from me," I hissed, starting to shake from the fury. "And it would've been somewhat fine if not for the fact you've done so consensually with everyone else!"

His silence broke. "You should be thanking me," he said, voice lower than before. "You should be kissing the ground I walk on for letting you live."

"You gave me no choice!" I snapped, inadvertently moving my ear closer to his mouth.

"Ah," he murmured, "so you wish I would have killed you instead?"

I tensed as my head filled with distant memories of urns and a bloody river. Cool perspiration coated my skin, and my breath turned shallow for entirely different reasons.

"Yes," I whispered. "You should have."

It felt like he froze too. "Why?"

Exhaustion hit me just then. I was tired. So, so tired. "Let me go," I said instead of answering. "Just . . . let me go."

Let me leave this place and never return.

"Only if you're going to behave," he said quietly.

Without any energy, I simply said, "I will."

To my surprise, he released me and stepped back. I turned around and caught his eyes slowly moving up and down my body before landing on my face.

Ignoring the flush I felt in places that had been cold for so long, I was about to leave when he said, "I didn't say you could go."

I stopped and whipped my head toward him. "I'm not a pet," I snapped before I turned back to walk away.

Between one blink and the next, he was blocking my path with his tall looming form. In another blur, his hand was grabbing my chin, forcing my head to tilt up and look at his eyes, which had gone neon blue. "You still don't understand how things work here, do you?" he said in a low, rumbling tone.

Blood rushed up to my face. "I already told you," I said tautly. "You should've killed me."

He stepped closer until our bodies were pressing together. I sucked in a breath at his proximity, and my chest rose, rubbing against his. This small movement made sparks shoot straight to my nipples. *Fuck.*

"I gave you a new life, a *better* life," he said quietly, and his eyes, no longer neon, were suddenly contemplative. "You're stronger than you've ever been. You have a community you can belong to, if you so choose. I've given you something people would kill for and, more often than not, don't get."

I grabbed the collar of his shirt, using the grip to get up on my tiptoes so our faces would only be inches apart. I could feel the rise of heat in deep places, which was getting more difficult to ignore.

"I never asked for this," I said, glaring at him. "I was happy up there. I was content. I was *free.*"

It was a total lie. My life above was shit. Go to work. Come home. Eat frozen dinners. Watch Cassidy's shitty band play. Go home. Do it all again the next day. It might have been meaningless, but it was my life. I was in control. Ragnor stole that from me.

"You took the one thing from me that meant something," I hissed, "and you're going to regret it."

His gaze caught mine, and for a moment, I didn't want to let go. I wanted to lean forward, take one more step until my torso was lined up with his, my breasts pressed against his chest, and my lips hovering over his—

Startled at the abrupt straying of my thoughts, I let him go as though my hands were scorched, turned around, and was about to make my exit when he said into the silence, "Everything would go far easier for you if you would stop fighting."

Part of me urged me to keep on going without replying. That continuing this little chat was dangerous. But my head and mouth had two different needs, and as I kept on walking, I snorted and blurted out, "I couldn't give less fucks."

"Have it your way, then," he said, and then I could feel him right behind me, his body heat seeping into my back as he grabbed my waist, pulling me to him, shooting electric currents down my spine. For a moment, I was frozen, turning even tenser when his hands smoothed their way to my lower stomach, spreading against my shirt, making my heart kick loudly in my chest, and those horrible thoughts from before returned with a vengeance, shooting images of him bending me against the wall, tearing off my pants, taking down his.

I gasped, shut my eyes, and attempted to escape his maddening touch when his next words froze me in place.

"Tomorrow at six. Be in my office."

CHAPTER 10

Before night breakfast the next day, I walked into the common room to find Zoey reading a book. But her face had an odd look to it, and it didn't seem like her eyes were moving. It was as if her mind was somewhere else.

I plopped down on the sofa next to her. "Good morning," I said quietly when she didn't respond to my presence.

She jolted and whipped her head to me. "Oh," she said, relaxing when she saw me. "Morning."

Frowning, I debated whether I should poke my nose in or not. Seeing the dark bags under her eyes, I made my decision. "Are you all right?"

She tensed for a moment before she let out a deep sigh. "No, I'm not," she whispered. "I'm not all right."

Hesitantly, I took her hand in mine. "I'm here if you want to talk."

Smiling grimly, she took a deep breath and said, "I just received a notice that my . . ." She shook her head. "That someone in my family died."

The first thing I wondered following her words was how she knew that. Our phones had been taken, and we had no way to contact the outside world—as long as we were newbies, that was. But that didn't matter now. What mattered was the grief coating her voice.

Squeezing her hand, I said, "You don't have to talk about it."

"I think it's better if I do," she said, voice shaking. "I do not miss my old life, you see. I do, however, miss some of the people I used to know."

She gently pulled away from me and put her arms around herself. "I'm from Brooklyn," she suddenly said. "My family is extremely conservative. I ran away from home when I was fifteen."

I listened silently, taking her words in.

"My relationship with my family is complicated, to say the least," she said, chuckling bitterly. "But some of them—my sister, for instance . . . some of them I miss like crazy."

It begged the question why, then, she signed up to be a vampire in the first place. But I didn't ask her anything. All I did was listen.

She raised her eyes to me. "Don't you sometimes miss your old life, Aileen?"

Of course I did. More than she knew, considering I wasn't here by choice. "Yeah, I do," I said, and in the spirit of sharing, I told her some bits about myself too. "I was on the road to get promoted at my job, you see," I said. "I was starting to get my life together, molding it into what I wanted. I even had this cute customer coming by sometimes."

I paused, looking away when Zoey's eyes filled with sympathy I couldn't quite process. "There was freedom there. I could do anything. Absolutely anything. But now . . ." *my fate was out of my control.* But I didn't tell her that.

In the silence that followed, something told me Zoey and I were both wondering why we were here, then. But like me, it seemed Zoey was reluctant to share that info. I could relate. What would she think if she knew my circumstances?

"There's another thing," Zoey said, breaking the silence. I raised my eyes to hers and saw her grief was gone, replaced by pain. "Have you heard about the Auction?"

I frowned. "I think I heard someone mention it once. Why?"

"I learned of its existence just yesterday, at dinner," Zoey said, shuddering. She was obviously shaken by whatever it meant. "One of the older vamps came over to our table to look down at us. He said that we shouldn't get too comfortable since the Auction would help our Lord get rid of us anyway. When we asked him what it meant, he didn't bother to explain, but it left us all wondering. Gus found a chapter about it in a book he found during his shift at the Archives."

A bad feeling crawled into my stomach, and I could only imagine what the Auction meant now. "Tell me."

Zoey's lips trembled as she explained. "Every few months, after each batch of new-vampire courses in all nine US Leagues is done, the Lords throw an Auction. They gather new Common vampires in one place, and they trade them for money and resources. It's just like a regular auction, only instead of objects, us newbies are on the stage being sold off."

This was disturbing on too many levels. "But what about the *waiting list*?"

"Apparently, it's worth shit," she said, tears in her eyes. "The *waiting list*, according to the book, is just a general list of potential vampires who have agreed to receive the Imprint. They can't give us the Imprint unless we agree to it. We're randomly picked up by each Lord at random times throughout our lives, with no guarantee that we will ever amount to anything down here. Then, if we don't prove to be useful to their League at any point up until the Auction, they can literally dispose of us by selling us off to another League."

"What happens if no one wants to buy us at the Auction?" I asked despite a million other questions racing through my head.

Zoey shuddered. "I have no idea."

That was messed up. Ragnor could afford to give me the Imprint because he would be rid of me for money anyway—that is, if anyone wanted to buy me.

"That means another thing," she said, giving me a pitying look I didn't appreciate. I drew myself back. "You can't tell anyone we live together. We also can't be seen together in public for risk of association by proximity."

I tensed. "Okay, but why?"

"Because you work in the kitchen," she said as though it was obvious.

And it was obvious when I thought about it for a moment. The way the other cafeteria workers trembled, Lon's behavior, Ragnor's table—it all made sense now. I was at the bottom of the food chain in this place. I was lower than groundskeepers and maids.

Seeing Zoey's face, though, I realized another thing. "I'll probably be auctioned since I'm not exactly a favorite among the League leadership," I said, "but you still have a chance to stay here, and you think being associated with me will lower your chances."

She nodded, grimacing. "I have nothing against you," she clarified, "but sometimes, life hands you certain cards, and you need to be smart about how you play them."

She was right. If I were in her shoes, assigned to a respectful enough job at the Archives, not being on Ragnor's radar, I would've thought so as well. It just sucked that after our earlier conversation, she had to go and say that being friendly with me should be a dirty little secret.

Still, it didn't change anything. So all I could say was "Understood."

Tansy entered the room then. She always seemed like she was floating, staring dreamily at nothing. She settled on the sofa near me and smiled. "I love my new job."

It seemed to be the last straw for Zoey, as she threw up her hands in frustration and stood up. "I can't deal with this right now," she half cried, half screamed, and went out of the suite.

I turned to Tansy. "Have you heard of the Auction?"

She cocked her head, her ridiculously long hair brushing her calves. "Material things don't scare me," she murmured.

"That's good," I said.

Suddenly, her eyes cleared, and her gaze turned piercing. "You're uncomfortable around me," she stated.

She was surprisingly sharp. "That's true," I said, not bothering to deny it.

"I know why," she said, her face somber. "You think I'm a freak."

"I don't," I retorted. It wasn't a lie. I just really didn't have the energy to deal with her.

She stared at me for a long moment before shrugging and jumping up on her feet gracefully. "See you tomorrow," she said airily and exited the suite.

I went to class alone. Everyone was already there when I arrived, but no one paid me any mind. In fact, it seemed like my classmates were all actively ignoring me. I guess Zoey wasn't the only one who thought keeping her distance was prudent.

I sat alone, waited for class to start, and listened to the others talk since I didn't have anything better to do.

"My meeting is at seven," Jakob boasted to the others.

"Why didn't I get a meeting with him?" Zoey pouted. "I would've liked dazzling him with my amazing personality if it means getting out of being fucking auctioned!"

"Don't fret, luv," said a guy with rock star hair and a heavy British accent whom I hadn't noticed until now. "This meeting has nothing to do with the Auction or popularity. I heard only *certain people* were asked to meet our Lord."

Jakob didn't like the sound of it. "What do you mean by *certain people?*"

"Who else here has a meeting with our Lord today?" Zoey asked, looking around the classroom.

Jakob was among the three who raised their hands. I didn't bother playing along. It wasn't like they would care.

Just then, Abe strode into the class, putting an end to all the chatter. Once everyone was in their seats, his black eyes studied everyone. "Today you're going to have your first physical training session," he said as a greeting. "After the break, you'll meet Logan up in the gym to work off some of your nervous energy."

Abe seemed to be eyeing a little more intensely those who'd raised their hands before. Even though I tried not to react when he mentioned Logan's name, my body betrayed me by shrinking down in my chair under Abe's gaze.

When he looked away and walked over to his desk, I exhaled the breath I had been holding in.

"Until then," Abe said, now shuffling papers on his desk, "we'll talk about the Auction."

Murmurs broke out around the room, but with one piercing look from Abe, they ceased. He took his usual position in front of his desk, extending his legs out in front of him and crossing them.

"The Auction is a tradition that goes way back to the first vampires. It allows vampires—both newcomers like yourself and older ones—to cross over to a new League and start fresh. For newcomers, it is compulsory to participate. Do you understand why?"

I had a guess. I believed Ragnor and the other Lords wanted to stack their Leagues with as many Gifteds as possible, leaving little room for Commons. Anyone would prefer having Gifteds after all, right?

Considering everything I'd learned so far, it seemed that there were way too many Common vampires around, and no League needed or wanted that many of them. And just like that, a realization crawled across my mind, so cold that it made me shiver. The people in my class were not just my classmates. They were my competitors. And we had better start figuring out how to distinguish ourselves from one another and from the Gifteds, or we wouldn't survive past the Auction.

"So if we're all Commons and there are more of us than there are of Gifteds . . . ," I mumbled from the back of the classroom. Abe looked at me with a small smile as if he'd been waiting for someone to get it.

"Continue, Aileen," Abe said, his smile getting bigger as he pointed to me.

Everyone turned to look at me, and I shrank a bit more in my chair, hoping Abe would let it go, ignore me, and keep teaching.

"Continue, Aileen. You're onto something," Abe said, now standing with his hands on both hips and nodding in my direction.

I cleared my throat before continuing, then sat up in my chair.

"If we are all Commons and there are more of us than there are of Gifteds and limited space in the Leagues, then some of us won't be here after the Auction. Some of us won't make it," I said, almost in a trance.

With a satisfied look on his face, Abe shook his head as if I had just solved the Da Vinci code.

"The Lords conduct a thorough background check on each candidate for the Imprint," Abe said. "Everything about you, from the day you were born until the day you ended up here, is known and discussed by Lords across all the Leagues. But what matters *now* is your performance as a part of your League. You need to contribute to earn your place, and this is why you've been given temporary occupations—to help uncover your hidden talents and see if you can become an integral part of a League. You then present your skills at the Auction, and the Lords have the option of buying out each of you if you fit their purposes and job vacancies."

It was a nice way to say we were all replaceable, and I believe that the occupations we were assigned played a part in it. For instance, Tansy got a job with Margarita at the Vampire Resources office, while I got kitchen duty. That said everything I needed to know.

Others seemed to think so, too, because Bryce, ever the cocky fucker, raised his hand. "Our jobs are a sign of future success, right?"

Of course he would think that. Bryce was the epitome of toxic masculinity. I was surprised Margarita hadn't put him in his place yet.

"That is correct." Abe nodded. "Some of you, the Lord wants here. He will bid on you at the Auction if this is the case."

Jakob raised his hand as well. "A few of us have a meeting with the Lord today," he said. "What does it mean?"

"Most likely, he wants to get to know you a little bit before the Auction," Abe answered. "All of you will have meetings with him throughout this week."

While the others seemed excited, I grimaced. There would be no getting to know *me*.

I was a monster in disguise, after all, and I doubted monsters would sell well.

Abe must've seen that classroom spirits had plummeted, because he gave us a twenty-minute break after merely forty-five minutes of class. Once Abe walked out of the class, my classmates launched a heated, furious discussion about everything Abe had explained about the Auction.

I didn't feel like listening. Instead, I felt like I needed to do something with myself before I went insane and punched someone. So I got up and stormed out of the room and walked down the hallway, just to put some distance between me and the others. I needed to be alone.

Unfortunately, alone time wasn't in the cards for me, because when I turned a corner, I almost crashed into someone. Pausing, I raised my eyes and saw Cassidy in front of me, her gaze like a deer caught in the headlights when she realized I was standing right there.

Seeing her, I snapped. Squaring my shoulders and jutting my chin, I folded my arms and snarled, "You owe me some explanations."

She looked anywhere but at my face. "Not now, Aileen—"

"Yes, now," I cut her off. "I played along when you wanted to pretend like we were strangers." I paused, seeing the perspiration glistening on her forehead. Her evident discomfort made me even angrier. "It's time you return the favor."

She paled and tensed. "What do you want?" she asked in a small, timid voice.

I didn't waste any time. "Were you on the waiting list?"

She was quiet for a few long moments, shifting from foot to foot, before answering. "It's complicated."

Now I was angrier. "Then explain it to me."

Stepping back, she shook her head. "I can't, Aileen." She hugged herself, her face paling further. "All I can say is that I'm sorry, if it helps."

Sorry? She was *sorry*? My hands clenched into fists. "Why?" I gritted out, my face flushing with rage. "Why did you do it?" Because by not saying anything, she was admitting to what I had suspected.

She had been on the waiting list. She'd planned to leave without saying a word. If I hadn't followed her that night, I would've never known what had happened to her. I would've stayed in the dark for the rest of my life, most likely, not knowing what happened to her. I would've died with the mystery of her disappearance weighing heavily on my soul.

But she seemed to think differently. "I was miserable out there!" she suddenly snapped, her cheeks flushing as her own anger rose. "I hated every moment of my horrible, pitiful life, and I couldn't take it any-more!" She glowered at me, her green eyes brightening as the vampiric glow lit them up from within, causing me to freeze.

She shook her head, shivering from head to toe. "I was never like you, Aileen," she said, her voice abruptly turning cold. "I hated every moment being in that fucking band, hanging out with men who thought they were better than me, and having loser friends!" She paused to sneer at me, no longer cowering—in fact, she was showing me her true self for the first time without any masks. "Do you think I *liked* you? That I liked having an unambitious friend who was ditzy and clueless about everything? Do you think I enjoyed being friends with Skye, whose self-centeredness was beyond annoying?"

I tried not to let it, but it hurt. It hurt to hear her say what she really thought of me. Of course I suspected that, but hearing it was strikingly different. It felt like she physically slapped me.

Folding my arms, I said flatly, "Unfortunately for you, you didn't get rid of me," coolly enjoying her eyes widening. "In fact, I'm going to be a constant reminder for you that you failed at putting your past behind you."

She realized what I was getting to. "Don't you dare, Aileen," she hissed, looking around the empty corridor as if Ragnor himself would appear out of thin air.

I smirked humorlessly and put my hand on her shoulder, squeezing it hard enough for her to flinch. "Oh, I didn't say I would spill the beans, Cassidy," I said, giving her a chilly look. "I'll just linger where you can always see me so you'll never be able to relax, in fear of me telling everyone just what kind of past you share with a lousy Common vampire."

She slapped my hand away and gave me a glower. "You know I'm Gifted," she deduced.

I kept my smile. "I'm not as stupid as you clearly think I am."

Her anger and fear were suddenly gone. She took on a contemplative look I didn't like.

"You know, I'm not supposed to use my Gift yet," she said conversationally as if we hadn't just had a huge fight. "But for you, I think I'll make an exception."

My smile fell. She smirked, opened her mouth, and would've said something, when another voice suddenly said, "Aileen?"

Both of us whipped our heads to the side. Tansy stood there staring at us with large round eyes, her fingers fiddling absentmindedly with her long braid. She looked at Cassidy, her expression as dazed as usual, before returning her eyes to me. "Break is over," she informed me.

For a moment, I wondered how long she'd been standing there and if she'd heard anything. But Tansy seemed to be as clueless as usual. Still, when I glanced at my former friend, I saw the hysteria written all over her face.

Somewhat smug, I said, "Thank you for letting me know," before turning to Cassidy with a triumphant look. "I guess you won't get what you want this time." *Suck it, Cassidy.*

She bared her teeth, her eyes now fully aglow. But before she could say anything, I gave her my back as I joined Tansy and walked away.

CHAPTER 11

Why did everything have to go to shit?

By the time I took my seat, my triumph from before was gone and was replaced with a deep sense of sadness. Needless to say, I didn't listen for the rest of the class, and when it was over and Abe said, "Meet Logan in the gym on the third floor," I felt a headache coming.

First Cassidy, now Logan, and later that meeting with Ragnor. I had a feeling this day was going to place in the top ten worst days I'd ever had, right along with that awful day years ago when I had to give my testimony to the police officer and spat lies to try and spare a criminal.

The gym was a huge empty hall filled with ropes dangling from the ceiling, thick mats piled in one corner, ladders of varying heights spread around the walls, and miscellaneous aerobics equipment scattered about on the floor. Logan almost looked small standing alone in the middle of the room, in a gray T-shirt and black sweatpants. "You have gym clothes in the locker room," he told us. "Go get changed, and be back here in five minutes, ready to work."

A few minutes later, all of us were again in front of Logan, wearing the same attire as him. Zoey had let her hair down and put on some makeup. She looked at Logan as if he was a snack. Just then, a little pang of jealousy hit me unexpectedly. It had been so long since I thought of Logan as anything other than an ex-boyfriend.

I pulled my brown hair up and pressed my lips together, thinking about how Logan used to tell me how much he liked that my face wasn't caked in layers of makeup. Now, as I stood before him in this ridiculously large gym, waiting to do whatever it was that he had planned for us, that time with Logan seemed like a million lifetimes ago.

Logan stared at us with a tight grin, searching the room and counting each of us. "Good, you're all here. Let's get started. Oh, and you . . ." He motioned to Zoey, who gave him a flirtatious smile as if she had been waiting for him to notice her. "Put up your hair."

She pouted and did as she was told.

At first, Logan had us do some warm-ups, though that was too nice of a phrase for what they were. We had to run forty laps, something that would have been impossible for me a few weeks ago. But now, I finished all forty laps without so much as a little sweat.

Afterward, Logan led us through a series of stretches, push-ups, pull-ups, and sit-ups. He circled us and moved between us to admonish or encourage or outright belittle us for our performance in each task. And only when we were pushed to the edge of our capabilities did he say, "Now, it's time for the hard part."

"So that was the *easy* part of the class?" Zoey asked, wiping sweat from her face. Her eyes, with eyeliner and mascara smeared all around them, reminded me of a panda bear's.

Logan's lips twitched. "Since you have something to say, *you* get to spar with *me first.*"

"*Spar* with *you?*" Gus asked, eyes wide. "That hardly seems fair. Surely, you're stronger and faster than all of us?"

"You think Muhammad Ali got to be the greatest by sparring with people who were slower than him? Weaker than him? You get better by working with people who have skills you need. You watch them, take punches from them, and learn to anticipate their next move. *That's* how you get better," Logan replied.

"Oh," Gus said in a defeated voice. "And what happens if we're not any good?"

Logan didn't respond directly and instead said, "I need to evaluate your starting strength and agility to see if any of you have potential to be selected to join the Troop. Can anyone tell me what the Troop is?"

There were some rumblings from around the room as Logan paced back and forth in front of us, sizing us up before his eyes settled briefly on me.

"The Troop is like our military," Zoey said as Logan turned his gaze in her direction.

"That's correct. You just got yourself out of having to spar with me first." Logan turned his attention back to the rest of us. "Not all Leagues have a Troop, but out of those who do, Rayne League's is the best, consisting of the finest martial artists and many Gifted individuals whose Gift resides in their physicality, much like mine." He seemed proud as he continued, "Because the Rayne Troop is top tier, the Rayne League is considered the safest, most secure League out of them all."

One of the girls raised a hand. Once Logan nodded toward her, she asked, "What do we need to be safe from?"

Logan's face became somber. "Vampires have many enemies out there. Which is why all vampires, not just members of the Troop, need to be strong enough to defend themselves against any and all dangers." He gave us a meaningful look before he said, "Once I assess you here, I will create individualized training programs for each and every one of you. I recommend complying with the programs unless you want your eternal life to end far too early."

I looked around. Gus and Jakob looked worried. Zoey looked elated. The others seemed simply nervous. I wanted the class to be over with.

"Contos, you're first," Logan said.

Tansy stepped forward slowly, her long hair pulled into a high ponytail that still reached past her waist. Logan studied her up and down, probably noting her waifish form, before nodding and taking a few steps back from her. "Attack," he instructed, arms at his sides.

Tansy walked timidly toward him and punched him lightly in the chest. Logan blinked as if waiting for her to actually punch him. "That doesn't count as an attack," he informed her. He hit himself in the center of his chest two times quickly as if to show where and how hard to hit him before saying, "Again. Attack."

Some of the others snickered at the pitiful attempt, and Tansy started trembling. Her eyes, as innocent and large as they were, grew bigger, something passing through her blue irises. I knew that look, though, and I recognized the trembling. This was a deer caught in headlights, wishing with every fiber of its being to be in the shadows.

Logan frowned, shaking his head and waving her away. "Come back when you're ready to actually attack," he told her.

Tansy nodded, looking grateful for the break. She was not the same Tansy I'd seen for the last few days. Here, in this room, faced with having to fight Logan, she was a frail, dull version of herself.

Stay away from her, my conscience whispered as if it knew something I didn't.

After Tansy took a seat in the back, she wrapped her arms around herself. Then Logan turned his attention to the class. "Martin," he called.

Gus approached him, and Logan gave him the same instruction he had given Tansy. Gus merely nodded before going at Logan full force. Logan evaded every punch and kick as Gus worked up a sweat. Logan had a bored look on his face, as though he would've been more interested in playing chess.

After a few minutes, Logan told him to stop and thanked him. Then it continued on in the same manner, with only Zoey managing to land a punch to his shoulder, gaining her an approving nod from Logan. She was almost preening when they finished, as though she'd just won the lottery.

"Henderson," Logan then called. His turquoise eyes latched on to me and were far less warm than before.

I walked toward him, then stopped when I was within sparring distance.

"Attack," he instructed, never taking his piercing eyes from mine.

At that moment, I had to make a decision. My instincts told me to ignore my training. To go easy on him. He was not a threat. I was not in any real danger right then. I should pretend to be weak, feeble even.

But Logan would know. He would know I was holding back because he *knew* me. Logan knew *exactly* what I was capable of.

It wasn't just that, though. If I wanted to get my revenge on Ragnor Rayne, I wouldn't be able to do that from the kitchen or if I moved to another League. I had to show I was good at something, and while I knew I wasn't physically any better than Gus or the others, I knew something they didn't.

Everything inside me rebelled against this decision. I was many things, but a sadist wasn't one of them. Besides, we were vampires now. He obviously wasn't the same needy seventeen-year-old boy.

Yet what choice did I have?

Ignoring my conscience screaming at me, I attacked.

At first, I purposefully aimed at all the places everyone else had—his face, his midsection, his crotch. And like with the others, he averted my attacks, one after the other. Once again, Logan looked bored. I had successfully led him to believe I wasn't going to be more effective than anyone else had been. That I couldn't *possibly* do *that* to him again.

His deduction would've been correct if it hadn't been for the Auction. The idea that I could be sent to a different League, my chance to get even with Ragnor gone forever, pushed me past all reason.

And for the first time in three years, I allowed the monster to take over.

The First Behest was *Gradus Diminutio*. Slowly, I began moving heavily, my punches and kicks weakening until it was as if I was moving in slow motion. It happened gradually, and Logan, oblivious to what I was doing, simply slowed his pace to match mine.

By the time he realized my pace was too slow to be natural, it was too late for him. Because then I launched the Second Behest—*Propero Incrementum*—and in about two seconds, I accelerated my pace abruptly and propelled my fist into his nose.

Logan barely evaded the would-be hit, pivoting just in time for me to miss him by a hair. But he hadn't seen it coming, and if I'd been a tad faster, I would've gotten him.

No matter. I still had a chance, even though Logan's eyes narrowed with barely hidden fury. He knew what I was doing now, but knowing wouldn't help him. This was the beauty of the Five Behests: unless you studied them, drilling them not just deep into your muscles but rather into your DNA, avoiding them was impossible.

Which was why the monster who taught me had been so good at the violent horrors he'd inflicted.

Before I let myself feel any sort of guilt, I used the momentum of my punch, turned, and feigned a round kick to his thighs. He jumped back, but I was already moving, letting my upper body rest while my legs worked—the Third Behest, *Crura Implacabilis*—and shot into the air, aiming my right knee toward his chin.

Logan was forced to squat, which was exactly what I needed since my right foot landed on the floor while my left shin was aiming for his head as if I were a soccer player and his head the black-and-white ball.

But I was still too slow, too *human* in my vampiric body, because Logan dodged, rolling back and climbing back to his feet. My body hadn't expected him to dodge, and I found myself falling on my side, unable to regain balance.

Any and all strength left me in a whoosh of air, and I was suddenly beyond exhausted. It had been so long since I executed the Behests, and while I knew them like I knew my own name, I needed better strength and stamina to maintain them for longer than a minute, which was apparently the maximum amount of time I was able to hold on to the Behests in my current state.

I lay there for a few moments, trying to catch my breath. The nape of my neck tickled, and a shiver cascaded down my spine. Suddenly on alert, I sat up, my eyes darting around to see what caused such uneasy sensations in my body, but aside from my fellow students and Logan, there was no one present.

Logan was standing a few feet away, his eyes wide and burning a neon shade of cobalt while his chest moved up and down. He was out of air, breathless; it had taken everything in him to avoid my Behests, and it showed. "What the fuck was that?" he snarled, furious.

My gut clenched as I forced on fake confusion and said, "I was attacking."

He glared daggers at me. He knew what it was. He knew what I had just done, and I could almost physically feel his hatred mingled with this old envy he couldn't quite hide. "Dismissed."

It was dinnertime, and my classmates were heading toward the cafeteria, but I didn't join them. The first couple of hours were always the most crowded, and I preferred having my supper in the last half hour.

As I made my way through the empty corridor leading to my suite, a familiar voice called behind me, "Aileen."

I tensed, paused, and turned around. Logan strode toward me, still in his gym clothes, eyes as bright as bolts of lightning. The enraged determination written on his face told me that if he hated me before, it was nothing compared to what he was feeling now.

"Logan," I said quietly, folding my arms. "I—"

He was suddenly in my face, looming over me menacingly. "You used Iovan's *Imperium* against me," he growled, his body shaking with rage. "Again."

That niggling regret was starting to kick in now, but I couldn't let it show. "I had no choice," I said quietly. His eyes flared with alarming rage. "I don't regret it," I added, lying to us both.

He stepped closer until he was a mere inch away, forcing me to tilt my head to look at his face. "You promised," he spat, disgust making his eyes flash brighter. "You *promised* you would never, *ever*, use that against me again."

He was right. Of course he was. And yet—"You've broken your promises too," I reminded him, grimacing when shock slammed onto his face. "You promised to never leave me, remember?"

It was a low blow. I knew it wasn't the physical pain that Logan was responding to. It was the fact that I had betrayed him . . . again.

He suddenly moved back, looking at me with fury and dread, horror and anger. "You really think I would've stayed?" He hissed at the question, disbelief contorting his face. "You really think I'm that much of a glutton for punishment?"

"Logan—"

"No, Aileen." He shook his head, glowering at me. "You don't get to accuse me of breaking my promise when *your* promises never meant shit." Logan's hands curled into fists. "After all this time, I expected some sort of decency from you. Shame on me for believing that you had changed. That you might be different. But I was stupid, and that's on me. You are a *fucking* monster. You are exactly what your father made you. And you *can't* change because it's who you are."

My heart boomed in my ears, and I opened my mouth, not knowing what to say, and ended up closing it, feeling so numb, empty . . . and cold.

CHAPTER 12

Ragnor's office was on the first floor. Inside the grand lobby were two secretaries seated at marble-top desks, typing on their computers and barely making eye contact with me when I declared my presence. One of them simply said, "Sit down and wait for us to call you."

After taking a seat on one of the overstuffed couches, I studied the room. Rows upon rows of books were neatly organized in sleek bookcases, and there was an oil painting of a hooded man I assumed was the asshole himself. The artwork seemed very old fashioned, as though it was painted during the Renaissance or something. And perhaps it was; Ragnor must be older than dirt to be a Sacred Lord. And if that thought wasn't unnerving enough, there was another painting of a man who faintly resembled him, wearing royal clothing, sitting next to a small table full of food, and looking like an aristocrat from the 1400s.

After I'd stared around the room for ten minutes, one of the receptionists called my name and instructed me to go through the door into his office. When I entered, I was surprised to find only a desk with a laptop and two chairs—one for Ragnor and one for a guest. The office was smaller than I'd expected, and there were no bookshelves or paintings whatsoever.

Ragnor stood in front of the desk with his arms crossed, facing the door. His longish dark hair was down in waves, and his height was as forebodingly intimidating as ever. His steely midnight blue eyes were on me, cold and assessing.

I stopped a few steps away from him, holding my hands behind my back. His eyes raked me up and down; it was a blatant perusal that ended with his expression growing dark. I tried to picture myself from his point of view: my long brown wavy hair was pulled up into a neat ponytail, my hazel eyes probably showed how tired I was, and my clothes were wrinkled from the way they'd been carelessly folded into the suitcase I'd gotten a couple of days ago, along with the rest of my stuff from the apartment I used to live in.

To think that Ragnor's men snooped around my shitty apartment, seeing how poor I'd been, how roughly I'd lived, I was ravaged by utter humiliation.

Ragnor didn't make small talk or tell me to sit down. Instead, he said, "You're aware your situation is different from the others'."

It wasn't a question, and despite the fact that he knew the answer, it seemed like he was waiting for a response. So I gave him a nod and said, "Yes."

His face tightened in warning. "Yes, what?"

Asshole. "Yes, *my Lord.*"

He started walking toward me, but it wasn't exactly a walk. It was like a lion stalking its prey, ready to pounce at a moment's notice. "Tell me why my team can't find a single piece of information about you."

Danger, my instincts whispered. *Tread carefully.*

I wanted to give a snide response, but something about him and the way he was looking at me told me that was a bad idea. He circled me, then stood in front of me, closer now, as if he was not sure what to make of me.

His eyes dropped to my body, making me tense. "What is this you're wearing," he asked, his voice dripping with discontent.

My mouth opened and closed with a click. I didn't know what to say. Now he was asking about my clothes?

Ragnor placed a hand under my chin and raised my face to him. "You're not getting enough sleep," he said as if I didn't know this.

I stepped back and out of his grip, which seemed to annoy him. I was breathing a little heavier now. I was suddenly aware of how close he'd been and how his eyes watched my every move as if he couldn't look away even if he wanted to. It made me feel warm all of a sudden and somewhat claustrophobic. Like there just wasn't enough space in this room to contain both him and me.

Did he feel that stifling tension too? Or perhaps it was all in my head.

Or maybe I was reading far more into this than I should. He was devastatingly, mouthwateringly, panty-dropping gorgeous, after all. He probably had dozens of lovers at his beck and call. Why would he feel anything for someone he considered a nuisance? An inconvenience?

That thought irritated me, and I folded my arms, lifting my chin up. "I doubt you called me here to discuss my clothes and lack of sleep." I paused, and when his eyes sharpened, I swallowed my annoyance and gritted out, "*My Lord.*"

He stepped forward, pushing his hands into the pockets of his pants, clearing his face from any emotion. "You're hiding your past, and I need to know what's in it and whether or not your past is going to be a problem for this League," he said flatly.

My fuse sizzled at his commanding tone. "My past is of no matter to you, and I can assure you I won't jeopardize either you or your League."

Ragnor's face didn't change, but his eyes turned colder. "If it is of no matter, Henderson, then why don't you simply tell me about it?"

Because there are some things better left buried. "I can't see how it's relevant," I replied blandly. "We were told the only thing that mattered was how we performed in the Auction. I'm focused on that."

He stopped a mere step away from me, and I had to tilt my head so I could look at his face. "Let me enlighten you," he said, voice dropping lower than it already was and catching an edge of a growl. "As you must've learned by now, there is a protocol before giving an Imprint. There is a very long wait list of candidates that are chosen very carefully by us Lords. We conduct a background check on all of the candidates to tell us about their personality and behavioral tendencies and to make sure they won't put our Society at risk. You understand now, Henderson, why the background check is not just important but mandatory?"

If he only knew what he was asking for. "You do not need my background to understand my personality," I said, my hands curling into fists at my side. "Your past doesn't make you who you are." This was a statement I didn't believe, but I was out of ideas as to how to dissuade him from snooping.

He stared at me unreadably for a moment before he said in a soft, threatening voice, "I've been watching you."

Run, my gut urged. *Run, run, run—*

"You have skills a normal person shouldn't have," he murmured, eyes raking me up and down again. They were less cold than before, and they left an almost tangible warmth in their wake. "You fight like a martial arts expert. You erased your past thoroughly enough to raise some questions. You're smarter than you let on. You keep your cards close, and you refuse to let anyone know what's going on behind these pretty eyes of yours." He was somehow mere inches away from me, making my breath get stuck in my throat. "You're a ticking time bomb waiting to explode, and that, Henderson, is a security issue."

I tensed. How did he know about my fighting skills? Did Logan tell him? Had he really said my eyes were pretty?

He must've sensed the question because his lips stretched into a humorless smile, and he said, "There isn't anything that happens in my League that I don't know about, and that includes you."

Not just dangerous. Ragnor Rayne was calculating and observant, and nothing could pass by him. It meant one thing only: until I had a solid plan for getting even, I should stay as far away from him as vampirically possible.

And he was also right. I *was* a ticking time bomb. This was why, in the past three years, I'd made sure to live the most unassuming life possible. I'd made sure to fill most of my human needs without any complications, be it having a social life and a steady job or maintaining a mentally and physically healthy lifestyle.

Perhaps this was my problem. Perhaps these stupid, irrational tingles Ragnor incited in my lady bits were there because I'd been abstaining for such a long time—years, really. Not including my sparring session with Logan, Ragnor was the first man I'd been so close to in the last three years. It was no wonder I felt all kinds of things.

Things that could've been prevented if he'd chosen not to save me. Which made me circle back to the one question I couldn't fathom the answer to for the life of me. "Why didn't you kill me?"

He stared down at me, his lips thin, but did not give me an answer. Instead, he said, "Don't make the mistake of thinking you're special. I don't care about you. I care only about the danger you may pose to my League. I care that I couldn't find a single thing about you or your past. Other than that, you are just another Common vampire, as disposable as the rest of your lot. I intend to keep close to the protocol for the next three months because we both signed an agreement." His eyes flashed. "But once the Auction is here, you'll go to the first bidder, no matter how cheap the offer."

A tense silence passed between us as we glared at one another. But then his eyes flickered up, and he lifted his hand. I closed my eyes, but then I felt him tucking a rogue strand of hair behind my ear. He let his knuckles trail the side of my face, and I gasped, an involuntary shudder cascading down my spine. My skin grew warm in response to his touch, and my breaths turned shallow. My eyes fluttered open. I looked at him, a tad too dazed, heat pooling in the pit of my stomach.

He stared back, his eyes such a bright, unnatural neon blue that they illuminated the dimly lit office. My lips parted at the stunning sight, and his gaze dropped to my mouth, his fingers trailing closer to that spot. When he cupped my face and his thumb grazed my lower lip, I sucked in a breath, my body leaning forward almost against my will.

He let go of my face so abruptly that I fell back, leaning against the closed door.

He stepped back, expression unreadable, eyes no longer aglow, and with a voice calm and cool like nothing had just happened, he said, "Make problems for me before the Auction, and trust me, Henderson, I *will* kill you."

The kitchen was in chaos, much like the last time when I arrived, and it was no less easy. Lon was screaming at everyone in the special way that only he could, his small eyes livid and burning a bright yellow. A few workers had to excuse themselves to go cry in the supply closet; he was so hard on them.

By the time night lunch approached, I was weary down to my bones. Some part of me wished Jada, the server from my first shift, were here—she was the only one in the League who'd been nice to me so far—but she was nowhere to be seen.

Again, I was picked by Lon to be a server, and again, I was given table fucking one. I was starting to think Lon gave me that table on purpose, that he was under instructions from Ragnor fucking Rayne to do so, but I didn't say anything. It would be like admitting defeat, and I refused to show Ragnor any sort of weakness whatsoever.

This time, the cafeteria was packed when Ragnor and his gang entered. He was again with Margarita and Magnus, his Lieutenants, and Magnus was attached at the hip to a woman who stared at him as if he hung the moon. Logan and Abe were with them, and Cassidy too.

Ragnor's presence overshadowed everyone else's, though. Wearing jeans tucked into combat boots and a dark tee, he looked like he'd come right out of a fashion magazine. His sun-kissed skin was on display, taut over his bulging biceps, and even from where I was standing, I could see the veins corded in his arms, making my mouth water.

Get a grip, Aileen!

Shaking my head, I didn't give myself time to think. Instead, I decided to pull my lips into a friendly smile and walked confidently toward the table.

Margarita saw me first and groaned. "Not *her* again."

Cassidy stared at me with a blank expression, as though our ugly fight had never happened. However, I noticed she followed my every move, as if waiting tensely for me to say something I shouldn't. Meanwhile, Logan placed his order without sparing me even a glance. Magnus was too busy whispering to his new girlfriend, who was biting her lip with a flush on her cheeks, and Ragnor simply said, "Roast beef, medium rare."

Neither Margarita nor Cassidy ordered anything. Cassidy didn't seem to think of food as long as I was there, while Margarita was pouting petulantly, her arms folded and her nose turned up in the air.

I went to fetch the orders and, in a split-second decision, made a plate full of things I knew Cassidy liked, such as spaghetti with Bolognese and schnitzel. Some part of me rebelled against this, but a bigger part wanted to show her that I was less petty than she thought I was.

I also made sure to get Logan's risotto and Ragnor's roast beef right, even though I was tempted to serve the latter well done instead of medium rare. Then I started my way back to the table, feeling the stares on me coming from the direction of Zoey's table.

My eyes were on the spaghetti and schnitzel plate. I wondered if Cassidy would appreciate the gesture. Probably not. Honestly, I didn't know why I bothered. Cassidy never appreciated anything anyone did for her. She expected everyone to treat her special and make a fuss over her. Hell, even after our fight, she probably still believed I worshipped the ground she walked on.

My friendship with Cassidy had always been . . . complicated, despite or maybe because of everything we'd been through together. And yet I wasn't immune to seeing her troubled. Fight or no fight, the old habit to take care of her, to protect her from herself and others, was too strong to break.

I was nearly back to the table from hell when something crashed at the far end of the cafeteria, followed by a scream.

Before I could even turn around to look, a commotion erupted. Vampires ran from the source of the crash, their faces slack with shock and terror as they pushed tables out of their way, shattering half-eaten plates of food and glasses of blood onto the floor.

I was staring at the mayhem before me, stunned, rooted in place, until someone shoved into me on their way out, sending my tray full of table one's orders crashing to the floor; then I finally discovered the source of chaos.

It was my classmate, Gus. At first glance, he seemed to be normal; his tall and lean figure was standing straight, with his pale skin gleaming under the cafeteria lights and his dirty-blond hair falling over his gray eyes.

But then I realized his eyes weren't gray anymore but rather shining a luminous white that encircled abnormally small pupils, and nothing about him was normal when he suddenly crouched unnaturally on all fours like a beast waiting to pounce, with his clothes completely torn to shreds. His fangs were out, and drool dripped from his mouth to the floor.

"Aileen!"

I whipped my head around to see Cassidy running toward me, her green eyes bright with fear. But then Magnus was there, his lady companion nowhere in sight, and he grabbed Cassidy around the waist with such speed that she couldn't have resisted even if she wanted.

She yelled something before being carried toward the exit by Magnus, finally snapping me out of my stupor. I turned my back to the man, *creature*, behind me and started running.

Far ahead, I could see Margarita and Logan. The female Lieutenant seemed to be arguing with my ex, her face livid, while Logan simply took her wrist and headed to the doors. Magnus, with his arms wrapped around Cassidy, reached the exit too.

I was almost to the doors myself when I heard a monstrous growl behind me. A moment later, hands grabbed my shoulders, flattening me to the floor; then a strong, heavy weight pinned me down. For a split second, I saw Gus's face before I felt sharp teeth, *fangs*, brushing against the skin of my neck.

Then I felt it.

The *power*. An undeniable force.

It commanded me to do its bidding as it snaked around me. Soon I could feel it down into my bones, a terrifying chill, an intimidating pressure that sucked the air from my lungs. This overwhelming force kicked my heart into gear, and it beat like a fluttering butterfly.

Both invisible and physical hands pinned me to the floor, not allowing for a fight or flight. All I could do was stay there, frozen to the core, forcing me to bear the unbearable, transparent, harrowing energy even if it swallowed me whole.

RUN! YOU HAVE TO RUN!

But I couldn't run, wouldn't have been able to run even if Gus wasn't on top of me; this unfathomable pressure pasted me to the ground, torturing me with the fear and terror it inflicted.

Faintly, I remembered when Ragnor had given me the Imprint. It was just like that back then.

"Stay still, Henderson."

Ragnor's calm, cool voice pierced through the terror, and in a flash, Gus's weight was off me, and his animalistic shriek reverberated through the hall.

His shrieks turned to horrible screams that curdled my blood, and I closed my eyes, teeth chattering. My entire body was wound up so tightly with the absolute, horrible need to flee, and yet I was unable to do so.

And just as abruptly as it came, it was gone—the oppressive, horrible agony; the powerful, invisible energy that had kept me still and engulfed me in terror—and like a soda bottle that had been shaken until its top burst, I stumbled onto my feet and started running.

I lifted my face and turned my gaze to see Ragnor facing the beast.

He grabbed the man-beast in a judo hold, his arm wrapping around his neck and his legs pinning his lower body to the ground. As his eyes burned neon blue, Ragnor's sharp fangs came out, and he sank them into Gus's neck.

And tore his head off.

Using only his fangs.

What the . . .

The twitching beheaded body of the man-beast spasmed for a second too long before it ceased to move. The severed head rolled on the floor, the radiant white eyes staring unblinkingly at the ceiling, blood all over the face.

Ragnor spat out the blood, his face both grave and taut with anger. He untangled himself from the dead body and climbed to his feet, wiping the blood from around his mouth with the back of his hand. He then turned and saw me, eyes no longer glowing.

I simply stared at him, face slack with shock at what had just happened. So many questions ran through my head.

He started walking toward me slowly, cautiously, face clear of any and all emotion. He looked like he was approaching a wild animal that could flee at any moment. But since I no longer felt that horrible, cold force, I didn't feel the need to flee either.

And while seeing him tearing someone's head off—quite literally— made my blood run cold, it wasn't the worst thing I'd ever seen.

Ragnor came to a stop before me and grabbed my hand. It was shaking. *I* was shaking. His free hand cupped the side of my face, gently tilting it until my eyes met his. "Are you all right?" he asked, voice low. "Did he hurt you?"

I searched his gaze just as he searched mine. I swallowed hard and croaked, "I'm fine."

Using his grip on my hand, he pulled me forward until my head lay against his chest, and his arms wrapped around me, his other hand holding the back of my head close.

I tensed, my arms freezing at my side, hands fisted. "What are you doing?"

His warm, strong arms tightened around me. "Nearly being attacked by someone experiencing Bloodlust isn't easy," he said matter-of-factly. "I'm trying to offer you comfort."

A spark of annoyance rose inside me, shaking off the shock. "I don't need your *comfort.*"

I felt him shrug. "You have it regardless," he said, his voice taking on an indifferent tone that grated on my nerves. "Until the Auction, you're still a member of my League."

That irritated me further. "Let me go."

He let out a breath as his head leaned against my hair, his jaw brushing it. When I jerked in his arms, he inhaled as though he was taking in my scent. My heart lurched in my chest at the thought. I raised my hands, flattened them against his stomach, willed them to push him away, but in vain.

His embrace feels so, so good—

"My Lord!"

Ragnor moved away so fast there wasn't even a blur. My shoulders slumped in relief as Magnus and Margarita came through the door. Their eyes were on Ragnor as they passed me, not sparing me a glance.

As the Lieutenants fussed over Ragnor, I used the opportunity to slip away, back into the shadows.

Where I will always belong.

CHAPTER 13

Lying with my first boyfriend in an old shed, I trailed my fingers over his skin where the moonlight touched, my entire front plastered against his as he was lying under me. He was immobile, letting my fingertips trail down his face to the weak point at the base of his throat, where I grazed my nails.

"Leenie," he whispered when my other hand crawled down his body to where his cock waited under me, "please . . ."

His plea made me close my eyes in euphoria. I grabbed at his member, felt him trying to jerk, but he was tied to the bars, unable to move.

"This is what I want you to do to me," I murmured, letting him go and raising my hands up. I wrapped them around his neck, pressing my thumbs against his windpipe as my nails dug into his skin, drawing pretty crimson blood.

He gasped, and I could feel his skin heating up and see the reluctant lust entering his eyes. Pleasure consumed me, and knowing I was in charge was so heady I almost moaned. I wanted to show him what I needed him to do to me, and what he always refused to do.

As he buckled against the bars, his face transformed, and his body grew taller, more muscular. His hair lightened from pitch black to dark chocolate brown, and his eyes darkened from turquoise to a familiar, eerie midnight blue.

I gasped when he suddenly tore his hands from the chains and flipped us over so I was on my back and he was looming over me. His hands pinned mine to the mattress, and his powerful, toned body hovered over mine as his eyes, hotter than I'd ever seen them, trailed down my body.

He licked his lips, and my heart drummed in my chest. Then his hands were on my naked thighs, spreading them, exposing my slick entrance to his hungry gaze. His hold tightened, growing painful, and I felt my loins clench.

This, I thought as he lowered his head and his teeth sank into the bundle of nerves at the apex of my thighs, making me arch my back and moan. This is what I want.

I felt the tension pooling, rising, threatening to burst out of me as he ate my pussy as if it was his favorite dessert. He licked and nipped and sucked, and the pleasure was so overwhelming I thrashed against the chains now caging my wrists to the rail, needing his mouth on mine and his cock inside me.

But when he raised his head and our gazes locked, I saw my reflection in his pupils and froze. It wasn't my face reflected there. It was someone else's. Older, familiar, and absolutely terrifying.

I woke up from the nightmare with cold sweat dripping onto the sheets of my bed and my heart drumming so hard I could feel my ribs shuddering. What began as a dream about how Logan and I used to fool around turned into a nightmare about Ragnor and me here in this place.

Sleep eluded me for the rest of the night.

"Let's talk about Bloodlust."

Abe folded his arms, his face grim. The general air in the League was grim, too, after what happened last night when Gus turned into a vampire-beast and went nuts in the cafeteria.

My classmates were out of it. Jakob, Gus's closest friend, stared at the wall, his face vacant but his eyes bloodshot from crying. Zoey, who was also close to Gus, wasn't her perky self and, instead, stared down at her hands, seemingly distressed. But the rest of the class were listening to Abe with rapt attention.

I was trying to focus and not linger on what happened after the vampire-beast's attack.

Or Ragnor and the dream that refused to leave my mind.

Abe began pacing back and forth at the front of the classroom. "Bloodlust happens when a vampire doesn't consume enough blood for a few days in a row." His face seemed set in his usual lecture mood, but there was a hint of something like regret in his eyes. "Similar to when humans become dehydrated, a vampire becomes blood deprived, and when this happens, Bloodlust occurs."

Whispers broke out throughout the class. Abe stayed quiet, watching the class with a worrying look. It made me wonder if Bloodlust was a common occurrence, and if it was, why weren't we told about it right at the beginning? True, Margarita had told me to keep to my blood diet, and Abe also mentioned that drinking blood every day was mandatory, but neither had explained about the consequences if we didn't.

Once the chatter died down, Abe's face cleared, and he gave us all a hard stare. "Bloodlust can hit you at any moment. One second, you'll be fine; then the next, you'll find yourself fangs-deep in your best friend's neck. Sometimes, there are signs that some may ignore—signs that someone is at risk for Bloodlust."

The room was silent. I glanced at Jakob. His face was no longer vacant but drawn, with his lips curled, his eyes welling with tears. He let his head fall, tears streaming quietly down his face. Not far from him, Zoey hid her face in her hands, her shoulders shaking from unheard sobs.

"Bloodlust will temporarily enhance your senses, speed, and strength to a point it will take a lot to subdue you," Abe said gravely. "But it also makes you lose your mind with the need for blood, *any* blood, and you become like a depraved animal, latching on to the first thing within reach."

Cynthia, an unusually quiet girl with rainbow-colored hair, raised her hand. Abe nodded in her direction, and she said, "This is what happened yesterday, isn't it?"

Abe sighed and nodded. "Yes." Abe grimaced before continuing. "Augustus was a very promising vampire," he said sadly. "He was smart and kind, and he will be missed."

He looked down at his hands before he started pacing again. "I hope that you can learn from this so we won't lose another vampire to Bloodlust."

One of the guys, Bryce, hesitantly raised his hand. "Why did our Lord kill him?"

"Because there's no coming back from Bloodlust," Abe said, voice loaded. "Unlike humans, who can be treated for dehydration, there is no treatment other than death for Bloodlust." Abe looked pained and affected. It was clear Gus's death was weighing on him. "It's our Lord's duty to protect us, even at the price of one of his own. Had he let him free, Gus would've gone on a killing rampage. Those afflicted with Bloodlust know no bounds, and their hunger is never satiated."

It was incredibly sad. I might hate his guts, but having to kill someone who hadn't hurt a fly was not something I wished on anybody, not even Ragnor. I couldn't help but pity Gus too. What a bad way to go, being remembered as nothing but a mindless mess of a man only because he forgot to drink some blood.

Cynthia raised her hand again—she seemed to be more active in class now that Zoey was silent—and Abe gestured for her to speak. "What happens if we consume too much blood, way above the average recommended levels?"

"Great question," Abe said, giving Cynthia a small grateful smile that made her smile encouragingly in return. "There is a reason why us vampires have restrictions on many aspects of our existence," he explained, locking his hands behind his back. "We are a dangerous species, and we cannot afford to run amok and expose ourselves to humans. This is why the restrictions exist in the first place."

He stopped by my table. "To answer your question, Perkins, if you consume too much blood, you will gain a sense of euphoria akin to what human drug addicts feel," he said, locking eyes with each and every student in class with a warning look. "Most who become addicted to blood eventually render themselves useless to the League and are forced out of the League System, or in certain cases, they'll be killed."

And on that positive note, Abe wrapped up the lesson and let us go on a break before gym class.

When we arrived at the gym, Logan was waiting, and he wasn't alone.

Ragnor was there, and so were his two Lieutenants.

Margarita didn't look at me; instead, she scanned the crowd with disgust written all over her face. Magnus followed Tansy's movements with an almost predatory focus that spelled *trouble*. Ragnor's face was impassive, and I realized it was the first time I'd seen him wearing sportswear; he had on sweatpants and a tank top that exposed his biceps and drew attention to his marble-hard chest.

My thighs clenched at the sight, and I lied to myself that it was due to nerves and nothing more. But then my mind turned to *that dream*, which, before it turned south, was definitely erotic, and a voice whispered in my head, *You're so full of shit, Aileen.*

"We have guest instructors today," Logan said without preamble, snapping me back to attention. "Our Lord Ragnor Rayne, his Lieutenants, and I are going to take turns sparring with each of you. You have one mission: make each of us use our Gifts—or, in our Lord's case, his Sacred power." He paused, gave us a quick reassuring smile, and added, "The point of this is not to set you up to fail but to gauge how you handle yourself in a fight with much older vampires and ones with Gifts and magic, something you, as Common vampires, don't have."

"This is bonkers," Cynthia murmured behind me.

"I don't want to spar with our Lord," Bryce whispered back. "He'll make a pancake out of me. I wouldn't mind tangling with the woman, though."

"Get in line," murmured Kastor, another classmate, which caused all the boys nearby to chuckle.

Logan took a step forward. "Each of us will randomly choose the ones who will fight us, starting with our Lord."

Ragnor didn't wait a moment longer. His stare went to me, and he said flatly, "Henderson."

I got pitying looks as I walked toward him and stopped right next to his towering form. *Randomly, my foot.*

Magnus was next. It came as no surprise, either, when he chose Tansy, giving her a hungry look when she went to take her place next to him, shaking from head to toe. Margarita picked Bryce, much to his excitement, and Logan got Kastor. In the next round, Zoey was picked by Magnus as well, which, on a normal day, she would've been happy about, and Ragnor got Jakob, whose face looked terrified despite him still grieving, and so on it went.

"We'll start with our first picks," Logan instructed once everyone was selected. "The rest will sit and wait on the benches."

Logan gestured for Ragnor, Magnus, Margarita, and their respective prey to take sparring poses throughout the gigantic gym. I faced Ragnor, whose eyes were fixed on mine, and waited for Logan to say start. The moment he did, everyone around us moved, and I tensed up, waiting.

But Ragnor was waiting too. He was as still as a statue, and I tried to decipher what he was trying to do. Was he aiming to intimidate me? Did he want me to attack him first? What was the point of this?

After a couple of minutes, Ragnor's face hardened. "Attack," he said, his low voice commanding, his midnight blue eyes blazing.

All right, then. I took a steady breath and walked toward him slowly, checking his body for any spot where I could launch my first attack.

Ragnor had the aura of a serial killer, giving off a vibe that shot my survival instincts into a hyperaware mode nudging me to run, run, *run*.

I stopped a couple of steps away from him, trying not to let his looming, ominous presence overwhelm me. I wished I could forget the memory of his arms around me or his finger on my lip or the dream where his mouth was on my pussy. I wished I could ignore how infuriatingly sexy he was.

Focus, Aileen.

Calculations ran through my head. I needed to aim for the last place he would expect. Catching him off guard was my only hope. But despite his supposedly relaxed pose, I knew he was ready for everything I might think of. He was old, older than all the vampires in his League, and he was Sacred, which was an obvious bonus. How old could he be, though? They said only the oldest vampires were Sacred, but what was old? One hundred years old? Two? Five?

All the plans I came up with had flaws. He would read right through anything I tried. If I used Iovan's *Imperium*, he might be anticipating that too. He already knew about my near takedown of Logan the other day, after all.

The clock was ticking. I had to do something. Fastening my hold on my haywire emotions, I purposefully flicked my gaze down to his legs and then up to his neck and launched myself at him. My fist went to his gut while I flung my leg to his waist, and for a moment, I thought I was actually going to pull it off, but then I blinked, and he wasn't there anymore.

Off-balance, I caught my breath and looked around frantically, trying to see where he could've possibly gone in the millisecond that had passed, when a big warm hand grabbed the nape of my neck in a tight yet not painful hold. Warmth spread from that point of contact, making my skin sizzle and my thoughts wander to that dream, his office, his embrace.

Until his voice came a moment later, speaking one low word. "Dead."

He let go of me, and I turned around, my skin burning, watching him with more cautiousness than before. His face went back to impassiveness, and his stance was still relaxed. *Bastard.*

Giving myself no time to overthink, I started attacking him with a series of punches and kicks aimed at any part of him that might prove to be weak. But he deflected everything as easily as if he was batting a fly, and his motions were so fast they were a blur. He let me take the lead and did nothing to attack me, much like Logan had done during that first evaluation three weeks ago.

After a few minutes of being on the offensive, I stopped and circled him, frustrated. I needed to get a hit or make him use his magic, which would be great since it would be very helpful to know what it was.

Suddenly, he was in my face, his hand grabbing my neck. "Dead," he growled.

Goose bumps broke out all over my skin. Before I could do anything, he was behind me again, his arms wrapped around my body. "Dead," he repeated.

My heart kicked, and I felt as if an electric current rushed through my blood. Right after, in a flash, he had me plastered to the floor, pinned by his enormous body, his hands around my neck again. "Dead."

I half gasped, half moaned, the position straight out of my dream. Then he flipped me onto my front as though I were a pillow and straddled my back. His mouth was right at my neck, brushing against my skin. My heart boomed in my ears, my breath caught, and I stiffened, feeling the heat warming my skin all the way down to my entrance.

His body was heavy on mine, his breath hot on my skin, and I couldn't fight the shudder that went through my spine, or how my skin was warm all over, or how it felt like a bolt of lightning shot from my neck to my chest and far south.

It's just the dry spell . . . It's just the dry spell . . .

It was almost like a kiss against the skin of my neck when his deep voice rumbled, "Dead."

I got the message loud and clear. Overriding my arousal and what his body's proximity made me feel, a new emotion flowed through me. A helplessness greater than I'd ever felt spread through me; I was full of disappointment at my lack of ability to stand my own against him in a fight.

I hadn't realized in my stupid rage exactly who I promised to get my revenge on. He was as fast as lightning and as dangerous as the air around him insinuated. How was I supposed to get revenge on someone this fast and this strong? How was I supposed to best him when he'd been cultivating his power for who knew how long?

And the worst thing was, his touch set every part of me on fire.

I was completely fucked.

He released me and put a foot's distance between us. "Try again," he ordered.

Rising to my feet, I set my eyes on him, ignoring everything and everyone else. I was going to hit him. I had to. It might be futile, but I would accept defeat only after I exhausted all options.

Once I was steady on my feet, I ran toward him and desperately aimed a kick at his crotch. His hand caught my airborne leg by the calf, and with the other hand, he grabbed the fist I was trying to sneak into his midsection. Effortlessly, he pushed me down on the mat and came above me, his hands on my wrists and his knees pressing against my thighs.

Even though I hadn't made contact with him, he seemed out of breath when he looked down at me with midnight blue eyes full of darkness. "Yield," he commanded.

I stared up at him, breathless, hot all over again. I couldn't yield yet. I had to best him somehow. But my concentration went awry when he lowered his body harder onto mine, his abdomen a mere inch from my chest. With his fingers on my wrists and his face right in mine, it all made me want to close that miniscule gap, to feel the lightning strike my—

I cut off that thought before I could finish it and sucked in a deep breath. *Focus, Aileen,* I admonished myself. *Just focus, for God's sake.*

The forced calmness I imposed on my body caused it to unwind underneath Ragnor's hard, strong one. Moderating my breaths, I schooled my face into the emptiest expression I could produce. He saw the change and felt it, too, I knew, since his eyes narrowed, his lips pursed, and his grip on my wrists tightened. In the distance, someone called out "It's time for the next round!" but Ragnor shook his head and replied in a voice the sound of gravel, "We're not finished."

No, we were not.

Ragnor released me and jumped back, then circled me like a shark as I rose slowly and unstably to my feet once more. His eyes were trained on me, not bothering to hide his disapproval. I didn't care about what he disapproved of. I didn't care about him at all, in fact. I cared about only one thing.

Winning.

Without thinking twice, I ran toward him and feigned a punch, which he of course noticed, but then I crouched on the ground and grabbed his ankle with everything in me. My fangs popped out, and I lowered them toward the skin of his leg.

He caught the nape of my neck and pulled me off him as though I was a misbehaving cat. Once we were face to face, he said, "Again."

I gave him a strained smile full of teeth. His eyes narrowed farther at the sight.

Like a pitcher, he threw me away; I landed on my knees but quickly stood up and attacked him again.

Ragnor quickly pushed me on my butt before yelling "Again" with exasperation in his voice.

At some point, I managed to get my fangs about an inch away from his left bicep, and that was when he flipped me over, forcibly cocked my head to the side, and grazed my skin with his fangs. "Yield," he said, and this time, there was no room for argument or more tries.

My skin burned, *ached* for him to do more than simply graze my neck . . . and the power of that frustrated desperation scared the shit out of me.

I needed him to let me go before I did something stupid, even if my body begged otherwise.

My need to win was strong, and it wanted me to best him, no matter the means. I knew I could do it by catching him off guard, like kissing him or something absurdly dangerous like that.

But my self-preservation was far stronger. With him over me, his hot breath on my neck, his fangs close to my skin, his soft hair brushing against my earlobe making me lose my mind, all thoughts of winning evaporated and were replaced by the undiluted instinct to protect myself.

And it was that blazing, pure terror that was my undoing. "I yield."

CHAPTER 14

The dishwashing team for today's shift consisted of four vampires: Jada, CJ, Bowen, and me. I was glad to see Jada again, and it appeared she wasn't the only kind vampire in the Rayne League; CJ and Bowen were just as welcoming.

It also helped that the dishwashing took place at the end of the day, when Lon was already gone, leaving a sense of quiet peace in his absence.

"Bowen's the oldest one working in the kitchen after Lon," Jada, the only talkative one of the bunch, told me as she rinsed the special-edition china plates and I dried them. "He's been in the League since 1984. Our Lord bought him at the Auction and had to fight for him, too—apparently, Lord Renaldi believed he would turn out to be Gifted later on, and our Lord thought so too."

A snort echoed from the pot-cleaning station. "The only Gift I have is staying out of our Lord's hair when he's angry," Bowen, the source of the snorting, said bitterly.

Jada shot him a disapproving look. "You should be thankful he hasn't sent you back to Renaldi, free of charge, you useless oaf."

Bowen showed her a middle finger full of dishwashing-soap foam.

"Anyway," Jada said, handing me a fine-china plate before taking a glass and rinsing it, "Bowen was lucky. Our Lord rarely buys any vampires in those Auctions; he only spends money when he's absolutely sure the vampire's worth it."

This wasn't exactly surprising, but no one had confirmed it before. Thanks to Jada, I now knew how slim my chances really were. I frowned, mulling it over as I wiped the plate dry and set it aside. "Why does he give the Imprint to so many of them, then?" I asked.

Jada grimaced. "Each Lord chooses people to give the Imprint to by only one criteria: if there's a chance they might be Gifted, or become Gifted the older they grow as vampires." Her washing motions turned fast and a tad bit too strong. "No Lord wants to be stuck with too many Commons, but that's inevitable, of course, since there's no guarantee any of those who received the Imprint will turn out to be Gifted, what with the Gifteds consisting of about fifteen percent of the vampire population to start with."

It appeared Jada was a fountain of knowledge and even more of a chatterbox than I previously thought. "So how do they choose?" I asked, trying not to sound too eager.

Jada let out a rough sigh as she practically shoved the glass into my hands. "The official Imprinting law dictates that every human who wishes to become a vampire should have that opportunity." She scowled. "That's how the waiting list came into being."

"How does it work, though?" I asked, thinking back to the Secrecy Agreement that Margarita had me sign. "Isn't the existence of vampires top secret?"

"It is." Jada put down the fine china and grabbed a glass of blood, then sipped it. "This is why each Lord has recruitment agents. They find the right people and the right circles to spread the word, have them sign the mandatory NDA, bring them to events, and put them on the waiting list."

"CJ used to be an agent," Bowen said, leaning against the counter near us with his arms folded. He jerked his head toward the tall, tanklike Black man who was looking at us from where he cleaned the kitchen islands. "Isn't that right, C?"

He nodded, not stopping his motions.

"Why did you quit?" I asked him, drinking in every piece of info they gave me.

CJ gave me a grin that turned him from simply handsome to scorching hot. "It reminded me too much of my job as a human." When I simply stared at him, he snickered. "Salesman, newbie. It's like being a fucking salesperson, telling bullshit to young and innocent people who don't know what they're actually signing up for."

"Of course that's not the only way to do it," Jada told me, and her eyes blazed with anger that wasn't directed at me. "The Lords found a loophole in that law that allows them to take a sneakier path: they go and find potential Gifted vampires themselves and have their agent insert them onto the waiting list about a day before they actually give them the Imprint."

Now I was confused. "I don't think I'm following."

"You're so bad at explaining, Jada," Bowen drawled as he drew closer, wiping his hands. "The Lords are supposed to choose randomly who to give the Imprint to from the waiting list," he said, sending Jada a grin when she glowered at him. "They're only *supposed to*, though."

"Let's just say it hardly ever happens that way," CJ commented, and Bowen snorted in agreement.

"Now, about the Auction," Jada said loudly, needing to hear her own voice. "It's meant to whittle out the number of Commons. Unfortunately for the Lords, us Commons are part of this Society whether they like it or not."

"We're lucky, though," CJ said, suddenly serious. "Our Lord is one of the few who actually cares for his Commons. He *sees* us, unlike other Lords who regard us as a waste of space."

Jada let a china plate drop to the floor and shatter. She glared down at it before raising her bitter gaze to meet mine. "CJ is right," she hissed. "We're worthless to the Lords, and while he doesn't say it, I'm sure our Lord feels the same way."

Bowen sighed. "Don't be ungrateful, Jada."

She put her hands on her waist and glared at him, eyes glowing. "I'm very grateful," she told him through gritted teeth. "But you have to admit I'm right."

Shaking his head, Bowen retorted, "If our Lord didn't care about us Commons, why would he put us in key positions?"

"Are you talking about Maika from VR?" CJ asked.

"To name one, yes." Bowen nodded vehemently. "There's also Sanu, who's in charge of the Archives, and Neisha, one of the four commanders in the Troop—"

Jada's snort cut him off. "Come the fuck on, Bowen. All these people you mentioned are obviously under the Lord's scrutiny because they have a chance of becoming Gifteds."

My eyes widened, suddenly remembering that Abe said this could happen.

As he swept up the broken china, CJ said, "Jada's right, Bowen."

Bowen grimaced; disapproval was written on his face. "You both don't know what I know," he said quietly.

I was about to interrupt their heated discussion and ask Bowen what he knew when Jada turned to me and said, "Remember what I said: *all* the Lords absolutely despise Commons." Her gaze turned sharp. "And if one of them tells you otherwise, make sure to stay as far away from them as possible."

Two weeks had passed since that gym lesson with Ragnor, and I hadn't seen the asshole Lord. Which was great. Fantastic, even. Because it gave me time to process everything I'd learned about him and helped strengthen my resolve.

During one of my kitchen shifts, working the soup station on the buffet, I was with a vampire called Hassan, who was serving fried chicken next to me, when a couple of female vampires came over, chatting among themselves.

"She's got it bad," the dark-haired woman said, snickering. "I heard her the other day threatening one of the noobs because she was staring at him too long. As if our Lord would be interested in a *noob*!"

I poured them tomato soup and handed it over. They didn't even acknowledge me as they moved to Hassan's station. "There was also that incident in the Troop a few weeks ago, remember?" the dark-haired one said.

"She's unhinged, I tell you." The blonde giggled.

The two moved on, and I turned to Hassan, who stared broodily ahead. "Do you know who they're talking about?" I asked him tentatively. He wasn't the warmest person, and unlike Jada and her friends, who were surprisingly tolerant of my noob status, Hassan was one of those who kept their distance.

But to my surprise, he scowled and said, "They're talking about the Lieutenant." He practically slapped a piece of fried chicken onto a waiting vampire's plate. "Word of advice, noob: never disrespect either of the Lieutenants."

Learning of Margarita's crush on Ragnor wasn't surprising. What did surprise me was that I had found out that she wasn't the only one and that he hadn't been with a woman in the past few decades.

Of course that was merely a rumor I heard in the kitchen when I mentioned his relationship status to Jada. "Many think that our Lord had his heart broken some time ago," she told me, eyes twinkling with her delight for gossip. "This is why, presumably, no one, not even Margarita, dares make a move on him."

She wasn't the only one who said that too. It seemed the topic of Ragnor's supposed abstinence interested some of my classmates as well. During one break between classes, I heard Cynthia talking about the same rumor with Jakob, who'd managed to get back to himself somewhat after Gus's demise.

Unfortunately, I didn't learn anything beyond that when it came to Ragnor's past lovers. I did learn some other things about the Lord of the Rayne League, though.

CJ and I were cleaning the cafeteria during our shift when I decided to ask, "Did Ra—our Lord ever give the Imprint to someone without their consent?"

That question seemed to catch CJ by surprise. "Not to my knowledge, no," he replied, frowning. "Our Lord is many things, but he never does anything without reason. Forcing the Imprint on someone without getting their written consent has been prohibited since 1815."

I paused in the middle of cleaning and straightened, staring at him. "What do you mean, prohibited?"

CJ didn't notice the change in my tone, the excitement that entered it, as he crouched behind a table and tried to get rid of a stain on the floor. "Exactly how it sounds," he replied, "though, I doubt anyone cares for that old law. I mean, why would a Lord do such a precarious thing? It's a waste of their valuable resources."

What resources? "I don't understand."

He sighed and rose back up. "You haven't learned about how a Lord gives the Imprint to a human yet in your course?" When I shook my head no, he stretched his arms and said, "Then I suggest you wait until then. Abe is a far better teacher than I am."

I was most definitely not going to wait. "Come on, CJ," I said, giving him a pleading look. "You can't leave me hanging now."

He groaned. "Fine," he said bad temperedly, leaning his back against the table and folding his arms. He might've said Abe was the better teacher, and yet he'd just taken the same position my teacher always did when he launched into a lecture. "When a Lord gives the Imprint to a human, they have to part with some of their Lifeblood."

I understood nothing of what he'd just said. "What the hell is Lifeblood?"

"I'm getting there, so shut up and listen," CJ said tartly, and I zipped my mouth, eager to learn. "Lifeblood is the essence of what makes us vampires instead of humans. It's what allows us to be stronger, faster, have better senses, and even become Gifted and Sacred. It's also what changes our liquid intake needs from water into blood. Every vampire has it, and the Imprint is the way to get it."

He held up his fisted hand. "Let's say we can quantify the amount of Lifeblood in each vampire. Commons have about this much." He put up his index finger. "Gifteds have something like that." He raised his middle and ring fingers. "Then Sacred have this." He raised his other hand and stretched out all ten fingers. "After giving the Imprint to one human, the Lord's Lifeblood count is reduced to this." He put away his left hand and left only his index and middle fingers up on his right one.

My eyes widened as I recalled that fateful night behind the Banner Bar. "So a Lord can only give the Imprint to one human per day?"

"Per *week*," CJ corrected, smirking at my evident shock. "Of course it varies with each Lord's power levels. Some of them can give the Imprint to two humans per week, maybe even three. But that normally depletes them entirely, and they have to sleep for days on end to regenerate the Lifeblood they lost."

My heart sank. "So giving the Imprint to two people on the same day . . ."

CJ shrugged. "I don't know of any Lord who did or would ever do such a reckless thing." He snorted. "Though who knows? Perhaps some of them might feel like it if the opportunity arises. Who knows what these Lords are thinking . . ."

And just like that, my resolve turned to steel. I was even angrier at Ragnor than I'd ever been. I couldn't contain my outrage, really.

Because the Imprint he gave me right after he'd given one to Cassidy . . . he could've avoided that. He *should've* avoided that—for his own damned sake. And yet he'd gone through the trouble of wasting his Lifeblood just to coerce me into this life, as if he'd done so on an impulse.

The loss of my freedom, of my past life, I had to endure it all just because Ragnor *felt like* giving me the Imprint too.

My anger had transformed into absolute fury by the time my shift was over. In the kitchen's locker room, I took off my apron, changed into simple jeans and a tee, then stormed off.

As I strode down the corridor leading to the escalator, wanting nothing more than to find a punching bag and draw Ragnor's face on it, I saw the bane of my existence himself, in all his glory, walking from the other direction.

Ragnor. Fucking. Rayne.

Just as I was thinking about why he had given me the Imprint, perhaps risking his own life, there he was, wearing jeans and a tee that put his toned muscles on display. Just seeing him made everything inside me light up in excitement I couldn't vanquish.

And yet my anger, resentment, fury . . . they overrode everything else, at least that was what I kept telling myself.

His strong jaw locked when his midnight blue eyes caught sight of mine, and he stopped, but I didn't, not until I was right in his face. Then I forgot myself and snarled, "I've had enough."

Ragnor's eyes narrowed, and he stared down at me with an arched brow as if taunting me to go on. "Your feelings are duly noted."

I glowered at him. "You should've avoided giving me the Imprint," I growled, shaking with rage. "For your own fucking sake, what with the whole Lifeblood thing."

He said nothing, simply stared at me unblinkingly.

That made my rage burn brighter. "Yet you gave me the Imprint anyway, ruining my life and risking yours because of some sort of a fucking *impulse*."

His eye twitched, and he said mockingly, "I didn't know you cared so much about me risking my life, Henderson."

"Don't twist my words!" I snapped, wishing I could hit him, smack that stupidly gorgeous face of his. "Just answer me once and for all: *Why the fuck did you give me the Imprint?*"

My words echoed in the empty corridor, followed by a loaded silence. His eyes didn't leave mine, yet I couldn't read him.

When he finally spoke, his voice was deep and low, and it felt like he was inching closer. "What would you do if I told you there was no reason?"

My spine stiffened as I blurted, "I'd kill you."

Before I could so much as blink, Ragnor grabbed my wrist and suddenly pulled me into an empty storage room smelling faintly of bleach. He then had me pinned in the tiny space against the shut door, his hand around my neck, his eyes glowing neon blue. "You really think you can kill me?" he growled, and I ignored how his voice made my belly drop and my skin tighten. *"You?"*

His pinning me to the door sent me over the edge. "Fuck you," I growled in return.

The grip on my throat hardened, and his forehead pressed against mine, his eyes burning with cold fury. "It's time for you to know your place, Henderson," he grated out before taking his hand off my throat and moving it to my hair, grabbing it, pulling it down, and tilting my head back.

I gasped, but before I could say anything, his mouth was suddenly on the skin of my neck, near my shoulder, his unsheathed fangs tracing it, softly almost.

Nothing prepared me for the moment when he applied pressure and his fangs tore through my skin, causing me to cry out as pain flared at the spot.

It wasn't what those movies made it out to be. It was like flames flickered to life from the bite, spreading through my veins, causing fire to erupt under my skin. But as he sucked in my blood and his tongue brushed against my skin, the pain slowly transformed into something far more frightening. Something that made me want to both push him away . . . and pull him even closer.

And when his thigh parted my legs, the hard bulge of his cock nestled against my crotch, and his free hand grabbed my waist, I suddenly realized it wasn't just me. He felt it too.

The absolute madness that blazed between us.

With my body on fire, a moan escaped my mouth when Ragnor rubbed his jean-clad cock against my clothed entrance. My arms were around his head, pulling him closer as he sucked my blood, and with every brush of his tongue, I felt myself grow wetter and wetter.

All the rage I'd felt transformed into sizzling, liquid heat that turned me temporarily insane. That was the only explanation for why I started moving my waist, rubbing against him, riding him, wishing there were no clothes or barriers between us so that I could *feel* him.

He abruptly dislodged his teeth and mouth from my neck, and I almost groaned at the loss, but then his tongue licked the wound and went up to my throat, swirling against my beating pulse. From my waist, his hands were slowly moving up under my shirt until they rested on my ribs right under my breasts. I sucked in a breath as my chest grew heavy and my nipples pebbled, his touch sending waves of need down to my throbbing entrance.

I wanted more, so much more that I couldn't think straight. My hands slid beneath his shirt to his back, and the feel of his glorious, supple muscles made me gasp and shudder. He tensed at my touch but then pushed his cock hungrily against my crotch, causing my gut to tighten and my loins to squeeze. His hands were now tracing the outlines of my breasts, driving me so mad with lust I almost begged for him to tear off my bra and cup them, skin to skin.

And just as unexpectedly as it all began, he pulled away, stepping back to put some distance between us. We were both breathless, sweaty, staring at each other in what felt like apprehensive wonder.

At that moment, I could tell we were both thinking the same thing. *What the hell are we doing? Should we be doing this? Will it even be worth it?*

Silence stretched between us, and it seemed he reached a decision first.

Wordlessly, he moved past me, opened the door, and left.

CHAPTER 15
RAGNOR RAYNE

Sitting in the musky pub owned by one of his League members, Ragnor kept an eye on those present. He watched a human couple sitting in the corner of the room, murmuring softly to one another. At the other end of the bar from where he was sitting, a trio of human friends celebrated a birthday, rambunctiously asking for beer refills. Behind him, his keen hearing caught the chatter of a few vampires from his League having a night out, shooting the breeze. He recognized those vampires, of course. He knew all 512 vampires in his League not just by name, but by sound and scent too.

He tapped his fingers on the bar, listening to the nearby conversations as he waited.

"You the man, Bill!" one of the human friends said, slapping another's back.

The woman of the couple in the corner murmured, "Warren will never fit Patricia. He's too much of a square . . ."

Behind him, the vampires Maika and Jason were discussing something a tad bit more interesting. "I'm worried about Logan," said Maika, the deputy director of Vampire Resources. "He's been in a foul mood for the past few weeks."

"Yeah, he's been a pain in the neck during Troop training." Jason sighed. "I think it has something to do with him becoming a gym teacher for the CNC—nobody wants to work for these damned noobs, after all."

"Whatever happened to Samuel?" Maika asked. "He'd been running the CNC gym class for as long as I've been a vampire."

"I tried asking our Lord about him a couple of weeks ago," Jason murmured in response. "Let's just say I got majorly stonewalled."

If they knew he was here, he figured they wouldn't have been able to relax. Thankfully, one of the perks of being a Sacred meant that he could conceal his presence. It worked so well that even his own vampires didn't realize he was there.

It doesn't work on one person, though, a niggling, annoying voice whispered in his mind, darkening his mood immediately.

He didn't have time to dwell on that thought, however, because he heard the bell of the entrance door ringing, indicating that someone had just come in. He recognized her by her scent and the light, too-quiet footsteps, but he still turned around, pulling his hood higher over his head, and watched as she walked toward him, the only one able to see him, for she knew he was there.

Eliza Wains would've been plain looking had it not been for the formidable scar running from her sealed-shut left eye down to her collarbone. Her right eye was dark brown, almost black, and it narrowed when she saw him. She pushed her curly sandy-brown hair behind her shoulders, and her short and petite body climbed the stool next to Ragnor.

Once she was seated, she gave him a hard stare, something she managed to do even with one eye. "What was so important that you had to have me fly all the way from Paris?"

He gave her a thin-lipped look. "Good evening to you too."

A waiter—a vampire called Moses—came by, and Eliza glared at him, obviously in a foul mood. "Get me some beer," she snapped.

Moses gulped and nodded, then turned to Ragnor. Unfortunately, the effects of the presence concealer were gone once someone saw his face, which Moses did. Suddenly pale, the waiter swallowed hard and asked, "Anything for you, my Lord?"

"AB positive with gin," he replied quietly, not wanting the other vampires in the room to hear his voice and realize he was there.

Moses clumsily—and unnecessarily—bowed and left to fetch their drinks. Then Eliza arched an eyebrow and said, "Well?"

He didn't like working with outsiders on anything regarding his League. Especially outsiders who weren't even vampires. But he was at the end of his rope. His best people couldn't decipher the latest mystery, so he had no choice but to turn to Eliza for help.

Everything in him rebelled against the idea of mixing her up in his problems, but he was out of options, and he could no longer avoid the matter. "I have an issue in my League that I've found no solution to."

That seemed to perk her up. "Ragnor Rayne is having a problem he can't fix?" she asked, her eyes widening. "I'm intrigued. Spill."

He shot her a look that said he disapproved of her tone, but Eliza wasn't one to take orders from anyone, and she simply smirked. "I'm waiting."

Swallowing his ego, he laid it out to her. "Over a month ago, I planned to give the Imprint to the last human on the waiting list for this quarter," he said, thinking back to that night. "I did everything as I usually do—I made sure to run a security check on her to confirm she wouldn't be missed if I or one of my agents approached her with the suggestion. She had no close family members, but she had these two so-called friends and a couple of emotionally detached lovers, so I ran a background check on them all."

"Let me guess," Eliza said. "One of them came out fishy."

Moses brought over the drinks, bowed again to Ragnor, and left quickly. Once he did, Ragnor took his drink and said, "It's more than that. One of those two friends she had—she came out blank."

She frowned. "Blank how?"

"Blank as in no information whatsoever," he replied grimly, taking a sip from the gin-tinged blood. "At first, I thought she was using an alias, but my team confirmed this is her real name. However, they found absolutely nothing about her family or past. They only found that she'd been working at some grocery store for the past three years."

The woman was quiet, mulling over the information before saying, "But how is that important? You gave the Imprint to that other girl. How is her friend still an issue?"

This is the biggest fucking question, he thought gravely. "Something happened," he said, feeling his pride urging him to shut up.

Eliza must've sensed it, because she promptly asked, "What did you do, Rayne?"

"I gave the Imprint to the girl on the list," he replied, then sipped from his glass. "But this friend of hers came sniffing. She hid behind the trash bins, and once I was done with the other girl, I found myself . . ." He trailed off, trying to think of a way to put what he felt into words.

"Was it Bloodlust?" she asked. "Did you kill her?"

"No," he said, scowling. "I gave her the Imprint too."

She stared at him for a couple of minutes, shock written all over her face. It was hard to surprise the constantly guarded Eliza Wains, and that he had said something about what happened. "Why would you do such a thing?" she demanded to know.

"Giving the Imprint to a human depletes a normal Lord's energy," he said, angry at himself. "Since I'm not a normal Lord, as you know, it does the opposite to me. Giving the Imprint to a person gives me a high as though I snorted coke, but I'm used to the intoxication, and I know how to handle it."

"You say you were *high* when you gave the Imprint to that other girl?"

"Even though I was, I wouldn't have given her the Imprint," Ragnor snapped, losing his patience. "Whenever there's someone who wasn't supposed to be in the place where I give the Imprint, that high makes me kill them, no questions asked. This time, the high urged me to do something different."

She was quiet again, and he could almost hear the wheels in her head whirring. "A few questions," she said, tapping her beer glass. "First, how come you gave the Imprint to someone in a place where anyone could see?"

He didn't feel like talking about this aspect of the whole issue, but he knew her well enough to understand that, in order for her to arrange her thoughts, she needed all of her questions answered. So, despite how hard it was to admit his mistake, he said, "I suspected the woman would be a Gifted. The one I planned on giving the Imprint to," he clarified when she shot him a look. "When she told me she was ready right there and then, unable to wait a few more hours until the appointment, I . . . agreed to do it on the spot."

Eliza didn't like his answer. "So you're saying," she drawled, "your eagerness to get your hands on a Gifted was what led you to this whole mess?"

He gave her a cold look. "I don't appreciate you taking this tone with me," he said, voice dropping in warning.

She pursed her lips, and they engaged in a war of wills. Eliza wanted to keep judging Ragnor's actions. He refused to budge or let her walk over him. In the end, she must've realized that pushing the topic would be a death sentence, whether they were friends or not, and she rolled her eyes. "You're so bullheaded," she grumbled.

His shoulders relaxed now that she backed off. "What are your other questions?"

Eliza took a sip from her beer before she asked, "Did it happen before? Giving the Imprint to someone you should have killed?"

He didn't like the answer he had to give. "Only once."

Her gaze collided with his in realization. "Do you think—"

"No," he cut her off, "and this is not what I came to talk to you about. Any more questions?"

She sat back, looking at him with obvious contemplation. "What do you need me to do?"

"This girl is now a vampire in my League," Ragnor said, feeling all sorts of things regarding this little happenstance. "The Auction is only a couple of months away, and I plan to sell her to the first Lord willing to bid on her. Until then, I want to hire you to dig up whatever you can about her."

Her face turned serious. "Your team is as good as me. What makes you think I'll find out something your people didn't?"

This wasn't a question; it was a test. He and Eliza might be on good terms, and she might be one of the very few he could call a friend, but just like he was zealous for the privacy of his League members, so was she with her own people. She was trying to figure out how much he knew about her so she would know not to give anything away.

He gave her a pointed look. "I've witnessed your abilities firsthand, Eliza. I know what you're capable of, and I know that while my team is as good as you are, you have more . . . *unconventional* means of getting results."

That seemed enough to satisfy her. "I'll see what I can do," she said, "but I don't understand. Why do you care so much about some Common vampire's past? You plan to sell her at the Auction anyway, so what's the point?"

Old pain rose inside him, threatening to color his eyes neon blue. He pushed it away, refusing to submit to those buried emotions, and said, "My instincts tell me she's not who she pretends to be, and I need to know why a random girl caused me to give her the Imprint against my better judgment and how she managed to recover from the Imprinting in no more than twenty-four hours, when it usually takes a new vampire at least three days."

That was one of the biggest mysteries surrounding the girl. No one, not even him, had woken up from an Imprinting that fast. The average time was seventy-two hours, and even Ragnor himself, when he received his Imprint a long time ago, needed forty-eight hours to wake.

Yet that girl woke up after a single day.

And she hadn't stopped aggravating him ever since.

Eliza didn't like the sound of that, he observed. "It all sounds like the making of a clusterfuck, Rayne."

"And this is exactly why I need you," he added plainly.

"Dammit." She sighed. "Do you at least have some files on her?"

He took out a crumpled piece of paper with the insultingly few details he knew about her. "Aileen Henderson," he said, handing the paper to Eliza.

She scanned the page. "Average height, average build, brown hair, hazel eyes, olive skin," she read out. "Claims to be of Scottish, Egyptian, and Ukrainian origins—" She paused and raised her eyes to him. "Are you *sure*—"

"Yes," he cut her off once more, irritation evident in his voice.

Scowling, she continued. "Claims to have no talents or hobbies . . . recovered from the Imprint earlier than ninety-nine percent of the vampiric population . . . assigned to kitchen duties . . . resides with Zoey Rittman and Tansy Contos . . . former friends with Cassidy Jones and Skye Garner . . . relationship status unknown, family members unknown, acquaintances unknown . . . Wow, you really know nothing about the girl."

"Keep reading," Ragnor growled.

"Personality unclear," she resumed. "Sometimes hotheaded and rash, but other than that has a tight leash on her emotions. Versed in martial arts according to Logan—who's Logan?"

"One of the Gifteds," he replied curtly.

"Fine. Targeted by Margarita—you mean Margarita Wallen?" Eliza's eye sparked dangerously. "Is that who I think it is?"

"She's my Lieutenant," he said warningly, "a Gifted one too."

Her eye was full of loathing for said Lieutenant. "Fine," she spat, "but just so you know, if that bitch despises her, it just makes me like this mystery girl better."

"I don't care about where your affections lie, Eliza," he grated out.

She made a face and turned back to the paper but found the only things left were the addresses for her old apartment and the store where she'd worked. "You really found nothing," she said, shaking her head. "What the hell, Ragnor? Who's this girl?"

"I don't know," he said, the words causing him physical pain to utter, "but I have a bad feeling about this. I've never met someone so . . ." *fearless, fascinating, infuriating.*

She folded the paper and put it in the pocket of her jeans. "Do you have a picture of her?"

He handed her a small photograph that one of his people had taken of the girl while doing a search on Cassidy. "That should be enough."

She sipped the rest of her drink. "With what little you have, I'll have to double my usual fee."

He might have enough money to last an eternity, but Ragnor had a better plan than to spend an astronomical amount of money. "How about a quid pro quo?"

She studied him for a few long moments. "I wouldn't recommend it," she said with the bluntness he always appreciated from her. "As an information broker, I doubt you know anything that can be of use to me."

She might be whip smart and a friend, but Eliza Wains was still young. Or at least younger than him. "As a gesture of good faith, let me share what I have with you, and you can see for yourself."

She leaned forward. "All right. Shoot."

Ragnor smiled inwardly. There was nothing he liked more than to have the upper hand. "A week ago, I got a visit from an old acquaintance," he said quietly. "The name Luceras ring a bell?"

For the first time since she arrived, Eliza was speechless, frozen in place with her eye wide and her hands clenched into fists. She stared at him with something akin to terror.

Some part of him liked shocking the hell out of her. Another part was far less egotistical. "Luceras and I aren't friends," he said quietly. "I keep him close for certain reasons." Reasons Eliza knew about all too well.

She averted her gaze. "What are you suggesting?"

The question was redundant. He knew that she understood what he was getting at, but she needed to hear him say it.

"I can become his friend," he murmured, "and dig deep enough to give you what you want."

Eliza might have access to 90 percent of the information roaming around the world at any given moment, but Luceras belonged to the circle that had the remaining 10 percent to which she wasn't privy. Ragnor could get her the in she needed.

She turned her gaze to him, lips pursed, and said bitterly, "Quid pro quo it is, then."

They got off the stools, and he said, "Your services are greatly appreciated."

Silently, Eliza nodded and left, while he paid for the drinks and hurried back to the compound. Despite what either Eliza or his subconscious wanted to believe, Aileen Henderson wasn't the only vampire in his League who required his attention.

CHAPTER 16

I had just finished a dinner shift in the kitchen, ready to take yet another shower to wash away the smell of oily food on my skin, when I saw Margarita waiting outside the door to my suite.

The moment she caught sight of me, she strode toward me, her pretty face wearing a menacing look I didn't like. "Come with me," she ordered, sending me a loathing look as she started striding down the hallway toward the escalator I'd just taken to get here.

Grimly, I decided to take Hassan's advice and not piss off the Lieutenant even if she irritated the hell out of me. She took me to an empty classroom on the second floor, closed the door once we were inside, and turned to face me.

Before I could speak, she glowered at me and said, "I saw you with him, you know."

I arched a brow. "With whom?"

She bared her teeth, her eyes glowing amber. "Don't act innocent, you bitch," she snarled. "I saw him before he dragged you into that storage room. You were drooling *all over* him."

Oh. I tried to speak, but I was at a loss of words. How the hell did Margarita see Ragnor and me yesterday? I recalled that the corridor had been deserted . . .

But then again, I was too distracted by Ragnor to be able to sense anything else. How much did she see, or hear? Did Ragnor know she had been there too?

Still, it wasn't like I did anything wrong. It was Ragnor who grabbed me and pulled me into that room . . . "I think you're mistaken," I said slowly. "Ragn—*our Lord* and I were simply talking—"

"I didn't allow you to speak," she interjected with a snarl, taking a few steps toward me until she was so close that I could see the slivers of gray in her green eyes. "You've been a nuisance to the Lord, to *Logan*, and everyone else since you came here," she hissed, "and it seems that even after everything, you still didn't learn your lesson. I'm warning you"—her eyes grew large and furious—"you better start knowing your place."

She stepped back and gave me a disgusted once-over. "Whatever the two of them see in you, I will never understand," she said as her gaze returned to my face. "If *I* can't have them, no one can—especially not a useless noob like you." She sneered. "You better remember that."

Two of them, she'd said. Could she have figured out Logan and I knew each other from before? Did she know about our past relationship?

I sure as fuck hoped not. Otherwise, this was going to be one hell of a problem.

The next day, coincidentally, I had no class and, for once, no shift in the kitchen. So for the first time since I'd become a vampire, I had the entire day just for myself.

After eating breakfast, I left the cafeteria and debated whether I should visit the Common residence lounge or go to the arcade I'd heard Jakob and Bryce talk about yesterday in class. I was halfway to the lounge when I recalled Abe mentioning a greenhouse in one of his classes.

Decision made, my steps hastened as I made my way to the work-shop floor, where I could find what I wanted. Once I had what I needed, I took the escalator near the cafeteria to the top level; from there, the only way to get to the greenhouse was by climbing a spiral staircase.

The greenhouse was a huge hall full of flowers and plants, surrounded by the same stone walls as the rest of the place, but its ceiling was transparent, showing the actual night sky beyond. It was my first time here, and seeing the dark sky outside full of stars and a slender crescent moon, I felt a tad bit freer than I actually was.

To my relief, the place seemed to be deserted as I settled on one of the benches scattered around, opened the sketchbook, and started scribbling with the pencil.

Yes, I didn't consider painting or drawing my favorite pastime. But it helped me cool my head and numb my thoughts, which I could really appreciate at the moment. It also helped that I was surrounded by greenery, flowers, and plants of many kinds, giving me the feeling I was somewhat outside this stifling League.

For a couple of hours, I sat there drawing the scenery before me. It was like meditation, enchanting me into a trance state of sorts with the repetitiveness of my hand motions, and for the first time in a long while, I felt somewhat okay.

I might not have all the answers yet, Logan couldn't stand the sight of me, Cassidy pretended we were strangers while hating my guts, and I'd done something stupid with the Lord of this place, which put me on Margarita's radar even more so than before, but right here, right now, nothing mattered but the sound of sharpened graphite over paper.

When I finally put down the pencil, I stared at my drawing. It was a loose sketch of the greenhouse, and it didn't do it justice. But it was mine. I did it. I created something from nothing.

I looked up from the drawing and stared at the row of pink and purple carnations to my right. The closest to me was different from the rest, though, what with it being orange, and I petted its petals, marveling at its beauty. I wish I'd brought some watercolors with me. I wanted to paint this particular carnation.

I released the carnation, closed the sketchbook, and tucked it under my arm, preparing to leave for lunch. When I rose and turned to the left, I saw a figure sitting at the other end of the bench, his hands in the pocket of his jacket, a hood covering his head. He wore black tactical pants tucked into familiar worn-out combat boots.

Narrowing my eyes, I folded my arms and came to a stop before him. "Are you following me?" I half asked, half barked.

He let out a breath and took his hood off. Cool midnight blue eyes crashed with mine. "No, I'm not," he replied flatly. "And frankly, Henderson, if you have nothing of importance to say, leave."

His dismissive tone made my blood boil. "There's no rule against me being here even if *you're* here," I said, pausing on purpose before I drawled, "*my Lord.*"

He pinched the bridge of his nose, exhaustion etched on his face. "You know what Lifeblood is, don't you?" he asked exasperatedly.

I frowned, letting my arms fall to my sides. "What about it?"

Pushing his hair back, he said, "My Lifeblood's depleted right now."

Freezing, I stared at him. "You've just given the Imprint to someone," I said. My heart rate increased, and I felt myself losing my calm. "Someone who was on the waiting list."

Shockingly, Ragnor gave me what I could only call a pleading look. *What the actual fuck?* "Leave, Henderson," he said, letting his head fall back. "I'm too tired to deal with you."

He acted as if he was drunk. Gone was the cold, aloof Lord. Here was a strikingly sincere and honest man who seemed to be trying to catch a break.

It was fascinating. So fascinating, in fact, that my anger disappeared, and I took the seat next to him, my eyes never leaving his tired face. "You know," I said quietly, swallowing a snicker, "you're acting pretty cute right now."

His head snapped in my direction; his eyes narrowed. But for some reason, it didn't have the same effect as usual; I wasn't cowed in the slightest. "Did you just call me cute?" he asked, refreshingly bemused.

My lips quirked. "Well, cute is a bit of a stretch," I said, thinking out loud as my eyes gobbled him up while he lounged on the bench, so weary he was utterly relaxed yet still powerfully tall and muscular. He was like a snoozing beast. Lethal yet harmless.

It left me wondering if this was what he looked like when he slept, lying leisurely over the bed without a care in the world. With effort, I tore my eyes away from him and looked ahead at the colorful lilies. I heard him shifting in his place until suddenly he said, "I thought you didn't consider art a hobby."

I froze at the whisper, then turned to face him. He was holding my sketchbook, examining the drawing I'd made. I hadn't even realized I wasn't holding it anymore, and I was abruptly on edge, amusement gone. Tense and embarrassed, I looked at his long fingers as he traced the pencil lines.

His front pressed against mine, his lips on my neck, hands on my waist, rubbing against me.

Startled by the assault of the memory, I snatched the sketchbook from his hands, closed it, and blurted, "I don't."

I was staring at the floor, and yet I felt his gaze like a physical touch before he said, his voice returning to its usual flat tone, "You have potential."

My cheeks prickled as a blush arose on my face. "I don't," I mumbled and jumped to my feet without looking at him. "Have a wonderful rest of your day," I added in another blurt while face-palming myself inwardly. Gritting my teeth at the humiliation, I strode toward the exit.

But then an arm snaked around my waist and pulled me back against a hard chest. Ragnor's breath came down to my ear. "It's quite refreshing, seeing you all flustered for a change," he murmured, and I gasped as goose bumps trailed down the side of my face to my fingertips.

When his lips grazed against my earlobe, I squeezed my eyes shut and bit my lip so I wouldn't moan. My thighs clenched as he put his other arm around me, grabbing my chin and tilting my head to the side, exposing my neck to his roaming lips.

I had no idea what had come over him tonight. I had no idea why he was doing what he was doing without any warning. Because this was not about a battle of wills. He was behaving like a totally different person, a sexy, devilishly hot specimen who flirted and teased me as if we weren't a Lord and his Common noob. As if we were on great terms. As if our relationship wasn't what it actually was.

Margarita's threats rang in my head. I might hate her, but she was right in a sense; I needed to keep my distance from him. Ragnor was dangerous. Really, really dangerous.

And yet when his mouth covered the skin of my neck, I shuddered, unable to move as pure need rode me hard, willing me to give in.

A crashing noise made him let go of me, and I jumped away from him. When I heard a loud chatter approaching from behind the corner where the entrance was, I didn't dare look back at Ragnor and simply followed my instincts, which came back with a vengeance, telling me to run, run, *RUN!*

But running away didn't erase his touch. No amount of running could make me forget how I felt when his lips grazed my skin as his strong arms wrapped around my waist.

Yet I tried anyway to scrub away the feel of his touch on my shoulders, my bare skin, my chin held in his powerful hand, and his cock rubbing me and his breath hot and tantalizing on my neck.

CHAPTER 17

To celebrate the end of the first month of classes, Abe had announced we'd be going on a two-week field trip. The chance to get out of here after not being able to leave was exciting. We'd had zero contact with the outside world and no idea what was happening beyond these walls.

"We'll be visiting the other seven Leagues in the States and meeting their respective Lords," Abe had explained in our last class for that month. "It's an opportunity for you to get acquainted with the Leagues you might transfer to after the Auction."

More like be bought into, I thought bitterly, but I was the only one who felt that way; my classmates were excited about the upcoming trip too much to care for such semantics.

Now, all fifteen of us were waiting with Abe in the old warehouse where I'd first opened my eyes after receiving the Imprint. What we were waiting for, I wasn't entirely sure; Abe had simply told us we'd depart in a few minutes.

Seemingly lost in thought, Tansy stood next to me, staring at Zoey, Bryce, and Jakob—the golden trio of our class now that Gus was gone. I wondered, not for the first time, what was going on in her head. Unlike my other classmates, Tansy was hard to figure out. Others seemed to think so, too, because everyone gave her a wide berth.

It was ironic that even among a group of actual vampires, no one accepted those who were different.

"Isn't it fascinating?" Tansy suddenly asked. I turned to watch the golden trio, trying to see what she meant, but they were simply chatting and laughing, excited for the trip, like everyone else.

"What is?" I retorted.

She motioned with her chin toward the trio. "Them," she said. "Friendships. How peculiar."

Look who's talking. "I don't follow," I murmured, frowning. This was why I didn't bother chatting with Tansy; I didn't mind her being a little airheaded, but more often than not, trying to understand her led to a throbbing headache.

She shrugged and whispered, "Neither do I."

Thankfully, I didn't have to listen to more of her ruminations, because just then, two people appeared at the end of the hallway.

Ragnor and Logan.

I tensed, seeing the two of them heading toward our group. Ragnor looked especially striking today, with a pair of faded jeans tucked into his signature worn-out combat boots, and a light-blue tee covered by his trademark trench coat. His hair was down and wavy, its tips brushing his shoulders, and a five-o'clock shadow covered his jaw—which was new, since his face was always impeccably shaved.

Logan, too, seemed quite refreshed, with hair glistening from a recent shower, sweatpants, sneakers, and a white tee under a black leather jacket.

My asshole Lord and ex-boyfriend were quite the sight, and I wasn't the only one who thought so; my classmates, both men and women, seemed mesmerized by their appearance. Even Tansy.

Then Abe spoke, and my little staringfest was broken. "Our Lord and Logan will be accompanying us for the trip."

That was great. Spending two weeks with my ex who hated me and the asshole Lord I had dry-humped, then had a strange sexual interaction with in the greenhouse, and whom I was absurdly attracted to despite hating his guts?

It was a disaster waiting to happen.

When I was in tenth grade, I'd gone on a field trip to Washington, DC, arranged by my high school.

I remembered being happy to be away from my hometown for the first time ever and being even more excited because Logan had gone with me, being my classmate at the time.

But Logan was popular. With his good looks, outgoing nature, and soccer-prodigy status plus being the captain of the school's soccer team, he had many friends, and a bunch of people fancied him to the point of blunt obsession.

And yet Logan knew that he was the only friend I had, and he spent the entirety of that trip by my side, ignoring everyone else. Tessa Garland, the head cheerleader and Logan's childhood friend who'd been carrying a huge torch for him without Logan noticing, gave me the stink eye the entire trip. She tried to monopolize Logan's time, but he refused to let her get away with it.

That field trip had been the first time our classmates were aware of our relationship beyond being simply friends, and it seemed none of them liked it whatsoever.

And yet here we were now, sitting in a spacious bus, with Logan surrounded by most of my current classmates, not paying me any mind.

It had been years since that high school trip. The water wasn't simply under the bridge; the bridge was flooded, drowned by a vicious downpour.

I always knew Logan would turn out okay, that he would do well. Now, seeing him here with Ragnor confirmed that despite what I had done, Logan had turned out just fine. In fact, he was better than just okay.

I sat by myself near the back of the bus, away from prying eyes, my beaten-up earbuds plugged into my rusty old MP3 player Ragnor's people packed from my former apartment. I laid my head against the bus window, watched as the New England greenery passed us by, and tried to find some sort of reprieve from the mess that was my life.

Tansy, who was sitting alone as well in the seat in front of mine, was sound asleep, her loud snores filling the air. Ragnor was somewhere up in the front, sitting by Abe, who was driving the bus. The rest were with Logan in the middle of the bus, their excited chatter loud enough to wake up the dead.

I unfolded the itinerary Abe had handed us yesterday. It included a map of the States and a red line showing where we were heading, including the stops. With the Rayne League being someplace in Maine, our first stop was the Atalon League in Rochester, New York.

Meaning we had about an eight-hour drive.

We were each given a large bottle of AB positive—the blood type most neutral in taste—an avocado sandwich, and a big chocolate chip cookie. I was currently biting into said cookie as I scanned the itinerary and the map and concluded a few things.

First of all, there were no Leagues in the Southeast. The western-most League was in Oregon. I wondered if there was some sort of a reason for that.

Secondly, out of the seven Leagues in the US, there was only one Lady: Maiana Kalama of the Kalama League in Oregon. It seemed that the Vampire Society was quite patriarchal.

And finally, there was the Gifted count of each League. All the Leagues had more or less the same number of vampires—roughly around five hundred—but only the Rayne League had close to fifty Gifteds, while the rest had, at most, about ten. How had Ragnor managed to acquire all these Gifteds?

I remembered Jada's explanation about the Imprinting process and the loopholes around it. Still, it seemed too drastic of an imbalance. And that begged a couple of questions: Why had Ragnor gone to such great lengths to get his hands on all these Gifteds, more so than the other Lords, it seemed, and why had no other Lord questioned him about that?

Or maybe they had. I knew nothing about the vampiric political climate, after all. Perhaps this field trip was a chance to change that. And that irritated me because I needed to know. Since I was to be a full part of this damned Society, I refused to stay in the dark. I refused to just go along with everything and not ask questions.

I folded the itinerary and put it back in my bag. For the next couple of hours, I dozed off with my head against the cool window, rock music playing in my ears.

Then something shifted in front of me, and my eyes snapped open. Someone had slid into the seat next to Tansy, and when I caught sight of a shaved head, I realized it was Bryce, a burly guy a couple of years older than me, and a friend of Zoey and company. Leaning forward, I turned my gaze to Tansy, who seemed frozen in place.

"Have you thought about my suggestion?" Bryce asked Tansy, spreading his arm along the back of her seat. He didn't seem to notice, or care, that she was tense, obviously uncomfortable.

Tansy's ponytail barely moved when she jerked her head tersely. I couldn't see her face, but I had a feeling it showed nothing good.

Bryce did not get the message. Through the gap between the seats, I could see the predatory look on his face, the eagerness in his dark eyes. "You should," he murmured softly, drawing closer to her, which made her tense even further. "I'm a good bet, you know. Magnus *really* likes me."

At the Lieutenant's name, Tansy whipped her head toward Bryce, her eyes impossibly wide. "I'm not interested," she whispered, her voice wobbly.

It seemed to spur Bryce on, because he leaned toward her, cornering her against the window. I tensed. "Trust me, babe," he murmured in a voice so low that I barely heard it. "All you have to do is lie on your back and enjoy the ride."

Wow. What a scumbag.

Bryce raised his hand. Tansy's eyes filled with horror before she shut them, trembling from head to toe, folding into herself. It made Bryce grin and inch closer.

But I was done watching. I jumped to my feet, got out of my seat, moved into the aisle, and grabbed Bryce's shirt collar, pulling him with major force away from Tansy.

"Fuck!" he yelled in surprise and annoyance before he turned to see me. His eyes then narrowed. "What the fuck, Aileen?"

I glared at him. "Go back to your seat, Bryce," I warned. I was bored, antsy, and annoyed with this long-ass road trip, and I was ready to burn off some of that energy. All Bryce needed to do was give me an excuse.

He shook off my hold, rising to his feet too. "You're interrupting a private conversation," he said, ignoring my warning. *Good.* "So fuck off and—"

My fist struck his jaw with such force that he stumbled back, lost balance, and would've fallen on his ass had Jakob and Cynthia, who were sitting nearby, not grabbed his arms in time.

Bryce shook them off and straightened, glowering at me. "You'll pay for this," he growled, baring his teeth. His fangs were unsheathed.

My blood thrummed with exhilaration. I didn't give him time to attack first. Instead, I propelled myself onto him in one swift step and pushed him to the floor. He yelped, but I couldn't care less. He might be burly, but I saw him in gym class. He always moved heavily and clumsily, as if he didn't know what to do with his own brawn.

I punched him in the other side of his jaw, making him grunt in pain. Pinning him under me using my thighs, I clasped my hands around his neck, feeling myself brightening from the inside. "Do you like it, prick?" I asked, my voice soft. "Do you like having no power, being at the mercy of someone else, forced into helplessness? Huh? Do you like it?"

His face started turning purple. He grabbed my arms, trying to get me off him, so weakly I almost laughed. Funny how these men who got off on weaker, meeker women being at their mercy were just as weak, if not more so.

Tears filled his eyes, and he managed to choke out, *"Please . . ."*

I tightened my hold and smiled. "Yeah, I didn't think so."

"Henderson."

I froze. Slowly, I raised my eyes and saw Ragnor crouching before me. His eyes were a bright blue and his face grim. "Let him go," he said quietly.

I dug my nails into Bryce's skin, drawing blood. "No."

He held my gaze. "You have to let him go," he told me conversationally, very unlike him. I'd half expected him to growl and grunt at me as he always did. "You're not his Lord. You do not have the authority to exact punishments."

His sudden change of behavior was the reason I had to raise my guard higher than usual. It wasn't like how he was back in the greenhouse. It wasn't his usual self either. And not knowing what was going on behind those eyes of his half scared me, half enticed me. "He harassed her," I said, voice low. "He deserves to have a taste of his own medicine."

"And he will," Ragnor agreed, which made my eyebrows shoot to my hairline. He wrapped his large, warm hand around my forearm, and his touch made goose bumps rise on my skin. "But it's not your job to do that."

When I simply stared at him without replying, his free hand went to my hands and slowly peeled my fingers off. My instincts told me to fight this, fight *him*, but his gaze was still locked on mine, and his face was so calm, his touch surprisingly gentle, that I found myself letting go of Bryce and allowing my emotions to give way to another feeling altogether: *comfort.*

Once my hands were off, Logan pulled Bryce to his feet, glaring at me. Then he glared at Bryce before dragging him to the front of the bus. I realized then that everyone was watching us. Abe hadn't stopped the bus, but the soft music he'd played in the background was now turned off.

Using his hold on my forearm, Ragnor pulled me up to my feet before letting go. "Come with me," he murmured, and I followed him down the aisle to the back of the bus, away from everyone else. He ushered me onto the seat and settled next to me.

He stared straight ahead at the onlookers who'd been staring at us, and growled loud enough for them to hear, "Show's over."

My classmates heard the angry undertone and made themselves scarce. Abe played music again. Chatter filled the bus once more as if nothing happened.

I turned to him. "Are you going to chew me out now?"

He turned fully toward me, crowding me against the window, much like Bryce had done with Tansy. Only this was different. Ragnor wasn't Bryce, and I was not Tansy.

"You crossed the line," he said in a low voice, his face serious while his eyes, which returned to their tranquil midnight blue, searched mine. "But I don't need to tell you that. You knew what you were doing."

I folded my arms, feeling the need to put a barrier between us. "Are you going to punish me?"

His eyes flickered to my mouth before they returned to my eyes. "No, Henderson," he said, surprising the hell out of me. "Showing me a glimpse of who you really are is punishment enough."

My cheeks burned as if he'd just slapped me, and I glowered at him. "I didn't show you anything," I said, voice on the verge of snarling.

He didn't reply; his hand moved forward, and he curled his fingers around a rogue strand of hair before tucking it behind my ear. He brushed his knuckles against my cheek, making me freeze. "I saw your face, your eyes," he said, staring into said eyes with a somber seriousness that set my heart aflutter in panic. "You liked it, having him at your mercy." His voice dropped, and he leaned closer, his mouth nearing my ear, his breath warm and hot against the lobe, making me shiver. "You looked like you needed the violence, or you would go mad."

He sees too much, a voice whispered in my head, a voice that sounded suspiciously like my father's. *You have to run before he catches you.*

But before I could so much as take a breath, he grabbed my face and cocked it to the side, exposing my throbbing throat. I sucked in a breath as his lips faintly brushed against the skin under my earlobe. "Next time you need to resort to violence," he said softly, "come to me."

My breathing was rough, especially when he flicked his tongue against my skin, the skin he'd bitten into not too long ago, and then when he spoke again, I felt like I couldn't breathe at all.

"This is an order from your Lord."

Then he was off me and striding down the aisle back to the front of the bus, leaving me breathless, flushed, scared, and utterly furious.

Because he wasn't my Lord. I hadn't seen him acting like he did with me with his other subjects, too, so he couldn't possibly be my Lord.

He was simply the asshole I couldn't get out of my head.

CHAPTER 18

The home of the Atalon League wasn't as surreptitious as the Rayne League's place. The entrance to the Atalon underground compound was placed in a skyscraper smack in the middle of downtown Rochester.

It was three o'clock in the morning by the time we arrived, and the area was quiet. Abe and Logan led us into the side entrance of the building, and we took the stairs down one floor. Ragnor acted as the rear guard and seemed to be on higher alert than usual. Bryce was walking next to him, looking pale and frightened, what with Ragnor keeping him close—and everyone knew what that meant.

We took a large, fancy elevator that brought us about half a mile underground, and when we exited, we were finally in the compound.

There were no major differences between the Rayne and Atalon compounds. Both had the same architectural style, with arches and escalators leading everywhere. But the colors were somewhat different; the Rayne compound was defined by its neutral colors, with black, white, and beige marble and some occasional wood. Here, everything was bright, full of all shades of red. I felt like we'd just stepped into a blood cell.

A welcome committee waited for us in the entrance hall. It consisted of three men—two of whom were identical twins, Black with curly hair and slightly slanted eyes, and the man between them looked the way fictional vampires have been portrayed in movies and books for ages: porcelain skin, a chiseled, clean-cut jaw, platinum hair, and a pair of pitch-black eyes. He was almost as tall as Ragnor but more on the lean side.

My first impression of him was that I didn't like the look in his eyes. There was something not quite right there. But it was hard to get a read on him since, much like Ragnor's, his defenses seemed to be up.

Ragnor stepped from the back of our group and approached the black-eyed man. That man reached his hand out, and Ragnor shook it, then turned to us. "This is Lord Orion Atalon," he said. "You will refer to him as Lord Atalon."

When Atalon smiled, it was a chilling sight. "It's good to have you fledglings here," he said in a smooth, melodious voice that quite contrasted with his cold, snakelike looks. "Let's show you around."

He flicked his fingers, and the twins moved, heading toward Abe and Logan. They led us toward the downward escalator, and we all followed, most of my classmates seeming just as eager and curious as me.

As we walked, Atalon lingered back with Ragnor, the two of them speaking quietly. I slowed my pace, making sure I was near enough to the end of the group so I could try to hear what they were talking about.

Unfortunately, they were speaking too low for even dogs to hear. I could barely hear the murmur of their voices, but it was all unintelligible.

"Our first stop is the Atalon League's pride and joy," said one of the twins at the front as we came to a stop near a grand double door. "Our League has many artists, both Common and Gifted, and as big believers in nurturing said artists, we built the Atalon Gallery back in the 1800s."

The other twin pushed the double door open, revealing a large, spacious chamber. It was filled with portraits and artworks hung on the light-red walls and a few immaculate sculptures scattered around the space. There was a thick column in the middle of the room, upon which a video art installation was screened, showing the evolution of column architecture through animation, starting with the Greek era and its different types of capital orders—Ionic, Doric, and Corinthian.

It was hypnotizing and utterly fascinating. I'd studied a bit about Greek architecture during one of those art courses I'd taken before.

Seeing the video art showing it so vividly in a three-dimensional way was breathtaking.

Before I knew it, my legs took me to the column, and I stood there following the movement of the ridges in the video with my mesmerized eyes. Faintly, I heard Abe saying we had about half an hour to explore, but I didn't care. I was too busy studying the column.

In another life, I might've been an art curator. Perhaps even an architect, though I doubted I was smart enough for that. But I could've tried. If I'd had a normal life, I might've been able to try.

But in this life that I had, before I even became a vampire, these kinds of thoughts were merely dreams, and since dreams had no place in reality, I'd crushed them before they could ever take root in my head.

Seeing this column, then moving toward the artworks on the walls, beautiful paintings of portraits, landscapes, and so much more, I was filled with heavy melancholy about what could've been.

I stopped before a certain painting that caught my eye. It was of a woman's back, her fiery ginger hair down in waves on her back, and she was standing in what looked like the Garden of Eden as depicted in classical paintings.

The painting was relatively simple, but something about it called to me, and the longer I stared at it, the more I started to realize why. The woman was painted in the act of running. But it didn't look like she was frozen in time; the artist managed to paint her in a way that made her seem to be in the midst of the motion, as if it was a frame in an aged movie reel.

The landscape beyond the woman had the same feeling to it. As though the waterfall was slowly flowing down and the clouds in the sunset sky were changing colors, like the sun was still setting, its rays reflecting differently.

"Beautiful, isn't it?"

I glanced to see Lord Atalon standing next to me, his contemplative eyes on the painting. I returned my gaze to the masterpiece and saw the initials in the lower right corner. "You painted it, didn't you?" I asked, considering the initials were O. A.

His lips twitched. "I did," he said but not with pride; instead, he sounded somewhat wistful. "When my magic first developed, this was the first painting I created."

I tensed. His words, his flippant way of saying the word *magic*, implied he was a Sacred Lord, like Ragnor. Meaning he had actual magic. "Is your magic tied to this painting?" I inquired, and when his black eyes landed on my hazel ones, I wondered if I should've kept my curiosity to myself.

He smiled wryly. "Yes, it is," he said but didn't elaborate. I was smart enough to not ask any more questions.

Just when I was about to leave him to it, he asked, "You are an artist, aren't you?"

Momentarily tense, I turned to face him fully. "How do you know?" I asked, worried that he seemed to know more about me than I assumed he should have. Had he talked about me with Ragnor?

His eyes bored into mine as he stepped closer. "I can tell when someone appreciates art more than the average art enthusiast," he replied, and his eyes dropped to my hands. He took them in his as he studied them deeply. "Though you lack the calluses of a true artist."

"I'm not so good at the actual craft," I told him, careful with what I shared, as I slid my hands away from his grip. "I do appreciate those who are, though."

Atalon's eyes returned to my face, searching it. "With the right mentor, you can always get better," he said, and there was something in his eyes I couldn't quite decipher. Something that made my spine grow stiff.

Silence stretched between us as he seemed to be waiting for me to say something, but when I didn't, he nodded and said "Carry on, then" and walked away.

And I could finally breathe.

The rest of the tour at the Atalon League proved to be just as mesmerizing as the gallery had been. Workshops full of any and all art supplies—from the cheapest to the most expensive—were spread across the entire compound. Artwork hung in every corridor, and fine sculptures decorated each nook and corner. There were grand windows with projections of landscapes to give the place an airy, spacious vibe, and the vampires we passed all seemed like those art-college students I used to be so jealous of, with their clothes marred with paint, and their hair a mess of colors.

The cafeteria wasn't as artsy as the rest of the place, though there were a few sculptures and portraits here and there. It was probably the most basic room in this place. Its layout was the same as the Rayne League cafeteria, but there wasn't a dome here like back there; instead, arches supported the circular ceiling, and there were paintings there that could've easily dated back to the fifteenth century.

A large king's table was prepared for our party, and we all sat down. Ragnor, Logan, Atalon, and the twins—who were Atalon's Lieutenants, I learned—sat at one end of the table together, with both Atalon and Ragnor sharing the head position.

A few servers came over to take our orders and pour us O negative blood—a type that was considered exquisite since it was rare to harvest—tinged with a fifty-year-old cabernet sauvignon. Once the servers were gone, Atalon raised his glass for a toast and said, "For our continued, cordial friendship."

Ragnor gestured with his own glass and clinked it with Atalon's.

We all toasted silently and drank. The blood was mediocre at best, and the bitter wine didn't add to the taste. I'd already found that AB negative was the most tolerable so far.

Everyone else seemed to think differently, though. They were downing their blood with obvious enjoyment, asking for a refill soon after finishing.

"Is it that good?" I asked Tansy. She was sitting next to me and downing her second glass with evident delight.

She turned to me, her gaze unclear. "Is anything really good?" she asked in her typical Tansy fashion. "Or is it what we were wired to think?"

I had no idea what the hell she was talking about, so I turned to my left where Cynthia was sitting and asked her the same question. She replied curtly, "Yes."

After my skirmish with Bryce, all but Tansy had given me the cold shoulder. No one believed Bryce had harassed Tansy as I had claimed. Bryce, being one of the popular guys, played the victim with his friends, turning them against me—that is, if I hadn't lost their favor already. It was a wonder I managed to get a reply from Cynthia at all.

Dinner passed in silence—at least at my end of the table. Tansy was daydreaming as she slurped her spaghetti. The others seemed to be doing the same. The rest of the table, however, was vibrant and noisy with chatter, laughter, and brazenness.

I was aware of someone watching me throughout the entire meal. The prickle on my cheek was hard to ignore. However, when I glanced sideways, trying to catch who was staring, no one seemed to be paying me attention. Ragnor was talking to Atalon; Logan was speaking to Zoey and her group, with the twin Lieutenants jumping in here and there; and the rest were either busy eating or talking to one another about this or that.

There weren't many other vampires in the cafeteria, and those who did inhabit some tables were in their own worlds.

By the time we were parting ways with Atalon and his League, I still had no idea who'd been watching me during the entire dinner, and I began thinking it might've been in my head.

Until Atalon approached me as everyone exchanged departing pleasantries. He stood next to me and leaned over, his voice a soft murmur as he said, "If things don't work out between Rayne and you, let me know."

I whipped my head toward him, eyes narrowed. "Excuse me?" I half whispered, half hissed.

He gave me a grin that was borderline wicked, his eyes flickering in a way I didn't like. "I've known your Lord for many years," he said quietly. "He's a master when it comes to keeping his cards close to heart, but he can't quite hide it when his emotions are riding him hard."

He suddenly stepped right in front of me and leaned down, his hands cupping my face. My heart lurched at the sudden move, and I completely froze, not sure how to handle what he was just doing. Atalon leaned forward some more until his breath was in my ear. "If looks could kill, I would be dead ten times over."

My eyes shot to the side where Ragnor was speaking to the twin Lieutenants, and I found him staring at us like he was considering tearing Lord Atalon's head off like he had done to Gus when he was full of Bloodlust. Before he could catch my look, I closed my eyes. "I'm not interested." *Either in you or him.*

Atalon let me go and stepped back, his gaze roaming down my body and then back up. "If anything changes," he said quietly, and this time, I could see the heat in his eyes. It made them glow a dark shade of crimson. "Let me know."

Lord Atalon moved to Ragnor to shake his hand. As I watched, Ragnor's face cleared of any indication he'd just acted like a possessive lover rather than a Lord who hated my guts as much as I hated his.

CHAPTER 19

The next stop was the O'Brien League, led by Charley O'Brien, a short redheaded Irishman with a heavy, almost unintelligible accent. His League was located in Indianapolis and focused mostly on trade goods. Their underground compound was similar in design to the Rayne and Atalon ones, but it felt different; it was like a large factory with many divisions, each for developing different kinds of goods. Its specialty was coffee beans, and the entire place smelled that way.

"Here ye can taste our special brand o' coffee," O'Brien now said after we all sat down in his League's cafeteria, which seemed more like a tavern than anything else. His Lieutenants, two women who were so tall they dwarfed the already short Lord, were personally serving us this special coffee, which could've passed for cappuccino if I merely went by its color. "Give it a sip, and let me know what ye think."

All of us took a sip, and the reactions varied. Zoey spat out the coffee with a disgusted scowl. Logan and Abe politely downed the entire thing despite both their faces showing a deep struggle. Bryce jokingly forced Jakob to drink his share too. Cynthia didn't bother touching her cup.

The only ones who seemed to have no reaction were Ragnor and Tansy. Ragnor was drinking it as though it was blood. Tansy had on a dreamy, contemplative look as she sipped the coffee.

I didn't understand what the fuss was all about. The coffee tasted like an espresso with a strange aftertaste but nothing worthy of a grand reaction.

O'Brien grinned toothily and leaned back against his chair, satisfied. He turned to Ragnor. "What do ye tink, Rayne?" he asked, his eyes bright, expectant. He looked like a puppy who wanted his master's approval.

Ragnor didn't bother glancing at him when he said, "The addition of powdered reindeer meat is certainly . . . a choice."

My eyes shot to Tansy, who didn't seem to be listening. Next to her, Jakob's tanned face turned a bit green.

O'Brien perked up. "Still as sharp as always! It's unique, innit?"

Ragnor gave a curt nod as he shifted in his seat and tapped his fingers on the table. Could he be . . . uncomfortable? His face was twisted with barely contained disapproval, and he seemed to be pleading with whatever divine power was up there to make O'Brien shut up when he launched into an explanation of his experiments with different types of coffee.

Seeing Ragnor so out of his element unleashed a smirk. The power balance was very evident, with O'Brien sucking up to Ragnor as much as he could, seeking his approval. And yet Ragnor, who had the upper hand, was trying to be on his best behavior, even if it meant drinking a bizarre coffee brew.

It was hilariously out of character.

His eyes suddenly shot to me and landed on my curled lips. His face darkened, which made my smirk grow, and I gave him a wink before returning to the food being served to the table by the regular servers.

Other than the coffee-tasting incident, the rest of our visit at the O'Brien League passed rather uneventfully. When we were back on the bus, though, loud conversations erupted among my classmates.

"This League is not for me," Jakob said, shaking his head so fast it was a blur. "I hate coffee. I hate the smell of coffee. I hate everything to do with fucking *reindeer meat* powdered into the fucking coffee."

Bryce laughed. "You should've seen your face!" He snickered. "You looked ready to pass out!"

"It's not funny, Bryce," Cynthia snarled.

Zoey then said, "Besides the whole coffee thing, Lord O'Brien doesn't feel very . . . Lordlike."

She was right. Lord O'Brien's perky personality was one thing. His looking up at Ragnor like one would do at a god made him seem like a doormat. I didn't know a lot about the vampiric Society and politics—at least not yet—but I could tell that, as Leagued vampires, we should strive to have a more grounded, self-assured Lord.

The discussions about the merits—or rather demerits—of the O'Brien League continued for a long time, and I dozed off, tired of listening to them talk back and forth about the same things.

Over seven hours later, we arrived at our third stop—the Daugherty League in Kansas City, Missouri. Lord Deion Daugherty, a slender, bony man with dark curls, was waiting for us at the entrance, accompanied by his own Lieutenants, a man and woman who could've been members of a rock-metal band, what with them wearing black, having colorful hair, and sporting a bunch of emo-like jewelry.

"Rayne!" Daugherty said when we stepped out of the elevator into the underground compound, which was painted entirely in black and purple, lit up by lanterns fit for Halloween. Daugherty came over to Ragnor and gave him a man hug—a one-armed hug with a pat on the back, which Ragnor did not return yet seemed to force himself to tolerate.

"Daugherty," Ragnor said darkly.

Daugherty was either brave or stupid, because he didn't seem to notice Ragnor's tone and gave us all a big smile. "Ready to rock 'n' roll, y'all?" he said and gave us all an excited grin.

I stared at him, at a loss for words. The others seemed to feel the same, because they looked at one another as if trying to discern what the hell was going on.

We followed Daugherty to a large music studio. I recognized the type; Cassidy and her band rented one of these for their rehearsals, but this one was on a whole new level: the recording room was huge, the studio included a music mixer the size of my whole studio apartment from before, and it was soundproofed with high-quality material.

Daugherty had us stand in the studio part of the room since there were about eleven vampires in the recording room, listening to something another vampire said. "Bring up the volume, Steve!" Daugherty ordered jovially, and the male Lieutenant pushed up the sound.

We could all hear as the talking vampire said, *"Now, each of you are going to grab your instrument of choice and show me what you're thinking of playing in the Auction."*

My classmates and I all tensed when we heard that last dreaded word. Abe noticed, because he told us quietly, "It's an Auction-prep class. You'll have one when we return too."

We watched as the first newbie vampire grabbed the violin and started playing some classical piece I didn't recognize. Another one played a classical guitar-solo piece by Isaac Albéniz—I recognized this one—while the next one went to the drums and executed some difficult beat I couldn't even follow with my eyes.

I was mesmerized by the talents of the Daugherty newbies, who must be Common like us since they would also be put in the Auction. I wasn't the only one entranced by the little concert we were watching; my classmates drank up the Auction-prep lesson, seemingly taking mental notes.

Daugherty's League was all about music, so much so that every room in the compound had something to do with music or musical instruments. There was a workshop for building instruments, a little auditorium for internal shows, a karaoke studio intended for both practice and fun alike, and even a hall of fame.

The Daugherty cafeteria looked like a jazz bar, with a small stage, a bunch of round tables throughout the room, and a bar near the end that served alcoholic blood beverages twenty-four seven. As we sat to eat dinner, a band took the stage and played light blues.

I was sitting close to where Ragnor and Daugherty sat chatting quietly between themselves. Since everyone else was silent, listening to the band, I could hear bits and pieces of their conversation while pretending to watch the show as well.

When their conversation took on a heated tone, I heard clearly when Ragnor said, "I'm not lending you any more of my Gifteds, Daugherty."

Glancing at them, I saw Daugherty staring at Ragnor with a hurt face. "But this is different!" he pleaded, voice rising. "This is a *nightingale* we're talking about!"

I couldn't see Ragnor's face—it was hidden by Abe's—but I could tell by his voice that this conversation was going even further south. "Moses is still picking up the pieces after what your members did to him," he growled. "I'm not going to put any of my vampires—Gifted *or* Common—at risk by allowing them to be here."

Daugherty's face flushed angrily. "I told you I don't give this shit to my members anymore!" he yelled loudly enough now to disrupt the music. "And my vampires are just as good as anyone's, including yours!"

"Oh, really?" Ragnor said, and I'd never heard him sound like this. There was hatred in his voice that made the tiny hairs on my skin stand on end. "Then explain to me why the drug-trafficking rates around this city have been rising ever since you moved your League here five years ago?"

Eyes glowing, Daugherty jumped to his feet, fangs unsheathed. "Are you looking for a fucking fight, Rayne?" he growled. Gone was the rock-'n'-roll-y'all man from two hours ago. "Because you'll fucking regret it, you piece of shit—"

It was so fast that I would've missed it had I not watched them so closely. One moment, Daugherty was taunting Ragnor, and the next, he was flattened on the floor with Ragnor standing over him, imposingly taller, more muscular, and far more threatening.

The jazz band paused their performance. The emo Lieutenants were standing close by, staring at their Lord and Ragnor with shock slammed onto their faces. Logan and Abe were behind Ragnor, ready to jump into action. Everyone else was watching, trying to grasp what the hell was going on.

I was trying to understand, too, because I got very little. What was a nightingale? Who was Moses? And what the hell did the Daugherty League do to him?

"You can run your little drug cartel for all I care," Ragnor now said, voice low, dark, and fearsome enough to make everyone stay still, "but do not expect me to provide you with my vampires to keep your business going."

He turned around, and I saw his eyes were glowing blue. They landed on me for a split second before he turned to Abe and Logan. "Let's go. We're done here."

We left the musical Daugherty League in haste after that, deafening silence in our wake.

CHAPTER 20

The bus was silent when we resumed our road trip, heading to Albuquerque, New Mexico. My classmates were sleeping, along with Abe—Logan was driving now—and Ragnor was in the back seat of the bus, emitting such a dark air that everyone gave him a wide berth.

For the past hour since we got back on the road, I debated whether I should approach him. On one hand, it seemed like I was asking for trouble; he was obviously in a foul mood, and everything about him screamed "Back off." On the other hand, some part of me wanted to take the seat next to him and give him comfort like he'd given me back when I'd attacked Bryce.

I knew it was absurd. I didn't need to be a genius to see it would be a death sentence, trying to comfort someone like Ragnor Rayne. And yet I recalled his odd behavior back in the greenhouse, where he'd shown me that he wasn't entirely emotionally invincible, whether he intended to or not.

Why do you even care whether he needs comfort? The voice of reason intruded in my mind. *It's not like you're lovers—hell, you're not even friends.*

And yet logic had nothing to do with how I felt.

So I found myself sliding out of my seat and walking down the aisle to where he was sitting near the window of the back seat. Then hesitantly, and trying not to think about it too much, I sat down right next to him.

His body tensing was the only indication I got that he knew I was there. His gaze remained on the window, his arms still folded.

I refused to be cowed, though. Looking down at my hands, I softly said, "I've been trying to figure out the Leagues we visited, seeing if they're better or worse than yours. Just to explore my options, you know. I even made a list of parameters that I think are important in any League."

When he remained silent, I started to feel embarrassed about what I was doing. *Why do I even bother?*

But then to my surprise, Ragnor spoke. "What's the list?" he asked, voice flat.

Fidgeting with the hem of my shirt, my heart drumming in my ears, I cleared my throat and said, "Power, wealth, and freedom." I paused, but when he didn't say anything else, I continued. "In terms of power, it's been a no-brainer for me to figure out who has the most out of all the Lords we've met so far."

From the corner of my eye, I could see Ragnor shifting, turning to me. "What about the other two?" he asked in a rough murmur.

Goose bumps trailed over my arms at the sound of his unfairly sexy voice. "When it comes to wealth, you all seem on par with each other, though I could be wrong," I said, feeling his gaze probing the side of my face. "But then there's the element of freedom."

All of a sudden, he grabbed my hand and held it on his thigh. I almost jumped out of my seat, my heart skipping a beat. "I guess I didn't rate high on that part," he said somewhat sarcastically.

I grimaced. He wasn't entirely wrong, and yet . . . "If I look at it subjectively, you're right, of course," I said quietly. "But objectively, everything points to the opposite."

From my time with Jada, CJ, and Bowen, I knew that Ragnor had given them more than enough freedom to do what they wanted. The other vampires in the Rayne League always seemed to be relaxed and content, much more than the vampires in either of the Leagues we'd visited so far—except maybe Atalon, but even that was questionable since we hadn't seen many of his League members.

The whole supposed freedom of the Daugherty League seemed forced, if not fake, like Daugherty was trying to be that cool, progressive parent, while actually being a bigoted, old-fashioned one. O'Brien League wasn't about freedom but some sort of anarchy, if anything—what with Charley O'Brien himself being the weakest Lord I'd seen so far and certainly not fit for leadership.

"Henderson." Ragnor's voice brought me back, and I chanced a look at him. His eyes locked on mine, seemingly searching for something, while his face wore an inscrutable expression. "What are you trying to get at?"

My cheeks tingled with a blush, and when I tried to scoot away, he pulled me by the hand until our thighs touched and his face was in mine. Swallowing hard and ignoring the erratic beats of my heart, I averted my gaze, took a deep breath, and said, "All I'm saying is that you don't need to be hard on yourself for losing control back there."

He froze. Closing my eyes and hoping I didn't fuck up, I blurted, "You did it for your League members. That's a noble cause."

His breath was in my ear just then, and I jolted at his sudden proximity. "Are you trying to comfort me, Henderson?" he murmured, lips brushing against my lobe as his soft hair tickled the side of my face.

Shuddering involuntarily, I tugged at my hand, trying to make him let go. He only tightened his hold. Heart in my throat, I mumbled, "I'm not."

"Liar," he whispered, and then he let go of my hand, then cupped my face. My eyes snapped open, and I stared at him, stupefied. The air between us was charged, especially when he brought his lips an inch away from mine. "You were worried about me."

I jerked my head in a shake. "I don't like you."

His lips twitched, making my heart attempt to bolt out of my chest. His midnight blue gaze ensnared mine in an unbreakable hold. "You sure about that?"

"My Lord."

Ragnor and I broke apart. He let me go, I scooted away, and we whipped our heads toward the source of the voice.

Logan stood in the aisle, staring at us with a tight face and almost glowing eyes. I thought he'd been driving, but he must've traded the task with Abe for him to be here, almost catching Ragnor and me red handed.

Face hot, I attempted a bored look before saying, "I'll take my leave now." I paused, glancing at Ragnor, whose eyes were on Logan now, back to their hard edge. I then turned to Logan, whose gaze went from me to Ragnor, before his eyes narrowed.

The Lord and my ex seemed to be engaged in a staring battle. It almost looked like they were having a telepathic conversation of sorts. Since I didn't want anything to do with whatever the hell was happening, I slid past Logan and hurried back to my seat.

Ragnor and Logan remained in the back seat for the rest of the drive.

When we arrived at the Bowman League compound, it didn't take long for me and the others to realize this League would fit very, *very* few.

Isaac Bowman had been a banker in his human life, and his League was basically a giant bank made solely for vampires, with branches in every League (I hadn't known that). It also had its own accounting and law firms for both vampire and human services. The League was made of depressing offices and cubicles, and every vampire we passed seemed to be just as dreary as their Lord.

It didn't help that Bowman's voice was so monotonous that it could've put an insomniac to sleep.

"I believe in the prosperity of the vampire race," Bowman said after we sat in the gray cafeteria, which also served gray, odorless, shapeless food. "Thus, I make sure each League's finances and cash flow run smoothly. In addition, we pay high dividends from any profit we make thanks to humans, and our stock system is also in accordance with the humans' economic state . . ."

Nobody listened to Bowman's endless boring chatter except for Jakob, the smartest in our class and the only one who seemed to understand what Bowman was rumbling on and on about. Even Bowman's Lieutenant didn't seem interested in his long lecture and, instead, chatted Abe up, from having nothing better to do.

"Is this even edible?" Cynthia murmured quietly as she poked her fork into a gray, jellylike piece of meat.

Zoey eyed the meat suspiciously. "I'm usually not a picky eater, but even for me this is too much."

Tansy, sitting next to me, slurped her gray soup as if she didn't have a care in the world.

Unlike Zoey, I did try a bite of gray meat. I regretted it immediately after and decided that even if Bowman's League were perfect (which it clearly wasn't), I would've prayed to God not to be bought into it, simply based on their food quality.

I glanced at Ragnor to see if he was eating, but he seemed to be talking quietly with Logan. Neither of them touched the unappetizing gray chicken breast on their plates.

Other than the horrible food and Bowman's boring rumblings, the visit ended without any sort of incident. Ragnor shook Bowman's hand, and the two seemed respectful of one another. I guessed Ragnor would tolerate any sort of dreary hosting by Bowman, considering Bowman led the bank operating the Vampire Society, including the Rayne League.

Much like the visit to the Bowman League, the drive to our next stop passed uneventfully. I mostly dozed, listened to music, and sometimes even pulled out my sketchbook and sketched some stuff, wishing I had colorful crayons instead of just a pencil—I could no longer see gray after the gray onslaught in the Bowman compound. Still, even though I tried my best with the sketches, they looked like bad re-creations of the masterpieces Lord Atalon had painted.

When we arrived in Las Vegas, however, our second to last destination, the strange sense of boredom and peace that had befallen me and the rest came to a screeching halt.

I'd heard of the Renaldi League a few times since becoming a vampire. None of the things I'd heard were good.

The entrance to the League was through a large casino on the Vegas Strip. At first, I didn't think much of the location—neither for the League nor for its entrance—but the moment the elevator stopped and all of us exited into the entrance hall of the underground compound, everything started to make sense.

Unlike the rest of the Leagues' compounds, which were designed more or less the same, the Renaldi League's was entirely different. For one, it looked like a combination of a casino, a love motel, and a brothel. The lights were red, the marble floor black, and the walls red and gold with lacelike patterns. Plush sofas in the same color palette were scattered around the room.

A man waited for us in the entrance hall, and when he bowed to Ragnor and said, "Hello, Lord Rayne," I knew he couldn't be Lord Renaldi.

Ragnor nodded. "Hello, Stefan. Where is Manuel?"

Stefan must've heard the disapproval in Ragnor's tone because he flinched. "I'll take you to him. Follow me, please."

Ragnor's face contorted. He was pissed off. I could deduce why; in every other League, the Lord had greeted us. Here, Renaldi seemed disinclined to show Ragnor the same respect, and it evidently didn't bode well.

All of us followed Stefan down the dimly lit corridor. Music drifted in from somewhere, the bass beats making the walls visibly vibrate, they were so loud.

Logan, walking at the front with Ragnor, whispered to him quietly. Ragnor barked something in return, making Logan grimace and stop talking. Abe, walking at the back, seemed alert, his eyes darting from wall to wall as if waiting for something or someone to jump out at us. The rest of us remained silent.

Since Ragnor, Logan, and Abe were on edge, we all were on edge. Zoey was clasping Jakob's hand, her face white as a sheet. Tansy's arms were wrapped around her. Cynthia clung to Bryce's side, who didn't seem happy with it but didn't shake her off, either, as if he needed someone to lean on too.

The corridor ended at a single black door. Stefan turned the lock and pushed it open; music blared from inside. "Welcome to the Renaldi League," the vampire said, smiling humorlessly.

When I stepped into the room, my heartbeat quickened at what I saw, heard, and smelled.

The room was full of veils and curtains, sofas and love seats, pillows, and various discarded garments. A huge chandelier hung from the ceiling, lit up by actual candles. There were candles scattered around the room as well.

A man was seated at the back of the room on what appeared to be a throne or a throne-shaped love seat. He looked as if he might have been a pro wrestler in his human life; his bare torso showed large, tight pecs covered by a huge tattoo of a Chinese dragon. He was tall, with arms and legs as thick as tree trunks and full of taut, toned muscles. His thick neck, square jaw, and face full of bristles and scars were just as overtly masculine as the rest of his body. The dangling earring of bones on his left ear didn't manage to soften any of it; in fact, it only added to his threatening looks.

Then there were the women. An actual harem. Some of them were half-dressed while others were entirely naked. They surrounded the man's seat, each of them doing different things. One was brushing the man's long, smooth black hair, her large breasts jumping with every movement. Two were washing his feet. Another leaned over the throne's armrest, her left nipple being sucked by the man as he kneaded the other. And one woman knelt between his legs, sucking his dick.

The reactions in our group were varied. Some, like Zoey and Cynthia, looked away, appalled. Others, like Jakob and Bryce, stared at the show, fascinated, and possibly even a little horny. Then there was Tansy, who seemed to stare ahead with a face gone blank and eyes unseeing. Logan tried to look anywhere else, disgust and anger on his face; Abe simply turned his back on the show, and Ragnor, face a mask, was unreadable.

The hedonistic display was too much, that was for sure, but my eyes were on Ragnor. I wanted to see what was going to happen. I couldn't care less if the man seated on the throne, who must be Lord Renaldi, was getting sucked off right in our faces.

When Ragnor stepped forward, heading toward Renaldi, the latter took his mouth off the woman's breast and turned with a wide, wild, predatory grin to Ragnor. "Rayne! My friend!" he greeted, throwing his arms to the sides before returning to fist the brown hair of the woman blowing him, pulling her so hard she made choking sounds. That seemed to delight Renaldi, and he kept on making her choke on his dick until he suddenly thrust, his face tightening, as he reached climax, emptying himself inside the woman's throat.

Then, using his hold on her hair, he threw her—actually *threw* her—to the side, making her cry out as she fell down. None of the other women seemed to care.

Ragnor came to a stop a few feet away. "Get down," he said, and even though his face was a mask, his voice betrayed what he truly felt: not just disgust but absolute fury.

Renaldi grinned as he rose from his throne, his limp cock resting against his thigh. He grabbed a pair of white pants from somewhere and put them on as he walked toward Ragnor. "Ah, still a square, I see," Renaldi murmured loud enough for us to hear as he stopped before Ragnor. Despite his tanklike figure and height, Ragnor was just an inch taller.

"It's been ten years already since you became a Lord," Ragnor said, looking down at Renaldi as though he was a problem child and not a huge man who seemed to have been in his late twenties at the moment of Imprinting, much like Ragnor. "It's time you start taking your League seriously."

"Hmmm," Renaldi murmured and turned to face the rest of us. "Well. Since the square here wants me to take this *seriously*," he drawled, "then heya there. I'm Lord Manuel Renaldi, but you can call me Renaldi." He glanced at Zoey, smirking when she blanched, before resting his gaze on me.

I tensed but returned his gaze. *Look away,* I pleaded silently. *Just look away . . .*

Renaldi's eyes flared, burning a sudden shade of gold. "What do we have here," he said, not taking his gaze off me as he walked forward. It was as if he was looking into me, capturing glimpses of something I hadn't even admitted to myself.

Ragnor's hand shot to Renaldi's shoulder and squeezed. "Take your depraved eyes off my fledglings," he growled lowly, his eyes cobalt blue with anger.

"Or maybe this one in particular, Rayne?" Renaldi's face split into a predatory grin while he kept his eyes on me, seemingly trying to uncover what I was desperately trying to conceal. Locked in place by his unrelenting stare and its surprising power over me, I found it hard to breathe. Ragnor stepped between us, body heat radiating from him.

Renaldi seemed pissed off at being cockblocked and returned Ragnor's gaze.

A silent war ensued between the two Lords. The tension in the air rose and rose until it was suddenly too hard to breathe. Some of my classmates stepped back from the two Lords, eyes wide with fear. Logan and Abe opened the door behind us, ready to usher us out if need be, their eyes glowing worryingly on high alert. The harem of women scooted away, and when they did, I suddenly realized all of them had something in common.

All were brunettes.

I heard he had a thing for brunettes, Zoey had told me the first time we met. It seemed like she'd heard right.

"Everyone, out."

Ragnor's voice was barely recognizable. At once, the women fled the room, and Logan and Abe ushered us all toward the exit. Though there was nothing I wanted more than to leave this stifling chamber, I lingered behind, staring at the Lords, who were standing as still as sculptures, their gazes still locked and aglow.

Then in a split-second decision borne of adamant curiosity to see where this whole thing was going, I jumped behind one of the love seats, wrapped myself in one of the blankets lying around, and stayed still.

When the ruckus of people leaving was over and the door was slammed shut, silence followed. Then I peeked from behind the love seat.

Ragnor pushed Renaldi back. The other Lord half stumbled and snickered, staring at Ragnor with a sinister glint in his eyes. "I didn't take you for a noob banger," he said lewdly, licking his lips.

I'd never seen Ragnor so pissed off. He flattened Renaldi on the floor in less than a second, his fangs unsheathed. "I told you what would happen if you used your magic on me again." Unlike his face, Ragnor's voice was completely civil, as though they were discussing the weather.

Renaldi laughed. "You can't kill me yet, Rayne. I still got your Imprint."

What?

"It seems you forgot," Ragnor murmured silkily. "Then allow me to remind you."

For a few moments, neither of them moved. Then out of nowhere, Renaldi screamed, thrashing under Ragnor's weight.

I couldn't understand what I was seeing. Ragnor hadn't moved, hadn't done anything, and yet Renaldi acted as if he was suffering through the greatest pain in the world. Ragnor seemed to be projecting out a force field of some kind, but it was invisible. He had to be because even though he hadn't moved an inch, his eyes were locked on Renaldi as Renaldi grabbed the sides of his head and pulled at his hair like he was going mad.

His screams grew louder, more horrifying, the more moments passed.

Then I felt it, as if I was sucked into Ragnor's terrifying force field. The pain. Horror. Fear.

It felt like I'd lost the one thing I was afraid to lose. It felt like I was dying. Like the air was sucked out of my lungs. It felt like I was back in that basement, watching the same cycle of horrors all over again. Like I had never left, never fled the nightmare that was my father.

It was as if someone was tearing me to pieces from the inside out, but not physically. It was my soul that was being torn. My very heart was being tormented.

It was worse than any physical pain I could've had. It was pain in its purest, most awful form.

I wanted to scream like Renaldi. I wanted to shout, to get this out somehow before I went insane. But I bit my lip until I tasted blood. I held on to the silk blanket on the floor beneath me, willing myself to be quiet, to ride this terror to its end, even though it felt like it would never end.

The torture went on forever, to the point where my limbs went numb and my breath got stuck in my throat. Tears filled my eyes as the excruciating pain streamed down my veins, making me wish I had died. Anything, even death, would be better than this.

Renaldi's screams faded. Nothing but pain filled my senses. It pulled me into a void of darkness, consternation, and fright so deep I could never claw my way out—

And just as suddenly as it began, it was gone.

The pain was gone, making me choke on breaths I hadn't let out. My numb limbs started waking up. I couldn't move, though, and the tears fell, pooling near my temples.

Faintly, I could hear Ragnor speak. "Never use your magic on me, or mine, again. Am I clear?"

Wait, what did he mean by *mine*? Had Renaldi been using magic on me too? A mumble followed a crashing sound.

"I said, *am I clear*?"

A cough, and then in a weak, defeated voice, Renaldi whispered, "Yes, my Lord."

CHAPTER 21

"I don't feel safe," Zoey whispered into the darkness from her bed in the shared guest room. "This place reeks of booze and sex, and I'm scared Renaldi will just pop up at the door."

All the girls, including me, hummed in agreement. None of us felt safe, especially after the day we'd just had. And the worst thing was, we were having to stay here for two more days.

After the showdown between Ragnor and Renaldi, everyone returned to that harem room, and I acted as if I'd just come back with everyone else. Ragnor then reintroduced Renaldi, who was far more cowed and haggard after Ragnor's treatment, and Stefan, Renaldi's Lieutenant, took us on the tour.

The Renaldi League dabbled in gambling and liquor making. It had its very own distillery and a chain of casinos spread across Las Vegas and beyond. The League swam in money just as much as Bowman's, and it showed; everything colored gold was actually pure gold. Every crystal was actually a real diamond.

None of us girls wanted to be here anymore, especially since it seemed that the women of Renaldi's League had only one role here while the men took over key roles of making sure the League ran smoothly. With all the women being brunettes, Zoey and I, and a couple others, felt like we were personally being targeted.

The contrast between Atalon's classy League and this slimy, sleazy one was staggering. It had me wishing we were back at the Rayne League already.

Unfortunately, when it was time to leave after the tour, Abe informed us that our rented bus refused to start, and that the mechanic said it would take two days to fix.

Meaning we were staying at the Renaldi League until our bus was up and running again.

Which didn't bode well for any of the girls present.

"Our Lord didn't seem to approve of Renaldi's . . . welcome show," Cynthia wondered out loud now from her bed next to mine. "Perhaps we can ask our Lord to get a room at some hotel."

"I doubt that," said Jane, another classmate. She sounded quite convinced too.

I didn't disagree with her, but I was curious. "Did you hear anything, Jane?" I asked quietly.

Jane sighed. "I've been sitting with Carlos at the front of the bus. I overheard some stuff."

At once, all of us turned to her. I flipped to my stomach and put my chin on my hands, staring at her with avid attention. She sat cross-legged on her bed right in front of mine, her dark hair falling in tight curls onto the mattress. She seemed to preen under the sudden attention.

"So Abe has been talking to Logan a lot this past week," she told us eagerly. "They usually chatted when our Lord was on phone calls and took to the back seat for privacy."

She straightened, jutting her chin as she projected an air of importance. "Apparently, our Lord's presence on this trip was quite a shock."

If I hadn't been paying attention before now, that would've slapped me into focus.

"It seems that our Lord joined at a last-minute notice, and his reasoning was that there are more dangers than usual out here, so much so that he needed to keep an eye on us for safety measures," she said, her voice dropping and turning mysterious.

The other girls gasped. Even Tansy to my right didn't seem to be in her usual head-in-the-clouds state as she stared at Jane with open worry.

"That's scary," murmured Aisha, another classmate.

Jane nodded gravely. "I know."

"So that's why you think he won't let us stay at a hotel," Zoey summarized.

"Exactly," Jane replied. "If our Lord believes we are in constant danger, he wouldn't want any of us to be anywhere he can't see us."

A strange feeling crawled into my gut. Could it be that Ragnor had come because of me?

Or maybe I was giving myself far too much credit. His world didn't revolve around me. He was a Lord of a vampire League. He had subjects to take care of, newcomers to protect until he could sell them off to the highest bidder, and a reputation to maintain. He wouldn't take a leave of absence for two weeks to join a road trip with his *noobs* just because I was there. That was a stupid, self-involved notion.

Maybe there really were dangers out there for us. I wouldn't know; when it came to Ragnor's enemies, or the Vampire Society's enemies as a whole, I was clueless.

That was an unnerving thought.

"If we're already talking about our Lord," Cynthia piped up, "then what do you think about him and Renaldi?"

Jane snickered. "You mean the fact that he practically holds Renaldi by a leash?"

"Yeah, that's been fun to watch." Zoey smirked. "Especially since Renaldi keeps giving him the evil eye."

I opened my mouth, but then closed it, choosing not to say anything. No need to tell them Renaldi most likely had initially been given the Imprint by Ragnor. Or that Renaldi had apparently used his magic, whatever it was, on Ragnor, and Ragnor had retaliated in a way I was still grappling to understand. They shouldn't know I'd stayed behind to witness it all either.

Then Cynthia said, "If I didn't think so before, then now I'm sure that our Lord isn't just hot but sexy as fuck."

I tensed.

"He is, isn't he?" Zoey sighed dreamily. "The things I would let him do to me . . . yum." She licked her lips.

"Don't you think he's too aloof, though?" Jane murmured. "Like, I can't see myself ever being with someone like him. He's too . . ."

"Intense," Aisha finished, nodding wisely. "Cold. Calculated."

"Yeah, but that's part of his appeal," Zoey argued, her eyes dazed. "I mean, him being a Lord, our Imprinter, and so self-assured and intimidating . . ." She shuddered.

"It's a turn-on, for sure," Jane agreed breathily.

Irrational anger burned inside me. *You don't know what he's truly like,* I couldn't help but think. *I might not know him well, but I sure as hell know more about him than you do, and you should keep your dirty little drool away from him.*

My mind screeched to a halt. *He's not mine,* I reminded myself, my heart pumping loudly in my ears. *I don't even* want *him to be mine.*

But the hesitance, the doubt in what should've been a full conviction, made fear bloom in the pit of my stomach. Because that couldn't be. I couldn't actually . . . *like* Ragnor, could I?

You sure about that? he'd taunted me a few days ago, and I couldn't help but question it again myself. Because if I liked him . . . then I was more stupid than I thought.

"I think"—Tansy's airy voice burned through my frightening thoughts—"that our Lord is reckless."

Everyone was so surprised at the clarity in her words, we turned to her with rapt attention. "Why do you think so?" Zoey asked, looking at Tansy as if she hadn't seen her before.

Tansy's huge blue eyes landed on me, more piercing than I expected. "How could someone as calculating as our Lord make such a big mistake?" she asked, her voice still dreamy but her gaze far more serious than I'd ever seen it.

I looked away, and Zoey and Cynthia exchanged confused glances while Jane asked, "What mistake are you talking about?"

I felt her gaze burning my cheek, so much so that I returned my eyes to her unblinking ones. "He didn't do his job," Tansy murmured, her eyes searching mine. "He didn't research enough." She leaned forward toward me as her eyes widened. "He should've known about the Morrow Gods."

The other girls burst out laughing. "And here we thought you were being serious for once." Cynthia snickered.

"As if!" Jane chortled.

They kept on laughing and talking, and Tansy's huge eyes turned away from me, regaining their glazy look, as if nothing out of the ordinary had just happened.

And yet I felt as if my entire existence tilted on its axis.

Tansy knew.

She had to know, if not all, then something at the very least, about my past for her to mention what she just did.

No one knew about the Morrow Gods.

No one but my father and me.

When I was little, back in the basement, we made sacrifices to them. We had to. *I* had to. I hadn't heard anyone except my father mention them. No one knew about them. But Tansy knew. And she knew that I knew. But how?

She'd looked me straight in the eyes as if trying to send me a silent message when she spoke those two words that made my entire world crumble at the edges.

I couldn't be here with these girls talking as if nothing had happened and Tansy acting as if she hadn't just dropped an atomic bomb. It was suddenly too hot, too crowded in this room. I needed out.

I stumbled out of the bed, murmured something about forgetting something in the cafeteria, and left the room for the dimly lit corridor.

I tried to walk, but my knees wobbled, and I had to lean against the wall for balance. Perspiration covered my skin, dripping down my face and wetting my clothes.

How can she know?

I sucked in a breath and could barely let it out. I needed air. Open air. I had to get out somehow.

What the hell did she know?

But my knees gave in, and I fell to the ground, my heart fluttering rapidly in my chest. Vaguely, I knew what I was going through, being unable to breathe, unable to move, feeling this awful suffocation as if I would never know how to work my lungs again, as all I could see were black dots spreading across my vision.

And through it all, a distant song played in my head; then the world went dark.

Deep in the forest, no bird is safe,

For crumbles of berries, the Gods shall grow;

Found in the heart of nature's womb,

The Morrow Gods shall come . . .

I woke up on the floor of the entrance hall, feeling groggy and exhausted. Slowly, I sat up and leaned against the wall, too weak to stand.

For a few moments, all I could hear were my shallow breaths. Someone was heading my way. The distant thudding of footsteps got closer by the second. If I didn't move, whomever it was would see me in my most vulnerable state.

Panicking, I crawled forward against the wall until I reached a side corridor. I moved around the corner and sat against the wall, trying to catch my breath. The footsteps echoed closer until I could tell they were in the entrance hall.

Then the footsteps stopped. I craned my neck, trying to listen as my heart fluttered hysterically in my chest; then a familiar voice said, "Good evening, Lord Renaldi."

It was Logan, and apparently he wasn't alone. Whose footsteps did I hear?

"What's a cutie like you doing roaming around my League?" Renaldi responded, his voice light yet mocking.

I could only imagine what face Logan was making, being called a *cutie*. "I'm patrolling to make sure none of our vampires are out of line," my ex responded with barely concealed apprehension.

"How diligent," Renaldi murmured, and I heard him shifting. Despite being in some sort of a daze, I was curious; I wished I could see what was happening instead of staring at the other wall of the dark corridor.

"If that's all, I'll leave now," Logan said, an edge to his voice that wasn't there before.

Renaldi chuckled. "But what's the fun in that?" he said. "Don't be such a stick-in-the-mud."

"With all due respect, Lord Renaldi, I'm busy," Logan answered through gritted teeth. "Now, if you'll excuse me—"

A crashing sound made the wall I leaned against vibrate. "Your eyes are really something," Renaldi murmured. They were closer to where I was now, and I wondered what the hell that crash was about. "Rayne doesn't see your true potential. Such a waste . . ."

"Let me go," Logan growled, "before I do something I shouldn't."

I was no longer groggy. I was far too invested in what was happening out there, so much so that I wanted to risk it all and take a peek, see for myself what was going on.

Another noise reverberated through the hall, followed by a third, familiar voice of someone I hadn't heard coming. "That's enough."

I froze. Ragnor.

Renaldi sighed before saying, "You're in luck, cutie. I'll let you go. But next time"—he paused—"we'll finish what we started."

Footsteps—Renaldi's, most likely—thudded away, and as they did, Ragnor said, "Go to sleep, Kazar."

Logan made a growling sound. "Next time, please don't interfere, my Lord," he ground out. "I was handling it fine by myself. Also, don't coddle me. I can keep on patrolling."

"It wasn't a request," Ragnor retorted coolly. "It was an order. I need you in top form tomorrow. I'll take over patrolling."

This didn't sit well with Logan, who snarled, "But—"

"Go, Kazar," Ragnor cut him off flatly. "Don't make me repeat myself."

There was a moment of silence before Logan let out a breath and murmured, "Yes, my Lord."

I didn't dare move as Logan's footsteps disappeared into the distance. Silently, I begged, *Go to sleep, too, Ragnor . . .*

After everything that had happened today, I was so fucking tired; I just wanted to get back to my room and sleep. Now that my panic attack was behind me and I could finally think clearly, all I wanted was to have a few hours of peaceful bliss before I had to face what happened and what Tansy had said.

"I know you're here, Henderson."

Fuck.

Pursing my lips, I held on to the wall and used it to rise to my feet. I still felt unbalanced and out of it, but I managed to remain standing. Still leaning on the wall, I exited the corridor and turned to see Ragnor facing my way, arms folded, wearing tactical pants, combat boots, and a black tee that showed his strong corded arms. His hair was messy around his face, and his midnight blue eyes were darker than usual in the dim light of the hall.

He looked so goddamn tasty that I couldn't help but feel somewhat self-conscious in my tights, tank top, and socks, with my uncombed hair down on my back.

In less than a moment, he was before me, my face in his hands, eyes searching mine. "What's wrong?"

So many things, I thought bleakly. "I'm fine," I said, but it came out slurred. I wasn't fine. I was still trying to recover.

"You're not fine," he growled, thumbs caressing my cheeks as he plastered me against the wall. "What happened to you?"

I wanted to say *nothing,* but his eyes were full of something I hadn't seen in them before. *Is that . . . concern?* I opened and closed my mouth like a fish, speechless.

His eyes flickered down to my lips before rising to my eyes again. "If you don't tell me what's wrong," he murmured quietly, "I won't be able to control my actions."

Frowning, I tried to read him, but he was wearing a look I couldn't quite decipher. My stomach was tied in knots over that look, though. And my thighs clenched when his eyes fell again to my lips, as if he couldn't help himself.

I forgot my exhaustion, forgot everything that had happened. My inhibitions went crashing down as all rationality left my head. For the first time in a long fucking while, I didn't want to think. I didn't want to question anything. I just wanted to do what I felt like doing, and to hell with the consequences.

I sucked in a deep breath, my hands found their place on his shoulders, and I said, "I'm not telling you anything."

His eyes went neon. He heard the challenge in my voice. Heard the invitation. The gauntlet was thrown down. All he needed to do was pick it up.

But then, as though he realized what was happening, he blinked, and the glow was gone. Slowly, he slid his hands down my face and stepped back, staring at me with his expression under lockdown. "You should go to bed, Henderson," he said quietly.

Disappointment washed over me until I felt my exhaustion being switched to utter frustration instead. "You're a coward, Ragnor Rayne," I told him, hands clenched into fists.

His face remained flat, but his eyes flared. "Be careful what you say to your Lord, Henderson."

There was something in the undertone of his voice, almost like I had hit a nerve. As if *he* was the one wary of *me*.

As if I mattered to him far more than he let on.

I would've laughed if I didn't feel so hurt. I let the wall go. "I hope you regret this moment for eternity because you'll never get another chance."

Then, before he could say anything else, I flipped him off and made my way back to the guest room, trying not to cry from the sheer pain of being so blatantly rejected.

CHAPTER 22

The next day, Renaldi threw a grand feast in order to mend the cracked bridges between him and Ragnor. That was my interpretation. The official reason was to "strengthen the unbreakable bond between the Renaldi and Rayne Leagues."

The feast would take place in the Renaldi casino and bar at midnight, so until then, we had time to prepare. Apparently, the feast was planned to last until the small hours of the morning, before it would be time for us to go back to sleep.

While none of the girls was happy about our stay at Renaldi's, the upcoming feast proved to be a welcomed distraction. Our guest room turned into a prep room, with Aisha, who'd been a makeup artist in her human life, doing all of our faces; Jane and Zoey, who were quite the fashionistas, recommending what we should wear; and Tansy, who was an expert when it came to hairstyling—with her knee-length hair, that was practically a given—doing our hair.

I was surprised to be involved in the preparations. Before this trip, I'd been a social pariah thanks to my station as a kitchen worker. But this trip—perhaps because of our unexpected prolonged stay at the Renaldi League, our least favorite one—made everyone put social ranks aside. It was as though we were all in the same boat, and the unexpected comradery was a welcome distraction.

Zoey, who'd brought many dresses on the trip, offered me one. "This will look great on you," she said excitedly, showing me a pastel-green summer dress.

I gave her a strained smile. "Pastel colors are not exactly my favorite . . ."

"No worries," Zoey said, rummaging through her backpack. "I have another dress here that you might like. Blue's good?"

I was about to say yes when I remembered the neon-blue eyes of the man, the Lord, who rejected me. "Do you have something black?" I asked hastily, pushing that thought away.

Zoey hummed and then pulled out a black dress. It was the most basic dress, a medium length with short sleeves and a modest neckline. "It's not really special," Zoey murmured, seemingly put out.

"I'll take it," I said, then grabbed the dress and put it on. It was a tad tighter than I would've liked—Zoey was thinner—but it fit.

Aisha fixed my makeup according to my request—nothing too hard or too soft, just as standard and natural as possible. Then Tansy motioned for me to take the seat before her so she could do my hair.

After yesterday, I expected Tansy to behave differently. Yet she seemed back to her usual self and treated me no differently than before. Maybe she didn't necessarily know anything about my past after all.

Tansy's touch was gentle, soothing, as she brushed my hair. "It's pretty, you know," she told me softly.

"Thanks," I said, lips quirking.

She didn't say anything until she finished brushing and began braiding my hair. When she spoke, though, she said one single word. "Gold."

I frowned. "Gold?"

She let out a breath. "Your hair. It should be gold."

I froze in fear. That was the second time in less than twenty-four hours Tansy had said something that could be directly related to my past.

After everything that went on with Ragnor last night, I hadn't even dwelled much on what had triggered the whole panic attack.

Tansy had said something that, on the surface, seemed like a typically nonsensical Tansy thing to say. But talking about the Morrow Gods and my hair being gold . . . it was too close to home. As if she knew what I knew.

And that didn't make sense because she couldn't possibly know about that. No one knew but my father and me.

But my father was also very much a liar. Perhaps Tansy knew of them because of her family too?

That thought was disturbing. I hoped Tansy's family wasn't like mine.

Could such coincidences exist, anyway?

Whatever it was, it put me on edge.

I didn't respond to her comment, and she didn't speak again.

The girls weren't the only ones who made an effort; the boys did too. Bryce and Jakob were actually wearing suits with bow ties, and the rest, while not wearing ties, cleaned up well.

Abe and Logan were dressed similarly in buttoned shirts tucked into black trousers. Logan especially looked good, with his hair brushed to one side, his bristles recently shaved, and the sleeves of his dark-blue shirt rolled up to his elbows.

All of us were waiting for Ragnor and Renaldi in the casino-bar lobby. It was located in a different wing of the underground Renaldi compound and was usually open to human and vampire customers alike, but tonight Renaldi had closed it for the event.

Ragnor appeared from the hallway, along with Renaldi and two others. The difference between the two Lords was staggering; Renaldi was dressed in a dark-red two-piece suit with enough buttons open on his shirt to show half of his chest, and his shoes were a white Mussolini-pointed type. He looked so extra that it was almost funny.

Then there was Ragnor. Dressed casually in his regular faded jeans, combat boots, and simple black tee, he was ten times sexier than Renaldi could ever hope to be. His hair fell in soft, dark-brown waves around his face, the tips brushing his broad, strong shoulders.

Ragnor's midnight blues met my gaze, but I averted them at once, looking stubbornly ahead, at Renaldi. I could feel Ragnor watching me still, though, his gaze making me feel tingly down south.

He rejected me, I reminded myself angrily. *He has no right, affecting me like this.*

My hands curled into fists.

"Welcome to my pride and delight, *Casino La Vrais du Nord!*" Renaldi announced, spreading his arms in a manner as pretentious as the name of his casino. "Since we have time till the feast itself, we'll fill our wallets with money and our bellies with booze!"

He seemed to expect clapping, and we gave it to him, though quite reluctantly.

He didn't seem to mind, however. "Now before we enter, let me officially introduce my two Lieutenants, who shall host you tonight," Renaldi exclaimed grandiosely. "Stefan Melendez and Armel Rivette!"

There were more claps. I glanced at Stefan, who smiled in an apologetic way as if to say *I know my Lord's an absolute menace, but please forgive him; he can't help himself.* Then I turned to Armel stoically giving us a nod of acknowledgment.

I looked away and followed everyone as Renaldi let us into the casino. I didn't care much for the gambling part—I was never interested in such things—so I made a beeline to the bar. If I was to survive this event, I couldn't be sober.

Thankfully, the bartender was an expert at his job. He took one look at me, poured me a strong Bloody Mary—with actual blood—and said, "Let's hope you'll only need one."

I chugged that Bloody Mary bloody fast.

I'd never been much of a lightweight, but I hadn't drunk in quite some time, and the Bloody Mary wasn't just strong, it was *strong*.

For the first time since I came to the Rayne League, I felt light and relaxed. I joined a few of my classmates at one of the poker tables and chatted with them about absolutely nothing.

And it was *amazing*.

Then I hogged a slot machine for an hour straight, trying to get a triple seven, and in the process, spent all the tokens Renaldi had given to each of us.

I went back to the bar and demanded another Bloody Mary. The bartender obliged, albeit a tad hesitantly, and handed me the drink. I grabbed it and walked—steadily, I might add—toward an empty space on the floor and started dancing to the techno music playing through the booming speakers.

Closing my eyes and sipping my drink, I moved from side to side, a smile spreading over my face. It was so freeing, being carefree and doing whatever the hell I wanted. At this moment, at the very least, I had control over my lack of control.

Swaying as I did a wannabe pirouette, I would've fallen on my ass had someone not caught me in time, arms around my waist. Blinking, I raised my head to see Renaldi leering down at me, eyes glowing. "Careful, beautiful," he murmured, eyes raking down my body so blatantly, you would think he hadn't just been blown yesterday while surrounded by dozens of pretty brunettes.

But since I couldn't give a fuck about anything, really, I gave him a dazzling smile and pushed him off, dancing as I stepped back. "Thanks, Mister Lord," I said with a grin, "but I can handle myself."

Renaldi smirked and stepped forward. "I think I can help you handle yourself," he said, eyes on my boobs.

I couldn't help it; I laughed. "You're one hell of a slimeball, aren't you?"

His eyes widened at the insult, then narrowed as anger sparked in them, making them glow brighter. "Careful, beautiful," he said again, only this time his tone wasn't flirtatious but warning. "You can be a sexy little minx all you want, but remember who you're talking to."

That made me smirk. "I suggest you go harass another sexy little minx, then." *Logan is right there,* I wanted to add but didn't dare when his eyes flared. Instead, I simply laughed, dancing away from him, downing the rest of my drink on the way.

I returned to the bar, shoved the glass toward the bartender, and gave him a grin. "I need a shot."

The bartender eyed me in concern. "Drink some blood instead," he said quietly, handing me a glass of bright-red blood.

I drank it, flipped him off—my middle finger was working overtime these days—and went away, pouting. I was finally feeling good, and the bartender was ruining my vibe!

"Asshole," I mumbled as I walked toward the washroom. Once there, I headed to the sink, turned the faucet on, and washed my hands. I didn't even know why I was doing that; it wasn't like I got them dirty or anything.

On the other hand, Renaldi was his own brand of dirt I needed to wash off.

Once I was done, I was about to leave when I heard a familiar voice from beyond the door saying, "Describe her to me."

It was Logan.

Delighted, I pushed my ear against the door, curious to hear who he was talking to and what about.

"Brown hair, hazel eyes, quite pretty," another voice said, and it was also vaguely familiar. I frowned. It was on the edge of my mind, who the other man was . . .

"You can't possibly mean Aileen," Logan said in a disbelieving, disgusted voice.

"I told you, Renaldi likes his brunettes," the other voice said, and it took me a moment to recognize it as Stefan's, Renaldi's Lieutenant.

I froze, my heart drumming in my chest.

Logan grunted something that sounded like a curse, before he said, "I need to tell my Lord about it."

"Why?" Stefan sounded startled. "Despite his *many* faults, it's within Renaldi's rights to interview a visiting noob as a prospective addition to his League."

"You don't understand," Logan said, obviously pained at the discussion. "If it's *her*, my Lord has to know before I bring her to you."

"Fuck, fine," Stefan groaned. "Tell your Lord, then."

There was a short silence, before Logan suddenly asked, "Does Renaldi want to add her to his harem?"

"What do you think?" Stefan murmured.

Bile rose in my throat. They were talking about me as if I didn't have thoughts of my own. As if I was Ragnor's whore Renaldi wanted to fucking hire.

"Shit, man," Logan almost growled. "Tell Renaldi to stay clear of her. He might be a piece of shit, but she's far worse."

I flinched. *Ouch.*

Stefan snorted. "I highly doubt someone like her is worse than *Renaldi*, Logan."

"You better believe it, Stefan," Logan responded bitterly. "Aileen fucking Henderson might look like a man's dream, but she's a living fucking nightmare."

I stepped back from the door. I couldn't listen to any more of this. Any buzz I might've had was gone. Any lightness I might've felt turned into unbearable heaviness. Overhearing that conversation had sobered me right up.

I stumbled back, my back hitting the sink I'd just used. I could taste salt, and I realized I was crying. My breaths turned shallow. My knees could barely hold me up. I wanted to scrub myself until I could be clean, untainted by the past and by who I truly was.

I needed out.

Closing my eyes, I put a hand on my chest and forced myself to take a deep breath in and a deep breath out. Emptying my mind from all other thoughts, I focused on breathing, the heaving of my chest.

When I got my breathing under control, I opened my eyes, turned around, and looked in the mirror. Aisha's makeup wasn't entirely ruined. My hair was a tad wilder in its fishtail braid, but other than that it looked fine. My dress had some new wrinkles from Renaldi's previous manhandling, but otherwise, I looked no worse for wear.

I walked to the door and listened. I heard nothing. Opening the door, I exited into the empty space, but instead of returning to the casino, I walked around the outskirts of the room, heading toward the exit as surreptitiously as I could.

Keeping an eye out, I saw my classmates were now playing roulette. Logan, Abe, Armel, and Stefan were having a drink at the bar. Renaldi was busy sipping a glass of wine while leering at my female classmates.

Ragnor was nowhere in sight.

Good.

Hurriedly, I rounded the room and reached the exit. No one was looking. I exited into the lobby and then moved through the corridor, taking off the short heels Jane had lent me.

Then I ran as if my ass was on fire.

Unfortunately, I didn't remember the way back to the League's main area. So when the corridor split into two, I had to go with my gut and chose the one on the left. I followed it until it curved and split into three different corridors.

I couldn't afford to stop. I followed the one in the middle for no reason.

When the corridor suddenly sloped downward, I couldn't stop in time. I fell down with a shriek caught in my throat, then slid down a curve and dropped unexpectedly into water.

Hitting the water with a loud, reverberating *splash*.

Tired but motivated, I swam up and gasped for air. Leaning my hands against the stone wall, I shuddered at how cold it was down here with the icy water swallowing me whole. I looked around.

I was in a small round cave with a stone wall so tall I couldn't see its end. The corridor that spat me out was a drainpipe in the middle of the wall.

Well. My plan had just backfired. Now instead of being stuck in an underground compound, I was stuck in a cave where no one would ever find me.

"Think, Aileen," I said aloud. My voice echoed ominously around the cave. "Try diving."

Right. Perhaps I could swim out from under the cave?

After taking a deep breath, I dived back into the water. I went as far down as possible and swam around the cave, looking for an exit, if there was one.

But it seemed luck hadn't completely evaded me, because I saw an opening in the lowest part of the wall. Hoping it was the right direction, I dived again, entered the underwater tunnel, and swam as fast as I could.

The tunnel, however, refused to end, and I was starting to suffocate. I didn't know if vampires could die from lack of air, but I sure as hell knew it felt like it. The longer I didn't breathe, the slower and more sluggish I became, which I really couldn't afford.

I was so close to freedom. So close to clean air, unstifled by Leagues and Lords and vampires.

What felt like hours later, the tunnel ended in open water. At once, I propelled myself upward, and the moment my head broke the surface, I sucked in a much-needed breath.

I was exhausted, but I needed to get to solid ground. So I swam toward a patch of green nearby and finally found myself out of the water.

I lay on the grassy ground, unable to do anything but breathe.

Unfortunately, the tiny bit of luck I'd had was entirely used up, because just then, something metallic pressed against the back of my head and an unfamiliar voice said, "Don't move, bloodsucker, or I'll rip your head off."

CHAPTER 23

I sat with my back against a tree and a man next to me, holding an actual, honest-to-God scythe an inch from my throat, making sure that no matter where I wanted to move, the sharp blade awaited me.

Blood poured from my temple where the same man had pressed the blade against my skin, my clothes were torn and wet, and my skin was full of scratches from when the other two men dragged me across the park away from the lake and into this secluded spot.

Now the other two men were hovering over a shiny laptop while one typed. "Signal's weak," one of them, who had a mole on his chin, told the other, who had waist-long dark hair. "Might take a while for him to answer."

The long-haired man tsked. "Should've given us his number," he muttered bad-temperedly. "Instead, he's so fucking paranoid, he—"

"Shut up," chin-mole guy cut him off. "You've been talking shit all night, and I can't hear it anymore."

"Fuck you, Yannis," the long-haired man snarled.

The one with the chin mole, Yannis apparently, glowered at him. "You better shut your trap before I break your neck, Felix."

Felix reddened but pursed his lips, remaining silent.

"You're one quiet vamp," the man next to me whispered, making me jolt. "Didn't even struggle when we captured you."

I glanced at him. "I'm tired," I told him, which was the truth. Also, I was trying to figure out a way to get out of this stupid situation I'd gotten myself into.

"Still, you're far too complacent," the man murmured. "I would've thought you bloodsuckers had more fight in you."

At that moment, I was more confused than anything else. First of all, how the hell did these men know of vampires? And second of all—"What makes you think I'm a vampire?"

He chuckled quietly. "Your kind can't fool us. Our noses are far superior to yours. You don't need to show your fangs or glowing eyes for us to get the memo."

That was disturbing, and it begged another question. "Who are you?" I asked as a sudden thought crossed my mind. Were they even human?

If vampires existed, it wouldn't be so far fetched to believe there was more than one supernatural being in existence. Who were our natural enemies? Going by popular fiction, I'd been made to believe it was were-wolves. But these guys didn't look like werewolves, or how I imagined werewolves would look. They looked like people.

Now I was scared.

"That's none of your concern," the scythe holder said. "All I can say is, we've been on the lookout for one of you to finally show up here in Vegas. Tonight is our lucky night . . . but not yours."

That was the understatement of the century.

A rustling sound from somewhere up ahead made Yannis and Felix jump to their feet, on high alert. "Stay here," Yannis ordered, pulling out what seemed to be a small handgun before walking toward the sound.

Felix glanced at the scythe holder. "Keep an eye on it, Wode. I'll be back."

"He told you not to leave, though," Wode said dryly, as if he couldn't care less.

Felix ignored him and entered the woods, his spine straight with determination. Leaving me and Wode alone.

"You know, I don't actually hate your kind," Wode said conversationally. I glanced at him again, trying to see his face from beneath the hood of his cloak but in vain. "Rigid and cold? Sure. But a complete waste of space? Not really."

"Then why?" I asked, my heart booming in my ears. "Why are you doing this . . . whatever this is?"

Wode chuckled. "Faith, my friend. Everything is always about faith."

Gunfire echoed in the forest, so nearby that I stilled. Wode grew quiet too.

Another rustling sound, and then a sight out of nightmares appeared. A tall, muscular man appeared, holding two severed, disfigured heads by the hair, which I could barely tell belonged to Yannis and Felix. His naked chest was dripping with blood, and his jeans and boots were soaked in either blood or mud. His eyes were glowing a pure, electric neon blue, his hair a mess, curtaining his face. His fangs were unsheathed, blood dripping from the edges of his mouth.

Wode proved to be smart. He took the scythe off me and jumped to his feet. His hood fell off in the process, revealing a rugged, handsome face. I was struck by his unforgettable eyes that shone like quicksilver and his tousled hair as black as the night. With a flick of his hand, the blade suddenly shrank until it was as small as a keychain. "She's all yours," Wode told the man.

The man dropped the severed heads onto the ground. He stared at Wode, his face the epitome of vengeance, as though he was ready to tear Wode's head off just as he had done to the other two, despite his offer to surrender me.

Wode seemed to like his head where it was. "I didn't hurt her," he said quietly before he nodded and took off with such speed, he could've been a vampire.

But any thoughts I might've had about Wode disappeared when I returned my gaze to the man. He was looking at me with eyes so bright the pupils were almost completely gone. He stepped toward me, and if I'd had just a little more energy left, I would've up and run just then.

He crouched before me, and his large hand reached forward and cupped my head gently. That's when my stunned mind finally computed who it was.

And the emotion that caught me in the throat was so unexpected, I almost cried again. "Ragnor," I whispered.

Shock and horror made it hard to connect the man I knew and the monster before me. I felt myself shake, staring at him with both terror and relief. Because he was here, saving me, and yet he looked as though he'd been pulled from the deepest depths of hell.

Then something warm engulfed me, and I felt my eyelids flutter shut and my muscles relax as a sudden, unnatural sleep took me under.

I woke up in the softest, coziest, most comfortable bed I'd ever lain in.

Squeezing the duvet, I wanted to remain in this bed forever. I was awake, I acknowledged, but still tired enough that I could go back to sleep for days more. My mind wasn't working properly yet anyway, and it was so warm and comfy here.

A weight fell on the other side of the bed, signaling I wasn't alone in this room, wherever this was, and that shook me right awake.

Slowly, I pushed away the duvet and sat up. The familiarly designed room took the back seat when I saw the half-naked, scarred back of the man who sat on the other edge of the bed. The soapy smell of men's bodywash tickled my nose, and when I saw he was drying his wet strands with a towel, I realized he'd just taken a shower.

Automatically, I looked down at myself. I was still in Zoey's dress, still dirty.

And I was in his bed.

Ragnor's bed.

As my mind slowly woke up, I looked around me and realized why the design of the room seemed so familiar. The room wasn't one I'd ever visited—it was a suite with its own living room—but it had the same marble floors and wooden walls, the same lantern shape and colors, and the same basic layout as my shared suite with Zoey and Tansy.

I was back at the Rayne League.

But *how?* How long had I been out? It couldn't have been *that* long. We were supposed to drive back by bus from Oregon, our final destination and the location of the Kalama League, all the way straight to Maine. Yet even if the bus had already been fixed, it still would've taken five days to get back, including rest stops and all that . . .

"How are you feeling?"

I jumped, snapping my head toward Ragnor. He turned to face me, his face no longer full of blood, his fangs sheathed, and his eyes their usual, pretty midnight blue. But my gaze couldn't stay on his face; my eyes had a life of their own as they roamed down to his chest, where his glistening pectorals made my mouth water.

"Henderson?"

In one swift motion, I got off the bed and was about to head toward the exit of what suspiciously seemed to be Ragnor's private quarters when the man himself grabbed my arm, bringing me to a stop. "We need to talk," he said quietly.

I whirled around to face him, feeling my ire and panic rising. "I need to shower," I said, searching his gaze—to find what, I had no idea. "I need to take this fucking dress off and shower before I—"

Between one breath and the other, I was suddenly in his en suite bathroom, with Ragnor in front of me. "Here," he said, his face unreadable as he looked at me. "You can shower. I'll leave you a towel and a change of clothes."

My mouth opened, gaping. "You want me to take a shower *here?*" I asked, my voice an octave higher.

He let go of me and folded his arms. "As I said, we need to talk," he said quietly. "And after that stunt you pulled, there's no chance I'm letting you out of my sight again."

Affronted, I glared at him. "Are you going to watch me shower too?" I asked bitingly.

To my astonishment, his lips twitched, and he leaned his side against the tiled wall, his eyes gleaming with interest. "Sounds like an excellent idea," he murmured, gaze dropping to my chest and lower, before snapping back up.

Hot and bothered yet so angry, I pointed at the door and snarled, "Get out!"

If I wasn't shocked enough, then I sure as hell was when the normally aloof, cold, and downright prickly Ragnor Rayne gave me a smirk. *A smirk!* The audacity!

My nipples grew tight, and I bristled. His fucking *smirk* shouldn't make my nipples tight. He shouldn't make me tight anywhere. He shouldn't make me anything!

Apparently, he was in a humorous mood, because, smirk still intact, he said "Let me know if you change your mind" before stepping out and closing the door.

Once he was no longer here and silence fell over the room, I let myself feel the full range of my disbelief. Who was this man? He couldn't be the Ragnor I'd come to know in the past almost two months. There was no way.

The nightmare who'd saved me from those kidnappers was closer to who Ragnor was. With that Ragnor, I could somewhat deal. This Ragnor was an unknown who was far more dangerous to me than anyone had ever been.

I stared at myself in the bathroom mirror and tried not to cringe. I'd done my best to get rid of the makeup using the water, but there was still some eyeliner that refused to come off. My hair was no longer wavy but full of kinks since Ragnor, in a typical male fashion, used an all-in-one shampoo and conditioner. Stuff like that did hell to my hair.

He'd somehow gotten my pajamas from the closet in my room, so I was wearing my comfy gray sweatpants and black tee. The only downside? I didn't have a bra to change into. I'd thrown the one I'd worn into the laundry hole, and now I was stuck with my tits free of their chains.

Which wasn't the way I wanted to face Ragnor, but what choice did I have?

I scowled at my rumpled reflection, threw the door open, and walked out. The bedroom was empty, so I headed to the living room. That's when I saw there was an adjacent small kitchen with a minibar and a coffee machine. Ragnor was running said machine right now, and without turning to me, he asked, "Coffee or tea?"

My scowl was replaced with confusion. Was Ragnor, the Lord of this League, offering to fix me a drink? "I can make it myself," I said. The thought of him making me coffee had me feeling like the world was tilting on its axis, and I couldn't deal with it at that moment.

Ragnor glanced behind at me, his brow arched. "I'm already on it. Black's fine?"

"Yeah," I blurted, then paused. "Seriously, I can make—"

"Go sit down," he cut me off conversationally, dismissing my suggestion. Grimacing, I folded my arms and was about to argue, but he must've sensed it because he suddenly sighed and said, "I doubt either of us has the energy to start a fight, Henderson, so just take a fucking seat."

He talked without heat, but with a resolute, definite intonation that made me want to kick something. Still, despite my irrational reaction, he was right. I was dog tired. Did I really have the mental capacity to engage in a verbal war with him?

Spine stiff, I took a seat on the large sofa, hugging my knees to my chest. It was surreal, sitting in this living room, warm and clean, while Ragnor, still half-naked and wearing only a pair of dark-gray jeans that snuggly cupped his stupidly bitable ass, was making me coffee.

It's as if I'd woken up in an alternate universe where Ragnor hadn't stolen my freedom and I hadn't become his troublemaking burden.

Because that's what we were, weren't we? Despite everything that went on between us, despite how I'd tried to get him to make a move not that long ago and was thoroughly rejected, we were hardly anything to one another. Until not too long ago, we couldn't stand each other, after all. He saw me as an insolent menace; I hated him for giving me the Imprint without consent, and we all lived happily ever after.

So why, oh, why was he changing this equilibrium?

There's never been an equilibrium in the first place, the voice of reason whispered in my head, making my teeth grit.

Ragnor turned around holding a kettle full of boiling coffee. He brought it over along with two mugs and sat down right next to me, placing everything on the coffee table. Silently, he poured the coffee into the mugs, took one, and handed it over to me with a steely expression.

With my lips thin, I snatched it from him and sipped it. It took quite the grit for me to grumble out a quiet, "Thank you."

Ragnor's face remained impassive as he sat back sipping his coffee, his toned arm lying across the back of the sofa, right behind me, so strong, muscular, and absolutely sexy.

Stop!

"So," I spoke again when he said nothing, needing to break the silence. "What did you want to talk about?"

His eyes flickered to me. "Finish your coffee first."

It'd become an instinct to do the exact opposite of what he commanded, if only out of sheer spite. I put the mug down on the table, turned to face him fully, and folded my hands. "No."

He looked up to the ceiling, as if he was silently asking God for patience. It was snark inducing.

"Need the help of a higher being to deal with me?"

His eyes returned to my face. "You give yourself a lot of credit," he informed me dryly.

I cocked my head. "Am I wrong, then?"

He let out a breath and put his mug down as well before turning to me, face suddenly serious. "You ran away."

Oh. Right. That happened.

With everything that followed my escape—say, being kidnapped and threatened—I'd forgotten what I even set out to do. I'd been so tired and, yes, still somewhat tipsy that when I saw Ragnor had come to save me, instead of feeling defeated, I felt absolutely relieved.

"I tried," I told him honestly, holding his gaze. "It was the perfect opportunity."

His lips stretched into a sardonic smile. "Not perfect enough."

"So is this why I'm here?" I asked, readying myself. "For you to make sure I won't run away again?"

"Partially," Ragnor said, leaning closer. "It's also because I need to know what happened with those three . . . *men*."

The hesitation in his voice wasn't lost on me. He wanted to say something else. "What were they?" I asked, ignoring his half request, half demand.

"Tell me what happened," he ordered, ignoring my question.

I leaned forward, my face a few inches away from his. "See, Ragnor," I said, ignoring the flare of annoyance in his eyes at my using his name instead of his title, "this is exactly why you piss me off. If you wanted good little soldiers, you should've become a dog trainer rather than a vampire Lord."

He grabbed my jaw, and I was suddenly on my back, with him looming over me, my body trapped between his thighs, both my hands held in one of his. "Did they hurt you?" he asked, his eyes less dark than before. "Did they take your blood?"

I glowered at him. "Let me go, then I'll talk."

He tightened his hold on my jaw. "I asked you a question."

Angry that he thought he could intimidate me into yielding to his demands, I felt like messing with him. "Actually, you asked me two."

He bared his teeth, fangs unsheathed, eyes suddenly neon blue. "Answer me."

This Ragnor I was familiar with. This Ragnor, while frightening, was far less dangerous than the teasing, coffee-making one. "I dare you, *Ragnor*," I said, smirking in pure satisfaction when his face contorted with fury. "Bite me. Suck my blood. Dry hump me against this couch. Then run away like the coward you are and pretend it never happened."

His eyes were blazing. "Last chance, Henderson," he growled, his hold on my jaw bruising me, which sent tingles down my spine. "What did those men do to you?"

I grinned widely now, my loins clenching. Seeing him so pissed off as he held me like this, his entire focus on me, these beautiful eyes trying to strip my soul bare . . . I was so turned on that I could feel the wetness pooling in my panties.

More, my body begged. *I need more.*

"You might be stronger than Atalon and Renaldi," I murmured, squeezing my thighs together when his gaze sharpened. "But you're much more of a coward than they are. At least they were upfront about what they wanted from me. What they wanted to *do* to me."

He stilled, and his eyes were suddenly back to midnight blue, his fangs retracted. The abrupt transformation from a nightmarish, predatory mode to a civil, conversational one was shocking enough to make my heart jolt.

He let go of my jaw and released my hands but didn't get off me entirely. Then in a voice no longer a growl, just matter-of-factly, as though he was talking about the weather, he asked, "Do you want Atalon or Renaldi?"

I searched his face, but he put on a mask. His eyes were a chilly kind of clue, carefully unreadable. *What was happening?* One moment, I managed to make him so brilliantly angry, and now . . . What the hell was going through his head now?

"Are you seriously asking me that?" I responded with a question, staring at him in disbelief.

He leaned his face closer. "Is it a yes or no?"

I swallowed hard, my confidence, my *control* over the situation waning, changing into something unclear. "Of course it's a fucking no," I whispered, eyes wide, studying his face as I wished for him to show me what was going on inside his head, or at least give me an indication to know how to act.

"Then," he said, voice dropping low, "what is it that you want from me?"

My breath caught.

Silence stretched between us as I tried to come up with an answer. My heart was beating so loudly, I was sure he could hear it. My skin grew warm and sweaty with anxiousness. My breathing grew shallow, unsteady.

All the while he remained completely still, staring at me unblinkingly, waiting for a response.

And suddenly, I couldn't find it in me to fight this anymore. Why was I even trying when it was futile anyway?

I raised my hands and cupped his face, giving in to the maddening inferno that had been burning between us since the very beginning, and finally admitted to myself, and to him, what I really wanted.

"You. I want you."

Then I kissed him.

CHAPTER 24

I pressed my lips against Ragnor's with every bit of desperation I had.

His response was immediate. His arms went around me, a hand cupping the back of my head, as he kissed me back, causing my gut to tighten and my blood to boil with sudden exhilaration.

He licked at my lips, making a pool of heat gather in my entrance. I parted my lips, and his tongue sneaked inside, tangling with mine. My nipples tightened as I tried to push myself up to press my front against his, and when he pulled me up and onto his lap, I pasted myself against him, wrapping my arms around his strong, delicious body.

I suckled his lip, and he bit mine in return. He trailed his hands down my back until they slid under my shirt, and then I felt his knuckles grazing the bottom of my breasts. Moaning into his mouth, I let my own hands roam down his gloriously naked chest, feeling his pecs flexing under my touch, growing as taut as my nipples.

He cupped both my breasts at the same time, making me break the kiss with a gasp, my back arching. His lips went to my throat and licked the skin before he bit down with his teeth while flicking his thumbs against my tight buds. I jerked against his touch, breathlessly grabbing his shoulders and digging my nails into his skin when he pinched my nipples, driving me mad with an abundance of lust.

He tore the shirt off my body and closed his mouth around one nipple while he kneaded the other. I tensed, so wet and hot and horny that I wanted him to feel just as crazy, just as wild as I did, if not more so.

I pulled myself on top of the erection tenting his jeans and started humping him like the depraved woman I was. He growled against my nipple, and suddenly his lips were off, and his eyes were searing mine, so bright and blue and full of unbidden heat that I melted right there and then.

We stared at one another as I rocked myself against him, feeling my orgasm building, wishing he was actually inside me and pounding into my pussy, holding me until I bruised, sucking my nipple until I felt blood.

His arms were suddenly around me again, and in a blink, as if he'd just teleported us, he had me sprawled on my back on his bed, his body between my thighs as he took off my pants and panties with urgency.

He loomed over me, his neon blues staring down at my body with a hungry expression that rocked me all the way down to my entrance. Then he licked his lips and I shuddered, somehow feeling closer to release than before. He kept on staring at me, studying every mound, every crease, every curve, until I couldn't take it anymore.

"Ragnor," I begged.

His eyes snapped up to my desperate ones. In one swift motion, he pushed my thighs up, buried his head between them, and took a slow, languid taste along my entrance.

The orgasm that ripped through me was so unexpected, I gasped. My back arched, my hands fisting on the sheets, as my body shuddered, trying to ride the wave of pleasure that made me spasm. But I couldn't even give in to the pleasure because Ragnor ravished my pussy like a starved man, licking and nipping and biting, while his thumb played with my clit, and I realized the tension was building again, stronger, more powerful than before.

"Ragnor!" I moaned as another orgasm tore through my body, making me squirt into his mouth, wetting the sheets, it was so strong.

He pulled his magical mouth away and looked at my flushed face. Then he pushed three fingers together inside me, making me buckle and thrash, the pain and pleasure were so great.

"Fuck," he growled, pumping his fingers in my pussy, making me see white with how good it felt. "Fuck, you're drenched."

"Please," I begged as he started rubbing my bruised clit again while pumping his fingers unyieldingly. I cried out as a mini orgasm soaked his fingers in my juices.

He took out his fingers and cupped my breasts as he rose until his face was right above mine, his hot, molten eyes watching me with pure need. He pinched my nipples and I panted, biting my lip, pleading with him with my eyes to stop torturing me and get to it.

"If I fuck you," he suddenly said as he rubbed my breasts as if he couldn't help himself, "it won't change anything."

I was so heady with euphoria that it took everything in me to grate out, "I don't care."

He stopped his motions, and I cried out in frustrated need. "Look at me," he said in a low voice, and I turned my dazed gaze to his. He was turned on, beyond turned on even, but he was serious. "You'll still be up for the Auction, and I'll still be your Lord."

Enough of this, I thought and almost growled. Shooting my hand down, I found his jean-clad erection and grabbed it, giving it a squeeze that made Ragnor's face go slack with pleasure. "I. Don't. Care," I snarled in his face. "So get on with it, or I swear to God, Ragnor, I'll dismember you."

A slow, wicked, sexy smile stretched his lips as he grabbed both my wrists in one hand and pinned them above my head. "I like it when you think you're in charge," he murmured against my lips while I heard his free hand unbuttoning his pants. "It's turning me on."

Before I could reply to his condescending remark, his lips crashed against mine, taking them with a fury that made me blind with need. When I finally felt his cock by my entrance, I gasped. "Condom?" I moaned into his mouth as his free hand grabbed my thigh, pushing it wide to accommodate what I could feel was one hell of a large, thick, hard cock.

"No need," he murmured against my mouth and shoved the entirety of his significant length in one smooth slide right inside me.

I screamed into his mouth at the sudden pain. It'd been three years since the last time anything but a dildo was inside me, and Ragnor was huge. So fucking huge that it made my tight pussy clench around him, making his cock jerk inside me, hitting my G-spot so effortlessly that the pain melted, giving way to mind-boggling pleasure.

Ragnor raised his head and stared at me, eyes as unfocused as mine. "All right?" he growled.

I spasmed around him in response.

He pulled back slightly before driving his cock back inside until it reached its hilt, and my back arched as I cried out, feeling both pleasure and pain at how his cock filled and stretched me thin to my absolute limit.

Then Ragnor started moving, and I was lost, utterly lost in the wondrous sensation of having the man I'd been wanting for weeks, the man who'd driven me to the brink of insanity, now burying himself so deeply inside me that it was almost as if he was trying to rip me apart, shattering everything I thought I knew about sexual pleasure.

I moaned and screamed. He released my wrists at some point, and I held on to his shoulders for dear fucking life. He held my ass in a bruising hold that made me so horny, it wasn't even funny, as he pounded his cock in and out of my pussy, making me grow impossibly wetter, causing my orgasm to climb high, higher than it'd ever climbed before.

Then he slid almost entirely out before ramming back inside right to the brink, and I exploded like a nuclear fucking bomb. So lost in pleasure, I didn't know if I screamed or moaned or begged or anything, because all I could feel was the release taking me under and breaking me to pieces. I stayed in place as my entire body shuddered, the orgasm tearing me apart from the inside out, shaking me to the fucking core.

I felt the liquid heat filling my pussy up, and I knew Ragnor had come too. His teeth sank into the skin of my shoulder as he pumped a few more times, emptying his hot seed inside me.

Even after I came to, I couldn't move. How could I, when I'd just experienced the best fucking orgasm-fest of my life?

Ragnor's lips trailed up my shoulder to my jaw, then, finding my lips, pressed against them almost as if he wanted another taste.

Then in a deep, low growl, he said, "Again."

I blinked, sure I heard him wrong. "W-what?"

He raised his face and looked at me with eyes as calm as the ocean yet as hot as the middle of August. "Did you really think once was enough?" he asked, as if he couldn't believe I was that stupid to insinuate such a thing.

I stared at him, half in horror, half in anticipation. "But you just . . ." My words disappeared as I could feel that he was still long and thick and hard inside me. My eyes widened. "How?"

He gave my hips a squeeze and grinned. It was such a masculine, smug grin that it made my belly flip-flop, it was so sexy. "I want this too" was his response before he pulled almost entirely out of me and pushed back inside with such force, I screamed.

And then he drove us both to the land of pure, unadulterated bliss once more.

Ragnor and I fucked five times.

Five. Times.

And it was transcendentally glorious each and every time.

Our bodies were far more than simply compatible. Our chemistry was just too combustible.

I'd reached heaven and back so many times, I didn't know what was heaven and what was earth anymore. My pussy was spent, used up more than it'd ever been, and bruises covered my breasts, hips, and ass.

Sex with Ragnor was rough, wild, and utterly dirty. I doubted the bedsheets would be able to survive the washing machine after our rough treatment.

We were now lying on the floor—I had no idea how we got there—curled into one another. His hand rubbed my arm up and down, and I made circles over his abdomen. Neither of us could move for the foreseeable future.

"So," Ragnor said simply, as if he hadn't fucked me five ways to Sunday.

"So," I said, as though I hadn't just ridden him like I was a rodeo expert.

"I think we should talk now," he said.

I glanced down at his tired dick, felt my broken pussy, and realized that he was right. It was time. "We have to get up for that."

He let out a deep breath. "You first."

Narrowing my eyes, I turned my head to face him. He looked at me with calm, night-ocean eyes. "Why not you?"

He arched his brow. "Do you want to argue again?"

My lips quirked. "If it leads to another amazing fucking . . ."

He sat up suddenly, bringing me upward with him, and bit down on my lower lip. He released it and gave me a serious look. "As much fun as it was, it can wait until after we talk."

To be honest, even though I knew he was right, that we did need to talk, I didn't feel like talking. Sure, fucking was out of the question right now, but I felt like I wanted to do just about anything else other than talk.

Because I had a feeling that once we talked, this little illusion we created in the past few hours would disappear, and I wasn't ready for that.

But Ragnor refused to budge, and eventually, we both rose to our feet, cleaned ourselves, put our clothes back on, and sat down like two proper adults.

"Let's start from the beginning," Ragnor said as he poured us freshly brewed coffee. "What happened with those men?"

I sipped my coffee before I responded. "I ended up in that park after my failed escape attempt," I said, not looking at him. "They caught me, called me a bloodsucker, and while they kept me captive, they tried to reach someone via email, I think, since they didn't have his number."

Ragnor didn't reply, simply sipped his coffee. After a few silent moments, he said, "As you probably guessed, those men weren't humans."

I froze, shocked that he'd actually answered my question from before. "What are they, then?" I asked hesitantly.

He let out a rough sigh. "It doesn't matter," he said, glancing at me. "I killed them already."

Something about the way he looked at me told me not to press this. So I changed the subject. "How come we're back at the Rayne League so soon?"

He looked away, sipping from his coffee. "After you passed out, I took you back here in our League's private jet."

That sounded suspiciously like a lie, but it also somewhat made sense. By plane, Nevada was about five and a half hours nonstop to Maine. Yet my gut told me he wasn't telling me something. "So, when are the rest coming?" I asked, pushing my suspicions to the back of my mind.

"They'll travel to the last League as planned and return here by bus in a few days," Ragnor said, putting the mug on the table before turning to me. "Considering you tried to run away, your trip permit was revoked."

I scrunched my nose. "It wasn't fun anyway," I said, thinking back to the Renaldi League and Stefan and his conversation with Logan. Shaking my head, I put the mug on the table as well and leaned back, folding my arms. Because I knew what was coming next, and I had no idea how I would respond to it.

Gently, Ragnor grabbed my chin and turned my head to face him. "We have two choices," Ragnor said, his gaze locking mine. "One, we can go back to the way things used to be and ignore everything that happened here today."

I was sick to my stomach at the thought.

"Or two," he continued, "we can continue this affair discreetly, away from prying eyes and ears, while keeping the same distance as before when we're out in public."

I kept my face clear of expression. I couldn't let him see what I was actually feeling, or he would take option one with or without my say. "We can do option two," I said blandly. "I mean, it's basically like the first option but much less dull and boring."

Ragnor's eyes searched mine as if he was trying to figure out whether I was lying. I wouldn't let him know, though, because I *was* lying through my teeth. I was lying so hard I almost managed to lie to myself.

"All right, then," he said, then cupped my throat and brought me in for a kiss that sealed the least wise deal of my life.

Because he'd said so himself: he would still put me up for Auction. I wouldn't be treated specially just because we were fucking. He would enjoy my body, and I his, until it was time for me to go.

As for me, I would have to pick up the pieces one way or another.

CHAPTER 25
RAGNOR RAYNE

"Your vamp sure knows how to bury her past."

Ragnor glanced sideways and saw Eliza coming around the table to sit before him. She'd called earlier this week to let him know she managed to dig something up about a certain vampire who made herself at home in his head. They'd set the meeting, and now, sitting in the pub owned by his League, it was finally time to solve the mystery that was Aileen Henderson.

"Before you say anything," he said after she ordered a cup of coffee, "I want to know one thing: Is she a threat?"

She stared at him long and hard before sighing. "Not in the sense you may think."

This didn't calm him, but he put his troubling thoughts aside and said commandingly, "Speak."

She scowled. "I'm not one of your minions, Rayne."

He didn't budge. "Talk."

She rolled her eyes. "Fine, you ass," she huffed out, then turned serious, grave even. "The first thing I did was access public files. Using your descriptions of the girl, I tried searching for profiles that matched that, thinking she might be using an alias."

It had occurred to Ragnor as well that she might be using a different identity. "And?"

"I found nothing, as if the girl was wiped off the face of the planet," Eliza replied simply, but gravity pulled her words, making them even more solemn than before. "I then accessed the dark net, much like you said your people did, and also—nothing. Once I covered these basics, I started thinking about different approaches. I broke into the prison-system database, and while I found absolutely nothing related to your girl, I did find something else."

She pulled a piece of paper out of her coat and handed it to him. "It was written in a section I didn't even think of looking into but just happened across while searching for something else, and had I not read carefully, I probably would've missed this."

Before he read what was written on the paper, he asked, "Why did you think you would find an answer in a prison database?"

She cocked her head. "People who want their past to disappear most likely committed crimes. I thought Aileen might've done time."

That direction of investigating had occurred to him briefly, but it seemed Eliza really did know how to do her job. Pulling up the paper, he saw it was a partial list of inmates who'd died in 2020 at a prison near Portland, Maine. The words were small, but Eliza had marked the name that was relevant to this investigation.

Amir Zoheir-Henderson.

"That's an Arabic name," Ragnor pointed out.

"That's what I was thinking too," she said, "but then I remembered that Aileen said she was from Egyptian, Scottish, and Ukrainian origins. Zoheir is a surname found in Egypt, while Henderson is Scottish."

Finally, *finally*, they were getting somewhere. "The Ukrainian part of her origins must come from her mother, then," he said, raising his eyes to his comrade. "So is this Amir her father? What did he do time in jail for?"

Her eyes flashed suddenly. "Once I had the name, I found the prison graveyard and visited it. Amir's age fits to be Aileen's father, so we now know that her father was in jail and died. Then with this name, I searched some more on the web and databases all around, but again, it seemed like your girl did a good job burying anything regarding the man. However," she added, "she didn't have access to *everything*."

"What do you mean?" Ragnor asked.

"I only thought of doing the most complicated research, then only later, it occurred to me to simply google him," she said, her eyes burning brighter, "and I found these articles."

She took out some crumpled papers and handed them to him. He unfolded them restlessly, and what he found made him feel his own eyes go neon blue. "He was charged for kidnapping, torturing, sexually assaulting, and murdering—"

"Girls under the age of ten," Eliza finished the sentence for him, her mouth pursed tightly. "Knowing this, think what Aileen must've been through."

That was sickening in more than one way, but he refused to contemplate it at that moment. "Did you find anything else?" he asked, controlling his emotions and turning off the beacons in his eyes.

"I found only one more thing," she replied. "Amir was arrested twice. The first time was eight years ago, and the second almost four years ago. It seemed that five years ago, he got released for good behavior, and then he continued with his crimes and got in again, this time for much longer until he apparently died in prison a year ago. The official statement was that he hanged himself, and we have no way of knowing if that is the truth."

"How did he even get released for good behavior?" he inquired, fury burning in his veins that the human authorities let go of such a fucker.

"Sometimes, lawyers do their job spectacularly." She grimaced. "Anyway, that's what I found. As for what happened to Aileen during the years Amir was in jail, I still found nothing, but I'll keep looking into it."

He was quiet for a while before he spoke again. "Is Aileen Henderson her real name, then?"

Eliza's expression darkened. "The articles call Amir by his first surname, Zoheir. Nothing is mentioned about him having any children. However"—she leaned forward, her eyes gazing at him darkly—"while public records don't have anything interesting to show, I did find the initials N. A. Zoheir as the only family member Amir has."

That didn't confirm whether Aileen Henderson was Amir's daughter, but everything else seemed to line up. If she was truly his daughter and she'd been privy to what Amir was doing with those girls . . . he didn't want to even think about it.

"Now." Her voice drew his gaze back to her. "My payment."

Ragnor studied her for a few moments. His head was still in a mess over what she'd shared, and yet he owed her the information. "Luceras called me the other day," he said quietly. "He's been studying some ruins in Egypt and shared with me some of his findings regarding the Bennu bird."

Her eye sparked with interest and terror at the same time. "You mean the bird associated with Ra, the sun god in Egyptian mythology?"

"One and the same." He nodded, thinking back to that disturbing phone call. "Luceras has been trying to find information about the Bennu bird for a long time now. What he's found so far isn't a lot. Mostly some folktales he can't rely on."

She stared at him with rapt attention. "Why is he researching some mythological bird?"

He gave her a grim look. He knew that what he was about to say would be triggering. Not just for Eliza but for him too. Because this was the thing that had brought them together in the first place. This was the one thing both of them were actually afraid of.

In his many years of existence, he'd rarely found anything scary, if at all. For him to feel such a weak emotion did not bode well.

"Luceras suspects that a certain group associated with one of the few folktales worth noting hasn't been entirely eradicated like we thought," Ragnor now said, looking carefully at Eliza to see her reaction.

Her eye widened. Horror dawned on her face. Her lips parted, and in a fearful whisper, she said, "The Children of Kahil."

He nodded and leaned back. He took a deep breath and said, "I'll find out more soon. Luceras will be back in the US soon, and we plan to meet."

As though in a trance, she nodded and rose to her feet. "Thank you, Rayne," she said distractedly before she looked again at the crumpled note with Amir Zoheir's name on it. She then took on a contemplative look, turned to gaze at him, and seemed to debate whether she should say something before she reached a decision and said, "I do want to ask you a question before I leave."

His shoulders tense, Ragnor gave her a curt nod as he said, "Go ahead."

"Are you still planning on selling her?"

It took him a moment to understand what she was thinking. They'd been talking about a different subject, after all. But he understood now, and his face became somber. "There shouldn't be a change in that plan," he replied with an irritated bite to his voice.

"But there is." She peered at him with a spark of dark curiosity. "I know you hate hearing my two cents, but you're going to listen to it anyway; I think there's more to it than your simple need to know about her history for the sake of your League, and I think you should *seriously* consider whether you're going to let this opportunity go or not. Think about it."

She departed soon after, leaving Ragnor feeling the need to break something, because she wasn't wrong, even if she wasn't completely right; something about Aileen Henderson rubbed him the wrong way. At least on the mental plane.

Physically, however, it was as if she was made just for him. And he planned on exploring every inch of her tasty body until, like all the others, he tired of her.

Because he *would* tire of her. Even if his cock thought differently. Even if it took all his willpower to make it so.

CHAPTER 26

Tansy sent a puny punch toward my midsection, and I pivoted, catching her by the arm before she lost her balance. She glanced at me, perspiration dripping down her pretty face, her eyes unfocused.

I let out a sigh and released her arm. "You won't get better if you keep at it like this," I told her softly. We'd been sparring in gym class for the last ten minutes, and it seemed that after nearly two months, she wasn't getting any better.

And here I was looking to get some of my anger out in a good sparring session.

Tansy's head fell, her long hair bursting at the seams of her tight, restraining bun. "I'm sorry," she whispered.

"You don't need to apologize," I admonished her. "You just need to take practice seriously."

"I do." She looked away, not convincing either of us. A thwack nearby made us both spin our heads to see that Zoey, sweaty, breathless, and smug, had knocked burly Bryce on his ass.

I turned to look at Tansy, and she winced, planting her gaze to the floor. My gut told me not to expect anything else from her today. Glancing to where Logan was barking instructions at Jakob and Jane, I said, "Let me be on the offense."

Her lips thinned and she nodded. She entered a defensive pose while I started launching soft kicks to her shins. Her eyes widened, and she seemed to know I was going easy on her on purpose. I also slowed down my attacks because this wasn't my focus at the moment.

"If you want to tell me why gym classes are hard for you, I'm here," I murmured so only she could hear.

She didn't reply as she weakly blocked my slow, anemic punch to her face. "You shouldn't," she said so softly that for a moment I thought I imagined it.

Frowning, I gave a frail kick to her ribs, allowing her to block it again. "Shouldn't what?"

Her light eyes were clear when she caught mine. "Be here."

I paused my attacks, staring at her. "I don't follow."

She shook her head and let out a shaky sigh. "Of course you don't. You never follow; you always watch. But, Aileen," her face suddenly took on a pitiful look I didn't like. "You can't watch forever."

Stunned, I stared at her, lips parted, and was about to say something—I didn't even know what, since it's not like she made sense—when Logan called, "Time!"

Tansy gave me a faint half smile and headed toward our gym instructor. It took me a moment to get ahold of myself and move.

As Logan barked explanations about improving forms and doing a stretching routine we needed to implement on a daily basis, my mind was not into it. Instead, I could only think about Tansy's cryptic words: *You can't watch forever.*

What the hell was Tansy talking about? And why couldn't I shake off the feeling that something was amiss and that perhaps she was far more astute than everyone else gave her credit for?

Either way, when Logan released us, I was lost in thought. I took the escalator up, heading to the kitchen, and as I passed by a door, a hand suddenly grabbed my arm and pulled me forcefully inside an empty, unused office.

I sucked in a breath when a familiar body pinned me to the now-closed door, and I looked up to see midnight blue eyes staring down at me. "Ragnor? What are you—"

His lips were on mine before I could finish, and he was kissing me like he was a parched man who'd found water in the middle of the desert.

And just like that, all thoughts of Tansy and her words cleared from my head, replaced by the electricity that shot through my veins.

He lifted me up, and I wrapped my legs around his waist, leaning into the kiss as I grabbed his hair, pulling him close. His erection rubbed against me, and I moaned, feeling the heat pooling, dripping to my panties.

Without taking his mouth off me or letting me go, he managed to take off my pants and panties together, exposing my slick entrance. He took out his hard, thick cock, and without warning, shoved it inside me, grabbing my waist to push me on top of him, bringing us together so deeply that I had to let go of his mouth to suck in a breath, my heart drumming in my chest.

"Fuck," he growled, eyes glowing, and with his arms around me, he held me as he walked, still inside me, to the neat office desk and put me down, flipped me, and had me bend over the surface. With his hands on my waist, he entered me from behind.

"Ragnor!" I half screamed, half moaned as he started ramming into me with such force that I held on to the edge of the desk for dear life. His thick length made my pussy squeeze around him, growing wetter and slicker as the tension built inside me, the pleasure almost too much to bear.

Then he did something he hadn't done before: he slapped my ass hard enough to leave a mark.

And that was my undoing.

"Fuck!" I screamed as the climax broke me, making me spasm around him. He slammed into me with such ferociousness, spanking my ass and grabbing the skin tightly, and the pain, the pleasure of the pain, the roughness made another, stronger orgasm shatter through me, making me gasp out, "Fuck, fuck, fuck—"

CRASH!

Ragnor got off me in a blink. I sucked in a breath, my heart a drumbeat in my chest, my ears, my slick cunt as I straightened, my knees wobbling.

Our gazes met. "Stay here," he commanded in a rough growl before storming out of the room.

Operating on autopilot, I grabbed my pants and panties, got dressed, and redid my ponytail. I was shaking, goose bumps covering my skin, as I paced around the office, waiting for Ragnor's return.

Minutes later, his sexy figure appeared at the door, his face sparked with a sliver of emotion he seemed to be able to recall at will. It was as though he hadn't just been buried deep inside me in the throes of lust. "A lantern collapsed." He cast his eyes down, a blandness in his tone that didn't match the fire I'd just seen in his eyes.

I stared at him, wondering what that meant, if perhaps someone had caused it to collapse. I was about to ask him about that when Ragnor grabbed his coat, turned to me, and said, "Let's stop here."

He might've said that, but I could tell he wasn't okay stopping here. His eyes ravaged my body, flickering with frustration, and yet it seemed like his mind was set.

Now that his touch wasn't driving me mad and the interruption had sobered me up like a cold shower, I remembered that there was something I needed to talk to him about.

I opened my mouth, but Ragnor was already closing the door behind him, leaving me as if he hadn't just been balls-deep inside me.

CHAPTER 27

It was unbelievable. It was the third and last month already. What was even more unbelievable was the fact the Auction was drawing near, and with it, so many things that needed to be done.

"The Auction has a few stages," Abe explained during our first class of the last month. "First, all the vampires put on auction will go through the Exhibition process. Who can tell me what this stage is about?"

Zoey raised her hand immediately. Once Abe allowed her to speak, she said, "It's about the Lords checking us out, measuring us up, and talking to us as prospective vampires for their Leagues."

"Correct." Abe smiled. "To summarize, it's the mingling part of the evening, when you can socialize with the other Lords and try to appeal to them." He paused and gave us all a hard look before locking his fingers behind his back and starting to pace. "Bribes, blackmailing, all this nonsense won't work on them, and I urge you *not* to try."

Abe motioned for Jakob, whose hand was up, to speak. "How do we appeal to the Lords?"

"That, you'll learn in our next lesson," Abe replied as he stopped pacing and turned to face us. "Now, let's talk about the Blessing. Who knows what's the Blessing stage?"

Again, Zoey's hand was up, but this time Jane's was up, too, so Abe nodded to her. Flustered, because she was picked over Zoey, Jane started to ramble. "I work for Maika in VR, and she told me that we need recommendations from our temporary employers for the Blessing part."

"It's true," Abe said, "but it's not all. Anyone else? Zoey?"

Jane deflated, and Zoey shot her a smug grin before replying. "The Blessing stage is when each Lord gives a few words about each newcomer and tells the audience about their performance in their temporary job assignments. The Lord then declares their favorite newcomer."

Abe gave her an encouraging smile. "Correct yet again," he said, and Zoey looked as smug as a peacock. "Now, let's talk about the third and final stage: the Auction itself."

Silence spread through the class as the *A* word echoed across the room.

"You would be called one by one to the stage and show off your best talent as Commons," Abe said quietly, breaking the silence and drawing our attention. "After you perform, the bidding will start until someone buys you out."

Hesitantly, Jakob raised his hand. "What happens if no one bids on you?" he asked, and tension filled the room.

Abe gave us a grim look. "Make sure you don't find out the answer for that one."

On that ominous note, Abe switched gears. "Since we're a mere four weeks away from the Auction, your preparations start today."

Abe offered us all a reassuring smile, as though he felt the anxiety that spread throughout the room. "You will go through a talent evaluation with the events committee members. It starts today after the break and will last until next week."

I was no longer calm, and neither were my peers. Zoey was biting her nails with nervousness, Tansy was more quiet than usual, Bryce tried to laugh it all off with a joke, while his eyes were full of fear, and the rest seemed as though doom had befallen on their formerly good fortune.

"After lunch break, you have an assessment class where you will discover which talent of yours is best suited to show off in the Auction and increase your chances at being bid on," Abe continued, ignoring the general dismay in the classroom. "Make sure to explore your options because, once you choose your performance, you cannot change it."

After that, I wasn't that calm anymore.

Because I needed to figure out a plan quickly. The problem was that I didn't know what I wanted. Did I want Ragnor to buy me? Did I want to be bought into another League? Or perhaps, should I give this all up and become Leagueless?

It was an opportunity to get away from everything. I had a chance to return to some semblance of a normal life in another League, or without one, and make sure I was back in full control of my life.

Fucking Ragnor in dark rooms was not part of said control.

Neither was Logan's renewed presence in my life.

Not to mention that Cassidy, the reason I was here to begin with, was like a constant reminder of how daring to care for another person led to doom.

The Auction hall was like an underground Olympic arena, with hundreds of seats surrounding a surprisingly small stage. On the seats nearest to the stage sat three people. Two of them I recognized—Magnus and Margarita, Ragnor's Lieutenants. The third person was a woman with a severe face and bushy eyebrows who reminded me of Frida Kahlo.

Margarita, sitting between the other Lieutenant and the stranger, rose to her feet. "Newcomers, take a seat in the first rows," she said. "We'll call each one of you for the assessment, and the rest shall wait. After you're assessed, you are to return to your seat and wait until everyone is done."

Once everyone was seated, Tansy was called to the stage. She seemed oddly serene as she went over to the stage. She looked tinier than ever, standing on her own, with her plait almost touching the floor. I glanced at the judges and saw Magnus's eyes were staring at her in a sharp, predatory way that gave me pause. Considering the way he licked his lips, it only affirmed my suspicions that whatever his intentions were, they were not holy.

"It is written here that you dance," Margarita said, looking at a piece of paper in boredom.

Tansy bobbed her head in a nod, sending strawberry blonde strands over her neck.

Margarita yawned. "Let's see it, then."

Tansy took off her shoes, closed her eyes, and moved.

"She's in," Zoey whispered to Bryce a row behind where I was sitting on my own. "I overheard Sanu from the Archives talking to Margarita. There is a reason she was on the waiting list for one year only. Our Lord has his eyes on her."

"But why?" Jakob, who was sitting next to them, asked in a hiss. "Yes, she can dance, but she's not Gifted."

"I remember Abe telling us that it's very rare, but sometimes, after you are given the Imprint and become a vampire, you might be able to develop a Gift as the years go on if you started as a Common." Zoey's voice was extremely excited about that.

"Really?" Bryce murmured, surprised. "I forgot all about that. I mean, it makes sense, even if it's rare; after all, vampire Lords become Sacred only after centuries of honing their vampiric powers or something, so turning from Common to Gifted isn't that far fetched . . ."

"She has potential," Jakob interjected softly. "This Auction is sold from the start. She's staying, while most of us won't."

I tuned out of their conversation and returned my eyes to Tansy's dance. She had fluid movements, her hair like a crown around her head, and she seriously had potential, as Jakob said. I knew extraordinarily little about dancing, but even I knew a star when I saw it.

Margarita stopped Tansy after a couple of minutes and scribbled something down. "Is dancing all you can do?"

Tansy gave a single nod.

The Lieutenant sighed. "Fine. Then your performance is set. Next will be Zoey Rittman!"

Zoey took the stage, and Margarita read out Zoey's hobbies—apparently, she'd listed a lot of them—before Margarita eventually said, "Logan mentioned you're doing exceptionally well in gym class. Why don't you show some of the movements Logan has taught you?"

Zoey's cheeks flushed at the compliment, and she nodded. She then started an offensive sequence Logan taught us a couple of weeks ago, which included many complicated movements. She executed them all quickly and accurately, though, and while I'd been vaguely aware of her talent in this area before, I was fully observing it now.

When she was done, Margarita gave her a disgusted look yet said in a saccharine voice, "Logan is never wrong. Magnus?"

"I think you should go with it," Magnus advised in an indifferent tone. "It might show our Lord you're worth buying and that you might be a good addition to the Troop."

Zoey grinned. "Then I'm going with it."

"Good," Margarita said, her face returning to a bored look. "Next, Bryce Sullivan."

One by one, the newcomers showed off what they could do best. Most were below average, but some surprised everyone with their hidden talents. Everyone went with flashy, exciting routines that would draw the eye, which was the right thing to do; in an event where you were practically fighting others for attention, the flashier your performance, the better your chances were to be noticed.

This was why I knew what I had to do—for better or worse. So when Margarita called my name, I went to the stage with an idea in mind.

The idea was solidified when Margarita sneered at me. "Ah, the talentless noob," she said, her voice taking on a nasty tone she hadn't used with anyone else. "So. What's it going to be? Striptease?"

Murmurs spread through my classmates like wildfire. I could feel their gazes on me. They were probably wondering why Margarita was picking on me.

I expected it, though. Margarita had hated me since the start, and she showed no signs of stopping anytime soon.

Yet I refused to stoop to her level. "I'm going to paint."

Margarita, Magnus, and the third woman looked at me as though I was nuts. "Paint?" Margarita repeated, as if she'd never heard the word before.

My hands curled to fists at my sides. "You don't think I can?"

"This is stupid." Margarita rolled her eyes. "I doubt you're good enough to capture the audience's attention."

"I don't care," I said, my blood boiling as I kept my smile intact. "Give me the canvas and let me show you what I can do."

Margarita smirked then. "You know, I'm going to enjoy this. Your future humiliation will be *extremely* satisfying." Her smirk turned nasty. "Get the noob some canvas and paints."

Minutes later, I was seated on a stool before a medium-size canvas with a brush in my hand and a palette full of oil colors. Margarita, whose sharklike grin made my blood boil, said, "You have five minutes. Start!"

It took everything in me to keep my hatred hidden as I sank the brush in pink and quickly painted the whole canvas. I let only one thought remain in my head as I took a red color and drew all over, marring the paint with my fingers on some parts in a certain way. Propelled by the hot sting of her words, I then shadowed it all with grays and blacks, until it was dead clear what I wanted to show with the painting.

"Time!" Margarita trilled triumphantly.

I lowered my brush and turned to look directly at her. Dark satisfaction filled me when I saw how her stupidly arrogant face turned a bright shade of red.

On her side, Magnus seemed to tense, as if readying himself for the worst kind of outcome, and the Frida Kahlo look-alike grinned. Murmurs and confused whispers came from my classmates.

After a few stunned moments, Margarita finally seemed to collect herself, and she sent me a look full of loathing. "Painting it is," she hissed, venom dripping from her voice.

I smiled, rose from the stool, and gave them a mocking bow. I then returned to my seat and watched the painting from afar. I had to admit, it was one of my best works, with writing that looked like scars that hadn't healed right, and the scars created four clear words:

He'll never be yours.

CHAPTER 28

The timer went off, and I dropped the brush with a jolt. After stopping the annoying ring, I then turned to stare at the canvas to review what I managed to accomplish in five minutes.

Unfortunately, it wasn't much: an abstract mashing of colors that should've been a certain landscape but didn't quite form into any shape. Five minutes weren't enough to create anything concrete, and so far, all my attempts turned out to be failures.

Annoyed with myself, with the Auction looming in the near future, I threw the canvas away and put my head in my hands. I had only three weeks to practice what I wanted to paint in the Auction, and yet I couldn't even decide *what* to paint. Meanwhile, in the training room down the hallway from this workshop, Tansy was working on her choreography while Zoey was perfecting her martial arts routine.

Even Jakob's juggling act was far more decent than what I'd come up with so far.

I heard the workshop door open and looked at the time on the digital clock Abe had given me. "I still have an hour left," I said irritably, believing it to be Margarita, my favorite vampire, who decided to be my personal mentor—each of us got a mentor to help us perfect our performances—which meant she made me fend for myself, the bitch. I hadn't seen her throughout the practice sessions, or ever since the assessment class. She was my mentor in name only; in truth, she was setting me up to fail.

Not that I wanted her to mentor me. Every time she came to tell me class was over, she gave me this sinister, fuse-igniting little smirk, making me want to choke her.

Strong, muscular arms appeared on the sides of my stool. A warm, hard chest pressed against my back. I froze. This was definitely *not* Margarita.

"Working hard, I see," Ragnor murmured. His hands went to my sides, grabbing my waist and pulling me back against him. Despite myself, a bolt of electricity shot through my veins, making every part of me tingle. "How about taking a break?"

The thought was tempting. We hadn't gone at it since the other day when we were interrupted in the middle, and I found that I missed the feel of his cock inside me.

But my body and my mind weren't on the same page. "I can do with a break," I said carefully, and before his hands could roam anywhere dangerous, I shot to my feet and put some distance between us before turning to face him.

He was wearing casual clothes, his hair pulled into a tiny ponytail at the back of his head. He eyed me up and down with a heated expression that made me wish I'd worn anything but my dirty, paint-covered overalls.

Giving myself an inward shake, I folded my arms, waited until his eyes returned to my face, and said, "I want to talk first."

His lips twitched as he walked toward me in lazy, leisurely steps. His eyes were now on my chest. "You can talk if you want," he said in a low murmur that I could feel vibrating through my loins. "Let's see how long you'll last."

My eyes widened. "Ragnor—"

He pounced.

I was weak in the knees when his mouth crashed into mine in a kiss. He swiftly unclasped my overalls and shoved them to the ground before lifting me into his arms, making me wrap my legs around him in mere panties and a tank top. He bit my lip hard, making me gasp, and snaked his tongue in, tangling it with my own as he walked us to a paint-splattered table nearby.

Once he sat me down on the table, he released my lips, tore my panties away, shoved his head between my thighs, and thrust two fingers inside me without warning.

My head fell back as I yelled, "Fuck!"

He pumped his fingers in and out, and the pleasure was too much. I tried to close my thighs, but his free hand pushed one of them back, keeping them open. I spasmed uncontrollably, all thoughts leaving my head, as he fingered me inhumanly fast.

The orgasm ripped through me so unexpectedly that I screamed, digging my nails into his arms as I rode wave after wave of pure, unadulterated pleasure.

When it was over, he took his fingers out and released me from his hold. I let myself lie back, trying to catch my breath, as I heard him unzipping his jeans.

Before any rational thought could return, Ragnor grabbed my waist and pulled me forward until he was between my legs. I felt his hot, hard, large cock against the wet lips of my pussy, and I gasped.

He pushed into me in a single thrust, causing me to arch my back and freeze. He was so big, he filled every inch of me, and when his thumb suddenly flicked my clit, I couldn't help but come again.

He fucked me hard and rough as I was still trying to collect myself after the recent orgasm, but he wouldn't let me. And when he flipped me so his chest pressed against my back, pasting me to the table, he thrust again, this time far deeper than before.

His hand grabbed my hair and forcefully lifted my head. His fangs tore through the skin of my neck, and he sucked in my blood while he rode in and out of me so relentlessly that I could only scream as pleasure tore through me over and over again.

When he picked up the pace, I tensed, feeling the orgasm building again. His hand grabbed my ass cheek so hard that I knew it would bruise, and the pain forced my pussy to clench in excitement. He must've felt it, because he penetrated me even harder and deeper than before while he slapped my ass, causing me both pain and absolute, undeniable bliss.

He took his fangs off me and growled "Fuck!" as he thrust a few more times before he emptied himself inside me. My release came soon after, his cock jolting inside me, his warm semen making me feel so full, it was pure ecstasy.

Ragnor leaned his forehead against my shoulder as we both panted. His cock was still inside me, and at that very moment, I wished it would stay there forever.

Before the thought computed, he pulled out of me and stepped back. I forced myself to straighten as well and turned to face him.

As he zipped up his jeans, he looked at me and said, "You wanted to talk."

I stared at him for a few dazed moments. Then I averted my gaze to the side, and my eyes landed on the canvas I'd thrown away before he arrived.

And suddenly, my dizziness was replaced by a dawning horror that propelled me into action. Lips thin, I quickly put on my panties and overalls before facing him again. "I need to keep practicing," I said, avoiding his gaze. "You can leave now."

That didn't sit well with him, it seemed, because he crossed the gap he'd put between us until he was right before me. "But you had something to say," he said, and when I reluctantly raised my eyes to his face, I saw he was staring at me with that little furrow between his brows that was the only indication that he was somewhat confused.

Despite the fact we'd just banged like our lives depended on it, his proximity was suddenly suffocating. I sidestepped him and went over to pick up the stupid abstract painting I'd made. "It wasn't important anyway," I said in a fake light voice. "The Auction is fast approaching. I have to prepare if I want to be bought."

He said nothing as I fussed about with the canvas, gently putting it along with the other discarded canvases in the corner of the room. *Leave,* I begged silently as I passed him to grab a blank canvas.

He grabbed my arm and pulled me to him. I looked anywhere but at him as his hold tightened. "You knew what you were getting into," he said slowly, almost gently. "I was clear about this affair not having any effect on the Auction."

A spark of anger lit me up, and I snatched my hand away, turning to glare at him. "I know," I said, seeing his eyes narrowing, his lips curling downward in disapproval. That just got me madder. "This is why I need to practice like a motherfucker so some better asshole will buy me."

It was the wrong thing to say. His eyes glowed neon, and he pushed me against the wall, his hands on each side of my head. "Do you want to be bought into another League that much?" he growled, eyes furious and unblinking on mine. "Because I would be happy to give you exactly what you want, Henderson." By the look on his face, I had a feeling he wasn't just talking about his League.

And that just pissed me off even more. Why did he suddenly care about whether I wanted to stay in his League or not? It wasn't like he cared about what I wanted to begin with!

I glowered back. "If there's one thing I learned, thanks to you, it's that I no longer have the freedom to *want* something," I shot back.

His face contorted. Ragnor was completely pissed off. "You haven't let that go, have you?" he said, voice rough with that realization.

A humorless laugh escaped me before I could stop. "How can I ever forgive the man who stole everything away from me and refused to explain his reasons?" I snapped, feeling so angry that I didn't know how to contain myself. "How can I ever forgive the man who had me come here without explanations about my abnormal situation and let me fend for my fucking self?!"

His hand came to my throat and wrapped around it warningly, as his face slowly cooled over, his fury turning stone cold. "If you only had told me anything about yourself, none of that would've happened."

I gritted my teeth. "Oh, so now it's *my* fault?"

"Yes, it is," he growled, hand tightening around my throat. "The name Amir Zoheir ring a bell?"

Everything stopped.

My anger disappeared.

My indignation was no more.

Instead, terror rose so sharp and acrid that I started to shake. "No," I whispered, searching his eyes, wishing he hadn't just uttered that name. That he hadn't just shattered my very core.

His face was no longer cold as he released my throat and wrapped his arms around me, pulling me close. "You could've told me," he said in a raspy voice as he embraced me tighter. "Did you really think I would hold his horrible crimes against you?"

I was frozen, stuck in place, unable to move. He was trying to comfort me now, after almost biting my head off. He was telling me I could've trusted him with this. As if Amir Zoheir's existence, and my entire past, was nothing but just dust that could be swept under the rug.

As if my father wasn't a monster, and I wasn't his abhorrent creation.

I put my hands on Ragnor's chest and pushed him hard. He refused to budge. "Let go," I said, and my voice sounded strange. Unfamiliar.

"Talk to me, Henderson," he demanded quietly, squeezing me tighter.

But I was through with talking. "Let. Me. Go," I gritted out.

For a moment, I thought he wouldn't, but then he released me and stepped back, staring at me with barely restrained frustration. He looked like he wanted to shake me until I spilled everything. Like he wanted to penetrate my mind and discover all my secrets. Like he wanted to *know* me.

But I couldn't care about that. I couldn't really care about anything beyond the fact he knew.

He knew who my father was.

He knew about what he'd done.

He might not know my part in all that—there was no record of it anywhere, that I knew for sure—but he knew enough.

Gazing at his eyes, I pointed at the door. "Leave."

His eye twitched. "I will not tolerate this tone, Henderson. You can't speak to me like that just because we're—"

"Please," I cut him off, my voice barely steady. He looked at me as if he saw me for the first time. My lips trembled. "*Please.*"

Without another word, he turned and left.

And when the door closed behind him, I fell to the floor, put my hand over my mouth, and hoped no one heard as I broke down.

CHAPTER 29

"Let's have sex."

Logan turned to look at me, his turquoise eyes wide. "What?"

"Sex," I said, shrugging. "Let's try it."

"But . . . ," Logan started, then looked down at the floor. "Isn't it . . . like . . . I don't know . . ."

"Everyone does it," I said, thinking of Daddy. "I bet your parents do it all the time."

His face turned green. "Ew!"

"Oh, come on." I rolled my eyes. "It's not like you didn't learn about how babies are made, Logan. Although you did look squeamish when Mrs. Holden said she was going to assign you that baby doll to take home and take care of. Come on, let's do it."

"But what if we make a baby?" he snapped. "Don't we need c-condoms?"

"We don't need condoms, silly." I grinned, cupping his cheek. "I haven't gotten my period yet, meaning I can't get pregnant. Besides, I think we have to do it, like, a lot to get pregnant."

He turned greenish again. "Maybe we can just like . . . fool around. You know. Like touch each other—"

A spark of fury lit up inside me. "Everyone else is doing it. Everyone's having sex! We're not babies! Besides, don't you want to have sex with me? Isn't that what boys want?"

Logan's eyes narrowed. "I . . . yes, but . . . but I feel like maybe we are going too fast—"

"*Too fast? We're thirteen, Logan!*" I cut him off, scowling. "*I know girls who have already had sex and who are way younger than we are! Don't you think about doing it? Don't you want to know how it feels? What it's like? If you love me, you'll want to do it with me.*"

Logan stared at me for a long while before something in his eyes broke, and he grabbed my hands. "*Will it make you happy if we do it?*"

I squeezed his. "*Yes.*"

He sighed, cupped my cheek, and kissed me softly before he said, "*Then let's do it.*"

"*What have you done to him?*" Ella screamed at me, her eyes bloodshot.

I looked anywhere but at her face. "*W-what do you mean, Mrs. Kazar—*"

"*My son is bleeding. Bleeding!*" she yelled, pointing at the emergency room door. "*And there is this horrible thing stuck there, covered in blood . . .*" Her face turned purple and red. "*What the fuck . . . what were you two doing . . . WHAT HAVE YOU DONE TO HIM?*"

I trembled. "*I-I'm sorry, w-we were just—*"

"*Ella, the doctor finished checking him,*" Logan's dad said, eyes empty with shock. "*It's . . . I can't believe it . . . he was . . . she . . .*"

After he whispered, Ella sucked in a breath and whirled around to me, fury and terror written all over her face. "*She did what?!*"

I'd tried to do to him what I'd seen my father do for years. I later learned that what I had done was considered abuse. That the things my father had done in the name of love were anything but. And while the things Logan and I had done were consensual, I realized now that he had no power in the relationship. That I had assumed authority over him as my father had done to me and the other little girls. That I had used my father's ways of doing things, horrible, horrible things, to show the boy I loved that I loved him.

Logan had trusted me because we had been dating for four years, since we were thirteen. I trusted him too. I trusted him to allow me to find pleasure in using his body in ways I shouldn't have. I was too broken then to know that what I was doing was wrong. That it was not normal. That this kind of blood play was something to be engaged in by mature, responsible adults. That my cravings, my desires, my needs were not wrong but, in the wrong hands, were dangerous.

As Ella, Logan's mother and my foster mother, screamed at me, restrained by her husband so she wouldn't physically attack me as we all stood in the ER corridor, waiting for news, I couldn't help but feel the filth clinging to my skin. The filth of what I was just realizing I'd done.

I hurt Logan. I all but sexually abused him. It might've been consensual, but it didn't make it any better.

It didn't make me any better than my father.

"My parents don't want me to see you anymore."

We were sitting on the grass in the backyard of my home. Logan, who seemed to have grown three times larger and more mature than the last time I'd seen him months ago, refused to look me straight in the face. I knew why. Our last time together had been bad. So bad, he'd been hospitalized for weeks.

"I want to touch you," I told him with frankness I usually avoided when I was with him. Because it was the horrible truth; despite everything, despite what I'd done to him, I still wished for his love.

I was selfish; I knew that. A better person would've set him free.

But I didn't want Logan to be free from me. I wanted him shackled to my side forever. And even though I knew I was a monster, I couldn't help but wish for it.

"I want to touch you too," he said softly, and a tear ran down his cheek. "I love you, Aileen. I've never loved anyone before, and yet . . ."

I raised my hand, was about to touch him, when he recoiled away from me and faced me, his eyes wide. "Why did you have to do that?" he asked, his voice accusing. "Why did you have to . . . to—"

"It's what I know, Logan," I said, my voice cracking. I thought back to my therapist, to our long sessions, and felt my chest ache. "It's the only way I know to show you I love you—"

"When you love someone, you don't send them to the hospital!" he snapped. "When you love someone, you make sure they're safe, that they're . . . they're—"

"I was lost!" I cried out, lips trembling. "I was stupid, and lost, and goddammit, Logan, it happened right after everything went down with my father—"

"We're not fucking kids anymore, Aileen!" he shouted back. "You're acting like you're still Daddy's little lost girl—"

"Don't you dare," I hissed, my hands curling into fists. "You don't know what happened—"

"Then why don't you ever tell me anything?" he screamed. "In the past four years, I've been dating a fucking ghost. A ghost, Aileen! I know nothing about you or your circumstances—heck, I only know the dry fucking details because I fucking googled it! And you told me shit-not! What did your father do? What the hell happened before you were brought over to our house?"

I was about to speak, but I couldn't utter a word. Everything that happened . . . despite it all, I could never disclose this information. Despite what I logically knew, I still wanted to keep my promise to my father.

And Logan had seen, experienced, far too much of what I'd gone through. What I'd witnessed. The nightmare that was my childhood.

But I saw it on Logan's face. I would lose him if I said nothing. So all I said was "Teach me how to love you properly, and I promise you—I will tell you everything."

Logan looked at me with disgust, but behind that disgust hid another emotion, bigger and warmer than anything I'd ever seen. "Love should come naturally, effortlessly," he spat out. "It should never be forced or taught. That you wish for it to be this way . . ."

Something burned inside me. Fear. "Don't leave me."

He let out a bitter laugh. "That's what you don't get about love, Aileen. Even though I'm so fucking angry with you, and even though you hurt me more than anyone else in this world, I will never be able to leave you. This is love in its most honest and brutal form."

He then put his hands on my shoulders, pushed me to the ground, ripped off my clothes, closed his mouth over mine, and gave me what I wanted.

I woke up, tears burning in my eyes.

It had been years since I'd had these dreams. Years, and yet I had them now.

I knew why I dreamed of Logan, of our broken, twisted relationship. I knew why my mind forced me to remember what happened to people I attempted to love and what happened to them when they learned of my past. I knew it was merely a reminder, a *warning* of what was to come.

The horror of who I was, *what* I was, would forever haunt me.

The memories of me doing to Logan what my father did to those girls would forever be a stain on my far-from-clear past.

After years of therapy, I was still sick with myself. Sick that I'd done all those things, first in the name of the Morrow Gods and then for my own selfish reasons.

It hurt, knowing I was not worthy of anything good. It also terrified me that Ragnor, who somehow learned about Amir, would find out about all this and would forever see me for who I truly was.

A monster. Or at the very least, the spawn of one.

That suffocating fear consumed me for the rest of the night.

The plate slipped from my fingers and shattered on the kitchen floor. CJ, who was sweeping nearby, came over, frowned, and tidied away the pieces.

Jada sent me a concerned look. "Go sit down. I don't want you near any plates if you're going to drop them anyway."

I gave her a silent shrug and took a seat next to her. It was my fourth plate since the beginning of my shift. Concentration eluded me now that it was only one week until the Auction.

Bowen took a seat next to me. "It's the Auction jitters, isn't it?" he asked as though he read my mind.

I nodded, though it wasn't only the Auction. I hadn't seen Ragnor in the past week, ever since our fight at the workshop. I was still struggling to find a decent idea to paint in the Auction itself, while my classmates were already settled on their acts. Logan's gym classes grew brutal in their intensity, causing every bone in my body to ache. Nightmares interrupted my sleep, only adding to my constantly growing exhaustion.

"I remember my first Auction," CJ murmured as he helped Jada wash the rest of the dishes. "It wasn't a good experience."

"First Auction?" I wondered out loud. Abe hadn't said anything regarding taking part in the Auction more than once.

Jada gave me a small smile. "CJ completely fucked up his performance." She snickered.

CJ shot her a wilting look. "I was nervous," he muttered, "and I forgot the choreography."

"You're a dancer?" I asked, surprised.

He shrugged. "Not really. It's more of a hobby, and I used it for my Auction performance, you see."

"Unfortunately, CJ fell on his ass when he tried to execute a backward somersault," Jada said, jumping in, and grinned saccharinely when CJ glared at her.

Bowen chuckled and turned to me. "In the end, our Lord didn't think CJ was such a waste of space," he said, smirking, and then yelped when CJ threw a soapy sponge at his face.

"Speaking of which, do you remember that girl who wasn't bought?" Jada asked, turning to Bowen. "I think it was back when you first arrived."

CJ tensed, and Bowen's face darkened. Tension filled the air, and for the first time since I met them, there was no hint of humor on any of their faces. "Yeah," Bowen replied quietly. "Luana."

"Right," Jada said, face suddenly sad.

When a tense silence fell on the room, I couldn't help but break it. "What happened to her?" I asked, recalling that Abe never really told us what would happen if we weren't bought. None of us talked about it, if only because we understood it couldn't be anything good, but I felt like I should know. Just in case.

Bowen gave me a faint smile. "Luana wasn't considered particularly beautiful or talented," he said, voice wistful. "But she was diligent. She was on the waiting list for many years before luck came knocking on her door, and so she worked her ass off to try and get bought into a good League."

"What a fool," CJ murmured grimly.

"She had stage fright." Bowen shook his head, lips pursed. "She walked up on the Auction stage and just stared ahead vacantly, motionless and speechless."

He sighed. "It's extremely rare when someone isn't bid on, and when it happens, the unbought vampire has three options." His eyes glowed in anger, and he fell silent.

None of them spoke for a few long moments before Jada let the last plate she was washing go and stepped back, wiping her hands. "The vampiric Society is vastly different from the humans'," she said, turning to me with serious eyes. "We're closer to animals than humans are. We have better instincts, better senses, and far superior strength and power. Our Society's Lords are the embodiment of all these attributes when they reach their highest peak."

She came to sit next to me and took my hand in hers. "To keep ourselves civilized, we created harsh laws that are practically set in stone," she said, squeezing my hand. "Without these laws, we would be utterly barbaric. Rampant. Far more inhuman than we already are."

CJ crouched before me, dark eyes somber. "The three options given to Luana show just that," he said quietly. "Because Luana displayed she was of no use to the vampiric Society in any sort of way—and unfortunately, the five-minute Auction performance is all the Lords have to go on to evaluate her abilities—she was given a choice."

Bowen snorted bitterly at that. "As if it's actually a choice," he snarled as his foot jumped up and down on the floor in rising fury. "She could either, one: become a slave at her initial League, two: become a slave at another League, or three: legally break the League System Agreement and become Leagueless."

I stared at him, dread and shock making my lips part and my breath get stuck in my throat. "You can't be serious," I whispered chokingly.

Jada laughed humorlessly. "You know what the worst thing about it is?" she said. "Luana can never participate in an Auction again. She's stuck as a fucking *slave* for the rest of her existence."

A cold shudder cascaded through my spine. "This isn't fair," I said quietly, my hands shrugging out of her grip and curling on my knees. "All of this just because no one bid on her?"

"It's not just that, I'm afraid," CJ said quietly, giving me a terribly sad look. "As I mentioned, I took the Auction again. Funnily enough, even if you are bought, you still have one more chance to participate in the Auction. This is what I did, because I didn't like the League I was in or my job as a recruitment agent." His lips curled downward in a sneer. "I didn't know back then that second-timers' fates are usually similar to the unbought ones', even if they're bought during their second round."

That was fucked up on so many levels, I started to feel sick. "Does it mean you're Rag—" I winced. "Our Lord's *slave*?"

CJ looked away. "On paper, I am. But our Lord isn't fond of slaves, so I'm a kitchen assistant instead."

There was a note of reluctant respect in CJ's voice. As though Ragnor had spared him a worse fate—which, according to what they were saying, was far more terrible than being on dishwashing duty. But while I didn't entirely understand what it meant to be a *slave*—and I sure as fuck hoped I wouldn't need to understand—it sounded bad enough that I couldn't help but feel horribly nauseous.

"CJ, Bowen, and I were lucky," Jada said softly, drawing my eyes to her. Her eyes were full of determination. "Out of all seven Lords, our Lord isn't just the best leader but the most fair, respected, and strong. So Aileen," she added in a louder voice, "you've got to make our Lord buy you. For your own sake."

CHAPTER 30

"No," I said, tossing the canvas aside.

"No," I hissed an hour later, poking the canvas so hard with the brush that it dented and tore.

"No, no, no," I snarled as I ripped the hundredth canvas with my nails in a fit of rage.

I panted, sweating after hours upon hours of trying to paint something, anything, and glowered at the utter mess that was the workshop.

I pitched the brush so hard it hit the wall with a blue splash, fell on the stool, and put my head in my paint-covered hands. There were only five days until the Auction. Five fucking days, and I had no concrete act ready.

It felt like the air was pushing down on me, its transparent hands gripping my neck. My heart rate was beyond-the-charts fast with dread, and my entire body trembled in trepidation.

"I can't do this," I mumbled, shaking my head as tears welled in my eyes. "I can't fucking do this—"

The workshop door slammed open, and I jumped to my feet with a gasp, tensing when I saw the familiar redheaded woman stepping inside, her nose scrunched in evident disgust.

It seemed the universe wanted me to feel even shittier, considering Margarita, my elusive mentor, was finally paying me a visit.

"It smells like mildew in here," she grunted and gave me a disapproving, repulsive look. "What the hell have you been doing here all this time?"

The last thing I wanted was to talk to her, but I knew ignoring her wouldn't make her go away. "Painting," I said stiffly.

With her foot, she nudged at one of the tossed canvases. "You're not doing a very good job," she commented haughtily, an undertone of satisfaction to her voice.

It made me wonder if Magnus, the other Lieutenant, treated his mentees—Tansy and Zoey, in his case—in the same manner. Something told me he didn't.

"What do you want?" I cut to the chase. Obviously, she wasn't here to help me.

She turned to face me fully and gave me an arrogant look. "Well, I just wanted to check up on my poor little mentee," she said and smirked. "Apparently, I was worried for nothing. You're doing quite well on your own."

Anger sparked inside me, but she wasn't done. Pacing through the room as she studied my disastrous artworks, she said, "I'm truly excited for the Auction now." She snickered when she eyed one of the torn paintings. "I can't wait to see what will happen when no one bids on you."

She was circling me like a shark, I realized, as she returned to face me. "I warned you what would happen if you didn't know your place, noob," she murmured silkily, stepping closer to me as her green eyes flashed triumphantly. "You dug your own grave."

I wanted to hit her. I wanted to spit in her smug little face. I wanted to scream and curse her to hell and back. But I remained silent and still, staring at her with so much hatred that words deserted me.

Snickering, she turned around and walked to the door. "By the way, our Lord's doing final private meetings with all of you noobs," she said as she opened the door and whirled her head to me with a nasty smile. "Yours is in ten minutes."

Once she slammed the door, I instinctively looked down at myself. I was wearing dirty jeans and a baggy tee, with paint patches all over my skin. My hair was like a bird's nest since I hadn't showered in more than twenty-four hours.

Margarita must've known about this meeting at least an hour ago. And yet she wanted me to look my worst when I went to meet Ragnor. *What a fucking cunt.*

Then I realized I was going to see Ragnor, and I felt myself pale. Hurriedly, I went to the workshop washroom and washed my face in the sink. Looking up, I was horrified to see my hazel eyes were bloodshot, with dark under-eye bags.

My heart was in my throat when I tried to comb my hair with my fingers. *I shouldn't bother,* I thought, feeling pathetic. *He knows about Amir after all. He hasn't sought me out since our fight too. It's not like our affair is still going on.*

But what I felt was beyond such reason. When Ragnor saw me wearing unkempt and dirty clothes and looking like I hadn't slept well in days, he would know I wasn't okay, and I refused to show him that side of me. I refused to show him any vulnerability, not like that last time I almost broke down in his presence.

But the bitch hadn't given me enough time to pull myself together.

"Fuck!" I snarled when my tangled hair refused to be combed, and then I strode out of the workshop, heading toward the escalator that would lead me to Ragnor's office, feeling just as disgusting as Margarita thought I was.

When I walked into the office reception, I didn't even bother to give my name to the secretaries. I simply threw his door open and walked in, then heard it close behind me.

Ragnor was standing with his back to the entrance, but when I entered his office, he turned around.

Since I holed myself up in the workshop, I only made short visits to the cafeteria during mealtimes. My kitchen shifts were also reduced in preparation for the Auction. That meant I hadn't had any opportunity to see him up until now.

And he looked so good that I almost broke apart right there and then.

His dark-brown hair was down, its tips brushing his broad shoulders. His mouthwatering body was dressed in a simple tee, pants, and combat boots, yet on him, the casual attire seemed as if he'd come out of a fashion magazine. His face, too, was just as gorgeous, his penetrating midnight blues just as beautiful.

He looked fresh and clean and droolworthy. With his face set in a hard expression, he seemed to be in control, calm and collected.

I wanted to close the gap between us and have him envelop me in his strong arms.

I wanted to press my lips against his so that he would kiss me until I saw stars.

I wanted for him to tell me that it would all be okay. That I had nothing to worry about. That I shouldn't try so hard because he would buy me in the Auction.

I wanted all of that so much that I felt the same sense of strangulation from before returning with a vengeance. Gasping, I stumbled back and leaned against the wall, my hand on my chest, feeling my heartbeat quickening and trying to get ahold of myself.

A soapy, addictive scent tickled my nose when Ragnor was suddenly before me, his hands on my shoulders. "Breathe," he said urgently, voice low, and I tried to suck in a breath, but all it did was make my vision blurry. "*Breathe*, Aileen, you have to breathe—"

My panic rose, and I couldn't hold myself upright anymore. Ragnor's arms wrapped around me before I hit the floor, and his voice became distorted as if I was drowning and he was above water.

It went on forever. The invisible hands didn't let me breathe. My vision refused to clear. My body spasmed as I tried to fight the unknown foe.

Slowly, the hands around my throat released me, and I sucked in a deep breath, attempting to fill up my lungs as fast as possible. My sight cleared, my body stilled, and I realized I was sitting on the floor in Ragnor's arms, and he was rocking me back and forth, murmuring unintelligibly.

I held on to his shirt as I gasped for air, and he tightened his hold on me. Minutes later, when I could finally breathe properly, I tilted my head up and caught him looking at me with eyes glowing neon blue, expression inscrutable.

Those eyes broke me. *So much for not showing him vulnerability*, I thought bitterly when tears welled in my eyes. "I'm sorry," I said quietly, my voice breaking as my hands moved to grab his shoulders so I could straighten myself. "I'm sorry for this whole thing. I'm sorry for last time too."

His eyes seemed to turn brighter. "Henderson—"

"Don't sell me," I interjected hastily, lips trembling with remnants of panic. "Please don't sell me, Ragnor. I'll be good." I gave him a wobbly smile. "I'll call you *my Lord* and I will worship the ground you walk on like the rest of your vampires. Just don't sell me." My smile fell, and I got up on my knees, digging my nails in his shoulders. "Keep me here."

For the first time, Ragnor seemed alarmed. "Let's talk about this, Henderson," he said evenly, but I could tell my words affected him.

And yet he didn't tell me he would buy me. "What do I need to do?" I begged, releasing his shoulders to cup his face. I locked his gaze with mine. "I'll do anything—"

His hands were suddenly on my waist, and he pushed me against the wall. "Stop it," he growled, looking at me with sudden disapproval. "It's not like you to beg."

Distantly, I could feel a flare of anger, but I drowned it in my desperate hysteria. "I'll beg for as long as it takes." I looked at him pleadingly. "I don't want to be bought," I added, and before I could stop them, tears fell down my face. "I want to stay here with *you*."

A shadow passed through his face. "You don't know what you're saying, Henderson—"

I pressed my lips against his and kissed him with every bit of desperation I felt. He tensed, but then I felt his arms around me as he kissed me back.

It was a war of attrition. I seduced his tongue with mine, and he fought back with his hands in my hair and his teeth on my lip. I grabbed his hard length through his pants, and he grasped my breast, squeezing it hard. I took off his shirt, and he ripped apart mine. I pushed his pants down, and he slid mine down, spreading kisses on my leg as he did.

He was between my thighs the next second, our arms enveloping each other tightly. *This,* I thought, gasping when his cock pushed into me with one deep thrust. *This is what I needed.*

His fangs broke the skin of my neck, blood spilling from the wound. A sense of utter elation spread through my body as I bled for him, for Ragnor, as he fucked me hard and deep, all inhibitions—his and obviously mine—completely gone as if they never existed. He took me over and over again, making every little muscle in my pussy clench around his magnificent cock as I screamed, shattering around him with an orgasm that took me by storm.

That took him over the edge, and he grunted as he pumped into me, faster and stronger than before, until he buried himself inside me, his thighs spasming as he came.

He slumped over me, licking the spot he'd bitten, cleaning it of the remaining blood. Having his big, hot body crushing me to the floor was a bliss as strong as the orgasm he'd just given me. We were both panting, spent, as if we both had been mutually frustrated and finally managed to let it all out.

After a few long moments, Ragnor pushed himself up on his arms and stared at me with languid, tranquil midnight blues, his cock still buried inside me. "It will be okay, Henderson," he said quietly, his fingers caressing my cheek almost lovingly. "It's going to be over soon."

His words were meant to soothe, I knew, but they had the opposite effect. Because he reminded me who we were and what was happening.

Now that I wasn't drowning in despair, reality returned with a vengeance.

The Auction.

My paintings.

Ragnor refusing to tell me whether he would buy me.

Ragnor knowing about Amir.

Fuck. How could I have forgotten about *that*?

I put my hands on his chest and pushed. He obliged, sliding out of me, and I climbed up on my feet and gathered my clothes. "So," I said, forcibly using as much of a casual tone as I could while I dressed. "It's supposed to be a pre-Auction meeting, right?"

He rose to his feet and started putting his clothes back on. "Yes," he said, voice strangely soft.

Once I was completely clothed, I walked to the desk and sat down on the guest's chair. "Then let's have it," I said monotonously.

He rounded the chair and leaned over, his hands on the armrests, his face inches from mine. "The Aileen Henderson I know doesn't beg," he said, eyes hard on mine.

I stared back at him, my emotions so spent that it wasn't so hard to clear my face from any expression. "I'm willing to do many things to get what I want," I said flatly, and his eyes narrowed. "You might know about my father, Ragnor, but if you think it means you know *me*, then you're mistaken."

He didn't need to know that he was right. I hated begging. I hated feeling so hopeless that this was my only resort. But I refused to show him any more of myself. I refused to let him see just how much of a mess I was, when he was the epitome of self-control.

He let my chair go and leaned against his desk, face hard. "Are you still mad about me finding out about Amir?"

I couldn't help but smirk. I wasn't mad. It was never about such a simple emotion like anger. "Yeah, sure, let's go with that," I said flippantly.

Apparently, my tone seemed to get on his nerves, because his eyes flashed dangerously. "If you're going to act like a petulant child, then consider this meeting over," he said in a low, threatening voice.

Smirk still intact, I rose to my feet. "Let's end it here, then."

I was about to turn and leave when he grabbed my wrist and pulled me back, crushing my chest against his. "Why aren't you fighting me?" he asked, eyes brimming with an emotion I couldn't decipher. "Why are you acting like we're strangers?"

I tugged at my wrist, but he refused to let go. Smirk falling, I gave him a hard stare. "Because that's what we are," I said, my captured hand fisting. "A Lord and his Common noob on the outside, and on the inside, two complete strangers hooking up."

His face contorted in obvious displeasure. "Is that all I am to you?"

And just like that, I came back to myself, and my fuse fired up. "That's all *I am* to *you*, asshole!" I burst out, tearing my wrist from his grasp as I stepped back. "Why should it matter to you, though? I'm just some random woman you *felt like* giving the Imprint to without any fucking explanations, and you're a fucking Lord who's going to sell me to the highest bidder!"

For the first time since I met him, Ragnor snapped. "Do you really think I *felt like* giving you the Imprint?" he shouted, closing the gap I tried to put between us in two steps. "Do you think I liked throwing you into the deep end of the pool without first teaching you how to swim?"

"*Then why?*" I screamed, pushing at his chiseled, immovable chest. "Why did you do it?"

In a blink, his eyes were glowing the brightest I'd ever seen them. "Because I couldn't fucking control myself!" he bit out, face utterly furious as he grabbed my fisted hands. "Because I saw your pretty hazel eyes, and any and all rational thoughts left me!"

I froze, my eyes widening as I stared at him, shocked. "What?"

An animalistic growl vibrated from his chest to mine as he plastered my front against his. "It's just as I said," he said gravely. "Right from the start, you've been driving me absolutely fucking crazy."

A gasp escaped me, and my heartbeat was in my ears. As I stared at his handsome face with his expression open and fragile for the first time ever, he took my breath away. It was as if I was seeing him for the first time. As if he was a different person—not a vampire Lord but just a man.

For a few moments, I couldn't speak. I was lost in those eyes that showed so many emotions, all of them raw and primitive yet absolutely enthralling. But then I replayed his words and found the words to ask in a soft, weak voice, "Why didn't you tell me everything from the start? That my situation was different, and I was an accidental exception?"

He let my hands go and looked away. I tensed, and for a moment I thought he wouldn't answer, that he would shatter the moment, but then in a barely audible voice, he said, "I didn't want you to know."

My heart stopped.

He let out a rough sigh. "I don't have a good excuse, Henderson," he said, returning his gaze to me. "I was just too pissed off at myself for doing something even stupid young Lords don't do, and I took it out on you."

I opened my mouth, but no words came out. All I could do was return his gaze with mine, trying to find something to say, to show him that I understood now, that I could finally get over this now that he came out and admitted it; then a mechanical voice came from his desk.

"My Lord, Zoey Rittman is here for you."

And just like that, the magical moment we'd just shared was gone. Within one blink and the next, Ragnor's face closed down like a door slamming shut, his eyes no longer a wild yet soothing neon blue but a hard and cold midnight blue.

"Time's up," he said, devoid of any emotion.

But I didn't take it to heart this time. Because I felt the same need to protect myself. To put my walls back up. To put that moment of raw, painful honesty behind me.

So I merely nodded, turned on my heel, and left, feeling that, after his revelation, I would never be the same.

CHAPTER 31
RAGNOR RAYNE

It was hours later when he was finally alone.

Ragnor opened the drawer of his office desk and pulled out a small oil painting portraying a woman, and his eyes moved over every line, every brushstroke. The colors were so vivid that the woman looked almost alive: her bright, fiery red hair softly falling in waves to her waist, her mesmerizing blue eyes looking to the side, a small half-laughing smile on her face, her skin a lovely shade of rose.

She was everything. She would always be everything. And yet another face was etched in his mind, a new face of a broken woman with shattered hazel eyes and long brown hair. She should be nothing. She should always be nothing.

Yet everything in him was urging him to go back, to take her in his arms, to never let her go.

But he couldn't. Not when he'd exposed so much of himself, shown his vulnerability in a way he hadn't done in centuries.

He recalled that night, that fateful night he saw Aileen Henderson hiding behind the trash bins. It was as though he'd been possessed; he was supposed to kill her, not give her the Imprint. But he couldn't help himself. He lost any sense of control and simply acted.

He'd tried keeping his distance from her. He'd tried to treat her like anyone else, but how could he when she was everything he saw when he closed his eyes?

Telling her some of the truth hadn't been the plan. But she'd pushed him, and at that moment, he wanted her to understand. He wanted to erase that look of desperation mixed with disgust from her eyes.

He glanced down at the portrait once more before closing his eyes. In truth, none of that mattered, not really. He'd made his bed and now had to lie in it, because that girl was not his.

There could only be one for him.

Ragnor opened his eyes, and instead of his office, he recalled that image from an eon ago, when the red hair sprawled across the marble floor, floating on a pool of blood, the pale body lifeless, the blue eyes opened and empty.

A knife twisted in his chest. Yes, none of that mattered. Aileen . . . didn't matter.

And so he made an oath. "I will never forget you again, Yulia."

CHAPTER 32

An ominous, foreboding cloud hung over the classroom when Abe arrived, his face stiff as he walked in and stopped to lean against his desk, staring at us grimly. "The Auction is tomorrow," he said as if we didn't know that already. "And it's time to wrap up this course."

No one responded. Everyone's faces were drawn with tension. I felt the same too. The Auction we'd all been waiting for and dreading was finally less than twenty-four hours away.

And I still didn't have a plan.

"Everything you've learned here will serve you no matter where you end up," Abe said quietly, shifting somewhat uncomfortably. "You'll be an asset to any Lord who welcomes you into their League."

Zoey raised her hand, and I realized it was shaking. Abe nodded for her to speak. "Will you be there?" she asked, her voice tiny and scared, very much unlike her usual strong, flamboyant one. "You and Logan, I mean."

Abe's face softened a bit at the quiet question. "Yes, Rittman. We'll be there."

"Who else's coming?" Jakob asked, glowering at the floor.

"Well." Abe interlocked his fingers. "The Lord and his Lieutenants, of course. Other Lords will be flying over, all of whom you've met already. They'll come with their own Lieutenants, newcomers for sale, and a few other VIP League members." He paused and seemed to think about something before he added, "There will be many spectators."

The class fell silent again. Abe gave us a concerned look that seemed genuine. "I've been in your spot before," he said suddenly, drawing the attention back to him. "I, too, was once put up for Auction."

He gave us a smile that I thought was meant to be reassuring but came out somewhat sour. "I don't have any special advice to give you," he said quietly. "All I can say is that as long as you give it your all, you won't have any regrets."

Abe meant well, I knew that, but this statement made me feel beyond irritated considering everything Jada, CJ, and Bowen had told me. "That's not really true, though, is it?" I said defiantly.

Abe's head snapped to me; his eyes were broad with surprise. "And why is that?"

"I heard what happens if no one bids on us," I said tartly. My classmates turned to look at me now, and the tension in the room rose.

"Whatever you heard, Aileen, you can rest assured it won't come to pass," Abe said hastily when he realized he was losing the others.

But I hated that he was trying to put everyone at ease while they were blind to what screwing up our Auction performance meant. And yet when I opened my mouth, Abe's gaze sharpened, and he mouthed something to me that looked suspiciously like *Don't say it*.

Glancing at the faces of my classmates, I paused. They looked on the brink of losing it. Even though most of them had their routines ready, they were all terrified of what tomorrow would bring.

Telling them would only make them feel worse.

Pursing my lips, I folded my arms and looked away, deflating. Nothing about this Auction was fair. Nothing about being a vampire was fair.

I couldn't stop thinking about what Ragnor had told me about why he gave me the Imprint. And now, his words were driving me mad instead of making me feel happy and confident about tomorrow. All I felt was terror and an anxiousness that I could barely contain as I wondered whether Ragnor would buy me tomorrow.

It seemed no one was in the mood to talk anymore after my little outburst, and so Abe said, "We'll end it here. But before you go," he added, and his eyes scanned the class, while a rare, sad smile curled his lips. "You've done well, and I wish you nothing but success."

The Comprehensive Newcomer Three-Month Course ended then. There would be no more classes with Abe teaching us about our new existence. There would be no more gym classes with Logan. And soon, there would no longer be job assignments.

Doomsday was upon us, and we would either survive . . . or face a fate worse than hell.

"Aah, Aileen," Jada said, grinning as she passed the plates she'd rinsed for me to dry. "I'll miss washing dishes with you."

"You never know," I murmured, not feeling the cheery vibe. "I might be right back here in two days."

CJ, who was wiping the counter next to us, snorted. "I highly doubt it," he said, and when I glanced at him, he gave me a somewhat pitying look. "I heard the Lord's thinking of selling every noob this time."

"*I* heard he's going to buy that little long-haired one, though," said Bowen, who was cutting vegetables on the island before us. "Rumor has it Lieutenant Magnus has his eye on her, and you know how he gets when he wants someone."

"Filthy business, the Auction," Jada muttered, her grin gone, as she grabbed more filthy dishes to wash. "The entire thing's all decided from the start, and everyone's pretending otherwise."

"This is true," CJ said quietly. "But don't worry, Aileen." He gave me an encouraging smile. "I'm sure that you'll do great."

"Unless Lord Renaldi buys her," Bowen murmured and received a slap to his head from Jada. "Hey!"

Jada scowled at him warningly before turning to me. "Here's something that might cheer you up," she said, eyes suddenly light and an amused grin on her lips. "I heard some people think that our Lord's taken a lover, so perhaps now that he's getting some for the first time in God knows how long, he might be in a much better mood."

I didn't stop what I was doing and forced my face to remain impassive. But my heart was fluttering, panicked, in my chest.

Ragnor and I hadn't had sex after our confessions in his office a few days ago. He hadn't sought me out, and I'd been locking myself in the workshop, trying to no avail to find something good to paint for the Auction.

Not seeing him had only added to my hysteria. I wanted him to embrace me and make me forget the Auction was happening. I wanted him to tell me he wouldn't let anyone buy me. I wanted him to lay my worries to rest.

Yet a dreadful feeling I couldn't shake told me not to keep my hopes up.

"Getting some doesn't mean you turn over a new leaf," CJ retorted dryly, drawing me out of my dark thoughts. "Though perhaps you're right. Maybe mystery girl is more than a fuck buddy too—"

"Don't be stupid," Jada cut him off with an eye roll. "Have you forgotten what he told Lissia?"

I froze. "Who's Lissia?" I asked, maintaining a bored yet somewhat disinterested tone that didn't show what was going on inside me. Because I was feeling many things, and none of them were good.

"His former lover," CJ replied before turning to Bowen. "But it's been over thirty years ago. Surely, he must've changed his mind."

The green monster reared its head. "What did he tell Lissia?" I pressed.

There was a pause before Jada sighed and said, "He told her not to expect love from him," she said gloomily, "because he already gave his heart to another many centuries ago."

The mug I held crashed to the ground.

Ragnor had been in love?

I didn't know why I was shocked. Logic dictated that he must've had relationships in the past—he was older than dirt, after all. It would've been weirder if he had never had any relationships.

But knowing it and hearing about it were two different things. And suddenly, I felt my resolve shattering to pieces.

The rest of my last kitchen shift passed in a blur. Jada had stolen a bottle of old scotch from the kitchen cupboard and had us raise a goodbye toast for me.

Normally, I would've enjoyed it—I liked the dishwashing crew the best out of all other vampires in the Rayne League, to be honest—but my mind was full of so many thoughts and my heart full of so many emotions that everything ironically became dull, numb, and empty.

Once the shift ended, I bid the dishwashing team one last goodbye and left feeling so out of sorts that when I took the escalator down, I didn't notice a certain man waiting near the end of the escalator until he said, "Aileen."

I raised my head and saw Logan. He was standing in the dimly lit hallway, wearing his usual training gear. His black hair glistened; his turquoise eyes narrowed when I came to a stop before him. "Logan," I said quietly, and it took me a moment to register that something was wrong. "Why are you talking to me?"

After our conversation almost three months ago, he never sought me out, and I never bothered approaching him either. He wanted us to be strangers, and unlike Cassidy, who argued I was beneath her, Logan had every right to ask that of me.

So what changed? And why now?

Logan gave me a pitying look. "Because, unlike you, I'm not a heartless asshole."

I couldn't help but wince, guilt crawling up my insides and gnawing at my conscience. "What are you talking about?"

He jutted his chin toward the room to the left, and I followed him inside. It was the Common vampires' residential lounge. I hadn't been there before—the lounge was a place for social gatherings, and I was invited to none of those—but it looked like what I imagined: sofas were scattered throughout the room, there was a bar near the other end, and a large TV screen was in front of a seating area full of cushions, near which stood table games, from table soccer to billiards.

Since it was almost morning, and tomorrow the Auction would occur, the lounge was empty, which made the room seem much bigger but also stifling.

I was here with Logan, after all.

Logan came to a stop in the middle of the room and turned to me. "Margarita knows," he said, voice loaded.

I came to a stop as well; his words caught me by surprise. I was about to ask what she knew when Logan gritted his teeth and bit out, "About the affair between our Lord and . . ." Disgust filled his face when he spat, "*You.*"

Tensing, I stared at him. He seemed as if he wanted to be anywhere else but here, and that begged the question, Why did he bother? It couldn't be just because of his conscience. How could he even have one when it came to me?

But more prominent was the question, How did Margarita know? I knew she suspected something was going on, but it wasn't like she had concrete proof.

"Why are you telling me this?" I asked, grateful that my voice remained steady. Did Ragnor know she knew?

He looked at me as if I was stupid. "She'll ruin you, if she hasn't already," he said slowly, his eyes searching my face with evident distaste. "You don't want Margarita Wallen as an enemy, Aileen."

Too late for that, I thought, recalling her spiteful provocation a few days ago. And that was bad. Because Margarita was a Lieutenant for a reason. She had some sort of a Gift—all Lieutenants were Gifted, like all Lords were Sacred, after all. Making an enemy out of someone like that wasn't my wisest move.

Not that my affair with Ragnor was wise either.

Yet Ragnor, while frustrating in different ways, at least didn't have it out for me like she did.

I studied Logan. There was urgency written on his face that he was desperately trying to hide, and that put me on high alert immediately, erasing any lingering thought I still had from before. "She's planning to do something to me," I concluded, a chill slithering through my blood.

His lips thinned. "I know Margarita like I know my own hand," he said in a low tone. "She didn't have to say it, but I *know*. I know the way she thinks. She's probably known of your affair with our Lord for a while now, and she's simply waiting for the right moment to strike."

Learning he was so close to Margarita made me mad. Didn't he have any self-preservation? Why was he so determined to self-sabotage? Because Margarita was nasty. Maybe not as nasty as I was to him but malicious enough.

I'd lost my right to question Logan about anything, though. So instead, I thought of what he'd just told me, thought of the Auction, and offhandedly said, "She has a flair for dramatics, doesn't she?"

Logan's face was grim. "I'd be careful tomorrow if I were you."

My heart drummed in my chest. Tomorrow was going to be brutal with or without Margarita's intervention. I was still out of ideas as to what to paint. My relationship with Ragnor and my future in this League were still up in the air. My nerves were already fried, to the point I was beyond hysterical.

Hell, after learning from Jada earlier that Ragnor used to have someone he loved . . . did I even *want* to stay in this League?

I'd been to the other Leagues—apart from that last one in Oregon, but still, I'd met most of the Lords. The only one who seemed remotely close to Ragnor in terms of power, wealth, and strong leadership skills was Atalon, and yet he rubbed me the wrong way. Then there was

Renaldi, who was probably the worst Lord of the lot. From Ragnor's interactions with O'Brien, Daugherty, and Bowman, they were far less influential, even despite Bowman being in charge of all the vampiric Society's finances and legalities.

In one of the CNC classes, Abe had told us that the Rayne League's main source of income was worldwide real estate holdings. Without getting into detail, Abe had said the Rayne League owned several properties in every major city in the world, and that alone let me understand the League must be extremely well off.

In addition to the financial status of the Rayne League, Ragnor was a well-respected Lord. Most of the other Lords went out of their way to accommodate him in their League.

I also couldn't shake what the dishwashing crew had told me before too: *Out of all seven Lords, our Lord isn't just the best leader but the most fair, respected, and strong. You've got to make our Lord buy you. For your own sake.*

Logan pulled me out of my frantic thoughts when he passed by me, heading to the lounge's exit. "How does she know?" I asked, panicked that he was leaving without another word. Because I needed to know how Margarita found out about Ragnor and me. I needed to be prepared for whatever stunt she'd pull tomorrow.

He paused and turned to me with an almost vicious smirk on his face. "You two weren't as discreet as you may think."

I remembered that time, while doing the deed, Ragnor and I were interrupted by a crash in the hallway. He went to check if someone was out there and didn't see anyone, and I forgot about it. But someone must've been there. Someone must've seen, either Margarita herself or someone else who tattled to her.

I'd been distracted by everything that was going on; stuff I should've noticed was coming to bite me in the fucking ass.

"I said my piece," Logan now said, smirk gone and an emotion I couldn't decipher in his eyes. "Make sure to watch your back, and good luck. I mean it."

I stared at him in shock. *I thought you hated me,* I wanted to say, but instead, I lowered my head, took a deep breath, and, without looking at him, quietly said, "Thank you."

"I don't need your gratitude," he snapped, and my eyes flashed back up to his face. He gave me a loathing look that made me visibly flinch. "All I care about is that you'll disappear soon enough and I won't have to see you ever again."

Not for the first time, I wondered how my life would've gone on if I hadn't followed Cassidy out that night. Would Skye have kept in touch after Cassidy disappeared? Would I have found other superficial people to hang out with? Would I have worked at the grocery store for the rest of my life?

Maybe I could've found someone to date. Perhaps I would've gotten a raise. Maybe I would've found something else to do with my life, found my purpose, and worked in some big corporation and earned the big bucks. I was only twenty-one. I'd had my whole life ahead of me. I could've been free and successful, maybe, if given the chance.

I'd never taken my freedom for granted, not after the incarceration of my father or the childhood I had. Yet even though I tried to protect it at all costs, it was still stolen away from me by the one person I found myself inexplicably drawn to.

And tomorrow, I was going to be sold off by the same man I wanted beyond reason, as if I was nothing but cattle.

A large, warm hand wrapped around my shin gently, making me jolt and sit up straight on the cushioned sofa in the lounge. I snapped my head up, and when midnight blue eyes met mine, I realized Ragnor was crouching before me, his brows furrowed. "You should go to sleep," he said as his hand rubbed up and down my shin as though he was trying to give me comfort.

But I didn't have it in me to accept that. I was emotionally spent and physically exhausted. Nothing could cure me of the numbness spreading inside me. It felt like I was mourning the death of my old life for the first time since I became a vampire, and receiving comfort from anyone, especially Ragnor, was beyond me at the moment.

His hand dropped when I didn't speak, and he moved to sit down next to me. "Are you all right?" he asked, voice low as he wrapped his arm around my shoulders.

As though my body knew what I needed before I did, I leaned against him and buried my face in his chest in response. He pulled me closer, embracing me to him, and leaned against the back of the couch, cradling me in his muscular, warm arms.

It wasn't about comfort. It was about human touch. And it felt good. So, so good. *Too* good. But my self-preservation had taken the back seat for now, and I burrowed deeper into him while he simply held me in silence.

It's an illusion, the voice of reason whispered in my head. *He doesn't care about you. He just uses you, like you once used Logan. He won't ever be yours.*

The thought made me wince, my heart dropping in my chest. I tried to pull away, but Ragnor's arms tightened around me. "It's okay," he murmured, his lips brushing against the top of my head. "Let me."

But it wasn't okay, was it? Because the man I was leaning against, the man whose arms I was finding solace in, was the very same one who'd brought me here and stolen everything from me, whatever his reasons, or lack thereof, had been, and who might be planning to sell me tomorrow to the highest bidder.

And yet I'd had sex with him multiple times. I jumped his bones thoughtlessly, blinded by lust and the absurd attraction that sizzled and was still crackling between us. I didn't bother to stop and think; instead, I succumbed to the feeling of being wanted. *Needed.*

I didn't need a therapist to tell me that was supremely fucked up.

So I pushed at his chest until he reluctantly let me go, then rose to my feet. "You're selling me tomorrow," I said as I stared at the wall ahead. Because by this point, I had the sinking feeling it wasn't even a question.

He didn't reply.

I would've laughed if my situation wasn't so bleak. "Then I guess nothing's okay after all."

He stood up and grabbed my wrist, pulling me back to him. "It's not that simple," he said quietly as his hand gently held my chin, tilting my head toward him. "You have to understand that."

"You don't see me as special," I gritted out. "What we have is just sex, isn't it?"

"That's not true," he said quietly, squeezing me to him. "Just accept this comfort, Aileen. It doesn't have to mean anything."

Something inside me broke. "Comfort should be given out of care, not out of pity."

I felt his chest rumble as he tensed. "I told you, it's not that simple—"

"I call bullshit," I cut him off, fury cleaving through my numbness like a knife. I shoved his hands away and stepped back, glaring at him. "You're a fucking Lord. You can buy whoever you want. It's not like anyone else has a say about it."

His eyes flashed and his lips pursed. He opened his mouth to say something but hesitated. Then he looked away, seemingly torn. And that was an answer all by itself.

I stepped back and feigned a smile. "I see, my Lord," I said without an ounce of irony, and his eyes snapped back to me, glowing and full of emotions I could not acknowledge. "All I hope for is that you sell me to a good League."

He took a step toward me and raised his hand as if to reach out to me, but I held out my own hand, silently begging him to stop. "*Good night*, my Lord," I said emphatically, giving him a deep, tense bow, before I fled the room.

CHAPTER 33

The day of the Auction had finally come.

It felt like the entire Rayne League had been waiting anxiously for this day, and so all non-Auction activities came to a grinding halt. The hallways were empty. The gym was deserted. Everyone was either in the cafeteria for breakfast or making some last-minute arrangements.

As for me, all I could think about was that Auction Day was no longer a distant threat.

It was here.

And it was then that I remembered one important detail. I had forgotten to get a recommendation from Lon. And if I wasn't already panicked enough, my fate was now sealed with that one mistake.

After looking everywhere for Lon and not being able to find him, I entered the cafeteria to try and grab some breakfast even though hunger eluded me, what with my stomach tied in so many knots that I felt sick.

After putting some *spaghetti aglio e olio* on my plate, I was about to grab a seat at one of the single tables when Zoey waved from her table with the rest of our classmates and called, "Aileen! Today we're all eating together!"

All right, then.

I took a seat next to Tansy and Zoey, with the rest of my soon-to-be-former classmates; put my plate on the table; and began eating. I didn't feel like talking, and no one seemed interested in hearing my voice as they continued speaking among themselves, so I just listened in, trying to gather some info while I was at it.

"I heard the Lord has been busy this past week," Bryce now said. "I wonder if he's going to show up for the Auction—"

"Of course he is," Jakob cut him off with an eye roll. "Remember what Abe said a couple of weeks ago? The Auction is about hosting other vampire Lords from different Leagues. I doubt our Lord would want to leave so many Lords in his territory without his personal supervision."

Tansy seemed to tune in to the conversation just then since her head whipped toward Jakob, her huge eyes surprisingly lucid as she said, "Don't you think it's a form of human trafficking?"

Everyone turned to stare at her. Zoey was the one to answer. "It's just the way it is, Tansy, and besides, we're not human anymore."

"But it's wrong," Tansy insisted, her eyes flickering to me. "Right, Aileen?"

I had no idea why she was addressing me specifically, but I answered her, nonetheless. "You're right. It is wrong, and it is unfair," I said. "But alas, you knew what you were signing up for when you got yourself put on the waiting list." Which was a luxury I, on the other hand, didn't have.

"None of us knew about the Auction until we actually became vampires, Aileen." Zoey sent me a pointed look.

"Well, I wouldn't know," I said, shrugging, anger unfolding inside my gut. "Since I was never on that list to begin with."

Everyone snapped their heads toward me now. "What do you mean, you were never on the list?" Jakob asked, his eyes narrowed.

I looked at my classmates. They seemed disturbed by what I just shared. But I was through with keeping this to myself. It's not like I had anything left to lose. So I told them, "My circumstances are different than yours. I was in the wrong place at the wrong time, and so I was given the Imprint without my consent."

They seemed to stare at me like they'd never seen me before. "You're kidding," Zoey said, searching my face for humor, and when she found none, she seemed stunned.

Jakob gave me a pitying look. "Must've been rough," he said quietly. "But hey, Auction aside, being a vampire is far better than remaining human." He gave me an encouraging smile. "You should consider your-self lucky."

I looked away; under the table, my hands curled into fists. He thought I was lucky? What part of this whole shitty situation was lucky? What if I *wanted* to stay human so that at least I would know my life didn't have just a beginning but also an end? What if I wanted to work at a grocery store and be my friends' punching bag forever?

This whole thing would've been tolerable if I at least knew what Ragnor was thinking. But I didn't. He barely admitted he'd lost control that night at the alley. He refused to tell me whether he planned on buying me in the Auction.

He never made you any promises, Aileen, the voice of reason whis-pered in my head, making my heart drop and my throat choke. *He never told you he wanted you.*

No. He never told me that. Could I really blame him, though? I was the furthest from a good woman. My very being would forever be tainted by my past sins. My soul would always be lacking. I would forever be my father's creation.

Perhaps I would be better off in another League after all. At least then I would spare Ragnor from finding out he'd slept with a monster.

I put away the brush and stared at the canvas I'd painted black in a fit of frustrated rage. My cheeks were still wet from the mix of perspiration and tears, but I had no energy to wipe them clean as I leaned back and stared at the workshop ceiling.

I can't do this.

A desperate, defeated part of me urged me to try to run away. But I couldn't, not when the elevator would only open with a handprint installed into the system.

There was nowhere to hide either. I'd seen guards patrolling the hallways on my way to the workshop after breakfast. They would be able to find me no matter where I went.

Even if in the unlikely event I managed to run away, did I want to live as a Leagueless vampire? I didn't know anything about the dangers waiting outside. That one time I got kidnapped by those men in Vegas was enough to tell me I was too ignorant and helpless at the moment to fend for myself.

If only I had a concrete plan, an idea as to what to paint, anything, really . . .

I hurled the canvas at the wall and bit down a scream. I rose to my feet and kicked the easel, knocking it to the side. I went to the thick pile of canvases and started searching them, tossing some aside as I literally fished for any inspiration.

But all my paintings were just not good enough. They were abstract and obscure. They had no deeper meaning. Even just for show, none of them had any appeal.

When I reached the bottom of the pile, I paused, staring at the first canvas I'd painted during the assessment class, with the scars and the four words aimed at Margarita. *He'll never be yours,* the painting said.

And I suddenly felt the impact of the words as if they were aimed at me, and I gasped, falling to my knees as fresh new tears rose to my eyes. Shakily, I grabbed the canvas and stared at the words, reading them over and over again, each time more torturous than the one before, until I no longer needed to.

The words were now etched in my mind.

Ragnor would never be mine. He'd given his heart away to someone else, after all.

So why was I agonizing over all this?

Because you don't want to be tied *to one Lord for the rest of eternity,* the voice of reason said, returning with a vengeance. *Because you don't want to be stuck in a position of utter helplessness. You promised yourself to never go back to that, Aileen. You promised yourself that you'd never again be a spectator but take charge of your life.*

Was that taking charge, however? Being Imprinted and now put up for Auction? How the hell was that considered taking charge?

I put the canvas away and buried my head in my hands. I took a shuddered breath, swallowed my tears, and forced myself to get ahold of my emotions. I had run out of time for tears, regrets, and resentment. All I could do now was grab another canvas and get to work once more.

Yet as I tried to rally myself into actions rather than words, my despair refused to leave and weighed so heavily on my body that I kept sitting on the workshop floor, surrounded by painted canvases and a fallen easel, unable to find the way out from the pit of hopelessness that burrowed deep into my core.

It took me fifteen minutes of searching my packed suitcase to find my one and only dress: a gray, sleeveless summer dress that reached my knees. I hadn't worn it since I was maybe sixteen, but when I put it on, it seemed to fit, albeit a tad tighter around the chest than before.

I paired it with black synthetic-leather boots since they were the least worn out of my shoes, and I pulled my hair into a wavy ponytail that flowed down to the middle of my back. As for makeup, I applied simple black eyeliner and light red lipstick.

With my emotions utterly drained, I found that I didn't care much that my attire was too casual for the event or that my chest, which had grown since the last time I wore the dress, was far too prominent in the tight cloth than I would've originally liked.

Stepping out of my bedroom into the suite's living room, I saw Zoey and Tansy waiting near the door. Much like me, Tansy wore a casual, flowery dress with simple sandals, and she'd let her strawberry blonde hair down, which meant it reached the backs of her knees. Her face was makeup-free.

Zoey, however, seemed ready for a gala event. She wore an off-white wide-leg jumpsuit with only one strap. Silver sparkles decorated the cloth, making her olive skin pop. She wore heavy makeup and even contact lenses that turned her brown eyes a fake gray, and her hair was pinned in a complicated braided bun that gave her a somewhat regal look.

When they saw me, Zoey was the first to speak. "You're packed?"

I nodded jerkily. "Yeah. Did you wait for me?"

Before Zoey could speak, Tansy took a step forward. "It was my idea that we would all leave together," she said, giving me a surprisingly lucid gaze. "It's the last time we'll be suitemates."

She was right; tonight, we would either leave to a new League, never to be back again, or we would stay. Either way, our time as suitemates, short and distant as it had been, was coming to an end.

Zoey let out a heavy sigh. "I can't believe it's been three months already," she said and turned to me with a sad smile. "I'm sorry for everything, Aileen."

Through the cold numbness, I felt surprised by the sudden apology. "For what?" I asked, baffled.

"For treating you like an outcast," she clarified, shaking her head in what seemed like self-reprimand. "Especially when you were thrust into this whole thing unprepared."

A pang of annoyance made me clench my hands. I didn't want her pity. "That's fine," I said flatly. "I understand, you know."

"But that's not who I am," Zoey said, leaning against the wall. "In any case, I hope today will go well for you."

She seemed to be sincere, and that made my annoyance leave, followed by the returning numbness. "Thanks. You too."

"I also would like to say something," Tansy suddenly spoke, more serious than I'd ever heard her, and turned to face me. "Meeting you has been enlightening, Aileen," she said, and I felt yet another wave of surprise splitting the dullness. "I never expected to meet you here of all places."

My surprise turned into full-on alarm. "What do you mean?" I asked, taking a step toward her as I felt my insides twisting up.

She shook her head and turned to the door. "Nothing," she said airily, sounding more like the Tansy I knew. "We need to go."

Before I could ask her about it, she threw the door open and left. Zoey glanced at me, seemingly just as confused, before following her out.

I knew that lingering on what Tansy said wouldn't do me any good, not now when the Auction was merely minutes away, so I sucked in a deep breath, forced my thoughts away, and exited the suite, closing that part of my new existence as a vampire behind me.

CHAPTER 34

The first stage of the Auction, the Exhibition, took place in the ballroom near the auditorium where the second and third stages would be held—the Blessing and the Auction itself.

The ballroom seemed to be taken straight out of some Dracula movie. Unlike the rest of the Rayne League underground compound, which seemed to be relatively modern in terms of architecture and design, the ballroom looked like it was built in the Gothic era. Large windows stretched from the ribbed vaults down to the dark marble floor. Lit from behind, their blue and purple stained glass created a flower pattern that was extremely pretty. It also added to the vampiric look, with all those present being actual honest-to-God vampires. At one end of the room, there was a bar that served blood and other drinks, and there was also a buffet with all types of nibbles on offer, from antipasti to nutty, chocolate ones.

Guests roamed the room, chattering, drinking, and nibbling. I had no sense for fashion, but even I could tell that the dresses and elaborate jumpsuits were designer brands and the three-piece suits were personally tailored. We newcomers—not just from the Rayne League but the others as well—stuck out like sore thumbs in this crowd; none of us wore clothes remotely close to that level. Not even Zoey in her sparkly jumpsuit.

Which was why it was easy for the Lords and their Lieutenants to spot the newcomers for some casual meetups.

The moment Zoey, Tansy, and I entered the already packed ball-room, Stefan, Lord Renaldi's Lieutenant from Vegas, approached us and looked at Zoey. "Please come with me, Miss Rittman."

Zoey seemed to recognize Stefan as well. She tensed but nodded and followed him into the crowd.

I doubted Zoey wanted to talk to Renaldi, but during one of the last lessons with Abe, he told us it was in our best interest to agree to talk with every Lord who wanted to chat us up. None of us wanted to get on any Lord's bad side by refusing to interact with them.

Once Zoey was gone, I turned to talk to Tansy, but I saw she was already a few feet away talking to a tall, brown-skinned woman with slanted eyes and extremely lush lips. She was wearing a bright-red three-piece suit that was evidently designer, and her dark, wavy hair elegantly fell over her shoulder. I didn't recognize her as any of the Lords' Lieutenants, and from the way she held herself—straight, squared shoulders, her chin high and proud—I wondered if she was Lady Kalama from the Kalama League in Oregon, the only one I hadn't visited during the field trip.

Since no one had sought me out yet, I used my marginal freedom and made a beeline to the bar. Some aperitifs were placed on the bar, and I grabbed one of them, hoping it was strong enough to tamp down my rising anxiety.

"Calm down," I muttered to myself as I leaned against the bar and watched the crowd. I caught sight of Lord Atalon's platinum hair and saw he was speaking to an unfamiliar newcomer—probably one from another League. The Lord was wearing a classic white tux with a red tie and highly polished black dress shoes. With his pitch-black eyes, ivory skin, fair hair, and sharp cheekbones, he looked better than I remembered. In fact, looking at his face, I thought he was rather handsome in a clean-cut kind of way.

Averting my gaze from him, I sipped my drink—some sort of cranberry cocktail tinged with AB-positive blood—and then saw Jakob. He was talking to Lord Bowman from the banking League, animatedly with exaggerated hand motions, but Bowman simply stared at him, face bored—though, to be fair, Bowman's face always seemed as if he wasn't even interested in himself.

I was about to take another sip when a flash of red hair suddenly appeared from the crowd, heading in my direction. I tensed, slowly taking the glass down, when I saw it was Margarita walking toward me.

As much as I hated her, I couldn't help but admit that she looked hot in a black, ankle-length skintight dress and extremely high black heels. She wore gold bracelets and matching earrings, and her wild red curls were tamed into a half-up, half-down do. Her face, too, was prettier than usual, with smoky eye makeup and cherry red lipstick.

She stopped before me. In her heels, she managed to top me by more than five inches. "Henderson," she said, a smirk on her haughty face.

Tersely, I gave her a curt nod and nothing more.

That aggravating smirk of hers widened. "I hope you are prepared," she said, her smirk turning into a nasty grin when I narrowed my eyes. My grip on the glass was so hard that I was half-afraid it would break.

"As if you care," I murmured quietly, staring at her with what I hoped was a blank expression. I refused to let her see just how much she raised my ire.

She snickered. "Of course I do," she said, voice low now as she scanned me from head to toe. What she saw made her eyes light up smugly. "I want to see you fail, after all."

Do not slap the bitch . . . Do not slap the bitch . . .

"But it seems I was worried for naught." She chuckled evilly as she pointedly looked at my dress before raising her eyes to my face. "It seems my wish to witness you not being bought will come true after all."

As I struggled to keep my anger in check, I studied her face. Yesterday, Logan had hinted to me she was cooking something up. What the hell could it be?

I got my answer a moment later when a menacing man built like a tank cut through the crowd. He was wearing a suit—it included black trousers and a black blazer—but the wine red shirt underneath the blazer was almost completely unbuttoned, showing off his chiseled, hairy chest inked with a grandiose Chinese dragon. His black tousled hair was messy, as though he'd just rolled out of bed, and his dark eyes were glinting with anticipation.

My body was beyond tense—it was frozen, rigid like stone—as I watched the man, the one and only Lord Renaldi, coming to a stop next to Margarita. "Looking good, Wallen," he said, giving Margarita a once-over so sexual it was a wonder Margarita didn't look uncomfortable.

Quite the opposite, in fact; the Lieutenant gave him a large seductive smile that made me feel sick to my stomach. "Thank you, my Lord," she said, giving him a smoldering look that made him smirk, before motioning toward me. "I wanted to introduce you to the noob I told you about: Aileen Henderson."

As though he only just realized I was there, Lord Renaldi's face snapped toward me, and his eyes widened in satisfaction. "I believe we met, Miss Henderson," he murmured quietly, intimately, as if we'd done more than simply talk back in Vegas. He took a step toward me, making my spine stiffen further, as he raised his hand to brush his knuckles against my cheek. "Though I must admit, I remember you being more . . . *appetizing* last time."

I wanted to gag, but I refused to give Margarita the satisfaction. "It's good to see you, too, Lord Renaldi," I said monotonously, voice tight as the bundle of nerves in the pit of my stomach grew.

He let his hand fall and returned his gaze to Margarita, who was trying to maintain a bland expression but couldn't quite succeed in hiding her triumph. "She's one of a kind, indeed," he said, a secretive smile curling his lips.

"So you've met," Margarita said almost gleefully before she turned to me, so smug and arrogant that I wanted to hit her. "She'll be a good addition to your collection."

It struck me then that Margarita had more than one plan. She didn't just want me to be unbought but if I were to be bought anyway, she wanted the disgusting, sickening Renaldi to buy me.

My heart was beating frantically in my chest as I felt true fear spread through me when Renaldi's eyes roamed up and down my body as though trying to see beneath my dress.

Was that how my father's victims felt?

His chest suddenly filled my sight when he stepped so close to me that he was less than an inch away from touching me. "Let's go somewhere private, Miss Henderson," he murmured quietly into my ear, making the wrong kind of goose bumps rise on my skin as I started to shake.

I heard Margarita's laughter growing distant. She left me with this horrible man without a care in the world.

She wanted him to ruin me before the Auction even started.

When his hands suddenly grabbed my waist and began roaming up the sides of my body and his repulsive, excited breaths were in my ear, I slowly lifted my leg, preparing to give him the strongest kick of my life, but then a familiar voice said, "Our Lord requires your presence, Aileen."

My eyes widened in shock, while Lord Renaldi let out a dissatisfied sigh. "I'll find you later, then," he murmured before he stepped back, gave me a promising grin, and left.

Then I turned to Cassidy, who'd just saved me from committing suicide.

"It's going to fall," Cassidy said with a scowl as she took the aperitif from my shaky hand and put it on the bar. She then grabbed my wrist and dragged me to the back of the room, where it was far less crowded.

I was so shocked that I hadn't resisted her hold, and when she let me go and faced me, it all finally sank in.

What Margarita had done.

What Renaldi almost had done.

What Cassidy was currently doing.

My eyes took in the sight of Cassidy wearing a surprisingly modest green maxi dress and silver high heels, then her pretty face with her pretty emerald eyes, and I blurted, "Why?" *Why did you help me?*

Because Ragnor couldn't have sent her to fetch me. If he wanted to talk to someone, he just did.

She folded her arms and looked away. "To settle the score," she replied somewhat bitterly.

I wasn't following. "Why do *you* need to settle a score with *me?*" I asked incredulously.

Shifting from foot to foot, Cassidy stared at the ground, gritted her teeth, and said in a strained voice, "You saved me from similar situations. I felt like I owed you." She then shot me a glare. "I'm not helpless, Aileen. I've never been. And yet, you couldn't help yourself trying to save me from Austin, just like you tried to save me from our Lord that night in the alley. Did it ever occur to you that I was with Austin because I wanted to be? That I stayed with him because I was getting something out of it?"

Shocked, all I could do was stare at her. "What could you possibly have been getting from an asshole who abused you? Beat you?"

Cassidy's lips curled. "Forget it. You don't know everything about me, Aileen."

"Then tell me, Cassidy," I said, ire rising. "How could you stay with someone like that?"

From the way she suddenly seemed uncomfortable, the slight tremble of her lips, and the refusal to meet my eye, I knew I wasn't going to like her answer. And I was right, because she said, "Austin's a vampire. He's the reason Ragnor saved me. He's the reason I'm here, Aileen."

My lips parted. What the actual fuck?

She shook her head at me and folded her arms. "He's a Leagueless. He introduced me to the world of vampires. He helped me sign up for the waiting list. He tipped Ragnor off about me. He did everything for me." She paused, refusing to meet my eyes. "And you butting in almost risked everything. Still . . ." She paused, letting her arms drop. "You had good intentions. So just say thank you and leave me be from now on."

I was absolutely stunned. It never occurred to me that there had been anything more to her relationship with Austin. I also never thought that she kept track of my attempts to help her out, since that's not what our friendship had been all about. It was about me being her friend, protecting her from herself, and in the end, I lost my humanity when I thought I was trying to save her life. It was never a give-and-take relationship. It was always about one side being constantly on the receiving end. Just as I wanted it.

I never kept a record of how many times I helped her so that she could pay me back in the future. It was something I just did because I cared about her. Because I wanted her to be safe and happy.

And instead, she remained in contact with her abusive ex. She saw me as an obstacle to her goal of becoming a vampire. She never saw me as anything more than both a convenience and an inconvenience in one.

But none of that mattered. Not now that we were no longer friends.

So all I could say was "Thank you" in a bitter voice.

Her eyes snapped toward me; she hadn't expected that, I could tell. She opened her mouth like she wanted to say something before she seemed to regret it and looked away again. "Sure," she murmured.

Awkward silence spread between us as we both seemed to struggle with our emotions. In the end, however, Cassidy mumbled something about being needed elsewhere and fled the uncomfortable reality that was our former friendship.

CHAPTER 35

After Cassidy's departure, I roamed the room aimlessly, observing the guests and hoping no Lord would engage me in some sort of conversation.

The Auction guests consisted of the seven Lords, their plus-ones and Lieutenants, special attendees from each League, and many of the Rayne League's leadership and Troop members (or so I was told—I didn't know anyone from the Troop)—and that was without counting the fifteen newbies each League brought along.

Needless to say, the ballroom was packed.

Which was why I managed to avoid conversing with anyone.

After my encounters with Margarita, Renaldi, and Cassidy, any patience or friendliness I had was used up. Now I was a ball of anxiety and nerves, and I felt like the room was closing in on me, the horribly familiar feeling of suffocation wrapping itself around my throat, threatening to take root and force me into creating a spectacle.

This was why I kept moving. I needed to stretch my limbs and physically tire myself so the hysteria would go away. Or so I hoped; to be honest, I had no tools to deal with these panic attacks I kept having recently.

In the first year after I left my hometown, I'd seen a therapist. She'd helped me get over some difficult emotions and guided me through the panic attacks I had back then. But these recent attacks had nothing to do with my past and had everything to do with stress causing me to lose my fucking mind.

As the walls began closing in on me with the more people I passed and the closer we got to the Auction itself, the more I began to truly panic. I searched the crowd, no longer content to simply watch but needing to find the one person I wanted—no, *needed*—to see.

Please, I begged silently, my eyes desperately darting from side to side. *Where the fuck are you?*

I reached the other end of the room and paused, and my eyes were drawn like magnets to the man leaning against a thick column. Unlike everyone else, he was dressed in a simple black tee, jeans, and his usual black combat boots as if he hadn't a care in the world. His dark hair was pushed back, and his midnight blue eyes were staring ahead, hard and cold, as a petite woman with long sandy-brown hair, her back to me, seemed to be talking to him.

In my panic, a burst of rage made me see red. How *dare* he flirt with another woman while my future, my life, my *entire fucking existence* was on the line.

And suddenly, I was through with it. *All of it.*

With my hands fisted at my sides, I strode toward Ragnor, baring my teeth in a low growl. He must've sensed my approach, because his head snapped toward me and his jaw locked, the only sign of emotion on his face. He murmured something to the petite woman with him, and she made herself scarce, hurrying toward the bar and leaving the path to Ragnor fucking Rayne open.

I stopped before him, beyond furious, beyond frustrated, and snarled, "It's all because of you."

His face remained impassive, but his eyes flashed. In a quick movement, he grabbed my arm and started walking toward a back door behind the column.

"Let me go!" I yelled, trying to push him off, but his grip tightened, and he kept on walking, dragging me along with him until we were behind the door in what seemed like a liquor cupboard.

Only then, he let go of me and faced me. Our gazes clashed, his growing brighter while mine was becoming far more desperate than furious.

The air became charged, and electricity sparked through my blood, making all the air leave my lungs. His eyes glowed; my stomach filled with knots, and almost simultaneously, we reached for each other, and our mouths collided.

The kiss was frantic and full of urgency. My hands were in his hair, and his arms were around me, one of his hands cradling my head while the other spread over the small of my back, pulling me forward so my front was plastered against his chest.

When his hands were suddenly on my butt, lifting me up so I could wrap my legs around his waist, a voice in the back of my mind whispered, *This isn't right.*

But my body begged to differ, because this felt like the rightest thing in my entire fucking life.

I never wanted it to be over. I wanted it to last forever. There was something between us, something undeniable, but *this* felt like goodbye.

That voice persisted when he tore his lips away from mine and pressed them against my neck while he freed one of his hands in favor of squeezing my breast through the dress, making my thighs clench around him and a heat pool in my panties.

When his fingers were suddenly spreading my slick pussy wide open, the voice screamed, *MAKE HIM STOP! HE'S GOING TO THROW YOU AWAY! DON'T LET HIM DO THIS TO YOU!*

And this time, I listened. "Wait," I breathed out and swallowed a moan when he inserted two fingers inside me and pumped.

"No," he growled, and his lips were suddenly on mine again, taking me so strongly and hotly that I wanted to give in to the blazing inferno between us.

But the voice of reason refused to let up. *He's going to sell you,* it viciously taunted me. *He brought you into this world, and now he's going to discard you like you're nothing.*

"Ragnor," I moaned, conflicted as tension rose deep inside me the more he fucked me with his fingers. I forced his head back and looked at his glowing eyes as he fingered me faster, stronger, rougher. "Ragnor," I whimpered, so broken by what I saw in his eyes. The absolute lust he felt where I was concerned.

This is just it. The voice of reason pushed relentlessly. Cruelly. *All he feels for you is lust and nothing more.*

Who can love a monster, after all?

Those last words finally did it. With tears in my eyes, I tremulously grabbed his wrist and plucked his fingers out of me and my panties. I then pushed at his chest, but he didn't budge. Instead, he cupped my head and brought my eyes to him. "Why?" he asked gruffly, glowing eyes frustrated.

I shook my head, forcing my tears to stay in place. "Step back," I said in a choked voice. "Please, Ragnor, step back and let me go—"

"I can't." He cut me off, his eyes searching mine in what would've seemed like panic on anyone else who wasn't Ragnor Rayne. "Not until you tell me why—"

"How dare you!" I burst out, hitting his shoulders as, despite my efforts, the tears fled my eyes. "You have no right, Ragnor—no fucking right—unless you're willing to promise me you're going to buy me!"

His face darkened, his hands falling from my face to my thighs as he unwrapped my legs from around his waist and set them back on the floor. "Why did you approach me, then?" he asked flatly, but his eyes couldn't quite hide his anger.

Why the fuck was he angry? And more importantly—"I just wanted to talk," I said, and humiliatingly, my voice broke. I looked away from him as I hugged myself. "Am I not allowed that courtesy anymore?"

I could see his hands fisting. "What is there to talk about?" he grated out. "It's the same fucking loop every time, Henderson. You won't tell me anything about yourself, and I don't have the answers you want."

That stung so much that I had to lean on the closed door, my entire body shaking. "That's why you only want sex from me?" I asked, feeling my heart dropping in my chest at the sinking, horrifying realization. "Is that all I'm worth to you?"

He didn't reply, and I didn't need to look at his face to know I was spot on.

I turned around and would've opened the door had Ragnor not put his hand on it, forcing it to remain closed while his front was pasted to my back. "That's what we agreed on," he said, his tone strange as his free arm wrapped around my waist. "That's all we're supposed to be for each other."

I was through talking to him. "Let me go, *my Lord*."

"I don't know if it can change," he said, tightening his hug. "I don't know if *I* can change."

Pain sliced my insides. "Then there's nothing left to talk about—"

"But I want to, Aileen," he said, and the sound of my name on his lips, not my surname, made my breath stick in my throat.

Neither of us spoke for long moments after that. I was still trying to process what he'd just said, what he'd confessed. The pain was still there, but now something else made my insides grow hot. Not anger. Not desperation or frustration.

Hope.

Slowly, I turned around just enough to lock my gaze with his, and as calmly as I could, I said, "Then prove it to me. Buy me in the Auction. Keep me by your side and use me to figure out everything you want."

I didn't wait for a response. I slipped out of his hold, flung open the door, and let myself out; the sound of my drumming heart was all I could hear as I let myself be swallowed by the crowd.

CHAPTER 36

The auditorium seemed larger than ever before now that all the seats weren't empty. From where I was sitting between Tansy and a woman from another League, I took in the sight of the crowded audience, trying to detect where Ragnor and his goons were sitting, but it was too dark for me to do so.

When everyone was seated and claps echoed around the auditorium, I stopped my search and turned to look at the stage. With how dark and big the entire auditorium was, the stage seemed too bright and too tiny. Thinking that soon I would be up there, painting God knows what, made my insides crawl.

A man climbed onto the stage. He was brown skinned and tall with large dark eyes, heavy makeup, and a fancy bright-pink suit. "Good evening, everyone, and welcome to the Auction!" he said into his mic, smiling as everyone clapped again. "I'm Kaylon, and I'll be your host for tonight!"

After another round of applause, Kaylon said, "Now, before we start with the heavy stuff, let's start this party off with some music!" He grinned widely. "Please welcome onstage Rayne League's amazingly Gifted newcomer, Cassidy Jones!"

I stilled as I watched Cassidy walking onstage, holding a mic. Once Kaylon left, the lights turned off, leaving only a beam showcasing Cassidy in all her glory.

Then the background music played, and Cassidy started to sing.

Goose bumps covered my skin as she sang a beautiful song I didn't know. Hearing her angelic, soothing voice was so familiar that I felt like I'd come home, if only for the next few minutes.

Without Fourcorns, that stupidly bad band of hers from before, Cassidy's voice was more beautiful than ever. It felt as though the melody wrapped itself around me, cocooning me like a hot duvet on a cold winter's night. Every note she hit was so lovely that it was like someone caressing my hair before I went to sleep. The vibrations of her voice synchronized with my heart, causing its fast, stressful thumping to slow down into an even, calm tempo.

Cassidy's singing was like a ray of sunshine in the middle of a dark forest. Like feeling truly awake after a good night's sleep. Like finding a rose in the middle of the desert.

When the song came to an end, I felt as though Cassidy had cast a spell on me. Every bit of anxiety I felt disappeared as though it never existed. The hysteria looming in the back of my mind, just waiting to take me under, was gone. Just like magic.

Was that Cassidy's Gift?

A lull spread in the auditorium even after Cassidy got off the stage. But then Kaylon said, "Give a round of applause to Cassidy Jones!" It seemed to snap everyone's attention, and roars and whistles filled the room with utter enthusiasm. The audience loved her.

I loved her at that moment too. If only for the peace of mind she'd brought me when I so needed it, Gift or no Gift.

"And now, without further ado," Kaylon said once everyone calmed down, "I present to you the hosting Lord, Ragnor Rayne, to start with the Blessing!"

Everyone clapped again, some even whistled, as Ragnor climbed up to the stage, his tall, imposing figure seemingly taking over the entire stage.

Kaylon handed him the mic, and Ragnor took it before he said in a flat tone, "Welcome to the Rayne League Quarterly Auction. I'll keep it quick and simple."

His eyes looked down on the first row. He seemed to be looking for someone before he spoke again. "All newcomers in my League showed certain potential, but only one stood out the most." He paused, his gaze seemingly stuck on someone, and then said, "Bryce Sullivan. His supervisors had nothing but praise to say about him, and I believe he will be an asset to any Lord who decides to buy him. To Bryce!"

"To Bryce!" the crowd called.

"Poor Bryce," said the newcomer to my right as Ragnor left the stage, replaced by Lord O'Brien, who started jabbering.

I turned to her. "Isn't it good that he was given the Blessing?" I asked, frowning. It was quite confusing as to why Ragnor had chosen Bryce out of everyone. I would've expected him to choose Zoey or Jakob, who were obviously the stars of our class.

The newcomer gave me a pitying look. "Your CNC instructor told you nothing, did he?"

I didn't appreciate her tone, but I wanted her to talk, so I simply shrugged and said, "Clue me in, then."

She returned her gaze to the stage as she spoke. "Each Lord gives the Blessing to the person he wants to get rid of the most. Whoever this Bryce is, I can't help but feel for them." She sighed. "Being on Lord Rayne's bad side, for whatever reason, can't be good."

We didn't talk after that and instead watched as each Lord gave their Blessing to their "favorite" newcomer. Of course I didn't take what the newcomer next to me said at face value, but I had to admit that it made sense; otherwise, why did Ragnor choose Bryce?

While the Lords were summoned one by one to give their Blessing, two vampires behind me whispered between themselves, loud enough for me to hear.

"It's here," one of them said, awe in his hushed voice. "Do you feel it, Naru?"

The other sounded worried. "I don't feel a thing."

"Strange," the first one murmured. "Perhaps you're not old enough to feel it?"

"You're only three months older than me, Morris," the second one, Naru, replied tartly.

They kept on whispering, but I tuned them out, trying to figure out what they were talking about. What the hell were we supposed to feel?

"Thank you, our Lords, for the wonderful Blessings!" Kaylon's voice returned my attention to the stage. It was Lordless now. "And now it's time for the part you've all been waiting for . . . the Auction!"

Roars and cheers filled the auditorium along with the wild, loud claps. For a moment, I was reminded of the movie *Gladiator*. It seemed as though the vampires in the audience were waiting for blood.

"Now! We'll begin with the Renaldi League—please welcome Helena Tate!" Kaylon shouted excitedly and got off the stage.

A curvy woman in a casual dress walked into the light. Her chestnut brown hair was braided. She took off her white sandals and then took a place in the middle of the stage. Once settled, she closed her eyes and took a deep, shivery breath. She seemed nervous as she drummed her fingers against her thighs, hands held tightly against her sides. She appeared to be praying quietly as her pale skin showed a greenish tint. And when the music began, she was out of time. Suddenly, she launched herself into a dance routine, lost in the music.

"She did the same trick last year too," the woman who was sitting next to me murmured. "Damn Lena, thinking she can run away."

"What are you talking about?" I asked her, frowning. CJ had told me what happened to those who chose to take part in the Auction a second time. Why would this dancer do that?

The woman gave me a scowl that seemed to be directed at someone else. "Every vampire is permitted to participate in an Auction once more after their first Auction. It's the only way to leave your League."

That, I knew. "But what is she trying to run away from?" I asked, grimacing. "Second-timers are fated to become slaves, aren't they?"

Her face clouded. "If you were given the Imprint by Renaldi, you wouldn't mind being any other Lord's slave for a fucking lifetime as long as it meant never being near him ever again."

I didn't need to receive the Imprint from Renaldi to understand *that*.

When Helena finished her dance, Kaylon said into the mic, "Bidding starts now!"

Animated chatters spread throughout the audience. Someone yelled, "Please bid on her, Lord Daugherty!" While another screamed, "Save your cash, Lord O'Brien!"

"I didn't know others could affect the Lords' decision," I murmured, staring at the spectacle behind me.

"They can't," said the annoyed newcomer next to me, who was apparently a second-timer. "The Lords' decisions are theirs alone."

Her words might've been resolute, but her voice was unsure. I could only hope she was right . . . though, maybe, it would be good if others had some sort of a say in it.

Thinking about Margarita, however, made me scrap that last notion.

"Two hundred!" Kaylon called now. "I see three hundred! Do we have three fifty? We have five hundred right there by Lord Renaldi himself! Anyone else? Going once . . . going twice . . . sold right back to Lord Renaldi!"

"Stupid girl," the woman next to me spat.

"I didn't know the Lords could buy their own vampires back for the second time in a row," I said, not commenting on the fact a vampire's life could be worth only five hundred bucks. That seemed so cheap and degrading.

"They can," the woman told me. "And in this case, the Lord is just being a selfish piece of shit."

Afterward, more of the Renaldi League were called to perform. Some of them were bought into different Leagues while others were bought by Renaldi, and the verdict was clear: those who were bought by Renaldi, men and women alike, seemed significantly less relieved than those who weren't.

The last Renaldi League vampire to be auctioned was the woman next to me. When Kaylon called "Isora Harland!" she rose to her feet, her face drawn.

"Good luck," I told her, meaning it.

She gave me an acknowledging nod before she took off.

Isora's act was singing. Unfortunately, Cassidy's earlier performance was still fresh in my mind, and in everyone else's mind, too, because she sounded like a poor downgrade. She'd picked a promising Whitney Houston ballad, and she had a pretty voice, but she couldn't possibly compare to Cassidy, neither in charisma, stage presence, or vocal abilities.

When she was done, she looked at the audience, trembling like a leaf from head to toe.

"Bidding starts now!" Kaylon exclaimed. "I see two hundred . . . two fifty . . . eight hundred by Lord Renaldi!"

Tears filled her eyes, and she shook her head silently, her eyes wide, pleading with the audience.

"Eight hundred going once . . ."

Her lips moved soundlessly. Was she praying?

"Eight hundred going twice . . ."

Her hands held on to one another for dear life.

Until—"We have a thousand from Lord Atalon!"

She froze. My heartbeat kicked up. It felt like everyone held their breath—or was it just me?—while Kaylon began the counting. "Going once . . ."

Please let Atalon buy her, I thought, feeling for the woman. I didn't even know why; it wasn't like I knew her.

But knowing who Renaldi was, I couldn't help but root for her.

"Going twice . . . ," Kaylon continued, and it seemed as if he was drawling on purpose. Didn't he see Isora was about to pass out from stress?

But then Kaylon finally said, "Sold to Lord Atalon!"

And just like that, Isora's knees gave in, and she fell to the floor, bursting out in tears. I couldn't help but clap along with the audience, feeling relieved for her. *Good for you, Isora.*

Since she couldn't move, Kaylon had to help her off the stage. Once he was back, the Auction resumed, and this time, it was the O'Brien League's turn.

As the vampires performed and were bought one after another, I couldn't help but notice that Ragnor hadn't bid on anyone yet.

It seemed that Ragnor really refrained from participating too much in the Auction, despite being its permanent host—since only the Rayne League had an auditorium big enough to hold the event.

One of the performances was a man showing off his robotics skills by introducing us to Tintin, a robot operating on an advanced form of artificial intelligence who was versed in psychology, thus able to act as a therapist (or so he tried to prove hilariously, causing the entire audience to laugh). During this act, Tansy, who'd been sitting quietly on the other side of me since the beginning, suddenly spoke. "Do you think they're here?"

I turned to her and saw she was gazing at the stage, her expression distant. Debating whether I should engage in a conversation with her that was bound to be fruitless, I waited until Tintin and the man left the stage before I asked, "Who's here?"

"Give a round of applause to the O'Brien League!" Kaylon roared, and the audience followed suit. "Now please welcome the newcomers of the Atalon League!"

Tansy's blue doe-like eyes turned to me, clear and wide. "The Morrow Gods."

I stilled, the applause around me transforming into blurry static as I stared at Tansy. With everything that had happened, I had pushed it out of my mind that she knew.

Heart racing, I searched her face as I forced my voice out. "Why . . . how . . . do you know about them?"

She cocked her head, eyes eerily unblinking. "They're here, aren't they?" she said instead of answering me.

My lips parted, and I attempted to talk, but I couldn't. And suddenly, not getting a recommendation from Lon seemed so insignificant compared to this.

When Tansy said nothing else, I pursed my lips and returned my gaze to the stage, my heart in my throat, my anxiety crawling back into my gut with a vengeance. I was so disturbed; I couldn't focus on any performance to save my life.

But time didn't stop, even if for me it did. It kept on moving until Kaylon announced it was the Rayne League's turn.

CHAPTER 37

I watched as Jakob, the first one of our League, took the stage. He was wearing a neat tux, but he was sweating buckets, so much so that, even though his jacket was black, we could still see the sweat patches in his armpits.

Despite his perspiration, which now was even more evident since he discarded the jacket and remained in a white buttoned shirt, Jakob managed to maintain an impassive face. As his music of choice began— "Macarena," of all songs—he started a complicated juggling routine that included twelve balls.

"You can do it, Jakob," I heard Zoey saying. She was sitting not that far away from me, and she was staring at Jakob with a mixture of pride and worry.

As though he heard it, Jakob conjured eight more balls from God knows where and bounced them all repeatedly from the floor back to his hands so fast that they became a blur. He gritted his teeth as he proficiently controlled the balls as though he was a conductor and the balls his orchestra, and when his act came to an end, he somehow caught them all by using the pockets of his pants, his sweaty armpits, his mouth, his bare feet, and his fingers.

The audience didn't need Kaylon's "Give your applause to Jakob Stornsky!" to go wild. I, too, found myself in awe. During the assessment class, I'd seen him juggling only three balls, so I hadn't expected much from him. Yet he'd definitely upped his game in the last month—hell, he completely nailed it.

And the Lords absolutely loved it, judging by their bids. "We have two thousand!" Kaylon screamed, he was so pumped after Jakob's act. "*Three thousand* from Lord O'Brien!"

"The Gods are with him." Tansy's whisper made me freeze. I pretended like I didn't hear her.

"We have three thousand and five hundred from Lady Kalama!" Kaylon called. "Anyone else? No one? You sure about that? Then going once . . . twice . . . *sold*!"

Jakob's shoulders slumped in relief, and he got off the stage with wobbly legs. Like all the others who'd already performed, he did not return to his seat.

Next was Bryce. After Jakob's brilliant performance, Bryce's playing the guitar wasn't as exciting. He was definitely decent enough, but his music wasn't so engaging. He was playing his own interpretation of the guitar solo in "Hotel California," which, while a lovely song, was very repetitive and didn't have much to offer in terms of harmony (or so Cassidy used to say, though I tended to believe her, all things considered).

In the end, Bryce was sold to Lord Daugherty for five hundred dollars. It was probably Daugherty's easiest buy so far.

Then Kaylon called, "Next on up—Tansy Contos!"

Next to me, Tansy froze, then turned to look at me. She was shaking just like Isora did before, and she whispered, "Pray to the Morrow Gods for me, Aileen." She rose to her feet, eyes unfocused. *"Please."*

How she ever came to learn about the Morrow Gods, something I believed only my father and I knew about, took a back seat when I saw her climbing onto the stage, looking more frail than I'd ever seen her. She was so small that the stage seemed to swallow her whole as she took off her sandals, put on pointe shoes—*What?*—and rose back to her feet, standing so still that only her knees-long hair moved in the soft breeze of the auditorium.

The first movement of Beethoven's "Moonlight Sonata" played, and Tansy began to dance. I stared at her, stunned; I had no idea she was a professional ballet dancer. When I looked to my sides, my peers didn't seem surprised.

It occurred to me then that I'd spent all my time during practice in the workshop alone. In the assessment class, I'd only seen her dance modern-style. I had no idea she was a freaking *ballet dancer.*

Because that's what she was; her languid movements and tight, precise poses were far too practiced to belong to an amateur. She was a pro through and through, and it suddenly made sense why she received the Imprint after merely one year of being on the waiting list. Ragnor must've thought she could become a Gifted.

And when I looked at her now and saw how the dreamy-eyed Tansy had transformed into a different person as she danced, I got the feeling she might become Gifted later on, against all odds. She was far too good to remain Common.

Tansy reached the end of her dance with a pirouette, only that pirouette seemed to last forever. With her back straight and her legs unmoving, she looked like the ballet dancers in those old music boxes as she twirled endlessly on her pointe.

When she finished, the applause was deafening. As I clapped along with the rest, mesmerized by what I'd just seen and the professional ballet-dancer bow Tansy now gave to the crowd, I couldn't help but think she didn't need any God—least of all the Morrow Gods—to be on her side. She was already blessed enough.

When Kaylon came back up to the stage, he opened his mouth, about to say something, before he laughed loudly. "Well, look at that! We have all seven Lords with their hands up!"

The roaring of the audience grew so loud, I winced.

Then I realized he said all *seven* Lords. Meaning that, for the first time, Ragnor was placing a bid—and on Tansy, no less.

I completely understood that decision, though. Tansy was magnificent. A rare commodity.

"Since all Lords want to bid, the rules dictate the bidding starts at ten thousand!" Kaylon said, grinning greedily, as though that money was going to him. "But it seems none of the Lords lowered their hands! How about fifteen thousand, then? Would you look at that—no one lets up! Then let's up the stakes, shall we?"

Kaylon paused, creating suspense, before he said, "Bidding starts at fifty thousand!"

Gasps echoed in the audience. "This is bonkers," I heard someone murmur, while another said, "The starting bid hasn't been that high in ten years!"

"We have three contenders in the running now!" Kaylon said. "Lord Renaldi, Lord Atalon, and Lord Rayne—let's see who'll win this wonderful ballet dancer! Who gives me fifty-two? Still all three. How about fifty-five? Ah, Lord Renaldi is out of the picture! It all boils down to Lord Rayne and Lord Atalon!"

At that moment, I knew who would win. So when, after two minutes of tough bidding competition, Kaylon announced "*Sold for seventy thousand to Lord Rayne!*" I wasn't surprised. Not like my peers, anyway, whose faces were slack with shock.

Ragnor's tenacity was legendary, so it wasn't surprising he won this bid. But knowing that didn't make me feel better. In fact, my feelings mirrored those of my classmates, whose shock transformed into pure jealousy.

All of us wanted to stay in the Rayne League, yet few of us would be able to, what with Ragnor bidding on only one so far.

The next few performances by my peers seemed to be affected by that knowledge. Jane, who rapped a Tupac song, messed up the rhythm and words, obviously distracted. She barely managed to get herself sold for two hundred dollars to Lord Daugherty, who seemed to bid on all musicians, good or bad.

After Jane, Cynthia recited a monologue from *Hamlet*, but it seemed the jinx was still on, because she forgot a few lines and tried to improvise new ones that didn't sound remotely close to the original vernacular. Her acting skills, while decent back in the assessment class, had turned to shit in this performance. Lord Bowman bought her for three hundred dollars without competition.

One by one, my classmates were bought into different Leagues. Ragnor didn't bid on any of them.

When Aisha got onstage, only Zoey and I were left. Zoey moved to sit next to me, and we both watched Aisha's storytelling act, and I knew I wasn't the only one who didn't listen.

Soon enough, I would be on that stage, and I would have to ad-lib my act because I'd failed to come up with a plan. What would happen to me if I messed up? Would Ragnor buy me? Or for the sake of keeping our relationship a secret, would he let me be bought by another Lord to save face?

I began to shake. The anxiety gnawed at my insides, making me feel sick.

Zoey's hand suddenly grabbed mine. "We'll be okay," she murmured to me, and when I glanced at her, I saw her gaze was on the stage, though she didn't seem to really watch Aisha's show. "We've got to be okay."

Receiving comfort from Zoey of all people humbled me. I squeezed her hand, took a deep, shaky breath, and whispered back, "We will, Zoey. We will."

Holding hands, Zoey and I stared as Aisha left the stage after a short bidding contest won by Lord O'Brien for three hundred and fifty dollars. We both tensed when Kaylon returned to the stage. It was either one of us now.

"Please welcome onstage Zoey Rittman!"

Zoey made a soft choking sound as she let go of my hand and rose to her feet. "You're going to be fine, Zoey," I told her as her face twisted in terror. "Show them what you've got."

Zoey glanced at me, shaking from head to toe, before she suddenly took a deep breath, tensed, and gave me a hard, blazing look. "You, too, Aileen," she said with a desperate sort of determination. "We've got this."

By the time she reached the stage, Zoey seemed to have pep talked herself. She was no longer shaking; her jaw was set in a stubborn line, and she took off her heels, leaving her in the pretty, sparkling jumpsuit. Her song of choice—"The Final Countdown"—played, and she launched into action.

She started with a series of impressive martial arts movements. She jumped and kicked a dummy that had been brought onstage, and she showed just why she was the best in our gym class.

The audience loved her—her strong, precise movements made it impossible to take my eyes away from her. She beat the shit out of the dummy with such power that she would've done some considerable damage if the dummy was a real person.

And when she was done, the host didn't even say "Start bidding," because five of the seven Lords already had their hands up in the air.

"Our first bid is from Lord Daugherty for fifty thousand!" Kaylon announced excitedly. "We have fifty-five from Lord Rayne! Fifty-six, anyone? Lord O'Brien doubles the number!"

My eyes focused on Zoey. She was panting, sweaty from the exercise, staring ahead with what seemed to be renewed trepidation, yet mixed with hope. Because Ragnor was bidding on her. And with Ragnor being the tenacious bastard that he was, he would definitely win.

Or so I thought.

"Sold for two hundred thousand to Lord Renaldi!"

Zoey's face paled and fell. Tears filled her eyes. She started shaking her head, taking a step back, when Kaylon came over to her and whispered something in her ear. She kept on shaking her head, her entire body trembling like Isora's did, only in Zoey's case, she didn't escape Lord Renaldi's clutches.

She was sold right into them.

Horrified, I watched as Kaylon practically forced Zoey off the stage. Right before she disappeared backstage, I saw fear clouding her face as tears escaped her eyes.

All her efforts . . . for nothing.

But I didn't have the time to feel sorry for Zoey, because my own time was up.

Kaylon looked at the paper in his hand and mumbled something to himself. He waved to someone offstage, who then came up to join him to also stare at the paper in his hand. They whispered among themselves and then looked back into the crowd as if something was terribly wrong. I was the last person from the Rayne League. Surely it was now my turn.

Kaylon and the other person were now joined by a third person, who peered out into the crowd, scanning it from the stage as if they were looking for something or someone.

Then Kaylon said into the microphone, "Lord Rayne, we appear to be missing the recommendation for one of your Commons. Might you join us so we can sort this out?"

The crowd grew restless; audible gasps fell from the lips of the spectators. I watched as Ragnor, with Margarita behind him, joined Kaylon and the two others onstage. They talked, and from the looks of things, the conversation was not positive.

I shrank lower into my seat, wondering if I would have a chance to participate in the Auction at all. I'd been so preoccupied with Ragnor and whether he was going to buy me and what I would do for my performance that I hadn't gotten around to getting Lon's recommendation. And now, my turn was likely over before it had even started.

Ragnor, Margarita, and the other two vampires left the stage. Margarita looked as if she had swallowed something bitter. Ragnor looked as if he was at his bullshit limit for the day, and the other two looked relieved.

And as if it had never happened, Kaylon smiled and said, "Please welcome to the stage—Aileen Henderson!"

CHAPTER 38

I climbed the stairs to the stage, watching the awaiting canvas on the easel. The claps of the audience were like a soft buzz in my ears; all sounds were overtaken by the war drum that was my heart.

My face felt warm when I reached the spotlight in the center of the stage. My stomach churned as bile rose up my throat. I felt sick. I felt too hot. I could tangibly feel the stares of the hundreds of vampires in the audience as they landed on me, expectant and exhilarated at the sight of another noob laid down for the butcher's knife.

I came to a stop near the easel, seeing the paint palette resting on the wooden chair, and was suddenly overcome by sharp, painful regret. I'd been stupidly arrogant in thinking I could take on the Auction with painting as my chosen act. It wasn't even about me not coming up with a plan—it was the fact I just wasn't good enough. Potential? Talent? I had none of those when it came to art. I was mediocre at best.

A desperate, reckless impulse told me it still wasn't too late. That I could perhaps do something else other than painting, like executing Iovan's *Imperium*.

But Abe had explained that once you chose an act, you couldn't replace it with another. It would disqualify me from participating, and the fate of those disqualified was the same as the unbought, if not worse.

The impulse disappeared, and I deflated. It was too late to change course.

I took a shuddering breath and knew that, ready or not, I had to start. I grabbed the palette, sat down on the stool, and stared at the blank canvas. I tried to come up with something to paint—anything would do at this point—but my head was just as horrifyingly blank as the canvas.

Pray to the Morrow Gods for me, Aileen. Please.

Tansy's words from before she left for her own performance reverberated through my head, causing a ripple in the blankness that was my mental canvas. My eyes widened as an idea, an awful, terrible idea, rose from the bottom of my mind, digging its claws in my psyche.

No, a deep, frightened voice whispered in my head. *Don't do that, Aileen.*

But that idea refused to leave. It dug itself deeper inside my head, taunting me, daring me to do what I had once promised myself I would never, ever do.

"You can do this, Henderson." The sudden murmur came from Kaylon, who spoke off mic from the foot of the stage near where I was sitting, giving me an encouraging thumbs-up.

But I wasn't encouraged. I was petrified. Because what Kaylon basically said was to move it, and I was too frightened of my one and only option to do that.

I glanced at the audience. Since the stage light was so fucking bright, the audience seemed like the black abyss, ready to swallow me whole. I just wanted to see Ragnor's face, even if for a split second. I wanted him to give me reassurance that he would buy me out.

Yet the darkness was too deep. As deep as the cold, chilly realization that I was on my own.

And my decision was made.

I closed my eyes, sucked in a deep, uneven breath, and, with my heart booming in my ears, let the paint palette drop to the floor. I then sank my nails into my left arm. I didn't wince; the sensation was too harrowingly familiar, and my nails tore through the skin, drawing blood.

Please, I silently begged, hating myself for what I was about to do. *If you're out there, please hear my call.*

I heard the gasps from the audience, but they sounded as though they came from an underwater tunnel. My senses were focused on the sensation of blood trickling from the wound I'd made.

A soft, almost unnatural breeze tickled my face as I opened my eyes and pressed my bleeding arm against the white canvas, smearing it across the surface, before letting my hand fall. Strangely, the breeze grew somewhat, cocooning me in its translucent blanket as, with my fingers, I began to draw.

Please, I thought desperately as I drew silhouettes of three men. *Please help me.*

I didn't want to leave the Rayne League.

I didn't want to be bought by anyone other than Ragnor.

I wanted to stay.

And right now, whether I drowned in self-loathing or fear because of my desperate decision, this was my only chance.

Quietly, in a soft, broken murmur, as I continued to draw, I began to chant:

"Deep in the forest, no bird is safe,
For crumbles of berries, the Gods shall grow;
Found in the heart of nature's womb,
The Morrow Gods shall come . . ."

I detailed the bright red bodies and then drew their limbs gently as I sang.

"The wind and the ocean caress your fears,
For love and its death are God borne;
Open your eyes and watch the miracle,
As the Morrow Gods return . . ."

The blood dried too fast, so I broke my skin again, spilling more and soaking my fingers in it. My hand began to shiver as I returned it to the canvas, and I forced myself, against all the barriers and walls I'd put up in my mind, to bring to the forefront the childhood stories my father used to tell me about the Morrow Gods.

"First away the birds will fly,
Fear is theirs to take;
For the Gods, whose eyes are singed,
Are the endless woven storm . . ."

I brushed my thumb above the men's eyes, drawing their brows. Then I dipped my finger in the blood and started drawing the background. The breeze was now a bit stronger than before, blowing wisps of my hair away from my face, attempting to wash away my misery as well.

"Fell and locked, they shan't know,
Just what is their fate;
From mournful bones, they will rise and bow,
For their fire's birthed the flames . . ."

It became harder to breathe as the breeze became constant, refusing to die down. Yet I still twirled my fingers against the canvas, laying out the flames of the infernal abyss. I made it the darkest shade of red I could, and my voice rose as my urgency did too.

"Deep in the forest, a well of bleeding blaze," I chanted as I drew the lines of distant trees, the breeze almost choking me.

"Scars the land bare and raw," I sang as I brushed my fingers against the would-be sky, creating a horizon full of crimson, while the wind rubbed against my skin, leaving a trail of risen hairs in its wake.

"Three beastly men share a golden cloak," I crooned as I rubbed my knuckle against the painted men's faces and leaned back, feeling the breeze in my throat.

"The Morrow Gods have come."

The painting showed three men standing side by side, their bodies silhouetted while their faces showed an identical expression of wrath—or so was my purpose. They were standing in the middle of a fiery forest, the sky beyond marred with smoke. The painting wasn't clear, with blood being the only pigment present and me not being as good as a true artist, but it was clear enough for my purpose.

Because this painting was one way for me to ask the Morrow Gods to take mercy upon me. To save me from this hell that was the Auction. From the hysteria and fear, sadness and agony that suffocated me from deep within.

Shaking, I climbed to my feet and, frightened at what the reaction would be, turned to face the audience. It only then occurred to me that it had been almost one minute since I finished my act, and yet the hall was entirely silent.

That didn't help calm my terror.

When I watched the audience, there was a stillness in the hall that hadn't been there before. I might've seen the crowd as one big black blanket, but the blanket seemed to be immobile. As if everyone was frozen.

Then I blinked.

And the Auction hall was gone.

I was in a field, an endless expanse filled with wilted gray grass and faintly luminous white flowers, with an empty sky of orange-tinted violet. Something about this field felt familiar, as though I'd been here before, but I knew that couldn't be. I would've remembered if I had.

A soft breeze, similar to the one from before, brought with it the scent of the ocean as it gently blew my hair.

A bright flash of gold made me freeze, and I grabbed my hair, feeling my heartbeat accelerating at what I found. Gone was the muddy-brown dye; my hair had returned to its original blonde, as if the entirety of the colorant had suddenly been neutralized.

Whipping my head up and letting my hair go, I looked around me, my eyes darting frantically throughout the field to see where the hell I was.

Because I was no longer in the Rayne League.

I was no longer in New England, that was for sure.

But was there a place like this on Earth? So tranquil yet oddly chilling, not a star blinking in the cloudless, sunless, unchanging sky?

As my heart boomed in my ears, I took a step forward; then a rustling to my right made me whirl around with a scream lodged in my throat. For a moment, I thought I must've imagined it, but then a few feet away, I saw something moving in the wilted grass.

Cautiously, I walked toward the moving thing until I was right before it, able to see it among the dry thistles.

It was a bird. A strange, naked bird with the head of an eagle, the body of a pheasant, a long tail that resembled a rat's, and large, featherless wings. Its skin was the same gray color of the grass it lay in, and its movements were jerky, its eyes shut tightly, as if it was fighting a terrible pain.

I crouched before the bird, watching helplessly as it writhed on the ground. As though it sensed me, the bird stilled, and its white beak opened. It let out a pained groan that did not sound like a bird at all.

Still, whatever it was, I couldn't just sit and watch as it was tortured by obvious pain. Gently, I gathered the bird in my arms, sat down on the dry, crackling grass, and petted its body as I would a cat's. "It's going to be okay," I lied, a knowing deep inside telling me that this bird was reaching its imminent end. "You're going to be okay."

The bird's lids trembled before they lifted, revealing a pair of dark rubies for eyes. Those rubies looked straight into my eyes, and the emotion within them seemed to contain far more than heartbreaking agony, but . . . sadness.

It gutted me, struck right against my chest. It felt as though I was staring at an old friend about to take their last breath, and before I could stop it, a sob escaped me, tears welling in my eyes. "Don't die," I begged, unable to think of anything but saving the bird. "Please don't die—"

I sucked in a breath when the bird's eyes mimicked mine, welling with tears.

Shaking, I stared at it as its lids fell over its eyes, its tears trickling out, falling to the ground.

The bird stopped moving.

It was dead.

And it felt like I was dying along with it too.

"No!" I yelled, hugging it close as the tears streamed down my face like water from a dam that'd been broken by pure force.

"No, no, no . . . ," I whimpered, grieving for the bird as though it was my own flesh and blood. Grieving for it as if I'd known it my entire life, despite having just seen it for the first time.

The hopelessness was beyond bearing. It felt like I would never be able to dream again, to feel, to hope.

It was as if God himself had just died.

Something shifted on my lap, and my eyes snapped open. Shocked and horrified, I watched the bird decaying right before my eyes, its body fragmenting into dust from the tip of its tail to the top of its head.

I tried to hold on to it. I tried to keep it in my arms, refusing to let it go, but by the next blink, I was no longer fighting to hold its body but its ashes.

Devastation tore through me, and I watched as the wind carried these ashes away from my palms until they were nothing but small specks in the distance.

My head dropped in utter defeat. I was crushed. I didn't know how I could go on from this moment. How could I go on living when I felt like I was being completely pulverized from within.

But then I saw the patch of wilted grass I was sitting on, and my shock, pain, and unbearable grief transformed into awe.

Because this patch of grass was no longer wilted.

It was as green as a ripe bell pepper. So green that it was almost painful to look at.

Raising my head, I looked around me, my heart beating quickly in my chest, but the rest of the grass remained the same. Only this patch right here had suddenly become healthy.

Shakily, I raised my hand, but then I winced in pain. Right. I'd cut my arm. But why did it suddenly ache? When I held the bird, it had been fine. Looking at my arm now, I saw that the wound had stopped bleeding. In fact, it seemed like it was pulsing.

Frozen in place with a sudden, renewed shock, I saw with my bare eyes the wound slowly seal shut as though an invisible needle was stitching it back together. Then it closed seamlessly, leaving no trace on the arm, as if I'd never cut it open to begin with.

Shivering, I wrapped my arms around myself, feeling a sudden sense of fear. I raised my eyes to the sky above, staring as it suddenly started to distort and ripple.

And just like the wound and the bird, the whole world, this dream-like realm, started warping as if someone was sloppily lifting a curtain to resume a show after going on a break.

The sky transformed into darkness. The healthy, pretty patch of grass became a blindingly lit stage with an easel and a blood-painted canvas. The rest of the wilting expanse was replaced by the dark void that was the audience.

I was back in the Auction hall.

As if all of what had just happened was only in my head, a faint, heartbreakingly realistic dream.

I was standing near the finished canvas. That soft, odd breeze from before was gone. I pulled my ponytail forward, and my shoulders slumped in relief. The brown dye was back. Or perhaps it had never disappeared in the first place.

Raising my eyes, I stared at the audience and frowned. Like before the whole thing happened, they didn't seem to be moving. Were they in shock? Had they been in that field too?

Then I turned to look at the host, Kaylon, who stood at the foot of the stage and seemed to be talking to someone. But something wasn't quite right. Their mouths weren't moving. Neither were their bodies.

An alarm went off in my head as I strode to the edge of the stage and crouched before Kaylon and the other person, needing to take a better look. They seemed to be frozen in time, almost like realistic dolls in a wax museum.

With my heart drumming in my chest, I scanned the first row, where the newbies of the remaining Leagues sat. They were all staring at the stage, but like the host and his friend, they seemed to be frozen, their expressions set in their faces as though they were merely portraits. I didn't even see them breathe.

My knees were suddenly weak, and I fell back on my ass, my breaths coming out so rapidly that I realized I was hyperventilating. Because what I saw couldn't possibly be real. There was no fucking way.

I stared at the vampires as seconds ticked by, and still no one moved.

Meaning that I was the only one in this room who felt the seconds go by.

Because for everyone else, time seemed to have stopped.

CHAPTER 39

The only sound in the eerie silence was my heartbeat drumming in my ears in a panicked rhythm.

I rose to my feet and began to climb down the stairs, leaving the stage, as I watched the faces of the people in the audience become clearer. Each of them wore different expressions and were frozen in different poses. It reminded me of that game I hated back in kindergarten—green light, red light. Only this was far creepier.

I walked through the rows, passing the frozen vampires, fascinated, confused, and yet terrified by what was happening. What was causing this . . . *anomaly*?

Maybe you *are causing it,* logic murmured in my head, and I almost laughed in hysteria. That couldn't be true. I was a Common vampire, and before I became a vampire, I was merely a human. Stopping time wasn't a power any living being should have.

Then why am I the only one not affected?

Something caught my eyes, distracting me from that disturbing line of thought. It was Margarita's red hair. Even in such a big audience, her distinct hair was far too prominent. She was two rows ahead, and I walked toward her, almost curious to see her face.

The first thing I noticed, however, was that she was sitting next to Logan. And when my eyes darted between the both of them, a sinking feeling took hold in my stomach. They were wearing expressions I'd never before seen on either face.

Margarita was staring at the stage with parted lips, her glowing green eyes wide and filled with trepidation. At any other time, I would've loved seeing such a look on her face, but when I saw Logan's face mimicking Margarita's, his turquoise eyes bright with a glow that on his familiar face seemed eerie, I couldn't find it in me to feel anything but sick.

Because they weren't the only ones who were looking like they'd just seen a ghost.

Raising my eyes to the row behind theirs, I saw Ragnor. He, too, was staring at the stage, at the canvas, with an expression that made me take a step back.

He looked like someone had slapped him, with his eyes wide with shock and his body leaning forward as though he would've stood up had time not stopped.

I'd never seen him make such an expression, and my fingers itched to cup his face, caress the creases near his eyes, as if to try and embed his visage as it was into my brain. I wanted to close my lips on his, using my touch to show him that whatever bothered him, it was all right.

But before I could do anything, a sudden, sharp pain cut through my head. Groaning, I stumbled backward, my vision blurring with the sudden, throbbing ache.

When it felt like a knife was trying to cut my eyeballs out, my instincts suddenly yelled, *GET BACK TO THE STAGE!* Gritting my teeth, I stumbled past the rows, vision blurry with tears of pain, and somehow managed to climb back up to the stage.

I fell onto the wooden stool near the easel and sucked in a breath, holding my head in my hands, shutting my eyes as I begged that this pain, this *torture* would stop.

The pain in my head became an unbearable pressure that made me scream.

"Resume time."

The torment must've been very severe, because I seemed to have hallucinated a familiar yet unfamiliar voice talking in my head.

The pain seemed to cascade from my head down my spine and even lower to my waist. I arched my back, trying to get away from the pain, needing it to go away, to leave me alone.

"Resume time, Aileen. It's your doing."

What the fuck?

Before my watery eyes, I saw what seemed to be another hallucination, this time vividly visual, that of a translucent, ambiguously shaped creature. It was glowing bright, making the pain impossibly worse, but then the voice whispered in my head, *"Release the time you have stopped, Aileen, or you shall die."*

Nothing mattered at that moment. Not even logic. I just needed the pain to stop.

Before I could question myself, I closed my eyes, and through the pain, tears, and sweat, willed silently, *Move, time. Please. I'm begging you, just continue on and release me from this terrible fucking pain.*

There was a clicking sound inside my head, like a grandfather clock's hands hitting midnight, and as suddenly as it came, the pain disappeared.

I slumped on the stool, breathing heavily, perspiration dripping down my cheeks, mingling with what remained of my tears.

For a moment, I was sure nothing happened. I was too occupied with feeling the sheer relief of having the pain go away.

So when Kaylon called out "We have fifteen thousand!" it took me a moment to realize what was happening.

Like I'd been sucked back to reality from whatever fever dream I'd just had, I snapped my eyes open and stared at the darkness of the moving audience. Next to me, Kaylon, whom I hadn't even noticed come onstage, was grinning at the audience as he said, "And Lord Rayne just upped the bid to twenty-two! Do we have thirty?"

I blinked and wiped the sweat and tears away before straightening on my stool. Time had resumed. The pain was gone. And everyone seemed to be none the wiser about what had just occurred.

Had anything really happened? The field, the stopped time, the pain?

Or had it all just been in my head?

"Fifty thousand from Lord Renaldi!" Kaylon suddenly called, drawing my gaze to him. "We have a bidding war, all right—and Lord Atalon just brought it up to seventy! Do we have seventy-five?"

The murmurs of the audience became louder with every announcement Kaylon made. And then he exclaimed, "Eighty-five from Lord Renaldi! Do we have ninety—and Lord Atalon brought the bid to a whopping one hundred thousand, folks!"

I realized, belatedly, that a bidding contest was happening right now to buy me.

And that the fight seemed to be between Atalon and Renaldi, and maybe Ragnor.

"*One hundred and ten thousand from Lord Rayne!*" Kaylon yelled excitedly, and I whipped my head toward the vague direction where I knew Ragnor was sitting. But I couldn't see him. I couldn't see a thing.

And then—"*One hundred and twenty by Lord Atalon!*"

My heart dropped. Atalon wasn't giving up.

Up the bid, Ragnor, I silently begged.

"Going once!" Kaylon declared.

My stomach somersaulted as panic rose with such vengeance that I suddenly felt faint. *Come on, Ragnor.*

Before I could think about it, I jumped to my feet and strode to the edge of the stage, searching for Ragnor with my eyes. *Don't sell me,* I thought, starting to get hysterical. *Bid on me. You want me, don't you? You said you wanted to try!*

"Going twice!"

No. This couldn't be happening.

Ragnor, I beg you, place the bid, I thought fervently, eyes darting from left to right, searching for him as sweat pooled on my forehead and my breathing grew short and shallow.

Nothing else mattered right there and then. Not my hallucinations of the field and the dying bird. Not the odd anomaly that happened and its possible connection to me.

All that mattered was that I was in an Auction and would be sold to the highest bidder.

And that the highest bidder was not Ragnor.

Desperately, I pleaded, *Please don't leave me, Ragnor. Don't be like Logan. Don't be like Dad. I will do anything for you if you just choose me, become your lover, fuck buddy, even a slave, just keep me here with you, please.*

"*Sold* for one hundred and twenty thousand dollars to Lord Atalon!"

I was led off the stage and into a back room where two vampires who'd been bought before me were waiting. The two were clinging on to one another, crying silently. Faintly, I realized one of them was Isora, the second-timer who managed to escape Renaldi's clutches thanks to Atalon.

The same Atalon who'd just bought me.

Because Ragnor had sold me.

He didn't fight for me.

He didn't care.

I could hear my heart breaking.

He left me.

Like my mother had left me when I was three days old.

Like my father had left me when he went to jail.

Like Logan had left me when we were eighteen.

Like Cassidy had tried to leave me, and would've succeeded if I hadn't followed her like Alice following the rabbit down the magical hole to fucking Wonderland.

But this was no wonderland. There was nothing wondrous about any of this.

How could there be when the man I wanted with every fiber of my being, the man I thought might feel, against all odds, the same way about me, tossed me aside like I did my practice canvases?

I went to the wall of the small waiting room and slid down to the floor, putting my head in my hands. What was it about me that made people want to leave me?

You know, an awful voice whispered in my head. *You know why they all leave you.*

I raised my head and stared at Isora and the other girl. I realized they were smiling, their bodies slumped with relief. Probably happy to be out of Renaldi's League.

Hopelessness weighed down on my shoulders, and I brought my knees to my chest, wrapped my arms around them, and wished that instead of time stopping, it had rewound, to before the Auction even started, when it was just Ragnor and me in that cupboard room.

Before he broke my soul to pieces.

Atalon had purchased a total of five vampires. Isora and the other girl from Renaldi's League, a man from the Daugherty League, another man from the Kalama League, and me.

Lord Atalon himself came to the waiting room, accompanied by the twins who were his Lieutenants. He looked as immaculately put together as before, and his penetrating black eyes stared at us with a gleam of satisfaction. "Good evening, my new vampires," he said formally. "Now that the Auction is over, it's time we leave."

One of the twins stepped forward. "Follow me, please."

Along with the other four, I rose to my feet. Numbness filled the place where my heart used to be, and I felt like I was on autopilot. When I attempted to join the other four following the twin, Atalon's hand wrapped around my arm, and he said, "A word, Aileen."

I paused and turned to him, gazing at his face apathetically. "Yes?"

He smiled. "I'm happy to have acquired you," he informed me, causing a sudden pain to split my gut into two. "And I want to assure you that I will treat you well. The Atalon League is a good place. That I can promise."

He was right. I remembered visiting his League during the field trip, and it *was* pretty nice there. If I had to be bought by anyone who wasn't Ragnor, then Atalon was definitely the best League to be bought into.

But Lord Atalon himself was a problem. His eyes were far too cunning.

And also, he wasn't Ragnor.

"Thank you," I said, meaning it despite the pain of betrayal cutting through my chest. Then I realized I hadn't addressed him properly and forced myself to say, "My Lord."

He chuckled. "Please, call me Atalon."

I smiled humorlessly. In my head, I could see Ragnor's eye twitching at my insolence and how much he hated that I didn't address him properly. And how he wouldn't care so much about that when we . . .

My thoughts came to a screeching halt. Enough. Just . . . enough.

Ragnor Rayne had thrown me away without a second thought. He didn't care about me. He didn't even take responsibility for bringing me into this whole new world against my will.

Yet despite it all, I'd let him inside me in more than one way, and he stomped on that as if I was trash.

But I was through with feeling sorry for myself.

I was through with Ragnor fucking Rayne.

Silently, I followed Atalon as he took me to the entrance hall of the Rayne League. Near the elevator stood Margarita, but I didn't even spare her a glance as she activated the elevator with her handprint.

We entered the elevator leading up to the warehouse where it all began, and once we were out and I followed Atalon out to the open air and beautiful dark sky, steel crawled into my chest—cold, hard, and biting.

Ragnor Rayne would regret this day for as long as he existed.

I would make sure of it.

EPILOGUE
ELIZA WAINS

The Auction hall was silent by the time Eliza went in. She had sat in the back, watching the Auction quietly, and seen everything that happened with a very specific vampire, and now, she was returning after observing said vampire leaving the Rayne League with her hand holding another vampire Lord's arm.

But now Eliza was back, and the hall was empty—all but for one man sitting in the front row, holding a large canvas painted in different shades of red blood.

She took a seat next to the man. Ragnor Rayne, a man she'd known all her life and who was like an annoying older brother to her, seemed to be absolutely lost.

Rayne was never lost. He was the type to guide lost ones to find their way.

And yet he seemed to be utterly defeated by his own stubbornness.

She turned to the painting. "It's pretty," she said. It wasn't a masterpiece, certainly not beautiful, but it was captivating, nonetheless. Aileen Henderson might not be a great artist, but she had the makings of one.

Rayne said nothing, simply looked at the painting with empty eyes.

Sighing, she put her hand on his shoulder and squeezed. "You've done the right thing," she told him. "You heard her singing that song. You know what it means."

Her words didn't seem to penetrate. She let her hand fall from his shoulder and leaned back, staring at the empty stage. "You should've bought her if you were going to be like this."

That seemed to grab his attention, and he whipped toward her, eyes turning neon blue. "Should I have?" he asked bitterly, voice low and on the verge of a growl. "She's been nothing but a nuisance. Arrogant. Insolent. Insanely maddening. Rude."

Eliza glanced at his hands. He was holding the canvas so tightly that his fingers dented the cloth. "Yet look at you now," she murmured. "You're a mess, Ragnor."

He turned away to glower at the painting. "I almost bought her, Eliza," he growled. "I would've bought her if the host had waited just one more second."

You snooze, you lose, she thought but didn't dare say it. Not now, when Rayne, for the first time ever, was showing actual human emotions. "In the end, it's good that you let her go," she said quietly. "You know that, don't you?"

He closed his eyes and slumped in his seat. "She never mentioned knowing about the tales of the Morrow Gods," he said through gritted teeth.

She refrained from snorting, but her words betrayed her cynicism. "Yes, because she told you so much about herself, didn't she?"

He put his arm over his face, taking a deep breath. "I'm tired," he said quietly. "I'm so fucking tired."

"I know," she said softly. "But you did the right thing. You know you did."

Because, Eliza knew, Aileen Henderson's very existence was dangerous. Whatever her association was with the Children of Kahil, it could only be dangerous—especially for Ragnor.

Before the Auction, Eliza had thought differently. She believed Aileen Henderson was Ragnor's saving grace she'd been hoping for, if only to save him from himself. She'd been delighted to see how twisted in knots Ragnor was over a mere twenty-one-year-old woman, so much so that no matter how many horrors the woman's past revealed, she still believed Aileen was good for him.

But her trying to summon the Morrow Gods had changed things. Eliza could no longer support whatever was going on between Rayne and the woman. She could no longer support Ragnor's interest in her.

Aileen Henderson was the enemy of Ragnor Meha-Seraphim.

AUTHOR'S NOTE

Dear marvelous reader,
   I hope you enjoyed the book as much as I liked writing it!

—Sapir

ACKNOWLEDGMENTS

I hereby acknowledge my mom, father, sister, brother-in-law, nephew, niece, friends, editors, etc.

Special thanks to Georgia McBride, my fabulous literary manager.

Turn the page to see a preview of Sapir A. Englard's book,
Blood of the Gods.

CLOAK OF THE VAMPIRE BOOK 2:

BLOOD OF THE GODS

PROLOGUE

Eight years ago
Lewiston, Maine

Darkness spread through the sky as Natalia and her father made their way to the Androscoggin River. They didn't talk, but Natalia wasn't bothered; her father was always silent when the time came for the second rite.

It was better than how loud he was during the first rite.

Though a silent monster was still a monster.

Her father came to a stop near the riverbank. Natalia paused next to him, staring pointedly at the river. Yet not looking at *that* didn't make its presence less prominent. But then her father started speaking, murmuring the words she'd been hearing every month for her entire life, and like every time, she felt the eerie need to gaze at him.

She'd once heard a few of her classmates' mothers calling her father handsome. She shared the sentiment, to a certain extent; at first glance, he seemed like a smart, kind man with warm eyes hiding behind a pair of square glasses. It also helped that he was a scholar, a biochemistry professor at the University of Maine.

What those mothers failed to notice was the fanaticism drawn in the depths of his hazel irises.

"Dear Gods of Faith and Divinity," her father muttered, eyes staring at the river unseeingly as though he was somewhere far away. "Let us draw from the well of our belief and embrace our true potential as vessels of your blessings."

He looked down at the large glass bowl he cradled in his arms. His eyes were alight with hot anger. "We have failed you," he said, voice louder and more bitter. Natalia jolted, perplexed; her father never deviated from the speech before. "Last time, we failed to provide you with proof of our faith. Rest assured this won't ever happen again."

Natalia felt her heart fall as she returned her gaze to the river. She hadn't forgotten about last month's incident. It still haunted her that there was someone out there, other than her, who knew about her father's true nature. She remembered her father's outburst when he had to forfeit the rite a month ago. It was a sight she didn't want to behold ever again.

And now, her father went to his knees, his body shaking in barely contained rage. "We present you with a worthy tribute to show our unwavering gratitude for all you've given us, O Sublime Ones, for our conviction in your powers is far superior to any other."

He turned his head to Natalia, and she realized she, too, was shaking at the utter, zealous devotion in her father's eyes. "Come now, Natalia. Show them your faith."

Natalia nodded jerkily as she stepped forward and pulled the penknife from the pocket of her jeans. She pressed the blade against her inner arm, feeling a sickening sense of familiarity, welcoming the pain as blood spilled from the wound, shining red under the moonlight.

Then she began to chant.

"Deep in the forest, no bird is safe . . ."

As Natalia recited the old psalm from the Book of Kahil, she put her arm over the bowl in her father's hands. It was filled with ashes, which slowly turned a light, distorted shade of red from the blood she spilled on it.

Natalia and her father were immobile, frozen in place, with Natalia's soft singing the only sound filling the loaded air.

When the last drop of blood fell onto the ashes, Natalia returned her arm to her side and straightened in her place. "The Morrow Gods have come," she whispered.

Her father climbed to his feet, stepped toward the calm water of the river, and poured the contents of the glass bowl into it, coloring the deep blue depths a faint shade of red.

Natalia and her father watched until the last drop of blood and ash landed and rippled over the water, waited for a few more moments, then clasped their hands together, closed their eyes, and murmured, "May the Morrow Gods bestow the Beyond with their eternal inferno."

Natalia was watching the Androscoggin River from the window of the living room as her father rinsed the bowl in the kitchen sink when there was a knock on the entrance door. Both Natalia and her father turned to look at the door, immediately alert.

Neither Natalia nor her father had any friends. Once upon a time, the neighbors had tried to befriend her father, but they realized quickly enough he wasn't interested in trivial things such as friendships. While Natalia had once wished she had friends, being homeschooled with no extracurricular activities didn't allow for such things.

Meaning there was no reason for anyone to visit them, especially when it was close to midnight.

Another knock on the door made Natalia jump. She put the workbook down and jumped to her feet, then tiptoed toward the door. Silently, she checked the peephole.

What she saw made her pale.

She stepped back from the door as yet another knock echoed in the silent house. She then turned to her father, who gave her an inquisitive look and mouthed, *Who's there?*

Natalia opened her mouth to speak, but no sound came out. At that very moment, many scenarios went through her head. So many of them, in fact, that she had a hard time breathing.

Her heart raced in her chest as cold sweat dripped down her spine. *This is a chance,* a little, distant voice whispered in her head. *This is the chance you've been waiting for.*

But there was a louder voice, a deeply terrified one, that screamed, *You have nowhere else to go!*

She had no time to choose, though.

The door was thrown open, and five police officers entered the house. They passed Natalia, heading straight to her father before one of them grabbed his hands and shackled his wrists. "Amir Zoheir-Henderson," the officer said in a disgusted, angry voice, "you're under arrest for charges of kidnap and rape. You have the right to remain silent. Anything you say can and will be used against you in a court of law."

Natalia's father did not resist. Quite the opposite, really; he remained calm as they dragged him toward the door. His eyes then turned to Natalia. "She has nothing to do with it," he told the police. "Leave her out of it."

She watched as the police then led her father out while one of them, a woman, remained behind, facing her. "It's going to be all right, Natalia," she told her, and Natalia saw the sympathy on her face she didn't bother to hide. "You're going to be okay."

Everything had happened so fast after that, Natalia hardly remembered any of it. She was put in a car, and some people talked to her, saying things she didn't quite understand, and through it all, she uttered not a word and shed no tears.

Until an investigator sat her down and asked, "Were you aware your father imprisoned young girls in the basement of your house?"

That's when she finally snapped out of her dazed stupor. And the first thing she said in many hours was a lie.

"No."

And the investigator believed her. Why wouldn't he, Natalia thought bitterly, when she was merely a thirteen-year-old, supposedly a little girl herself?

In the days after her father's arrest, Natalia didn't sleep. Couldn't, really. She was awake, staring at the ceiling of the motel room the police put her in, wondering what the hell was going to happen to her now.

Because she knew her father's fate was sealed. She was smart enough to know the police wouldn't have arrested him without some sort of evidence.

But what about *her* fate?

Natalia sat in front of the square glass window, a telephone pressed against her ear. On the other side, her father sat wearing the orange prison clothes she'd seen many times on TV. It was surreal that her father, the one who always wore those nerdy khaki pants and a buttoned shirt, was now wearing that.

"Natalia," he whispered into the phone. He seemed more tired than she'd ever seen him before; his eyes were bloodshot with heavy bags under them that reminded her of her own. His dark hair was disheveled, and he'd begun growing a scruff, when before he was always so clean shaven. The only thing that seemed normal was his glasses.

"Dad," Natalia mumbled, her emotions all over the place. She didn't know what to feel, didn't know if she could feel again, really, what with the cold numbness that had taken root in her chest since the night of his arrest.

"We don't have much time, so I'll make it short," her father now said, his eyes searching hers. "You must continue applying everything I've taught you."

Something rippled underneath the numbness. Something hot and ugly. "How can you think about *that* right now?" she hissed incredulously.

He gave her his disapproving look, the one she used to dread when she was younger. "This is the only thing that matters, Natalia," he said fiercely, a spark returning to his eyes. "We're the last Children of Kahil. With me gone, you have to carry on the legacy. To continue to prove your faith."

It's not my faith, Dad; it's yours, Natalia wanted to respond, but she bit her tongue and looked away. She would break him if she denied him this, she knew. He cared far more about the Morrow Gods than he'd ever cared for her, after all.

Her father had the uncanny ability to read what was going on in her mind, however, because he said, "I'm asking this for your own sake. You know I love you more than anything in the world, Natalia. I would do anything for you."

Lies.

"Look at me, please," he whispered, and reluctantly, she did. His gaze was desperate. "The Book of Kahil is in my office. Take it. Read it. Do what needs to be done."

She wanted nothing but to go back to her childhood home and burn that book. Because that book had brought nothing but misery upon her life—even before her father got arrested. Everything he'd done, all the things she'd witnessed, her part in it all, pretending to be oblivious when she heard screams from the basement . . . it was all because of that damned book.

"Natalia, my love," her father pleaded, and she could look at him no more. "Do not let all of our hard work go to waste."

She pursed her lips and stared at her hands. He tried to speak to her again, but she wasn't listening, unable to listen when all he uttered were pleas for her to commit the same crimes he did in the name of a long-lost faith.

Natalia stared at the milkshake that Amy, the social worker, had bought her, wondering whether she should show she was trying, after days upon days of barely nibbling an energy bar per day.

She wasn't hungry, though, and hadn't been for almost a month now. The Augusta orphanage workers tried to feed her relentlessly, and Amy, too, brought her burgers every time she came to visit. On better days, she pretended to eat while actually passing it to Carter, an exceptionally hungry boy her age in the orphanage, but usually, she just flat-out refused to eat.

If there was one thing she hated, it was adults trying to control her.

Amy now walked back into the room, and a couple in their forties followed her in. "You should drink the milkshake, dear," she said kindly, gesturing to the vanilla-strawberry mix.

But the milkshake was no longer on her mind now. Instead, she stared suspiciously at the couple, who gave her wobbly smiles and hopeful gazes as though she was the answer to all their prayers.

That did not make her any thirstier for that stupid milkshake.

Seeing that she wasn't in a cooperative mood, Amy cleared her throat and motioned toward the couple. "Natalia, please meet Ella and Roger Kazar."

Ella seemed to be on the verge of tears as she stepped toward Natalia and crouched so they were eye level, what with Natalia sitting down. "Hi there," Ella said softly, smiling tearily.

Natalia did not smile back. "Hi," she said flatly.

"Roger and I have heard so much about you," Ella continued as though Natalia had said nothing, "and we can't wait to introduce you to our son, Logan."

Alarmed, Natalia whipped her head toward Amy, requiring an explanation. Amy smiled widely. "Ella and Roger are your foster parents starting today," she said excitedly. "Isn't it great, Natalia? You get to have new parents, a new home, and even a brother your age!"

Natalia felt her heart sink. She didn't need a new family. Sure, the orphanage wasn't the best, but she only ever had one family. Her father. And despite everything he'd done, she loved him. She loved him dearly.

But when she turned to Mrs. and Mr. Kazar, she knew she had no choice in the matter. This had all been settled already. They were simply informing her of what was to come, not asking her if she was okay with any of it.

In their eyes, she was a little girl who needed to be taken care of.

In truth, Natalia's maturity was far beyond her years.

And because of that maturity, she knew she had to adapt, and quickly, to what was to come. Frosting her heart, she gave the woman a thin smile and said, "Thank you."

Ella melted. Roger was now crying too. Amy was beside herself.

Natalia was angry.

And that anger made her make an impulsive decision. Something she didn't think through but felt she had to do. If she was going to pretend she was an innocent clueless girl who went along with everything she was told, she had to do this.

"Also, please address me by a different name," she said, causing everyone's eyes to return to her. She feigned a shy smile in response. "I want to start fresh."

Ella was perplexed, but she softened and smiled widely. "Of course, darling," she said. "And what is your new name?"

Certainly not Natalia Zoheir-Henderson. Not with these people. Not when her father was locked away, perhaps forever, and she, too, was about to move from one prison to another.

She would go by her middle name. The one her father had given her, unlike her first name, so she would always remember where she came from and who she really was.

With a conviction far superior to the one she'd ever had as to the Morrow Gods' existence, she said, "Aileen Henderson."

ABOUT THE AUTHOR

Photo © 2023 Monika Fitz

Sapir A. Englard is the author of the massive digital hit The Millennium Wolves. Published in 2019 on the Galatea app, the twelve-book series has amassed more than 125 million reads. Englard's success has been documented in the *Boston Globe*, *Forbes*, *TechCrunch*, and more. A graduate of Berklee College of Music, Sapir is a full-time writer and musician. The Millennium Wolves series is published in French by Hugo Publishing.